D0090188

Praise for *FATE OF FLAMES*

"With its cast of diverse, well-drawn heroines, colorful world building, and action-packed story line, *Fate of Flames* is an immersive and monstrously fun read."
—Elsie Chapman, author of *Dualed* and *Divided*

"Raughley depicts the cost of power, the lure of fame, and the trauma of overwhelming stress in a compelling story with memorably flawed heroines. . . . An engrossing kickoff to the Effigies series."
—*Publishers Weekly*

"This series opener has it all: strong females, intrigue, a dash of romance, monsters, and a sequel in the wings."
—*Kirkus Reviews*

"It's a compelling concept, and the mix of fragility, defiance, strength, and utter exhaustion that plays out in the girls feels authentic. . . . A sequel will likely be eagerly anticipated."
—Bulletin of the Center for Children's Books

Also by Sarah Raughley

Fate of Flames

Book Two in the **EFFIGIES** series

SIEGE OF
SHADOWS

SARAH RAUGHLEY

Simon Pulse

New York   London   Toronto   Sydney   New Delhi

To the whole fam.

SIMON PULSE
An imprint of Simon & Schuster Children's Publishing Division
1230 Avenue of the Americas, New York, New York 10020
First Simon Pulse hardcover edition November 2017
Text copyright © 2017 by Sarah Raughley
Jacket photo-illustration by David Field and Steve Scott
Jacket photograph of manor house copyright © 2017 by Neil Holden/Arcangel
Jacket photograph of clouds copyright © 2017 by Toa55/Thinkstock
For information about special discounts for bulk purchases,
please contact Simon & Schuster Special Sales
at 1-866-506-1949 or business@simonandschuster.com.
The Simon & Schuster Speakers Bureau can bring authors to your live event.
For more information or to book an event contact the Simon & Schuster Speakers
Bureau at 1-866-248-3049 or visit our website at www.simonspeakers.com.
Series design by Karina Granda
Jacket and interior designed by Steve Scott
The text of this book was set in Adobe Caslon Pro.
Manufactured in the United States of America
2 4 6 8 10 9 7 5 3 1
Library of Congress Cataloging-in-Publication Data
Names: Raughley, Sarah, author.
Title: Siege of shadows / by Sarah Raughley.
Description: First Simon Pulse hardcover edition. |
New York : Simon Pulse, 2017. | Series: The Effigies ; book two |
Summary: After Saul reappears with an army of soldiers with Effigy-like abilities,
threatening to unleash the monstrous Phantoms and bring death and
destruction to the world, eighteen-year-old Maia and the other Effigies
hope to defeat him by discovering the source of their power over the
four classical elements, but they are betrayed by the Sect and bogged down
by questions about the previous Fire Effigy's murder.
Identifiers: LCCN 2017012151 (print) | LCCN 2017038207 (eBook) |
ISBN 9781481466820 (eBook) | ISBN 9781481466806 (hardcover)
Subjects: | CYAC: Four elements (Philosophy)—Fiction. |
Superheroes—Fiction. | Psychic ability—Fiction. | Soldiers—Fiction. |
Monsters—Fiction. | Secrets—Fiction. | Fantasy. | Science fiction.
Classification: LCC PZ7.1.R38 (eBook) | LCC PZ7.1.R38 Si 2017 (print) |
DDC [Fic]—dc23
LC record available at https://lccn.loc.gov/2017012151

PART ONE

You have shown me a strange image, and they are strange prisoners.

Like ourselves, I replied; and they see only their own shadows, or the shadows of one another, which the fire throws on the opposite wall of the cave?

True, he said; how could they see anything but the shadows if they were never allowed to move their heads?

—Plato's *Republic*

1

"I NEED TO THROW UP," I SAID.

Not the kind of words that inspired confidence before a secret mission. Still true, though.

Our helicopter's electromagnetic armor protected us from the phantoms outside, but I could still hear them thrashing in the sky, screeching through the violent Saharan winds that battered the metal. Between the howls and my motion sickness, my stomach was lurching. "No, really, I feel nauseous."

"Oh, so it wasn't just me, then?" On the opposite bench, Lake laughed nervously as she finished strapping on her parachute with the help of the agent assigned to monitor us. "It's actually kind of funny, but my lungs seem to be having a hard time, um, inhaling." Lake pulled at the maroon fatigues she wore under the vest, the same as mine, then turned to the agent. "Are you sure this parachute vest thingy is supposed to be on this tight?"

Mine was definitely a bit too cozy, but then one did have to be serious about safety measures before taking suicide jumps out of a flying vehicle.

"God, you two are so *pathetic*."

Chae Rin. For the purpose of the mission, she and Belle were in other helicopters, but I could still feel her biting presence. Her laughter battered my skull through my inner earpiece. "Like, is this your first mission? Suck it up."

"Excuse me for showing a bit of *humanity*," Lake bit back. Somehow it sounded even more dramatic in her British accent.

"Okay," I said. "I'm seriously throwing up now."

"Swallow it," a voice snapped at us through my earpiece.

It was the glorious lack of compassion I'd come to expect from Sibyl Langley, director of the Sect's European Division. The woman had spent the last two months unapologetically delivering me directly into harm's way, so I knew it was stupid to expect anything else.

"You're a mean lady," I complained.

"So I've been told. But I'll get over it, and so will you."

She was at the London facility, monitoring us from Communications, which meant every stupid thing I said would be heard by an entire room full of people who were probably endlessly thankful that they were several thousand miles away from danger. Lucky bastards.

"Now," Sibyl continued, "we only have five minutes before we get to the drop site. This is a sensitive mission. We're going over the mission details one more time."

"Seriously?" Chae Rin sounded annoyed. "You know I typically like to relax before flinging myself headfirst into danger."

"We've got one shot here to capture Saul, so I want to make sure you are one hundred percent clear on what you need to do today. Now stop talking."

Only one shot. But that's how it was with Saul, the man who'd somehow managed to harness the power of the phantoms to reign terror upon the world. Under his command, phantoms had attacked cities, including mine, and murdered thousands. I'd seen it with my own eyes, seen the bodies left in the wake of his cruelty. We Effigies—Lake, Belle, Chae Rin, and me—came together in the first place to stop his murderous spree, to find out who he was and why he was wreaking havoc. We captured him, yes, but we weren't able to uncover all of Saul's secrets. Maybe we would have if he hadn't escaped.

We almost had him. Two months ago in April, we stopped Saul from blowing up a train full of innocents, but he still managed to get away. The Sect had been trying to track his frequency all this time. Didn't have a lead for weeks—until today. In that respect, Sibyl's urgency was understandable. Needless to say, since Saul had escaped from Sibyl's custody in London, she was under immense pressure from the world's governments *and* Sect higher-ups to deliver his head on a platter.

Which is where *we* came in.

I peered at Lake, who busied herself by fiddling nervously with the pair of goggles the Sect had given us to guard against the sandstorm. Neither of us was particularly keen to face Saul again, but this was our job. We were the Effigies. He was the terrorist. No-brainer.

I gave her my best reassuring nod anyway. "Okay, so this is a simple grab mission. We capture Saul and get out, hopefully with our limbs still attached."

"With Saul, nothing's that simple," said Sibyl, and I could almost see her straightening her back, brow furrowed. "On the one hand, according to our intelligence, Saul's hideout should be at these coordinates."

They flashed on the monitor bolted in the corner, just above Lake's head. She twisted around to see it too—the blinking red square above a satellite image of desert dunes.

"Nice to see Saul found a hole to hide in," I said. "With all the other dirt-dwelling creatures."

"Fitting for him, annoying for us, since we're the ones who have to ferret him out." Chae Rin's voice came through loud and clear in my inner ear. "Scratch that—*I'm* the one who has to ferret him out." She paused. "None of you pay me enough."

"Yes, Chae Rin will dig out the hatch," Sibyl said. "His bunker should be approximately one hundred feet below the surface. Lake will aid in the descent from the helicopter."

"You guys don't pay *me* enough," Lake muttered under her breath.

Sibyl's sigh was enough to quiet them both down. "We have a lock on his spectrographic signature, so we can confirm that he's still at the location."

Spectrographic signatures were how the Sect was able to trace phantoms—and, when they needed to, Effigies. The Sect could trace the frequency of a special mineral, cylithium, existing naturally in both. For us, it pops up on the Sect's radar whenever we use our powers, even if they can't tell from the signature itself exactly *which* Effigy they're tracking. But Saul wasn't like the rest of us Effigies. Somehow, he'd found a way to mask his frequency. If we'd kept him in Sect custody for a little longer, we might have been able to find out how. But for now all we could do was chase him down along with the questions he'd left in his wake.

A shiver suddenly tightened the muscles in my arms. I guess I was still getting used to thinking of Saul as an Effigy like us.

"On the other hand, like I said, with Saul, nothing's that simple. For several days after the train incident, Saul's spectrographic signature had been unstable, as if he couldn't control his ability to mask it from us. Your encounter with him may have destabilized his psyche."

"Well, you did kind of cut off his hand," Lake said.

I sure did. Not that he didn't deserve it.

"Then the trace went dead—until now. But we can't let our guards down," Sibyl continued. "Even though we've traced him to these whereabouts, there's a risk he could—"

"Disappear," I finished for her. One of the many perks of being able to vanish at will.

"Hang on." Lake fidgeted against her parachute straps. "If he ends up poofing before we get there, then wouldn't this whole thing be a waste of time?"

She sent a worrying look past me, and I knew why. Following her gaze, I turned and peered through the window behind me, into the sunset peeking through the torrent of dust.

Where the phantoms were waiting.

"We knew it was a risk," Sibyl answered. "But we may not get another chance. Capture Saul. And if the situation doesn't permit, then gather as much information as you can from his hideout. I want to know what he's been doing and, more important, who's been helping him."

Right. Saul didn't have his ring anymore, which meant he couldn't control phantoms. So why would he pick a hideout in the middle of a Dead Zone? Surely an area protected by society and technology would have been the safer choice for someone who didn't want to get ripped apart in a phantom free-for-all. The only way he could last for so long in an unprotected area was if he'd had help from the kind of black-market tech commonly used in illegal Dead Zone trafficking networks.

Speaking of tech. I dug my hand into the lower left pocket of my thick vest and pulled out the sleek metal ball that had been nestled inside—one of three antiphantom devices we'd been given. Lake and I had this one. Belle and Chae Rin each had their own.

"We can only do so much to keep the phantoms at bay as you're reaching your drop sites," Sibyl said. "Once you land, it'll be up to you to activate your handheld APD at your specific coordinates by entering in the code."

"Hopefully before we get eaten," Chae Rin added.

On the monitor, three little blue lights flashed around the blinking red square indicating Saul's hideout, each four hundred meters away from the site. Together, they made a perfect triangle. The three APDs—or antiphantom devices—worked as a trio. It was why we were in separate planes. Each antiphantom device had to be set up at its respective corner of the triangle. Lake and I took the southern coordinate, Chae Rin the northeast, and Belle the northwest. Chae Rin and Belle had to activate their devices at their respective coordinates within the same time frame that Lake and I activated ours. As long as we didn't screw anything up, we'd be able to triangulate a protective field around Saul's hideout. It would be large enough for us to maneuver and bring in extra troops if need be. With Saul, we had to be ready for anything.

"We'll be monitoring you from here in Communications via satellite."

The agent came back in from the cockpit. "Thirty seconds to the drop site," he said. "Get to your positions."

Her dark brown skin graying by the second, Lake pulled the goggles over her eyes and motioned at me to do the same. "This is just bloody fantastic. You know, I *just* got my first Teen Viewers' Choice Awards nomination since leaving that *evil* girl group. The damn awards show is in a couple of weeks, and those *hags* are going to be there because they got *several* nominations they *clearly* don't deserve." She said this all in a single breath. "I'd better not get killed before then, I swear to god." She fitted the goggles around her eyes. The strap pinned down her long black ponytail. "No way am I giving them the satisfaction of my death."

"Technically, *we* got nominated," I corrected her, putting on my goggles. "Didn't think you'd be this excited over a Canadian awards show. Honestly, I forgot it was even happening."

Vancouver resident Chae Rin snorted through my earpiece. "I'm not even mad at the shade you just low-key threw at my country."

"You're going to be okay, though, right, Lake?" I asked her.

Lake hesitated. "Yeah. I think. Maybe. You?"

I hesitated too. The past few weeks had been a learning experience for the both of us. We were both stronger now, but we'd always been paired with one of the other girls if we weren't fighting in a group. This would be a test for both of us.

"We can do it," I said, and despite the painful pounding in my chest, I think I actually believed it. "Yeah. We can. You, me. All four of us. We can do this."

Lake's gaze drifted to the window. "Sure about that? It's looking pretty bad out there."

"Yeah." I squeezed my hands tight. "We're a team."

We were a team now.

Lake seemed a little taken aback, but she gave me a resolute nod nonetheless.

"At least let's try not to die," I added with a half smile.

One minute to the drop site. It was go time.

"Remember," Sibyl said. "You have to activate the three APDs at the same time. We haven't found any evidence of other human hostiles in the area, but stay on your guard. Gather up whatever information you can, and then give the signal for retrieval."

"Roger that."

Belle. She'd been so silent this entire time I'd almost forgotten about her, but she was in her own chopper, listening, quietly preparing. Her voice had the serenity expected of an Effigy who'd been handling suicide missions since childhood.

How I wished, as I wiped my sweaty palms on my fatigues, that I could have siphoned even a tenth of that confidence. But I'd spent the last two months away from home training for situations like this. I couldn't wuss out now.

Lake and I nodded at each other. Twenty seconds. Ten seconds. The hatch opened.

"Begin the mission."

At Sibyl's word, I leapt out of the helicopter. The long snouts of serpent-like beasts snapped in my direction, baring their ivory teeth. Dark smoke sizzled off their black, rotting hides, their ghost eyes shining against the dimming light of the darkening sunset. They knew us intuitively. Effigies, creatures of magic like them.

But we were their enemy.

They launched at us, but the helicopter's EMA did its job. The Sect's protective electromagnetic armor was top-grade, stronger than what even rich people could afford for their cars and yachts. The field stretching out from the helicopter's armor had a wide enough circumference to keep us momentarily safe from the phantoms even as we descended, but I knew that if they didn't tear us apart, the desert winds would. The wind whipped past my skin, battering against my goggles, tossing my clothes and my thick, curly hair relentlessly. The force was so great, it was all I could do to keep my lips pressed against the onslaught.

A few seconds of falling and I could already start to see the Sahara desert below.

"Deploy your parachutes," Sibyl ordered.

We did. The upward force hoisted me up with a jerk so violent I thought I would snap in two. The wind was too gusty for an easy descent. I could feel it veering me sideways.

"Lake," Sibyl yelled.

Through my goggles, I could see Lake's arms raised in front of her, her long, thin legs kicking in the air. I could almost imagine her closing her eyes, her breath straining under the pressure of maintaining the delicate balance needed to control her element.

Trap and release.

The words Lake always used whenever she trained me in elemental control. For Lake, it came naturally, but controlling a torrent like this over such a wide area would be difficult even for her.

She did the job; the air around me calmed and I could breathe normally again. But I knew it was only a moment of respite. Even with the darkening sunset reflecting off my goggles, I could see them through the glare: the phantoms twitching and twisting in the desert wind, their long, serpent-like tails floating behind them. Waiting. The helicopter's EMA had good reach, but soon we wouldn't be able to rely on it anymore. The second we were out of this protective bubble, we'd be on our own. Survive or get eaten.

Eventually, a male voice from Communications confirmed what I knew and dreaded. "Thirty seconds until the subjects leave the EMA circumference."

"You're close enough to the ground for a safe fall," said Sibyl, "but you'll need to detach your parachutes immediately once you're out of the safety zone."

The horrible minutes between now and the time we set up our APDs would be a free-for-all. We'd have to be fast.

We'd have to fight.

Twenty seconds. Ten seconds.

"Good luck, girls."

The phantoms' cries pierced the skies. They were ready. So were we.

2

FIVE PHANTOMS BARRELED FOR US. LAKE couldn't calm the wind and fight at the same time, so the violent gales rushed back. She used them to her advantage, pressurizing them into little blades that shredded the first wave of the phantom attack, but the recoil blew her right into me. She lost control as the collision, amped up by the wind, drove us in the wrong direction.

"Detach your parachutes!" ordered Sibyl.

We did. With a yank, they flew into the air.

"Lake, grab my hands!" I yelled, reaching for her.

She took them without a second thought and we fell, twisting in the wind. My combat boots landed on the ground hard, the shock waves shooting up my legs, but I was sturdy—

—until a phantom burst out from the ground at my feet.

I had just enough control over my wits to leap out of its way, dodging its attack when it bulleted toward me, but soon I felt the sting of bone pounding into my boots from beneath the sand, lifting me up. Another phantom emerging out of the ground.

Phantoms came in different shapes and sizes, often mimicking the forms of beasts that, unlike them, were naturally of this world. Like so many of the phantoms in the sky, like so many others I'd faced before, this phantom beneath me took the form of a giant serpent—its long, slithering midnight-black hide erupted through the sand as if it'd been lying in wait the whole time. Parts of its rib cage jutted out of its body through layers of flesh and smoke.

I jumped off as two more followed it, launching themselves into the air. I was good at dodging them, but Lake was even better, using the wind to twist herself midair, avoiding the phantoms' attacks.

"You're about thirty meters off-site," said a Communications agent as I dove onto the sand.

"What?" I heard Chae Rin exclaim through the comm. "What happened? Jesus, how did I know you two would be the ones to screw up?"

"You'll have to find your way back," said Sibyl.

Gritting my teeth, I pushed myself up. "How do we do that?"

The moment I turned around, a phantom's face snarled at me from behind.

Trap and release.

Digging my feet into the ground, I slammed the palms of my hands into its large, pointed teeth. The force of the phantom's charge sent me deeper into the sand, but I didn't budge.

God, the *smell*. It was the saliva. Thick and foul, it came down from its mouth and slipped between my fingers until I couldn't hold it back anymore. I rolled to the side, letting the phantom launch itself into the air. But it wasn't done. Arching its long back, it made a beeline for me, jaws gaping.

I could do this.

I used the few seconds I had before impact to shut my eyes and concentrate. I could do this. I'd done it before. I could do it.

I could do it.

I felt the heat swallow up my body first, then the smooth pole, obsidian black, materializing in my hands. The sight of the tiny flames flickering at my feet made my heart speed up in panic, like always, but I couldn't indulge it. The phantom shot at me, but I managed to flip out of the way just before it made contact, landing awkwardly on my feet. I was no gymnast. My head was still spinning when I swiped the blade of my scythe at the phantom's neck, chopping its head off with one swing.

Effigies could summon weapons unique to each girl. Not many did in their time, but enough had for the Sect to realize we were capable of it. Maybe that's why they called us the Four Swords. And this was *my* sword.

"Watch out!" Lake cried.

Another phantom screamed at me from behind, but Lake dealt with it before I could lift my weapon. It was as if an invisible battering ram had slammed into it. I could see the rotting black flesh of its belly as it flew back with the wind.

Which gave me an idea.

"Where exactly do we need to go?" My body was still on alert as Lake fought behind me.

"Sending you two the locations right now," said a Communications tech. "Tap the tiny switch on the right arm of your goggles."

Switch? I hadn't even noticed it was there, but once I felt around, I found a little raised nub in the right corner and pressed it.

"No way." Tiny red lights appeared on the inside of my goggles' transparent screen as if I were playing a VR game. *Awesome.*

"It's got camera function too!" Tech Guy said before collecting himself. This wasn't really the time to be geeking out, but it's not like I could blame him. It was really goddamn cool.

I could see our position lighting up as a flashing red dot. And at the top left-hand corner was the drop site where we needed to triangulate our antiphantom device with Chae Rin and Belle's.

This could work.

"Lake." I twisted around. "We're hitching a ride. On a phantom."

The pop star looked back at me as if I were insane. "What?"

"We'll get killed out here. But we can ride a phantom to get to the drop site, Chae Rin–style."

"Good idea," said Chae Rin through the comm. "A little dangerous, but it's doable." An ex–circus performer would know, especially one who had once dabbled in phantom riding. "It's like riding one of those mechanical bulls. Just make sure to dig your fingers in there and grab the bone or you'll get flung off real quick."

"Lake can use her power to keep us going in the right direction," I said, my hands sweating against the pole of my scythe.

Lake panted heavily. "Really kind of you to make me do the heavy lifting, mate."

We didn't have time to argue. Three more phantoms barreled at us from a distance.

Closer. Closer.

"I'll make it up to you later." Closer. "Now stop whining . . ." *Closer.* ". . . and get us a phantom!"

Lake pulled a phantom into her vortex with a tortured yell. After letting my scythe dissipate back into nothingness, I ran for the phantom at full speed and jumped onto its back, Lake following quickly behind me.

"Ow!" I yelped as the phantom's bone struck my tailbone. My legs slid uncomfortably against the thick, fleshy hide, my hands disappearing behind a thin veil of smoke as I felt for something to hang on to.

The murderous roaring behind us grabbed my attention just long enough to see the phantoms chasing after us. "Lake!"

"Oh, hell. Okay, let's go!"

The phantom flailed violently, but Lake's will was stronger. My hands dug through wet flesh to grasp hold of the bone beneath. Lake's right hand grabbed the back of my vest as she pushed and pulled the wind to get us to the drop site.

It wasn't an exact art. The phantom swerved and thrashed as the other phantoms pursued us relentlessly, snarling and snapping at the air. My legs were wearing out from clutching its body. Riding a phantom was terrifying, and Chae Rin was insane for even trying it. But as Lake directed the beast's kinetic energy to the drop site, I could see our location moving closer and closer from behind the screen of my goggles.

"We're hopping off!" I gripped Lake's arm. Pulling myself to my feet, I leapt with her onto the ground as the disturbed phantom screeched upward, but another was coming down from above.

Tapping off my goggle's monitor screen, I lifted my arms above my head. *Trap and release.*

Lake narrowly dodged another phantom. "Maia!"

Fire burst from my fingertips, climbing up the phantom inch by inch, starting from its gaping jaws snarling just a few feet from my head. I fell back. The fire swallowed half its body, turning flesh to char and smoke. I dove out of the way as the rest of the body crashed to the ground.

After two months of training, I was still having a little trouble controlling fire. Just thinking of the searing flames and the heat licking against my skin made the hairs on my arm stand on end. It took everything I had to stop myself from imagining my dead family in the fires.

But I was trying. For now that would have to be good enough.

"What are you doing?" Chae Rin yelled through the comm. "You guys still alive? We've got to activate the APDs at the same ti—" She ended in a grunt as she battled a phantom. It was dark now. I couldn't see either Chae Rin or Belle through the sandy wind. But I knew we weren't the only ones fighting.

"Lake, Chae Rin, Maia," said Belle. "If you're at your sites, then get your devices out."

Belle hadn't spoken much since the mission started, but the moment she did, my hand found my vest. I pulled the device out from my left pocket. The APD had a square monitor carved into its sleek metal surface. It was kind of like the electromagnetic armor you'd find in a really expensive car. You had to type in the code to make it work.

I placed it carefully on the surface of the sand. "Okay. I'm ready."

"Hurry up!" Lake cried, eyeing the rumbling ground several feet away.

"Now," said Belle.

My fingers moved quickly.

4EXX#G7

The monitor lit up blue and the metal ball gave a few curious shivers before going rigid and sinking a little into the ground. I poked it. Nothing. Even against the shifting sand, it was immovable. Then, in the next moment, a blue haze of light shot out from beneath the device, drawing a clean line in the sand as far as my eye could follow in the darkness. After turning my goggles back on, I saw them—blue lines shooting out from three different positions triangulating around the blinking center that marked Saul's hideout.

"It's activated!" said Chae Rin.

"Get into the field now," Sibyl said. "Quickly!"

We didn't need telling twice. Another phantom was already after us. Together, Lake and I dove into the protected zone before its twisted jaws could reach our skin. It collided with the hazy field instead, its flesh and bone bursting into smoke and dissipating into the air.

Grasping the sand in her delicate hands, Lake crawled a little deeper into the zone until finally collapsing onto the ground, panting heavily. I flopped over onto my back, chest heaving. The field was faint, but the particles reflected enough starlight for me to see the thinnest, wavering curtain shooting up into the sky above me.

"This mission is time-sensitive, girls," said Sibyl. "You'll need to make your way to Saul's hideout."

According to the Sect's intel, Saul was somewhere in this area, underground. It took a hell of a lot of work to get him into Sect custody the first time. This time, we wouldn't lose him.

With a half-haphazard tap of my hand, I jostled Lake before she could lose consciousness. "Come on, we're getting up."

"You first."

Wiping sand off my cheeks, I dragged myself to my feet, helping Lake up. After one last glance at the monsters roaming behind the protective field, we started our trek to Saul's hideout.

The winds were gradually starting to calm on their own. Respectable gusts shifted the sands across scattered green shrubs dotting the desert hills. I ignored the sound of phantom cries to concentrate on the stars above me lining the dark sky.

When I was a kid, my sister, June, would look at the sky from behind the window of our bedroom in Buffalo. She was the stargazer, the dreamer. She'd stare at the stars, maybe imagining the impossible. What would she think if she could see me here, battling phantoms in the middle of a desert?

For me, impossible was just another day. That's what it meant to be an Effigy.

"Oi." As we neared the location of Saul's hideout, Lake pointed at Chae Rin's running figure in the distance. "How the hell does she still have any energy after all that?"

Chae Rin's stamina and strength were incredible, even for an Effigy. But Chae Rin hadn't gotten out of the phantom onslaught without a scratch. She had a few up her arms, her pale skin and blood exposed to the air through the tears in her sleeves. Her short black hair grazed her shoulders back and forth as she continued toward us.

"You okay?" I called out to her.

Slowing down, she lifted her slender arm. "It's not as bad as it looks." She looked around. "So, where's the Warrior Princess?"

If she meant Belle, she didn't have to wait long. Soon, she emerged out of the darkness, her body veiled only momentarily by sudden gusts of wind carrying tufts of sand into the air. As her blond ponytail fluttered behind her, she lifted up her goggles to reveal those icy blue eyes, tired but steady as they found us in the night.

My body instinctively seized when I saw her, a tinge of fear that months ago would have been unimaginable. Back then I would have been fangirling in the truest sense of the word. The coldly beautiful but aloof Effigy whose years of experience had hardened her into a badass warrior. This was the girl whose posters and collecting cards were still somewhere in my New York apartment, probably in my bedroom closet along with all the other stuff I hadn't brought with me to London. For so many years, I wanted to *be* her.

It wasn't until I actually met her that I realized I never really knew her at all.

Chae Rin rolled her eyes. "Took you long enough," she said once Belle was near us.

Belle stopped in front of us, and I twitched. Just slightly. I didn't even notice at first, but once I did, I berated myself. *There's nothing to be worried about,* I told myself. *Just stop thinking about it.* I steadied my body.

"Wanted to make an entrance, eh?" Chae Rin continued to prod her, but Belle wasn't biting.

"These devices are specially made by our R & D department for missions," Belle said, ignoring the comment—a slight that did not go unnoticed by the visibly annoyed Chae Rin. "But their power is limited, which means this electromagnetic field is too. We'll have to work quickly."

"You mean, *I'll* have to work quickly," Chae Rin muttered.

"You're both right," Sibyl said through the comm. "You've got fifteen minutes before the field gives out. But once you go underground, we'll lose contact. Make sure you keep track of the time from your visors."

The countdown started at the top right hand of my goggles' translucent screen.

"Roger that." Belle lowered hers back over her eyes.

It was hard not to look at that straightforward fearlessness without feeling an awkward mix of awe and insecurity. It was almost reassuring seeing her focus back in full force, even if it was confined to the battlefield.

It always was, these days.

Chae Rin cracked her knuckles. "All right, then. Clear a path."

Belle, Lake, and I made sure we were well behind Chae Rin as she brought her hands low. Effigies didn't necessarily need to use their hands to manipulate elements, but it was just easier to—like our limbs were a lightning rod, the perfect conduit for such immense power. As she lifted her arms, the earth rose with her.

She did good work, moving away the sand, but I couldn't help worrying. Saul would surely hear the sands shifting above him, wouldn't he? And then just disappear. There were so many risks in this mission, but it couldn't be helped. Sibyl wasn't the only one under the world's pressure to deliver a terrorist—we were too.

Sand slid away from us in sheets and billowed up into the night sky with the wind Lake summoned. It wasn't long until we saw the white metal hatch, dirtied around its perfect right edges, big enough to fit only one of us at a time.

The four of us stood facing each other, exchanging steady glances. This was it. We were to work together. Beat the bad guy. That was the reason why the Sect gathered us, after all. We were an uneasy alignment created out of necessity, forged through a shared destiny.

The Effigies.

Sometimes, if I let myself, I could feel it: that unspeakable force linking one to the other. A connection. A bond. Or maybe it was just me. We'd already fought together and bled together. That may not have made us friends, but it made us something.

A team.

Yeah. And it wasn't all that bad.

"No time to waste." Chae Rin rolled up her sleeves. "If he's down there, let's go."

"Wait—" Lake put out a hand to stop her. "Director Langley . . . are you one hundred percent sure that Saul is in that bunker?"

"We can still detect his frequency at the below location," responded a Communications techie.

"He's there." Sibyl's voice was solemn.

"We can only climb down one at a time," I said. "He'll definitely hear us coming. If he hasn't heard us already."

"I'll go first," said Belle. "I have more experience. I'll neutralize Saul quickly."

Bending down, she gripped the handle and, with care, lifted the heavy hatch.

"Belle—" I started, but she put up a finger to silence me, nodding meaningfully toward the open hatch.

Her foot hit the steps swiftly and silently, maneuvering down each rung until she disappeared into the darkness.

We waited. Chae Rin watched the dark open hole grimly, ready to react to any sign of trouble. Lake's legs fidgeted, but not too much to shift the sand beneath her feet. Still nothing. I rubbed the sweat and dirt off my face and sucked in a quiet breath.

A blast shook the ground beneath us. My head snapped up. That was as good a signal as any. Each of us lifted up our goggles.

"Let's go." Chae Rin leapt down the hatch. After a slight hesitation, Lake climbed in next.

It was now or never.

I descended through the hatch last. The metal bars were greasy and dirty—easy to slip on. I made sure I didn't. The moment I hopped down onto solid ground, I felt the chill. And when I turned, I found a forest of ice blooming in the small bunker. Frost sparkled under the dim lights, speckling the hot, humid air of the dingy room—a room empty but for a single cot covered in dirty white sheets. Belle's ice crawled up to the ceiling, covering the black shadows on the wall.

Black shadows. Shadows of people. They were drawn in black spray paint against the red brick. Long and short, they lined the walls, their limbs thick and crudely sketched as if by a child.

And maybe Saul was the one who'd painted them. His form was distorted behind Belle's cocoon of ice as he stood suspended inside. In a navy-blue armored bodysuit and black boots, he almost looked like a soldier. But his face was obscured inside a pure white metal helmet. It wasn't like anything I'd ever seen before.

"He looks like a cyborg," Lake said.

I could see that too. The wide, dark slits where his eyes would have been looked like they would suddenly light up bloodred at the slightest computerized command.

"Has he said anything?" Chae Rin paused. "I mean, *did* he say anything? You know, before you literally iced him?"

"No." Belle put a hand on the ice gently with her fingers, just over Saul's face. "It was strange. He didn't say a word. But he made a move toward me."

Lake clutched her chest. "He attacked you?"

But Belle shook her head. "No. He just . . . moved toward me. At first I thought it was an attack, but there was something about his demeanor. As if—"

I stepped closer to her. "As if what?"

Belle paused. "As if he'd already been defeated."

With a tap of her hand, she melted the ice just enough to create a hole through which he could fall into her arms. His limbs dangled limply, but I could tell from the way his head twitched that he was still alive. And his left hand was clutching something desperately.

"How do you take this off?" Placing his body on the ground, Belle began struggling with the helmet covering his face. "Help me."

Lake and I looked for a lever, a groove, a latch, anything.

"Wait. There's a switch here," I said.

It was more like a tiny button tucked away by his ear. One click and the helmet shuddered and shifted open, steaming at the sides.

But the face inside was not Saul's.

"Who the hell is *this*?" Chae Rin loomed behind us for a better look.

The young man was barely out of his teens, blond hair matted against his pale forehead, scars riddling his thick, angled face.

"What's going on?" I studied his face. "I thought Communications said that they tracked Saul's frequency here."

Belle was quiet for too long. All the while the timer was counting down. Seven minutes and forty-five seconds. Seven minutes and forty-four seconds . . .

"Well?" I urged Belle.

"The Sect tracked the cylithium frequency of an Effigy here," she said finally.

The bunker was silent. That is, until the boy's lips parted in a cough.

"It's okay," I told him, surprising myself. What if he was an enemy? But there was something about his feeble moaning and the way his eyes fluttered helplessly that made me wonder otherwise.

Kneeling by his side, Chae Rin grabbed his shoulder and shook him. "Hey! Who the hell are you?" After a pause of silence, she shook him again. "We don't have all day."

"Chae Rin, be careful!" Lake scowled at her. "He looks half-dead already."

But if Lake was looking for sympathy, she wouldn't find it. "The APD field's about to go out," Chae Rin snapped. "We don't exactly have all the time in the world."

"Sir. Who are you?" Belle asked, more quietly.

The young man sputtered. I could just hear the beginnings of words carving themselves out from the sounds he made.

"What?" Belle leaned in as the young man's lips moved.

"Are you . . . Sect?"

"We're the Effigies," I answered quickly, tentatively touching his arm when it started to tremble uncontrollably. He looked relieved with my answer. "Who . . ." I paused, maybe because I didn't want to know the answer. "*What* are you?"

"I ran here . . . I ran from them . . . I hid . . . I wanted you to find me." He coughed, breathing heavily. "They were going to force me to . . . I couldn't . . . stop myself. . . . I waited until it stopped working . . . and then when I was free, I ran. . . . I needed you to find me. . . ."

It was like trying to solve a jigsaw puzzle with pieces missing. It was almost impossible to stitch his words into a coherent picture.

"I don't understand." Belle straightened her back. "Who was forcing you? How? To do what? Tell us who you are."

It was obvious that just speaking was agony for him. He couldn't answer right away.

"If you wanted the Sect to find you, why come all the way out here?" I asked him, trying to be as gentle as the urgency of the situation would allow. "They have facilities all over the world."

"*Not the Sect*," he blurted before taking in a sharp breath. "You. *You.* I . . . knew they'd send you once they could track me . . . looking for *him*. I have to trust you. My . . . family . . ."

Family? What was he talking about? As I shivered, he opened his left palm, revealing a gray flash drive just long enough to fit in his hand. He'd been holding on to it so tightly that after Belle took it, its indent remained in his palm. As the blood pooled in his veins where it'd been, he let his hand fall.

"What's on this?" Belle asked.

"I stole it from the lab . . . I ran . . . I wanted you to find me. . . . Others like me are coming for you. I was just . . . the first. . . ."

I gripped his arm tight until it stopped convulsing. He was looking at me. Only me.

"Tell me who you are," I said again, quietly.

I wasn't ready for the sight of his green eyes welling up with tears. It wasn't what I'd thought awaited us at the end of this mission. I swallowed the lump in my throat as he parted his lips one more time.

"It's too late for me. . . . No one can heal me. . . . Please find Alex. . . . He's . . . still . . ."

His head rolled to the side, and his body stopped twitching.

3

DEAD. HE WAS DEAD. BELLE CHECKED FOR A pulse, but it was clear even before she shook her head.

"I think I'm going to be sick." Lake said it before I could. Turning away from us, she crouched down and buried her head in her knees.

"Belle. You said Effigy." Chae Rin's mouth parted as she considered it. "What do you mean? Whose frequency did we track here?"

"He said we were *family*," I whispered. "What if he meant—"

"No." Chae Rin shook her head resolutely. "He was clearly delirious."

"Everything else he said was coherent enough," I argued. "It has to mean something. What if it meant—"

"That he's an Effigy?" Chae Rin looked like she was having trouble accepting it. Furrowing her eyebrows and scrunching her lips made her beautiful face shrivel like a dried prune. "He said 'my family.' Those exact words. He could have meant anything. I mean, he was dying. His cognitive abilities were probably on the fritz. That's it, isn't it? Right?"

If Chae Rin was having a mini-freak-out, I couldn't blame her. I'd learned in school what we all had learned growing up: that there were four Effigies, each with the power of different elements—fire, earth, water, air. And when one died, another took her place in an endless cycle. Despite all the resources the Sect and various government agencies put into researching where we came from, where the phantoms came from, no one knew for sure.

Four girls and a world full of phantoms. That was the only truth we could cling to. Until Saul appeared as the fifth.

The rules had changed.

But if there were more . . . where did it stop? Were there dozens? Hundreds? Thousands? We already knew so little about the world. Now we couldn't even trust what we *did* know.

"Belle, what were you thinking before?" The several seconds Chae Rin waited for Belle to respond was clearly too long. She grabbed Belle's arm. "Hey! Did you hear me? What's going *on*?"

"I don't *know*," Belle snapped, pulling her arm out of Chae Rin's grasp. "Just stay calm."

But the look of dread on her face betrayed her.

My eyes drifted back to the young man in her arms. Dead. And I was close to the body. With a sudden surge of panic, I stumbled back, almost slipping on the sheet of ice covering part of the floor. The whites of his eyes popped against the dark dreariness of the bunker as they rolled to the back of his head. Belle must have seen the expression on my face because after a quick glance my way, she closed his eyelids.

"Well, good job, Barbie. Dude's dead. You *killed* him." With her arms folded over her chest, Chae Rin scoffed in disbelief. "At least we could have pumped him for information that actually made sense. Like who he is. And what *that* is."

Belle turned over the sleek drive in her hand. "My attack wasn't . . . It wasn't forceful enough to kill."

"But you attacked him anyway when he was clearly no danger to anyone. You basically admitted that yourself," Chae Rin pressed. "Look at this place." She motioned around the hideout. "It's a freaking winter wonderland. You panicked. Just admit it."

Belle's attack did scream *overkill*. It wasn't like her to jump the gun. Wasn't like her.

A phrase I'd been thinking a lot these past few weeks. Since France.

Since the consciousness of her dead mentor had found life again through my body, even if just for a moment.

And then I remembered the dull fear that had seized me that day as she'd turned her curious gaze from Saul's ring to me. As she'd mulled a dangerous thought over and over in her head. The flicker of decisiveness that shattered almost as quickly as it'd appeared, dissipating into tears.

Weeks later, she was still struggling against something. I could tell by the way Belle wavered despite keeping a brave face, swallowing and tightening her jaw.

Belle didn't have an answer for Chae Rin. Instead, sucking in a deep, silent breath, she looked at the young man lifeless in her arms. "This man . . . He said no one could heal him. . . ."

"He also asked us to find Alex." I remembered the soft glow in his eyes, soon to be dimmed forever. "Alex . . . Is that what he meant by family?"

Frowning, Belle leaned over sideways, her sharp eyes trained on the young man's neck.

"What are you looking at?" I asked, afraid to step closer.

Gingerly, Belle shifted the body onto its right side so that she could inspect the white flesh more carefully. "What is this mark?"

Guess I didn't have a choice. Steeling myself, I inched close enough to lean over Belle's shoulders. The body had many scars, but the one I found at the back of his neck looked almost deliberate. A deep red, circular bruise, the size of a penny, right at the base. The jagged slashes across it told me he'd scratched at it more than once. Secrets etched bloodred into his flesh.

Short staccato warning signals came from each of our goggles. I pulled mine down over my eyes. "Five minutes," I said, then pulled them back up. "We don't have much time here."

"This place must be phantom-proof. Maybe EMA." Chae Rin looked around until she nodded and pointed at the corner of the room. "There it is."

She pointed at the small gray metal half circle drilled just below the ceiling like a CCTV camera, except without the camera inside. From behind the glass, I could see the wires and machinery sparking a light blue charge.

"Traffickers usually use some crude technology out here in Dead Zones," Chae Rin continued. "This might be a base that a group of them once used. That guy said he ran here. . . . Maybe he knew about it too. Was Saul ever even here?"

"Traffickers usually take their tech with them, don't they?" I'd learned a little about it during my training.

"They obviously meant to come back. Otherwise they wouldn't have left that there."

"That's not what I mean." I peered around the room. "They're nomadic. They'd have to take certain technology with them to travel in, out, and around Dead Zones."

"She's right," Belle said quietly. "They take their equipment with them wherever they go."

I nodded. "But this guy said he ran here, probably by himself."

"So?" prodded Chae Rin.

"So, how did he get here on his own? Do you see any antiphantom tech on him?"

No. Nothing but his uniform and helmet.

"He had to have had help getting here." I paused. "Right?"

"No idea, kid." Sighing, Chae Rin traced her hands along the brick wall. "Wait." She inched closer to the wall. "What is this?" She was peering at something tucked in the corner of the room by the hatch.

"What do you mean?" I went over to take a look.

It was hard to see since the dim lights above didn't seem to reach the dark corner, but I could still make out the pattern: a swirling circle, spiraling into itself. It had been carved into the brick with something sharp but inexact, like a rock. The edges around the circle were harsh and jagged, but even still, as my eyes traced the line curving up into a point, the image forming in my mind took shape, growing stronger the longer I stared at it.

"A flame?" I whispered. "It looks like a flame."

Without thinking, I turned to the painted shadows on the wall. "What . . . what is this?"

"Take a picture of it." Belle began pulling up the dead body. "Take a picture of everything. Use the function in the visors. And Lake—Lake, get *up*."

With a whimper, Lake wiped her face and turned around with red eyes.

"Search the room. We'll do a quick sweep before leaving." She stood, hoisting the corpse over her shoulder as if it were half its weight. The young man's helmet dangled from the fingers of her free hand. "We don't have much time. Work quickly."

With a crisp, derisive chuckle, Chae Rin pulled her goggles down over her eyes. "Okeydoke," she said, giving a humorless smirk. "Let's make this quick."

Maia . . .

   Maia . . .

   Are you listening . . . ?

Not for the first time, I heard her voice, softly, dangerously whispering in the recesses of my head. It'd been happening like this for weeks. It was how I knew I'd fallen asleep. It was how I knew I had to wake up.

The slow, deliberate notes of a secret melody drifted out from the dark. Humming. I couldn't see her—I couldn't see anything—but if I calmed my breath, I could hear her calling.

   Maia . . . ?

Then I saw it emerge from the dark—the image of an arm going limp over a couch, of a glass cup slipping from the grasp of Natalya's long fingers.

No, not again. I tried to tear my gaze away, but it was as if I'd been petrified. That's when I saw him slipping out of the shadows, his hands shaking as the woman tumbled out of her living room chair, his head lowered as he stared at the body on the floor.

"I'm so sorry." Tears stung Rhys's eyes as he whispered it.

   Maia. Don't be afraid, Natalya told me. *Come to me. . . .*

"No!"

My eyes snapped open as a stream of short, violent breath escaped from my lips, erratic, uneven. Bending over in my car seat, I placed my head in my hands.

Don't think about him. Don't think about him. Don't think about any of it. I repeated it until the image of his sweet face, his strong jaw, and his soft lips disappeared completely from my mind's eye. Once it did, I could breathe again.

"Hey! You okay?" said Lake from the seat next to me, shaking me by the shoulder. "Breathe, girl, *breathe*."

"Yeah." My mouth was dried-up and tasted bitter. I swallowed whatever saliva was there and gave her a reassuring nod. "Just a nightmare." One I'd been having far too often lately. One I wanted to never have again. "It's okay. I'm good."

"Had me scared for a second there." Lake tilted her head before leaning in to inspect my face. "Um, you've got a little . . ."

After she pointed to the corners of my mouth, I wiped the drool off and sighed.

The clay walls of the Sect facility shimmered orange and red under the sun. The gentle breeze in Marrakesh, Morocco, was a nice change from the desert torrents we'd faced hours ago, but the heat was just as relentless. Our Sect van was parked outside the premises, the dulled black automatic gates locked behind us. But the air-conditioning was broken, which meant that to keep ourselves from cooking, we had to keep the car doors open. A couple of flies buzzed in with the heat, one flitting annoyingly close to my ear. Waving it away, I lay back against my seat, wincing from the sun's onslaught.

Her voice lingered somewhere deep in me. *Maia . . . Maia . . .* steady like a drumbeat, each strike an assault on my nerves. My fingers twitched as I brought them up to my forehead and shut my eyes, trying to block her out.

Effigies fought and died, and each death opened up the door for another girl to inherit the power of the last. No, not just the power— the legacy, the memories, and the consciousness, even if just in pieces. Natalya Filipova was the last in my line. That meant parts of her lived on inside me. The Russian-born legendary fire Effigy who had lived as a hero.

But she hadn't died as one.

And she would never let me forget it.

It took me a moment to realize my hand was shaking against my forehead. Quickly, I brought it down and stared at it. The soft, sandy skin tone was mine. The dark lines stretching across the red of my palm. The white nails, cut short. This was my hand. Mine.

Even though I could remember how it felt to have Natalya move it through her will alone.

Mine. I clamped my hand shut as if the sharp pain of my nails digging into my skin sealed my desperate thoughts as truth.

Shivering, I checked the time on my phone. I hadn't been asleep for thirty minutes, but that heavy, languid feeling lingered stubbornly in my bones. It still took my body time to recover from these missions. I'd traveled here and there, back and forth so many damn times, all the cities were starting to blend together—as was, apparently, my vision, right now. I rubbed my eyes. The weight of the stress of battle came down hard on my bones. Belle always said that the more you train, the more you get used to it, but apparently nobody told my muscles.

Well, at least I wasn't the only one who'd conked out. Having taken the whole back bench for herself, as she usually did, Chae Rin curled up on her side with her headphones plugging her ears and slept peacefully, her bare legs sticking to the leather through the natural adhesive of heat and sweat. She was out of her Sect fatigues and back into her civilian clothes. We all were. It was hot enough in Morocco without torturing ourselves needlessly.

In the seat next to me, Lake fiddled with her phone with one hand and kept her minifan trained on her with the other. "They're still out there?" she asked, peering out my door. "Should it be taking this long? Didn't they already take the . . ." She paused and bit her lip. "The . . ."

Body. The body of the mysterious young man we'd found in the desert hideout. Sibyl ordered that he be processed at the African

Division headquarters several miles away. This meant that even after surviving a dangerous, body-breaking mission, we still had to stick with the body, stowed safely away in its sterilized white bag, as it was transported to Morocco to ensure its successful arrival. The moment we passed through the tall black gates, a medical team was already waiting for us. We should have been able to leave by now, but after half an hour had passed, Belle was still outside talking to the director of the facility.

"While the untalented and undeserving are releasing rubbish singles that get rewarded with money and praise, I am going on secret missions, fighting for my life, and hauling away dead bodies." Sighing, Lake closed her eyes against the fan-generated wind lapping against her face. "My one consolation in this whole dreadful scenario is Sibyl okayed us going to the TVCAs. Attending an awards show because you're nominated for something and not because your agent wrangled an invite from some poor underpaid intern. How novel!" With her eyes still closed, she grinned. "It's gonna be so great. I'm back in the game!"

I stared at her. "You've got to be kidding me."

But Lake was already checking out the nominations list on the awards show's home page. There we were, under Favorite Badass Role Models, next to an eclectic list comprised of a teen physicist, a social media star, an Olympic athlete, and a pop star fresh out of rehab. The weird thing about being an Effigy was you could fit in perfectly among any of them.

Ah, the strangest beast of all: celebrity.

Well, Effigies were known all over the world. Even as we fought monsters in a kill-or-be-killed lifestyle that usually ended in our bloody, gruesome deaths, the media still reported on us as if we were no different from your typical reality star or starlet stumbling drunkenly out of a limo into the latest LA party. When I was a kid, I worshipped the Effigies. I bought the posters and the trading cards the Sect put out just like every other obsessed fangirl. But it was the hero part that thrilled me. The fame part I could do without.

"You're not actually still planning on making us go to that," I said wearily. "Are you?"

"In fact, I've already picked out your dresses!"

"Oh god." My head rolled to the side and came to a rest against my seat belt. Unlike me, Lake relished the spotlight and thrived in it. Going from auditioning for some cheesy televised British talent show to debuting in a pop group to becoming an Effigy, staying famous wasn't something she had to worry much about. Still, it'd been months since her solo pop single was supposed to drop, but her record label was delaying the release, and her fans were beginning to think it was a myth.

"Did you check out Doll Soldiers? Wait, let me go there." On her phone, Lake signed in to the online forum of Effigy enthusiasts, the site I'd spent an unhealthy amount of time on before I'd, somewhat ironically, become an Effigy myself. I leaned over for a better look. Ah, the Belle Kill Count thread was still racking up the views, as expected.

Lake pointed at what was creatively called the Official TVCA Thread and grinned widely. "Our fans are organizing mass voting parties. Isn't it awesome?"

She clicked the link. She really shouldn't have.

"Oh . . ." Lake grimaced as she read the screen.

> [+299, - 173] LOL @ Icicles acting like they're too
>
> good to vote for a damn Teen Viewers' Choice Award.
>
> Like don't you think if Belle were "above it all" she
>
> wouldn't be going? Think again, they've all been

confirmed by their publicist. What now, bitches?

[+230, - 101] People honestly think Swans are pushing for this shit just because of Lake and her personal
career. Well, the reality is we're not, and if you think
that, it just makes your bitterness toward her that
much more obvious. Doing this kind of stuff helps the
girls. Do you know how much pressure they're under?
Every Effragist that supports OT4 should take this shit
seriously, so Icicles need to get over their damn selves
and *vote*.

"What's OT4?" Lake asked me because she correctly assumed I'd
wasted enough time on the internet to know the lingo.

"One True Four," I said. "All four of us. The whole crazy Effigy
gang."

"That's exactly what I'm saying!" Lake nodded excitedly as I read
another comment.

[+220, - 180] Okay, but Belle fans don't actually call
themselves Icicles and never did. We'd like you to stop
this immediately.

"Yeah, when the hell did that start?" I narrowed my eyes because it
only got messier and messier down thread.

[+218, - 194] I love the girls, but Swans are so desperate, pathetic, and transparent. Like fave, like fan!

[+218, - 150] I'm voting for Aaron. He just got out
of rehab and hasn't shown any dick pics or peed in a

public establishment in like a month—that takes real

courage.

[+210, - 130] I'm *screaming*—these girls are supposed

to be warriors; there is literally no reason for them to

be attending parties designed for the detritus of the

entertainment industry! *Wake up!*

They had a point with that last one. Unfortunately, after Saul's escape from the London facility and the PR disaster that followed, embracing our Effigy fame was the best option we had to distract the masses while the Sect pulled its shit together.

"When *did* they come up with 'Icicles'?" Lake cocked her head to the side. "A bit on the nose, isn't it? And *why* in God's name are they all fighting each other instead of voting?" She scrunched up her face as she whined, like a child throwing a tantrum. "Ugh, be *unified*, you wankers. I *want* this win."

Even I knew that expecting unification in Effigy fandom was like asking time to move backward. And in fact, you'd have a better chance of achieving the latter. The angrier people were, the longer and more frequent their online vitriolic rants. Hell, I was the former poster child of messy Effigy fans, so I had no room to judge.

Leaning back in her seat, Lake kept on scrolling through comments. With nothing else to do, I laid my head against the car window, readying myself for another nap, when the door opened with a yank. I would have fallen straight out of the car if I hadn't grabbed the seat.

It was Belle. "You three, come with me. *Chae Rin*," she added sharply and, being the gentle girl that she was, picked up a pebble off the sandy floor and threw it hard at Chae Rin's forehead. The Effigy awoke with a start, swearing the typical profanities I'd gotten all too used to during the past few weeks. She looked as subtly murderous as she always did whenever I had to venture into her dark jungle of a room in the morning and force her awake to start our training.

"Director Chafik has some information to show us in Communications," Belle said.

"Is it about the dead guy?" I asked, admittedly with little tact or respect for the dearly departed. "Or the flash drive?"

Belle quickly looked over her shoulder to where Chafik was waiting by the front entrance of the building. "I haven't given it to him. Not yet. Just a feeling."

"But—"

"Don't mention it to him either until I decide what to do." She straightened up. "Come, let's go."

None of us much liked being bossed around, but we stumbled hot and groggy out of the car anyway.

"Not feeling the new arrangement," Chae Rin, never one to let her displeasure go unnoticed, grumbled as she shut the door behind her. Lake shrugged and obediently went ahead of us. I was about to follow when Chae Rin grabbed the short sleeve of my T-shirt. "Look, I know back in that hospital after France, I was the one who said we should stick together, and we all agreed. And that's fine, but are we really just going to let Belle call the shots?"

"Isn't that what she's been doing?" My nonchalant shrug couldn't mask the weary sliver of dread in my voice.

"Hey, guys!" Lake called to us just as she, Belle, and Director Chafik were about to enter the facility. "You coming?"

"Yeah, we're coming!" I called back with a little wave. "Give us a sec!"

"You know as well as I do, kid." Chae Rin peered over at Belle and Lake as they disappeared through the entrance. "Something hasn't been right with Belle since—"

"Since she almost wished for Natalya to take over my body for good."

Chae Rin straightened up and sighed. "Since she found out Natalya's death wasn't a suicide like the Sect had told everyone it was."

And that the Sect could be involved. I was the one who'd seen her death scene myself in my dreams. The perks of having other Effigies' memories live on inside you.

Perhaps that was why Belle wasn't keen on handing over the flash drive.

"We have to cut her some slack," I said quietly. "This isn't easy for Belle. She's going through stuff."

"Like none of us are?" Chae Rin shook her head, exasperated. "I'd ask why you're so willing to overlook her bullshit, but then you are her number one ass-kisser, so maybe I shouldn't be surprised."

"That's not it!"

"It's not? Then what is it?"

I couldn't tell her. I couldn't tell her why my fingers were curling with guilt. Why my heart beat a bit heavier with dread every time I saw Belle.

I hadn't told Belle yet about the memory Natalya had shown me in France. I hadn't told anyone.

Chae Rin flicked me right in the middle of my furrowed eyebrows—a soft flick, thankfully. With her strength, she could have caved my skull in. "Come on, you can't tell me you're one hundred percent comfortable with this. You saw what she did in that hideout."

I did. But it was all the same. After our penultimate run-in with Saul two months ago, we'd decided that we had to work as a team from now on if we were going to be able to face the challenges up ahead. Well, every team needed a leader. That was Belle. I guess. It wasn't a verbal agreement. We didn't shake hands or anything. It was just . . . understood. Belle had the most experience out of all four of us. Unlike Lake and Chae Rin, who had only become Effigies in the past two or three years, nineteen-year-old Belle had somehow managed to survive fighting phantoms for six years. For an Effigy, that was pretty damn massive.

It was the Seven-Year Rule. Belle had told me once before. A little saying among the Sect. If you could survive more than seven years fighting monsters, you had either spent your life hiding or honed your skills enough to become a godlike fighting machine. Natalya held the world record, having spent fourteen years battling as an Effigy. Only fourteen.

Effigies didn't live long. The truth of it still terrified me.

"Regardless, she's the best equipped out of all of us for the job. Besides, it's not like it's a dictatorship. If she gets out of line, we can do something about it," I told her, but I wasn't too confident about that.

"Yeah." Chae Rin's expression darkened as she cracked her knuckles. "*I'll* do something about it. Better believe it."

Great. I sighed as Chae Rin went on ahead. As if I didn't have enough to deal with. An Effigy brawl was the last thing anyone needed. But these days, despite our "arrangement," you could never really know when one bad day would get us there. We were a team. We were supposed to be. I kind of wanted us to be.

Maybe "team" was too strong a word.

4

AT WELL OVER SIX FEET, DIRECTOR CHAFIK with his stocky build towered over all of us, except maybe for Lake, who was model tall in her own right. After a short greeting, we followed him into the facility.

There must have been one standard design for all Sect facilities. So far I'd been in two headquarters—one in Argentina and one in London—and the twisting, sterile corridors looked just the same. Communications, too. Once Chafik typed the security code into a keypad by a set of wide silver doors, and once the small screen scanned and verified his face with a gentle blue light, the door slid open and there it was, two stories of busy agents in suits hurrying past one another as they carried information to different stations. Most of the agents sat at rows of computers, typing away at a furious pace, speaking into headsets to whom I could only guess were agents in different parts of the facility, or maybe even agents at other facilities.

Since the Sect was an international nongovernment organization, they had facilities all over the world, some specifically for training agents while most were for base operations. Others, like the headquarters in London, were equipped for training Effigies. Not this one. This one was more research-based than anything else. Judging by what Chafik told us, their Research and Development building was even bigger than the one in London. That's where they'd taken the mysterious young soldier.

"We are holding the body there," said Chafik in an accent that made it sound as if he were slurring his words a bit. "First we will perform the autopsy and then continue on with other examinations. It will be a few days before we can send over any information from our findings."

Director Chafik's thick black beard stretched to his ears. The wrinkles across his face may have come from age, but I was sure the permanent frown lines cutting across his sandy brown forehead could only be attributed to having an intense stare as his resting face. As he and Belle kept pace with each other through Communications, I could see that they both matched in the severity of their expressions. It was like each was trying to outserious the other.

"Thanks, we appreciate it," I said, my footsteps heavy against the tiled floor.

I looked over at Belle, who probably had the flash drive still on her somewhere, maybe in the pocket of her checkered flannel shirt. It was a delicate dance, trusting the Sect without trusting too much. Natalya's own parents had warned us against them, and as it turned out, they'd had a point. The Sect was involved in Natalya's death. But we were still part of the organization, still party to their rules. And if we were going to recapture Saul and get to the bottom of the mysteries that surrounded him, we had no choice but to work with them. Even though there was no telling how many agents had played a part in Natalya's demise.

Agents. My mouth dried again, and my chest felt tight just like it always did whenever my thoughts drifted to him. I squeezed my eyes shut. *Don't think about him.*

Shaking the half-formed thought away, I crossed my arms over my chest, about to speak again when I caught the eyes of some agent who swiveled back around in his chair in an instant.

Sigh. Now that we were here, some of the agents couldn't help but peek up from their computers to take a gander at us. No matter how many weeks it'd been, I still couldn't get used to the curious, unsubtle glances of those who didn't, *couldn't*, see Maia Finley the Girl because to them, I was only, *always*, Maia Finley the fire Effigy. They gave us that quick, self-conscious look, the kind people give when they know they shouldn't stare but can't help it. Lake stood a little taller when she noticed their eyes on her, while Chae Rin sighed with obnoxious volume. Belle never seemed to care. I, on the other hand, shifted on my feet, uncomfortable in my skin. It was like walking into every room perpetually smelling like a litter box.

"You said you had some info for us?" I said once he'd reached a terminal at the center space of the room. Unlike the rows of benches in front and behind us, this small, circular area just had the one terminal with two flat-screens sutured together on the surface. I guess this was specially made for the director of the facility. "What kind of information?"

Chafik gave me with a curt nod as he tapped the computer screen awake. "Yes. Rousseau has told me the circumstances by which you came to find the body. You tracked an Effigy frequency to the desert."

"Yeah, we figured it was Saul's," Chae Rin said before adding under her breath, "But after finding that other guy instead, we're not so sure anymore."

Every once in a while, when Chafik was deep in thought, he'd breathe out a deep, baritone grumble like the one I heard now. It sounded a little like the earth should have been trembling beneath my feet. "Yes. This is a strange situation. Stranger than usual. Our facility has been checking for Saul's spectrographic signature."

I perked up. "And?"

He only needed to tap the computer screens with his fingers to bring up the satellite map of the world. A dull red circle blinked over the Sahara hideout like a pulsating heart. The thick green words hovering over it spelled out LAST WHEREABOUTS.

"This is the only signal we've been able to pick up in weeks," Chafik said.

"The only signal in weeks," I repeated. "And it may not have even been his." I sucked in a breath to calm myself down. The Sect's scanners may have actually been picking up Dead Guy's frequency all along. It was a possibility. But none of us knew what to do with its implications. The discovery of Saul, a man with Effigy-like abilities in a world that only had room for four of us, was shocking enough. The mere idea of countless others grew more disturbing each time I considered it.

"We did have reason to believe it might have been Saul's," Chafik continued, thankfully sparking a little glimmer of hope. "According to our scanners, an Effigy signal did appear *just* after your battle in France. First it popped up suddenly outside of London." As Chafik spoke, he tapped the screen so that the blinking lights representing his frequency appeared over their location. "Then, shortly after, it reappeared in Greenland before vanishing. We searched the area, of course, but didn't find him. He was off the grid."

"Saul fled shortly after Maia cut off his hand," Belle said, and when she turned her head, her blond ponytail swished gently to the side. "He must have gone back to London. Why? To see someone? And why would he then go to Greenland? Why would his signal end there?"

"Usually, an Effigy's signal will show up on the monitor, pulsing at a particular rate. However, while we were monitoring his signal, it was erratic, arrhythmic, even as he jumped from area to area."

"Sibyl said Saul's spectrographic signature had been unstable for several days after we faced him in France," I told him. "Then nothing until now."

I thought back to that day I'd watched Sibyl interrogate him in lockup when we had him captured at the London facility. I could still picture him clearly: caged in that cold, metallic chamber, drugged and rambling. But the tired fear in his eyes as he sputtered out incoherent phrases eventually dissolved into an expression wholly different—and sinister. The fear and desperation had flickered out, leaving only that glimmer of malice I was too familiar with . . . and that vile smile. The same he'd worn as he and the phantoms under his control had torn through bodies in New York.

"Well, I mean, Saul's nothing if not unstable. The last time Saul was in Sect custody, they measured his spectrographic signature and his brain waves," I said. "That's how we learned that Saul actually has two personalities: Alice and—"

"Nick Hudson." Chafik tapped away the satellite map and, in a few seconds, there he was. Saul—no, Nick.

He was handsome, almost beautiful. It was a fact I couldn't escape even after all the evil he'd done. Then again, Nick wasn't Saul. The black-and-white image Chafik showed us was of a young man in a nineteenth-century frock coat and trousers smiling boyishly without a care in the world outside a stone building. He was just one of a group of boys packed into the stairwell leading up to the grand entrance, but he stood out through his beauty alone: the same full lips, petite nose, and sculpted face, which was maybe a little chubbier in this picture. He was still slender, though with the slight muscular build of a casual athlete. If the photo were in color, I might have seen the ghostly sea blue of his eyes.

The hair alone was enough to make the difference. His was dark, not the silver I'd come to associate with Saul.

"After the interrogation you spoke of, Ms. Finley, we were able to research his history. Nick Hudson, born in 1847 to a wealthy British family that owned a small but lucrative railway company in Argentina before it was bought out and absorbed into a larger British firm."

"So Nick was a little rich boy." Chae Rin scoffed.

"But then he became an Effigy," Belle said.

"Alice is the more vicious personality," I said, thinking back to that terrible night in New York, the bodies strewn across the lobby of La Charte hotel. Saul had stood atop his serpent-like phantom as if it were his personal steed, lapping up the sight of the corpses like it were the only oasis that could quench his thirst. But it was Nick I'd faced in France, a boy who'd maintained an almost gentlemanly etiquette even as he held me against my will while threatening a train full of innocents with the phantoms at his beck and call. It made no difference. "Even still, they're both murderers." My lips pursed as I stared at Nick's gorgeous face beaming in monochrome.

"But then who's Alice?" Lake asked. "Did you find any information on her?"

Director Chafik shook his head. "We have not found anything so far. With only her first name to work with, we've cross-checked the name against all known Hudson associates and acquaintances, but nothing has come up."

"But if he's an Effigy, then she was the last one before him," said Chae Rin. "The little voice in his head. Only she is the one driving." And after a short pause, she laughed as the joke dawned on her. "Grand theft *body*," she said with a little chuckle. "Whoever Alice is, she sure took the poor guy out for a joyride and . . ."

The words died on her lips once she turned and looked at me. She must have seen the way my body was hunched over, my head lowered, my eyes downcast as I recalled the feeling of being ripped away from my own flesh and trapped inside my own mind. Another perk of having someone else's consciousness bubbling just under the surface. One wrong move—

I held my arms tightly, squeezing the flesh for reassurance before lowering them again. "If Alice is really the last Effigy in his line, then she would have lived and died in the same time period," I said. "But people aren't immortal. Even as an Effigy, Nick should have died by now."

"What is Saul?" Lake said. "What else can he do beyond teleporting? Oh, wait, he can control phantoms!"

"Nah, he used the ring to do that," said Chae Rin, and she would know because her old circus boss had used the one she'd stolen from Natalya's apartment for a phantom-Effigy performance act. I always wondered whether Chae Rin missed the feeling of riding phantoms for fun and profit. Having recently done it myself, I could safely say it wasn't an experience I wanted to relive.

"Accursed," I whispered, thinking back to that night in France. "He'd called himself accursed. Like us. He said his life span was just one part of his burden. Maybe he can live forever." A terrible thought. What if we couldn't kill him? "We have the power of the elements, but for him . . . teleporting and immortality . . . it's almost as if he can bend space-time."

"One of the researchers at your London facility, Dot Nguyen, has a theory," said Chafik. "For hundreds of years, philosophers have been theorizing the existence of a fifth element: ether. Experiments were conducted in the nineteenth century to examine its properties as a medium for gravitational and electromagnetic forces. Nguyen believes it's possible that there were originally five Effigies created, not four, and that Saul has the elemental power of ether. But all we have are our theories. What we need is a way to test them."

He brought up the satellite image again. "Like you said, Saul can appear and disappear at will. Weeks after Saul's signal went dead in Greenland, London Communications once again caught hold of an Effigy frequency, this time in the Sahara desert. Of course, they thought it was his, which is why they sent you to capture him. But this time something was different. This time, the signal did not just appear at the location. Rather, it developed gradually tens of meters away from the site before resting at the location."

He played the footage sent over from the London facility, and sure enough, I could see the red blinking dot materializing from nothing, fading *into* existence as it traveled through a phantom-infested Dead Zone. It grew brighter and brighter until it came to a resting point, a bloodred heartbeat.

"We know from the time that Langley had Saul in custody that his ability to mask his spectrographic signature *only* appears when Alice's personality is in control," Chafik said. "It would have been Nick that we tracked after your battle in France. Like Sibyl suggested, the fight may have destabilized him. However . . ."

He trailed off, pursing his lips tight, his exhale seeping out from his throat in another deep grumble.

"However?" I prodded him.

"He can still appear and disappear at will," Chafik said. "Indeed, it would make little sense for Saul to risk traveling through a nest of phantoms to reach that location, especially since he was injured from your fight."

"So the signal you tracked to the desert may not have been Saul's, but that dead guy's," I said, my mind filling in the blanks. "I mean, if the guy can't vanish and materialize at will, then he'd have to go *through* the Dead Zone. Vanishing is Saul's power, after all, and Effigies . . ." I raked my tongue over my dry lips. Effigies each had their own unique ability. "There really are more Effigies out there. . . ." I shook my head. No matter how many times I thought about it, I couldn't accept it.

"Perhaps. However, an Effigy's signal does not fade or grow stronger, nor is it ever unstable," Chafik continued. He tapped the screen again, and three silver dots appeared just a few miles away from the desert hideout. In Marrakesh. The blinking lights were us. "This is why the Sect can track you once you have come into your powers. Wherever you go," Chafik added, unhelpfully. I don't think he realized how creepy it sounded.

"So, number one: That signal we chased out into the desert probably wasn't even Saul's." Chae Rin counted it off with her fingers. "And number two: Even if it *did* belong to that soldier we found, he may not be an actual, legitimate Effigy? He may be something else?" She pressed a hand against her forehead, fingers sliding against the sweaty black hair matted to her skin. "Then what the hell *was* he?"

"We need answers." Chafik stared at the monitor. "How was this soldier able to travel through the Dead Zone on his own? And what are the circumstances behind these unstable frequencies—Saul's signal in Greenland and the one that appeared in the desert hideout? Is masking a frequency one of Saul's abilities? Or is it a special property that appears only upon the reappropriation of the current Effigy's body by the previous Effigy in the line?"

Still too many riddles. Effigies, like the phantoms, were discovered in the nineteenth century. Even after all the studies, all the research, there was so much we didn't know about them. But I was more concerned over where this conversation was heading. Especially once Chafik's eyes were on me.

"The truth is, Sibyl Langley spoke to us while you were waiting in the Sect van. We both think it may be time to use our own assets in order to seek out the answers to these questions. For that, we need you."

My breath hitched. Some of the agents from the bench in front of us were listening even as they worked at their terminals. I caught the shift in their heads as they waited to see how I'd respond.

"What . . . exactly do you need me to do?" I asked, my hands feeling strangely numb.

"It's our understanding that you have scried before." Chafik scratched his black beard as he considered what he must have been told by Sibyl. "In New York. Intimate contact with Saul forced you to prematurely open up the connection between your mind and the scattered psyches of the fire Effigies inside you. It is perhaps because of the connection between Nick or Alice and an Effigy in your line. The contact might have awoken that girl, if even just for a moment."

"Marian," I whispered. The girl both Alice and Nick were desperate to find for the answers she carried with her.

"Whatever that 'connection' was," Lake said, "had to have been pretty intimate if a kiss woke her up."

Intimate. Romantic? It seemed so by the way Nick had talked about her the last time we faced each other in France. That faraway look as he said her name . . .

"In either case, Maia's ability to cross through the psychic barriers into another Effigy's consciousness can give us a way to study this issue with the frequencies. Are both Saul and the now-deceased soldier you found Effigies? Is it the unstable crossing of two personalities—in Saul's case, Nick and Alice—that makes the difference in the ability to mask one's signature? Langley has proposed that we use you, Maia, to look into the matter. And I agree."

My jaw clenched. "You want to experiment on me?" I took a short step back. "You want to, what, keep me locked up here like a lab rat?"

"We only want to measure your brain waves and spectrographic signature as you scry. It should not take more than a few hours."

"But the whole point of this is to see what happens when one personality takes over the other. Like Alice did with Nick." The implications of everything tore through me like a scream. I felt numb from the neck down. "You want the same thing to happen to me."

"Natalya," Belle said with an odd, wistful quirk in her voice. It sent a violent shudder through me.

"No. No, no, *no*." My head was shaking side to side with each "no." "She took me over the last time. Do you understand what that means? There's no way—"

"We will be monitoring you *precisely* to make sure that doesn't happen." Chafik looked sincere enough, the seriousness in his small, dark eyes easing a little as if it'd make the blow any softer. "We want you because of the instability of your scrying. We see you as a closer estimate to Saul's own psychic battles than, say, Belle, who's studied and practiced the skill over a period of years."

My mind was a better measure to figure out what was happening in Saul. We were alike. Nick and I. Unlike Belle, we'd both experienced the horrors of having someone move your bones and stretch your limbs without your say-so. But this was still too dangerous. I didn't . . . I *couldn't*.

I looked at the other girls for help, and thankfully, Lake and Chae Rin looked just as skeptical as I did. Belle, on the other hand, had a pensive tilt to her head that told me she was mulling it over.

"It may be of help to us," Belle said. "We need to figure out the nature of Saul . . . and the soldier. This could be a crucial first step. And perhaps understanding the pattern behind Saul's frequency can give us a way to track and capture him."

"She . . . has a point, kid." Chae Rin gripped my shoulder. "I'm not totally sold on this, but there are questions that need answers."

"That's easy for you to say," Shrugging off her hand, I wrapped my arms around my chest. "You and Lake have never even had to scry before, so how would you know? And none of you know how horrible it feels to . . . to . . ." To have your body taken over. I shuddered.

"No, we don't," Chae Rin replied coolly. "But what other options do we have?"

"This is kind of an urgent situation," Lake chimed in.

I knew it too. But I didn't have to like it. With a heavy sigh, I looked up at Chafik with my teeth gritted. "You're one hundred percent sure you won't lose me in there? *Ten* hundred percent sure?"

Chafik nodded. "Don't worry. Our technicians will do everything in their power to make sure you are safe and secure. We already have a lab prepared in the Research and Development wing. Like I said, we will be monitoring you carefully to make sure there are no accidents. We only want Natalya's consciousness to graze the surface. We want to see what happens when your minds interact. We won't let it get beyond that."

"Don't worry . . . um . . . we're all here," Lake said reassuringly, though she didn't seem too sure if it was worth anything. "It'll be fine."

"You say that now. Just watch. In a few hours you'll have Natalya as a roommate instead of me."

Lake thought about it. "Well, then, hopefully she won't snore as badly as you do."

She waited for me to catch on to her smile, but I couldn't say I appreciated that joke. Once Lake realized her misstep, her shoulders slumped sheepishly.

Chae Rin scratched her head. "Look, kid, I get that we're not exactly best friends or anything, but none of us want you gone. Right?"

"That's a no-brainer," Lake answered. "You said it yourself: We're a team, yeah?"

But Belle took a little longer to respond than I would have liked. Her languid eyes stared off in the distance. She looked tired suddenly, as if all the energy had been sucked out of her in a moment. Perhaps fatigue had finally settled into her bones. But you never knew with Belle.

She nodded absently. "Let's go," she said in an almost whisper.

5

"CONSIDER IT A PHYSICAL," I TOLD MYSELF AS I entered the lab alone from the observatory room, but then, most of the physicals I'd had in the past were the normal kind with doctors and stethoscopes. There was indeed a doctor in the room, from what I could tell by both his long white lab coat and the way he just kind of stood around looking important. But instead of nurses, he surrounded himself with technicians tinkering with monitors and wires and all sorts of medical equipment I couldn't name if I tried.

"Ah, she's here," said the doctor when I shut the door behind me. "Maia Finley? My name is Dr. Rachadi." He was young, slender, dark, and handsome, but having a pretty face to look at made me feel only marginally better. "Have a seat over there. This shouldn't take long."

Before I even had the chance to follow his instructions, a couple of technicians started dragging me toward a long examination table. I couldn't see any of the other girls or Director Chafik, but I knew they were behind the large black screen on the left side of the room, watching me as I lay down on the table, as the technicians hooked me up to a set of monitors and wrapped black straps around my arms.

"Fix the tripod," Dr. Rachadi ordered a technician, who ran to reorient the camera stuck in the corner.

"What are you looking for?" I shivered, longing for the warmth of a bed. The room was unusually cold. "What is all this stuff?" Long tubes coiled around the floor and over the tables like metal vines.

Dr. Rachadi grabbed the long neck of a thin, clear monitor and rotated it so I could see the screen. "This entire apparatus," he said, patting the mass of complicated equipment, "will simply help us measure your spectrographic frequency and brain waves concurrently. We will monitor your cylithium levels, which should spike as you attempt to make contact with Natalya."

Make contact. They made it seem like they were leaving me stranded on an alien planet. They might as well have been.

"Cylithium. Right. Where all the magic comes from."

"Through studies in the past, we've come to conceive of cylithium as a kind of conduit or medium that not only enables your ability to control the elements but also allows for the connections between the psyches of the Effigies. Through previous studies on Effigies, we've found that the cognitive experience of scrying correlates to cylithium production, which goes into overdrive during the process. Now, you won't be scrying by yourself. For your safety, we'll be inducing your meditative state, adjusting cylithium levels to a premeasured amount. And we'll be using the instruments at the far panel behind me to ensure that the levels never get out of control."

When I lifted my head, I could see the technicians at the front wall turning various metal knobs of different sizes.

"That way you maintain the delicate psychic balance between the two minds," he said.

"Just don't kill me."

He swept his fingers along the screen and with a few taps an image of my body appeared, all outlined in metallic blue, bordered by stats and figures in writing too tiny for me to read from my table. "Maia Finley, age sixteen, blood type AB, weight—"

"That we don't need to say out loud," I said, and I would have sat up if I weren't hooked into so much weird stuff. I wanted to rub my arms. The hairs were standing on end, and I couldn't tell if it was because of my own fear or because of the subzero temperature of the lab. Everyone else was wearing layers. They could have warned me.

A voice rang out from the intercom. "Finley, please calm down." It was Director Chafik. *Calm down.* Easy for him to say. As if he had any idea how nerve-racking this was.

"Yeah, don't worry, kid. We're all here." Chae Rin.

Lake chimed in too. "We won't leave until it's all over, 'kay?"

Belle said nothing.

I wondered what the other girls were doing behind the black screen. Maybe they were laughing at me. Well, Chae Rin would under normal circumstances, but I had to believe that she'd be a bit more sensitive even though we weren't, as she'd said, best buds.

It's not like we disliked each other either. None of us exactly saw eye to eye when we all first met. But battling side by side had brought us closer together. I liked Chae Rin's straightforward personality, envied her mercilessness when it came to being as blunt as humanly possible. I'd come to expect it. Enjoy it, even—well, most of the time. Lake and I got along a lot better for whatever reason, maybe because we had the least harsh personalities out of the four. And Lake was just accommodating to everyone. I was sure she was as nervous for me as I was for myself.

Belle, on the other hand . . . I couldn't say I knew one way or the other. And that scared me.

Belle used to be my hero. Her strength, her skill, her focus. I still envied them as much as I used to worship them. Back then, I'd just wanted to be strong too. And I'd wanted her to acknowledge that strength as if that would somehow make it real. But right from the time we first met, the more I interacted with her, the more I realized how little about her I really knew or understood. And these days, after all we'd learned about Natalya, after Belle had come so close to seeing her again—through me—in France, it felt like things had only gotten worse. She was more distant and aloof. And then there were the missions where she was all too ready to strike the first blow. Dead Soldier was proof of that.

I thought back to her tired and unfocused gaze in Communications. In the past few weeks, in those quiet, unexpected moments, I'd seen her dulled eyes staring off into the distance. Something wasn't right. But then, nothing's been quite right since Natalya's death, not for either of us. Anyone could see that.

We both had the same ghost weighing our souls.

Only difference was, *I* was the one about to face her.

Dr. Rachadi tapped his monitor. A washed-out yellow light waved through my body diagram from head to toe. The two red bars on the right side of the screen began to fluctuate.

I shivered. "Why is it so cold in here? I can't scry properly under these conditions."

"Exactly. The psychic boundaries between your mind and the next in your line have already weakened from previous contact." He said it as if it weren't supposed to terrify me. "You know that to enter another Effigy's subconscious safely, your mind needs to be perfectly calm."

I lifted my head as much as I could. "Yes, or else I get taken over. But then again, that's what you want."

"Creating conditions of discomfort will ensure a scrying experience that will allow Natalya's mind to *just* graze the surface. Don't worry. Like I said, we'll be monitoring you carefully."

Natalya's mind. A sudden burst of fear gripped me. This was real. They were really going to do this. No, they said they'd monitor me. They'd take care of me. This wasn't a trap. We had to do everything we could to figure Saul out. And the girls were on the other side of that glass. If these people tried anything, they'd be here to stop them.

But who would stop Natalya?

She'd moved my body in France so well, fighting against Saul and his phantoms. She'd moved it much better than I ever could. I'd watched her from the deep recesses of my own mind, suffocated by darkness as if I'd been buried alive. That feeling of hopelessness started to crawl back into me as I imagined her face. Natalya Filipova, a girl I'd once considered my hero.

"I changed my mind." My words came out in short rasps. "I don't think I can do th—"

A hard prick in my arm gave my heart a jolt. One of the technicians had practically attacked me with a needle filled with a pale blue liquid, completely oblivious to the panic on my face. How the hell could I be sure these people weren't just trying to *murder* me? What had I gotten myself into? A warm liquid oozed into my bloodstream. I shut my eyes with a shudder, but I suddenly couldn't move my jaw. I felt nearly weightless, my body just barely anchored to the table upon which my limbs lay lifelessly.

I wished my uncle were here. Uncle Nathan. I hadn't seen him or talked to him since I'd left New York months ago. If he were here, I'd know for sure I was safe. I'd be . . . at peace . . .

"Raise the transducer frequency to twenty megahertz. Beginning . . ."

". . . cognitive penetration successful . . ."

". . . and eliminate the artifacts from the cylithium return signal . . ."

The voices weaved in and out, lyrics to an eerily pleasant song. Peaceful.

"Raise the frequency higher," someone said. Director Chafik, maybe. His voice was much deeper than the doctor's, a milky murmur that matched the steady rhythm of my calm breaths. "We have to allow Natalya to get to the brink. She'll survive."

Survive. I rolled the syllables along my tongue without ever parting my lips. Sur . . . vive . . .

Survive . . . survive . . .

Live . . . I want to live . . .

I want to live, Maia.

It was dark. In my T-shirt and jean shorts, I lay on a ground I couldn't see because the darkness had cloaked everything.

This wasn't what scrying looked like. There was a right way and a wrong way to scry, typically. Belle had explained it before. There was a difference between using the front door and being dragged in through the back window. When Saul had first kissed me in New York, that sudden, shocking contact weakened the already penetrable barrier between my consciousness and Natalya's, the last fire Effigy to die before me. Even now if I wasn't careful, I'd see her memories in my dreams, but this left me vulnerable. True scrying required meditation and concentration. It was different from just slipping into her memories. It was a controlled experience.

This was neither. I didn't know *what* this was, couldn't fathom why the darkness had drained away until I was back outside the Marrakesh facility. Our Sect van was still parked outside. The sun was still blazing hot. Wiping the sweat off my forehead, I shifted my gaze to the sparse row of palm trees by the guard towers, their long, stiff leaves stretching into the sky.

"Maia."

My body warmed at the sound of his voice, soft, deep, and darkly sweet. He stepped out of the driver's seat and shut the door behind him, the wind tousling his black hair, which had grown a little since the last time I'd seen him.

"Rhys." My arms were useless at my sides, the blood thumping in my body as I drank in the sight of his lean body dressed in the black suit typical for Sect agents to wear when not on the battlefield. A strange look for him; in the short time I'd known him, he'd worn mostly faded, worn-out jeans, baseball jackets, and, the first time we'd met, a bow tie.

"Oh good, you're here." He smiled as he straightened his pin-striped tie and walked up to me. "There's something I've been wanting to do for *ages*."

Wait. I'd had this dream before.

Many times. In many surprising locations.

I'd been having them since I'd first met him in La Charte's hotel lobby. The contents were embarrassing to admit, but since I'd had this dream before, I wasn't surprised when he wrapped his toned arms around me and drew me closer.

Stupid. What was I doing? I shouldn't be doing this. Not when he—

He kissed me. Long. Deep. Yeah. That was how the dream went.

Strange how you could become attached to someone so quickly. But then so much had happened while we were fighting together . . . while he was silently protecting me, keeping me steady each step I took down this painful path. A sinfully handsome boy who cared about some geeky shut-in with self-esteem issues. I guess I was bound to get attached.

But as he pressed his chest against mine, his fingers sliding down my back and curling roughly against the base of my neck, my heart was aching with dread as much as longing. A chill slid up my spine, my arms stiff against my hips. But as I felt the moistness of his lips, I wondered if I had the strength to ask him that awful question. The one that had kept me up so many nights. The one I didn't dare utter.

Don't be afraid, Maia. Go ahead. Ask him.

Her voice caused me to rip myself away from Rhys's lips, my fingers curling into fists by instinct. Fear pulsated through me as Natalya's voice echoed in my mind.

With a sharp breath, I whipped around.

She stood behind the black gates, graveyard still, as the gentle breeze died around her.

"Natalya." I'd spoken the word so quietly, I couldn't be sure if I'd mouthed it instead. Her short, black hair cropped to her skull, the straight nose and haunting, piercing gaze of her brown eyes. It was unmistakable. "What's going on?" I asked. "Isn't this a dream? Or am I really scrying?"

Your dreams . . . my memories. My memories . . . your dreams . . .

The breeze ruffled my hair. I could feel its caress whistling past my ears, but the hem of Natalya's white dress, cut just over her knees, did not so much as flutter. I was scrying, wasn't I? Or was I dreaming? Were our consciousnesses that inextricably linked that it didn't matter anymore?

Yes, I could feel her. Even though she stood several feet away from me, her presence weighed down my entire being, heavier and heavier with each passing second. As if she would overcome me at any moment.

Natalya's scarred hand clutched the hilt of her sword, its tip just grazing the dirt.

Zhar-Ptitsa. The sword of Natalya Filipova, the legendary warrior who'd carried the mantle of fire Effigy before me.

But the flush was gone from Natalya's small, angular face. She'd entered into my dreams, and she had taken with her the pallor of the dead.

I followed her right arm as it moved slowly, deliberately upward, her sword glinting in the sun as she raised it—to me.

Panic seized my entire body, my heart crashing against my chest. Natalya was here. Natalya was here. She was going to take my body again. She was going to take me. I couldn't breathe. I clutched at my throat, willing myself to calm down, but to no avail. She lifted her sword high above her head. I couldn't move, not even when the sword launched from her hand. I closed my eyes, ready for the impact.

It was the sound of Rhys's helpless whimpers that snapped my eyes back open. Blood dripped from his soft lips as his hand grabbed at the hilt of the sword piercing his chest.

It was a dream, I reminded myself over and over again as Rhys fell backward onto the dusty ground before I could catch him. It was a dream. The real Rhys wasn't dead. I knelt down and pressed my hands against his cold cheeks gingerly, suppressing the sob threatening to escape me. He wasn't dead. "Rhys . . . Rhys!"

Take heed. Such is the fate of those who betray.

"What do you want?" I cried, standing up again. "You want my body? Huh? You want to freak me out and take me over like last time? Is that what this is?"

I didn't have to wonder what she wanted for long because she made it clear the moment she raised her free hand and beckoned me with her finger.

A smile flashed on her face.

I want you to catch me.

She took off.

It must have been some invisible force propelling me forward because I didn't actually want to run full tilt for the gatekeeper's booth. But I was following her. I was following the girl who wanted to hijack my body.

My foot found the ledge of the empty booth and boosted me up, high enough that I could grab the roof. I flipped myself over onto the roof from the momentum and dashed across the moss-green metal roofing sheets. I could still remember the blood dribbling down Rhys's cheek as I jumped over the gate.

I saw the edge of a white skirt fluttering around the side of the building. It rippled in the wind as Natalya ran across the roofs high above me, jumping from one building to the next. Her feet tapped the rooftops so lightly, so quickly, they may not have even touched the metal at all. I chased her into the city, through the narrow, dusty streets of the same busy market the Sect driver had taken us through on our way to the facility. But this time the bystanders were moving in slow motion, their hands filled with food, baskets, and money nearly frozen in the air, their mouths parting too slowly for me to hear what they had to say before I breezed past them. A dream. I was dreaming still. But where was Natalya taking me?

Keep your eyes on me. Catch me, quickly.

Natalya's consciousness was particularly strong being the most recent death, and she used that to her advantage. The messages, the dreams. She'd even appeared once among the living, the day I took my oath as an Effigy. There, in that echoing cathedral, she'd become something like an omen. Back then I thought it was to warn me about the Sect. When I'd found out that she'd been investigating Saul during the last moments of her life, when I'd found out that the Sect had lied about her committing suicide, I'd decided to trust her.

But I learned all too quickly: Even in death, Natalya always had her own plans.

She jumped down, disappearing behind an alleyway. I slipped between two white wooden buildings and—

—and then I was in a museum.

I was taller. My arms long and white. These weren't my arms. This wasn't my body.

I was . . . I was turning around. There was a crowd of people here on the main floor of the museum. The National Museum of Prague. I was here on a mission, but I couldn't complete it. I'd only managed to leave my message for Belle in Castor's volume when I turned and saw him coming through the door—the door I thought had been locked.

Yes. Aidan. He'd come to the museum on the same day with friends I'd never seen before. He hadn't seen what I'd done and didn't ask questions, and I was grateful for it. Now that we were back in the lobby, he'd left his friends by the long, winding staircase to talk to me.

"Hey, Natalya, I'm so sorry I startled you before," Aidan said. He'd come dressed in a black striped T-shirt and jeans, wearing that cute grin I'd come to know over the years. "It's just that I saw you sneaking around the museum and couldn't help but be curious. I was surprised to see you here in the first place."

"I didn't even notice you, Aidan," I said.

He laughed. "Well, I'm pretty good at sneaking around too."

It was strange that he'd be here on the day I'd decided to carry out Baldric and Naomi's mission to find the secret volume. So strange. But then again, his laughter had a way of making you think otherwise.

"Aidan, about what I was doing—"

"Honestly? Don't even worry about it. If you've got something to do, then do it. It's got nothing to do with me." He smiled at me reassuringly.

It was the nice smile of a nice boy. I'd known him since we'd worked together on a mission near his post in rural New York three years ago.

Only fifteen, but still so capable. He'd been a good friend to me ever since, fighting with me, standing by my side as a comrade. I had no reason to doubt him, but I had to maintain my guard nonetheless.

"By the way, are you interested in coming to see the dinosaur exhibit, by any chance? It's why I'm here. I even dragged a few of my friends along."

His friends were waving him over. He always did have a bizarre love for large creatures, even knowing the damage they could do. On more than one occasion, he'd tried to get me to go to some circus with him in Canada. Monsters as entertainment. It was beyond me.

"Why don't you come with us?" he offered. "Life isn't all about blood and glory. Have a little fun for once in your life, Natalya."

But you weren't there for a little fun, were you, Aidan?

Natalya's voice, violent and murderous, jolted me out of her body and into a dark abyss through the pure force of her fury and pain.

He was spying on me. He followed me. Then he killed me.

"No . . ." I hadn't wanted to believe it when she'd shown me the first time in France. I didn't want to believe it now. "No, you're just saying that to take my body from me."

He killed me!

"He wouldn't!"

You don't believe me . . . because of your crush?

Natalya was laughing. It felt as if I were drowning. Her consciousness was swallowing me whole.

Pitiful. This body. This life. You don't deserve it.

Without mercy, her consciousness buried mine deeper and deeper. "No . . . Get away from me!" Deeper . . . deeper . . .

"No . . . no!"

I was screaming.

"Maia? Maia!"

"No!" I screamed, waking with a terrible shudder. Chae Rin pinned me to the table, hissing at me to calm down. I stopped thrashing and surveyed the room, now silent but for the beeping monitors. Dr. Rachadi gaped at me. I could see the sweat lining his forehead.

Director Chafik and the other two girls were hovering over me.

"Well?" I heard Lake say. "Did you get what you wanted?"

My limbs ached, and my head throbbed. Tears were welling up behind my eyelids.

"The frequency's instability during the process of scrying matched Saul's," Dr. Rachadi said, wiping his forehead. "For a few minutes, Natalya's consciousness surfaced. But the frequency didn't stabilize the way Saul's had once Alice's consciousness resurfaced during his interrogation. We can hypothesize up to this point that Saul's ability to mask his own frequency may not be something we can see in the other Effigies. Also—"

"Did you see her?" Belle. The naked desperation in her eyes was almost too much to take. Did she see me at all? Did she even care?

"Yes, I did. Natalya . . . She won't stop." My body shook as I lay back against the table, tears dripping down my cheeks. "She won't stop . . . until I'm gone for good."

My flesh was weak and tired, my muscles worn, my mind wounded. I passed out, praying I wouldn't see Natalya again.

I awoke to the sound of curtains rippling with the gentle breeze that fluttered in with the moonlight through the open window. It was dark. Were we still at the facility? Most facilities had rooms for agents and trainees, and this hard bed was about what I expected for the kind of dreary accommodations the Sect usually had available for them. Pushing off the gray covers, I turned my weary body onto its side. They must have brought me here after I passed out. When I picked up my phone by the side of my flat, white pillow, the text message Lake had sent me an hour ago said as much.

Sibyl called after you conked out. Said we were to come back right away for a debriefing and continue your training. ☹ ☹ I KNOW IT NEVER ENDS!!! But don't worry! We'll leave first thing in the morning! Lots of love <3 <3

I let my phone slip from my fingers and lay back against the pillow, resting my wrist on my forehead. What never ended was the lingering feeling of danger that came with the knowledge that Natalya was deep inside my mind, waiting for her chance. At least I hadn't dreamed about her again, not yet. But traces of the last one still haunted me.

I'd dreamed about Natalya skulking around the National Museum in Prague two months ago. Or more specifically, I'd scried into one of Natalya's memories in my sleep. There, she'd left a message for Belle in a secret room, but the dream had abruptly ended the minute she'd heard someone behind her. I could still remember her fear and shock. I thought perhaps it was an Informer, one of the specialized agents that shadow Effigies and bring information back to the Sect. And now I knew that it was Rhys who'd followed her.

Rhys . . . I thought of the blood dripping from his mouth and the light dying from his dark eyes. It wasn't real, just Natalya's memories and my dreams blending too seamlessly together while Dr. Rachadi messed around in my head.

Or maybe Natalya's consciousness was becoming too strong.

You don't believe me . . . because of your crush?

I squeezed my eyes shut. Two months ago, when I'd brought up Natalya's trip to the museum with Rhys, he'd been uncomfortable with my even pursuing the subject. And that was before the night I'd faced

Saul in France, when Natalya had finally shown me the scene of her death in full: her poisoning at Rhys's hand.

A dull pain began throbbing in my chest as I considered it. I couldn't recall every detail of the dream, but I did remember Natalya's heart calming upon seeing his boyish smile because that's how I'd always felt. His honey sweetness underlined by the dark charm of a warrior raised from youth for battle. I hadn't seen him since he'd gone back home some weeks ago. In the short time I'd known him, I'd attached myself to his kindness, caving in to my own attraction. But like Natalya, I hadn't realized just how little I knew about him.

Until it was too late.

Rhys killed Natalya. Or did he? Natalya was desperate to live again, and the only way she could do that was to destabilize my mind while I was most vulnerable—when I was scrying into her memories. Then she could slip into my body. It worked the last time in France. All she had to do was show me Rhys killing her. A lie. The perfect scheme. Or the truth.

It was why I hadn't told anyone about it. Not even Belle. I just didn't *know*.

And now I couldn't even trust my own mind. I covered my eyes with a shaking palm. What if she got me one day? What would I do then, trapped helplessly in my body? I tried to stop them, because I knew I had to pull myself together and be strong, but a few tears leaked out anyway, slipping through my fingers and trickling down to my ears. Sometimes it was too much.

"Don't cry, Maia."

My eyes shuddered open at the feel of his whisper grazing the skin of my ear, his hand on the side of my face. A tender touch. He'd sat down on the bed so quickly, so quietly. My whole body burned from his closeness.

No.

"You've been looking for me," Saul said. "But I'm here now."

I had already launched at him before the scythe had fully formed in my hand, flames erupting around my body. He moved off the bed with several steps back, quick and careful, side-stepping my first swing. The blade of the scythe lodged into the wall.

I had to calm down. Calm down and capture him. This was my chance.

Yanking the scythe out of the wall, I swung again. Saul could have disappeared just as easily as he'd appeared. Yet he didn't. A shadow cast from his wide plum hood covered the top portion of his face, but not the upward turn of his full lips. His robes fluttered from the impact of my blade against his hand—a *metal* hand. Silver and shining, its thin fingers connected by bulbous joints that whirred noisily as he held my weapon in place.

"I thought I cut that off. Where'd you get a replacement?" I asked coolly, trying to break through his grip with my strength alone, but Saul was strong too. "Couldn't have been while you were hiding out in Greenland."

He stood perfectly upright, shaking just a bit under the weight of my attack when he answered. "So you've been tracking me since we last spoke." And he began squeezing the blade so tightly I thought it would break. "You remember, don't you? What you did to me then?"

"I remember what *you* did." The bodies of innocent people strewn about the La Charte hotel lobby. The train passengers screaming as they were torn apart by phantoms. "I *remember.*"

I let go of my scythe, banishing it quickly before kicking him back and summoning it again in another whirl of flames that licked the curtains—but all I could see was him. Saul. I had to capture him. Jumping at him, I brought it down, only to have him dodge. The blade plunged into the floor. "How did you even find me?" I demanded, yanking it back out.

"I heard you were here and thought I'd stop by."

"Heard? From who? Only . . ." My breath hitched. Only the Sect knew we were here.

"Aren't you happy to see me?"

There was a whimsical note in his voice that made me think of Alice, but the sociopathic, dead Effigy in his line wouldn't have been this calm in the heat of battle.

"Nick. Is that who I'm talking to? *Is it?*"

"I'm sure you can tell. Though, strangely," Saul said, his voice a breath, "it doesn't seem to matter much these days."

The two personalities were constantly warring, battling for control over Nick's body. I knew what it felt like. But I had no sympathy for Nick, no matter how human he tried to make himself appear. Neither was to be trusted. He just so much as said it himself.

One strike. Two. He dodged well, grabbing my wrist with his metal hand and squeezing it tight.

"Relax, Maia. Don't you notice?"

Releasing me, he shoved me back, not too hard, perhaps, because Nick was still trying to pretend to be a gentleman. But when he pointed to the bed, I finally noticed—the flames were eating at the gray covers, licking the walls. And for a moment, I was paralyzed. For a moment, all I could see was my house in Buffalo up in flames, the bodies of my family being carted out in bags. Mom. Dad. My twin sister, June . . .

No. I could handle this. I'd been training for two months for this. I *could* handle this. But the scythe had already vanished into the air, my hands trembling as I watched the fire spread.

"Banish the flames, Maia. Go on. Don't be afraid."

Saul was too close to me. I could feel his hard body against the dark curls spilling down my back, his chest a breath away from my head. If he wanted to kill me, he could have done it already. I had to concentrate. This time I would do it.

I breathed and raised my arms. It was like the reverse of trapping and releasing. I drew the energy back inside my body, like depriving the flames of oxygen. Releasing a deep, shuddering breath, I collapsed back—into Saul's arms.

I stayed crumpled in them, too shocked to move at first, even with my brain screaming at my muscles.

"Good. Good." Saul's heavenly face beamed down at me, his sea-blue eyes glinting in the moonlight. "The better control you have over your powers, the easier it will be for you to find Marian."

A sudden spurt of adrenaline shot through my limbs. He didn't just have the power to disappear. He could take me with him if he wanted. Like last time.

I pushed myself out of his arms, but Saul grabbed my wrist before I could back away. "I'm not here to hurt you. I can't take you yet. I have too much to do before then. You can rest easy for now."

"Yet," I spat. "So you're still after me."

"It's not me you'll have to worry about, Maia," he said, sliding down his hood so I could see the long, loose silver hair that had been dark in the picture Director Chafik had shown us. "Truthfully, I was in an awful state after you hurt me in France," he said. So Sibyl's theory was right after all. "But I did gain control of myself. Control. Focus."

His gaze wavered strangely, but for just a moment. Or did I imagine it?

"Right now there are other things I have to take care of before we can see each other again," he continued as steady as ever.

"What do you mean?" A hard rhythm pounded against my chest.

"Alice and I are going to achieve what we've set out to for many years. Decades."

He sounded as eerily calm as the night I'd faced him in France. It'd frightened me more than Alice's murderous frenzy.

"I told you before. We both have a wish to grant. With Marian's help, we're going to reshape the world."

With his hood down, I could see his face in full, long and slender, beautiful with its high angles and sharp edges. The smile playing on his lips was gentle, unassuming—Nick's smile. But I knew better than to trust it.

"This is a world of shadows, Maia," he told me, leaning so his silver hair fluttered over his shoulders. "And the secrets hide themselves there in the dark. You'll understand that soon enough. I'll give you a sign." His breath was hot on my skin as he spoke, his melodic voice dancing in the heavy, spiced air. "You won't miss it."

Then he walked backward a few steps before disappearing, leaving me alone in the dark room.

6

WE WERE TO REPORT TO SIBYL IMMEDIATELY. Between Saul reemerging suddenly in Morocco and the mysterious man we'd found instead of him at the desert hideout, there were already too many variables to sort out. Still, I had to be careful. Some things we couldn't share with the Sect.

The Sect van took us from the streets of London down the phantom-proof highways to the facility. As I watched the dying evening sun through the window, I thought of Saul gripping me in his arms and shivered.

"Maia? Are you feeling better?" Lake asked for the thousandth time and leaned in from her seat beside me. The other girls hadn't stopped looking at me sideways since we'd left Africa. "That scrying session was pretty intense. Then Saul shows up in your room."

Chae Rin smacked the side of my head when I didn't answer. "Hello? We're asking you if you're okay."

Rubbing my head, I shot her a glare. "I'm fine. I'm still breathing, anyway."

"What about the scrying?" Over the months, Lake had gotten

comfortable enough with me to poke me in the arm, the cheek—it was annoying, but I didn't tell her not to. "What did you see when you were in there?"

I noticed Belle's head shift from the passenger seat.

"Not much," I lied, stifling a sudden nervous thump in my chest. "What matters is that I am okay now." *I can't tell you here*, I wanted to say. *Not with Sect agents around.*

Natalya's death had too many imprints on it. Saul. The Sect. And—

My hand twitched against the car window ledge. *Forget him*, I ordered myself. He wasn't even here anymore. He'd gone back home. He was *gone*. He didn't matter.

Rhys.

The sensation of his arms around my waist, his hand gripping the back of my head lingered even if it'd just been a dream. The blood dripping from his lips and the grin he'd given Natalya in the museum . . . *No.* With a slight jolt of my head, I shook his image away.

The Sect was what I had to focus on now. The Sect had lied about Natalya's death. And even now, Saul knew where I was because he'd been told. Who else would know but the Sect?

How far did this go?

Until I was sure I could trust Sibyl, I couldn't tell her about my visions of Natalya. There were some things I had to keep close to my chest.

And not just hidden from the Sect.

My eyes drifted to Belle's reflection in the rearview mirror.

The Sect had several main divisions, one for each continent. The London facility was the headquarters of the European Division. Tucked away in Epping Forest, a few miles out from the city, its massive buildings and connected wings remained hidden in the evergreens. There were Sect facilities all over the world, but just a few of them had the resources and equipment necessary to house and train Effigies. After passing the first set of gates, the car took us along the winding path slotted between the trees. Peaceful.

"What the hell?" The driver's exclamation snapped me out of my daze. He leaned over the steering wheel to see them better, but even from here, I heard the clamoring crowd outside the inner gates. A few moments later, their flashing camera phones and signs were fully visible.

I grabbed the back of Belle's headrest. "I-is that a banner? With *my* name on it?"

Yes. Yes, it was. FIREFLIES 4 MAIA FINLEY, it read. "Fireflies," of course, was the newly christened name of my personal fandom. Not that I minded, but I would have chosen something better.

Lord, not this again. *Fans.*

Fandom names never even used to be a thing. You had hard-core fans of certain Effigies, of course, but they weren't *that* organized, besides Lake's Swans, and that was a runoff from her pop music career. But the fandom trend had picked up fast once the four of us had gotten together. Along with Swans and Fireflies, you had Belle's Icicles and Chae Rin's High Wires. Of course, this was all encouraged by the Sect's PR team. Supposedly, promoting fanatical devotion could only help keep the public on our side. But some of these fans were a little *too* devoted.

The gates opened. Security was already there to keep the crowd from entering the premises, but most of the fans didn't even bother; they were swarming our van. A young women tapped a life-size toy replica of Natalya's sword against Belle's window, waving excitedly as if it wouldn't piss her off. On the other side of the car, an overweight man held up one of Lake's magazine covers. With a shaky hand, he reached underneath his glasses and rubbed his teary eyes. My stomach crawled with embarrassment as it always did when I saw crowds of people waiting for us at the facility, or at events. Is this what I looked like back then when I was running from event to event trying to get Belle to sign my shoes, my posters, whatever I could find? It was such a different view from the other side of the veil.

"Effigy nerds!" Chae Rin looked disgusted. "How the hell did they get inside the premises?"

A twinge of indignation made me glare at Chae Rin. Okay, yes, they were Effigy nerds. And it was weird and slightly bizarre, but the disdain was unnecessary.

I should have realized something was wrong when we didn't see them crowding the streets outside the first set of gates, like they had done since our battle in France. But there usually weren't this many people. I covered my eyes from the flashes until the sound of frantic rapping against my window gave me a start.

It was the girl holding the banner. Her long, straight chestnut hair parted in two braids running down both shoulders. She couldn't have been more than thirteen. If her skin had been a little darker, she would have reminded me of June. Of myself.

She already did.

I pressed my hand against the window and leaned in closer, watching that pleading expression from behind the glass.

"This is crazy. Hey . . ." Chae Rin poked me. "Tell your people to get lost."

"My people?"

"I don't speak *otaku*." She snapped her fingers. "Go on. Get to it."

Again with the disdain. I glared at her before turning back to the window. What could I say? Especially to that young girl practically begging me to roll down my window. The desperation in her green eyes was too familiar. The tremor in her voice as she said my name. The pen and notebook in her shaking, outstretched hands. I knew it all too well.

In the front seat, Belle ignored the rabble, her eyes closed, her hand rubbing her forehead wearily. She didn't see them. Why would she? She didn't see me back when I'd waited for her outside Lincoln Center last Fashion Week, before I'd become an Effigy. She wouldn't see them now.

But I did.

"Belle!" one fan said, only to be met with a deafening silence I remembered too clearly.

The same chill that I used to admire in Belle now spurred something rebellious in me. I started rolling down the window.

"What are you doing?" the driver barked as he watched me through his rearview mirror.

"Maia!" The poor girl was being crushed against my car door. "Maia!"

"Please get back." I hadn't rolled it too far down, but the girl seized the opportunity. Quickly lowering her banner, she reached inside her pocket and shoved a pink envelope through the sliver of space. As it fell into my hand, I wanted to say something to her. Whatever words I'd wished Belle had said to me: *Keep your head up, kid. There's nothing wrong with you. You're good just the way you are. You're strong.*

Words I still wish she'd say.

But before I could speak, the girl had already disappeared back into the rabble.

We finally got through the gates, only to be swarmed again as they closed behind us.

"Reporters." Belle's narrowed eyes reflected in the window.

Paparazzi would often find ways to ambush us in expected places. I'd already read about someone digging through the trash outside my New York apartment. But they weren't supposed to be inside the gates.

As our van came to a stop, I clutched the letter in my hand. "What do we do?"

With one swift movement, Belle was out of the car. The vultures descended.

"Well," the driver said, "you don't exactly have a choice, do you?"

Lake had already been reapplying her lipstick. After fixing her black hair, twisted into a bun at the crown of her head, she tapped me on the shoulder. "Make sure to look above it all, but still kind of relatable, you know?"

After reaching into her tote bag and slipping on one of the three pairs of shades she always carried, she opened the door and fed herself to the ravenous crowd. With a heavy sigh, I slipped the girl's letter into the front pocket of my hoodie and followed the others.

"Maia!"

"Maia Finley, do you have a minute?"

Sibyl would never allow reporters on the premises, and there was way too much security for them to just sneak in. Clearly they hadn't. Now that the gates were closed against the fans outside, the security officers were just standing around watching us get utterly devoured by disorienting camera flashes.

"Maia, do you have anything to say about—" started one reporter.

"Do you know anything about—" said another.

"Can you give us some room?" I cried over the din, wincing when someone tried to grab my arm, pinching the skin. "Back off, *seriously*!"

Only when I heard the words "secret mission" did my feet halt against the pavement.

"What did you say?" I blinked, guarding my eyes against the flashes. "What's going on?"

"Everyone, please calm down." A deep, baritone British voice rang out over the din. "Our Effigies have only just returned from the mission. Please be so courteous to allow them room to breathe."

Because of the commotion, I hadn't even noticed the double doors of the London facility's main building spit out a tall, well-built man. He was dressed well too, his long, black jacket heavy atop his maroon vest. His penny loafers clicked against the pavement as he walked toward us. But then Bartholomäus Blackwell was never one to shy away from extravagance.

He looked all too comfortable with the media attention, despite the fact that as the representative of the Sect's governing Council, he wasn't required to interact with the public much at all. Each division had a director, like Sibyl, who was the director of the European Division, or Director Chafik, who ran the African Division. They coordinated with the facilities in their jurisdiction, major and minor, as well as sharing information among one another. Then there was the Council, the shadowy presence that oversaw the Sect's operations in its entirety.

Blackwell was a diplomat, offering himself to foreign leaders of countries as the voice of the Council, the members of which stayed hidden in secrecy. When he wasn't doing that, he was off somewhere watching symphonies or hanging out in that huge mansion of his in the countryside, endlessly delighting in being a rich asshole.

Now, as he approached us, he reveled in the spotlight, the camera flashes blanching his already pale skin, his lips stretched into a self-satisfied smirk.

"Thank you all for coming," he said, and when he was close enough, I could see the diamond cuff links glittering on his sleeves. "Although I should apologize. I know some might consider it impolite to be late to your own press conference."

I should have known he was the one who'd called it. It wasn't the first time, either.

His thick black brows arched the moment his eyes found us, the Effigies, peppered through the crowd of journalists.

"Ah good, they've arrived. Girls!" He motioned us forward. "Join me. And, everyone, please give them space. I promise you, your questions will be answered."

The reporters finally backed off. The breathing room was appreciated, but I wasn't about to move at his command. It wasn't until I saw Belle turn to the three of us and nod that I reluctantly dragged my feet forward. At the end of the day, Blackwell was still a high official within the Sect. We couldn't appear to be "disobeying" him, not in front of all these cameras.

And he likely knew that.

"Don't be shy." He "welcomed" us with outstretched arms, though none of us came anywhere near them. We followed Belle's cue instead, lining up by his side like little pageant princesses on display for the consumption of greedy eyes.

My skin crawled as I stared into the crowd of men and women who grasped their recording devices tightly, eager for a sound bite. I could tell by the stiffness in the other girls' expressions that I wasn't the only one. Even Lake, who draped media attention around herself like a security blanket, went rigid as she stared up at Blackwell with her shades lifted, waiting for his next words with the slightest hint of dread in her eyes.

"Well, we should start. Don't worry, I'll keep this as brief as possible." He adjusted his white panama-style hat over his long, black curling hair. "I know the world has been anxious about the lack of information concerning the Sect's ongoing security issues. I've decided to call you here to stem any worries. The Sect, as it has and always will be, is functioning at peak efficiency. Thanks to the hard work of our courageous young Effigies"—he flashed us an empty grin—"and our Sect officials, especially the efforts put in by Director Langley, who has been leading the charge on this front, I can confidently relay to you new developments that have come up through the recently conducted mission."

I straightened. *Mission?* The mission that was supposed to remain a secret from the public? Belle kept her gaze dead ahead, but I could see her jaw tighten.

"Sir, when you mention the Sect's ongoing security issues," said one male reporter in the front, "are you referring to the Sect's failure to capture the international terrorist Saul?"

"Among other things." His finger ran along his square jawline as he thought. "Luckily, I have good news to report. After successfully tracing Saul's whereabouts, I've just been informed that we have been able to find and extract the target."

What the hell was he talking about? I stared at him in disbelief, but he wasn't finished.

"I can now confirm, given my sources, that he is presently within Sect custody at the Marrakesh Sect headquarters, thanks in large part to the efforts of these four."

"It doesn't look like this particular Effigy agrees," said one suspicious reporter.

And they were looking at me. That was when I realized my mistake: my face.

You have to think of the camera as the ultimate frenemy, Lake had told me weeks ago in our dorm room. One of the many PR lessons I'd been given by the master. *Like, if you love it, it'll love you, sure. But it's always waiting in the wings, ready to take you down the moment you show even the slightest hint of weakness. The camera's a snake trying to tear you apart every second. That's why, like I said, you always have to keep calm. Mind your reactions. Control the narrative.*

Mind your reactions. Control the narrative. Two good tips. And once I realized that my face had been contorted in confusion and panic, I knew I'd blown each one.

Relaxing my face and snapping my mouth closed, I stared back at the journalists, whose eyes were now trained squarely on me.

"Is there something we're missing here?"

"Are you telling the truth?" another asked. "Is the terrorist in custody?"

The floodgates opened, and it wasn't just the reporters. The fans were still outside, yelling over one another as they pressed up against the gates.

What did I do?

I could feel the sweat begin to bead my hairline. This had to be some sort of trap. It wouldn't have been the first time. Blackwell's last press conference ended with the world knowing that a number of agents, including his own former right-hand man, had helped Saul escape in the first place. But as he stared at the four of us, the congratulatory smile streaking his pale face disappeared. He looked at us with as much confusion as we looked at him.

"*Haven't* you captured him, girls?" He asked it quietly, but I still prayed to every deity in existence that his words hadn't been picked up by any of the journalists' recording devices.

This was a mess. So many people already distrusted us even before Saul's escape. Who would give Blackwell this false information? Who even let him call a press conference?

The gates opened, and a parade of Sect vans drove through so suddenly, the reporters scattered. Sibyl Langley could barely wait for her car to come to a complete halt before she kicked opened the passenger door and stalked up the paved path toward us. Her milky pantsuit highlighted her dark skin and the standard black suits of the agents flanking her.

"Director Langley!"

"Director, can you comment on—"

The reporters' questions fell on deaf ears as she made for Blackwell, her hawklike gaze ready as daggers. She didn't stop until their bodies were inches from each other.

For a fleeting moment, the two were locked in a battle of wills, neither able to yield to the other. Sibyl was much shorter than the large man, but in the end, her intimidating gaze made up the difference. Defeat settled into his features, his shoulders relaxing, his jaw setting. Just as he turned his head, Sibyl whipped around, her short black hair catching the wind as she pivoted on her feet.

"Thank you for coming. This conference is over. The guards will show you out," she said to the stunned reporters. Then to us: "Girls. Can you follow me, please?"

None of us were stupid enough to think that she'd asked a question. We followed her, leaving Blackwell behind.

"A press conference."

"Sir . . . ," Sibyl started, but the red-faced man on the jumbo screen made it all too clear he wasn't finished when he lifted up a hand to silence her.

"A press conference on a *secret* mission that ended in *failure*."

No one in the vast conference room dared speak as he barely held in his rage. Instead, we stared at Blackwell, who, of course, had taken the head of the table for himself.

"The amount of foolishness . . ." The man shook his head. "The utter incompetence."

But Blackwell leaned back into his seat. "The only incompetence I've witnessed is in whatever broken system of communication that led to Sect personnel giving me false information about their recent operations. That reflects a general incompetence within the operational structure of the Sect, does it not? Which in turn reflects a general *incompetence* in leadership." Blackwell tilted his head just slightly, letting his black ringlets slide down his broad shoulder. "Should you really lay that incompetence at my feet, Arthur? The role of the Council's representative is very different from that of you directors."

Arthur Prince, the director of the North American Division. I didn't know much about him, but given how comfortably he berated Sibyl, it was clear he saw himself as above her although they both had the same job. I could gather as much from that domineering sense of importance. If it weren't for his inscrutable composure or the intimidating broadness of his frame, he might have looked like a tax accountant instead, with his short dirty-blond hair, his gray suit, and his pin-striped tie.

Prince answered Blackwell with a deep scowl. As his wide jaw tightened, the skin around his neck and chin, loose from age, gave a slight tremor. "You called a press conference to prematurely disclose delicate information. The optics were bad enough with the Sect's inability to bring Saul into custody. We directors have had to coordinate search teams for Saul across the globe while aiding governments in repairing the devastation he's caused on top of dealing with phantom attacks. We are under enough pressure. *Langley*—"

Sibyl answered with a slight turn of her head.

"I know you're up to this job. I oversaw your training in Philadelphia myself. I was the one who prepared you to replace Director Bradshaw as leader of the European Division after he died."

He'd trained her. That might have explained why she still referred to him as "sir" even though they were technically of the same rank—why she listened to his rantings quietly instead of tearing him to shreds like I knew she could. It was either a seniority thing or a force of habit.

"I remember," Sibyl said in a measured tone.

"When I, along with the other directors, agreed to the Council's decision of putting *you* in charge of the Effigy initiative to capture

Saul, I did so under the assumption that you would be able to handle the operation."

"It was the Council's decision, sir," replied Sibyl coolly. "None of you had a choice to begin with."

"But your management of the situation so far has only placed the Sect under a heightened scrutiny that we cannot afford right now while we are dealing with our own internal issues."

"With all due respect, sir," Sibyl said, and I'd never seen her more careful with her words. "I endeavored to stop the press conference, which should never have been held in the first place"—she glared at Blackwell—"the moment I got wind of it."

"Which wasn't soon enough." He looked uncomfortable in his chair as he sat back and placed his hand on his desk as if it were all he could do to keep himself from trying to jump through the screen to get to us. "Not to mention your handling of the Effigies."

Lake and I exchanged a glance. The four of us sat quietly at the long, rectangular table like we were told, but it looked like it was our turn for a scolding. When Sibyl had told us we were going to the briefing room, I'd expected more angry faces around the table, but it was just us and a host of empty seats under the blinding ceiling lights.

"My handling of the Effigies?" Sibyl repeated.

Blackwell, who looked amused as he watched the former teacher berate his former student, found a strand of his hair, twisting it around his finger. "Ah, yes, your handling of the girls," he said. "Well, with your experience running the all-girls' training facility in Botswana, the Council felt that you'd be able to relate to the Effigies better than any of us. And so they gave you the go-ahead to mold the girls' public images."

"But embracing the spotlight means training the girls to manage themselves in it," said Prince. "Just like we need to manage the Sect's public image."

Chae Rin kicked me under the table, but I wasn't about to be the one who interrupted the very mean, scary man yelling at us. I gritted my teeth.

"The Sect has had trust issues with the rest of the world for as long as I can remember. That didn't start with this press conference." Sibyl turned to Blackwell. "The bigger issue is that you seem to have gotten a taste for telling the media information they shouldn't have."

Sibyl's glare would have made me squirm in my seat, but Blackwell only crossed his legs, amused.

"As the representative of the Council, it's not unexpected that I might appear in front of the cameras."

"Maybe. When you meet with foreign leaders. But giving out information on our operations is a sloppy move, and not the first you've made."

"I would suggest you search your own house before you launch any accusations." Blackwell leaned back in his chair. "It was under your watch that multiple agents helped Saul escape your custody."

"It was Vasily Volkov, *your* personal agent, who led the charge of his escape," Sibyl fired back.

Vasily. Both of my hands curled into fists atop the cold table. As an agent of the Sect, he would have been used to the battlefield, but he was far more violent than I ever thought possible, from cutting off a man's finger to almost choking me to death in the backyard of Belle's old foster home. I could still feel his rough fingers around my neck, could still see his fox grin and his long, faded blond hair grazing my face as he bent over me, straddling my body. My fingers twitched, aching to go to that spot on my neck, but I stayed still.

"*Ex*-agent," Blackwell corrected. "Vasily has been dealt with. I have no need for traitors."

"A traitor to you or to the Sect?"

I hadn't even meant to speak. But the words flew out of my mouth regardless. I glared at Blackwell from my seat.

He looked shocked and almost insulted that I'd dared to enter the conversation between "grown-ups" without permission. "I beg your pardon, young girl?"

"Is Vasily a traitor to *you* or to the *Sect*? As I recall, when Vasily tried to kill me in France, he'd said he was only following orders. So whose orders was he following?"

Blackwell's smug exterior cracked for just a moment, and I didn't know if it was because of guilt or because of the affront of being accosted by teenager. It was back up in time for his response. "Believe me, little girl. My will is the Sect's. If the Sect wanted you dead, the Council would have ruled it during your oath, and you never would have left the cathedral." He watched me suppress a shiver before continuing. "If the Council did not want you dead, then the Sect did not want you dead. In that case, why would *I* want you dead?"

To keep me from discovering the message Natalya had hidden for Belle. The box under her floorboards. Alice's letter. There was no other reason.

"Like I have already told the Council and assured the directors, Vasily acted against my own wishes. The Council has already assessed as much. And you know I have no say over what the Council does or does not decide. *However . . .*" He turned to Sibyl. "It was under your watch that agents are relaying false information about a classified mission—a *failed* mission, atop of that. Like Director Prince said, we can only do so much, but hasn't your mishandling of the situation led to this outcome?"

As Sibyl's eyes narrowed to slits, Prince rubbed his brow with a throaty sigh. "This is ridiculous. Like listening to children bicker."

Or listening to parents fight. The other girls looked as stiff as I felt.

"Neither of you need worry. You both have a part to play in this mess and thus have earned the brunt of my disgust." He spoke bluntly, and though he'd managed to bring the rage in his grizzled voice under control, it still simmered beneath his words.

"You should watch your tone, Arthur." Uncrossing his legs, Blackwell leaned in, propping his elbows up on the table. "Regardless of what you might think—and the mistakes *your* students have made—I'm still the voice of the Council."

"What you are, Bart," said Prince, spitting out the name, "is a member of the Blackwell family, who have and always will be the useless ceremonial crust on the Sect's toe. A glorified mouthpiece for the Council. A messenger." Prince gave him a derisive smirk. "The only reason why Langley and I allowed you to be part of this conversation is because I correctly assumed you would have nothing better to do. Is that why you've taken to calling press conferences?" He tilted his head, curious. "Were you under the assumption that taking the position of an underpaid media liaison would finally give you a role better than relaying messages and occasionally dining with whichever prime minister has time for you?" His disgust was palpable. "A spoiled little boy with nothing to offer anyone. Like father, like son, I suppose."

Blackwell's face had turned to stone.

After a short pause, Sibyl cleared her throat. "It's time we move on from this," she said. "I called you specifically, sir, because I needed your advice on what our next move should be in regards to Saul. Maia?"

I jumped a little at the sound of my name. It was the first time anyone had actually acknowledged our existence without prompting.

"During our last communication, you told me that Saul had appeared before you in Marrakesh."

I nodded. "He told me a bunch of cryptic nonsense, then disappeared."

"But our scanners didn't pick up his signature," Sibyl continued. "We wouldn't have even known that he'd been there if you hadn't told us. Saul must be able to mask his frequency again."

The Sect couldn't trace him for weeks after his signal went dead in Greenland. What if that was where he'd regained control of himself? If Saul had gone back to masking his frequency weeks ago, then it had to have been the dead soldier whose Effigy frequency Communications tracked to the desert hideout. I shook my head, considering the possibility.

"Saul could have taken her in her room." Belle folded her arms across her chest. "Even if she is his final goal, we have to assume he's planning something bigger."

"Like an attack?" Chae Rin asked. "Maybe. Right?"

"He told me he wanted to change the world." I squeezed my fingers into my palms. "But we've got his ring, so he can't control phantoms anymore."

"He'll come for you regardless," said Sibyl. "He's been fixated on you from the start."

I sucked in a deep breath, closing my eyes to keep calm. Yes, Saul wanted me. I was his gateway to Marian, the Effigy swimming around somewhere in my subconscious with all the others. Only she had the information he wanted—where to find the rest of the stone from which his ring descended. Only then could he grant his ultimate wish, whatever that was. Belle was wrong. *Marian* was his final goal. I was just the sack of flesh standing in his way.

The sound of metal scraping the hardwood floor stopped the conversation dead. Blackwell pushed out his chair slowly, deliberately drawing out the noise.

"Ah, yes, good," he said, pleased, maybe, that he'd succeeded in gaining our attention. "Plan your next operation. I won't stop you."

Standing, he adjusted his long jacket over his shoulders. "But I should remind you of this, Arthur. I am the voice of the Council." He looked menacing as he said it. "The Council wants results. And if they don't get them, they'll surely make adjustments needed to the organization itself—including the chain of command."

The two men glared at each other.

"None of that is a worry to me, though," Blackwell added, his fingers playing with the cuff links on his sleeve. "A handed-down, ceremonial position offers its own benefits, Arthur. Job security, for one."

And with that, he left, the slam of the double doors echoing across the ceiling.

Prince's bottom lip curled, but he kept himself in check. He shut his eyes. "What are you proposing, Sibyl?"

Sibyl tapped her fingers against the table. "If Saul is planning an attack, he'll need his rings. With them he could control phantoms again."

"Both are still in your custody?"

Sibyl nodded. "Yes. Fortified and under twenty-four-hour supervision. But we—"

The director put up his hand once more to silence her, much to her annoyance. This time, it was to take a call he'd just received. He gave a few curt nods before answering back. "Very good. If he's already arrived at the facility, then tell him to head directly to the briefing room. I'll speak to him there."

"Sir," Sibyl said once he hung up. "Who are you referring to?"

"To be honest," Prince said, "I've been considering this ever since it was clear that you were struggling to recapture Saul." His Adam's apple slid against his skin as he swallowed. "Like you said, Saul wouldn't launch an attack on the Sect or make another attempt for Maia without arsenal. At this point, he's at a disadvantage. He'll need at least one ring. However, with the current situation of our recent breaches, I'm not confident that the rings are safe at your facility under your care."

"Since Saul escaped from our custody, I've made sure to conduct intense screenings of our agents here at the London facility," Sibyl said in a low voice. She didn't let on, but her rigid posture told me she was on the defensive. "I've done everything I can to ensure their security."

"You'll forgive me if I'm not convinced," Prince answered flatly. "Don't worry, Sibyl. This is good timing. I've already been preparing for the possibility of moving the rings to a more secure location. It's a delicate operation that would require the support of the Effigies and only a handful of trusted agents. I have a few I can spare."

"A task force," Sibyl said.

"I've already generated a short list of agents from my division. Some have worked well with your team in the past. I sent them to London the moment I heard about the mission's failure. Especially now that Saul's declared his intentions, I think it's time we move up my original timeline."

Sibyl frowned. "Which agents have you contacted?"

"He should be here shortly."

We didn't have to wait too long.

I was already on my feet by the time he walked in.

I should have known.

Two months since he'd nearly died protecting me against Saul. He looked perfectly fine standing in front of me, his black hair trimmed, a healthy flush to his high-angled cheekbones. During the weeks he'd spent at a London hospital recuperating, I'd visited only when I knew he'd be asleep. And once he was released, I ignored him, even after he'd gone back to his own post in rural New York, together with all of his unanswered texts, to resume his original job as a run-of-the-mill field agent. His voice messages were still saved on my phone.

And for a time, I thought it would work. I thought that if I didn't see him, didn't speak to him, didn't talk about him, and didn't think about him, then I could properly deal with the fact that he may have murdered Natalya. I could take the information Natalya herself had given me, real or not, and stow it back in the recesses of my mind. I could forget him.

I should have known.

"Rhys." I stupidly stared at him with my jaw slack, my shoulders slumping hopelessly.

But Aidan Rhys did not look at me, did not even respond to the sound of his name from my lips. His eyes had already found the screen at the front of the room, and the man whose stone gaze he matched.

"Aidan." Prince clasped his fingers together, peering down at the young man with a businesslike chill in his expression. "Good, you've arrived."

I'd never seen Rhys so stiff. "Yes," he said with a formal voice and straight back, though the sharp glint in his eyes told a different story. "Hey, Dad."

7

"WAIT." LAKE LOOKED AT RHYS, THEN TURNED to Prince. Then back to Rhys. Then back again. "You guys are father and son . . . seriously?"

The two men left the question unanswered as they stared each other down.

Rhys *had* told me once that he belonged to one of those Sect legacy families—the ones who'd been loyal for generations.

My dad fought. I could hear his voice in memories. *My brother, too.*

What he hadn't told me was that his father was the *leader* of an entire Sect division. He'd left that little detail out.

"Not 'Dad.' Director Prince," Prince said, correcting Rhys's initial greeting, and it was then that I noticed the difference in their surnames. Was Rhys a pseudonym? Code name? Was it for security reasons? Personal reasons? My mind raced. There was so much I didn't know about him. Too much.

"*Director Prince*," the older man repeated.

Rhys straightened his jean jacket with a sharp tug, but said nothing. The delicate contours of his lean face tightened with his frown, the muscles in his long neck stretching as he lifted his chin. Even with his soldier-like, attentive posture, he was challenging the man childishly. But then, he didn't outright disobey him either.

Standing, Sibyl approached him to shake his hand. Only then did he seem to relax his body. "It's good to see you again, Rhys."

"Yeah, it's been a while, hasn't it?" It was like the spell his father had cast had finally worn off. His expression softened. Rhys gave Sibyl one of his friendly good-boy grins that seemed to light up his soft brown eyes. Then, finally, he turned our way. "Girls, hello again. And sorry, Lake: Yeah, this is my . . . dad."

His inviting smile strained at the word but didn't waver until his gaze passed over me. His body quirked curiously once we made eye contact. But not even that lasted long. "Good to see you," he said in one breath before he turned back to Sibyl.

"I already heard some of what's been happening on the way here. The mission to capture Saul." He snuck in a wry grin. "And that press conference. Phew! That was a nice bit of theater, but it doesn't help us much. It's already all over the news."

"The increased public scrutiny puts us in an even more delicate situation," Sibyl said.

"Director Prince has already discussed with me the possibility of moving the rings," Rhys said. "I know we'll have to operate in secrecy. I came here ready."

Prince responded with a curt nod. "This mission must be executed with the utmost precision. Sibyl will catch you up on our present situation. The three of us will consider the plan of operations and go over the short list of agents from the North American Division I've generated. We need to get preparations under way as quickly as we can."

Chae Rin leaned in, glancing at the rest of us. "What about us?"

"It's late and you've just come back from a mission," Sibyl said. "If this is going to go smoothly, we all need to be at our best. Eat. Rest. Train. Like usual. We'll handle the operational logistics."

"But—"

"We'll send for you once you're needed, not before."

Chae Rin jerked her head back, but Sibyl, who'd already turned away, didn't notice. Sibyl probably hadn't meant it so bluntly, but Chae Rin knew the ropes as well as I did. We were the muscle. What did that pigeon-faced conservative senator Tracy Ryan call us once? Right. Biological weapons of mass destruction. A little dramatic, but the point was clear: We Effigies only pretended to be heroes for the rest of the world and the adoring fans with their homemade signs and hand-written letters. The reality was, we were tools of the Sect. They pointed us at whatever they wanted blown up and we did our best not to die.

We followed orders. But Natalya's death had already taught us that working for an organization with as many secrets as the Sect meant trust was a luxury.

"She's right," Belle said as I watched Rhys from the corner of my eye. "There's a better use of our time. Let's go."

She didn't need to say much else. Following her cue, we stood up to leave.

With the breaches plaguing the Sect, Prince was being careful, controlling the variables of the mission right down to the agents he allowed in his task force. But we Effigies had our own mission. We'd have to be careful too.

Rhys turned his head slightly as I passed, as my shoulder grazed his arm. It was even worse than not being acknowledged at all. For one fleeting moment, my heart sped up. I almost hated myself for it.

I was the one who needed to be careful.

"Rhys." I caught Prince's voice just as I reached the door. "You know that I chose you to be a part of this task force because despite everything, I trust you. You are and always will be a soldier of the Sect."

I knew it. Natalya knew it too.

My stomach hit the couch hard, my legs awkward and stiff over the armrest. That's when I felt something crinkle in the pocket of my sweatshirt.

The fan letter. I reached inside and pulled it out. The pink envelope was sealed by an adorable bunny sticker.

"What's that?" Chae Rin shut the door behind her. "Is that the fan letter?" She came up to the couch and, before I could shove it back into my sweater, snatched it out of my hands.

"Hey!" I tried to get it back, but she danced out of the way.

"Let's see what we have here." Quickly peeling off the bunny sticker, she slipped out the letter. "Ooh, it's handwritten!"

I could see the girl's tiny cursive writing through the thin note-paper. Chae Rin made sure to annoyingly alter her voice as she read.

Dear Maia,

You're so cool! All my friends like Belle, Lake, or Chae Rin—

"Damn right." Chae Rin puffed out her chest.

—but to me you're totally the coolest because I feel like you're kinda just like me. I hope you don't read the comments online and feel bad about all the people saying you're not super-hard-core enough. You started like a month ago—and your scythe is so cool! I'm even making one out of cardboard!

"Did you hear that?" Tilting her head, Chae Rin let out a loud, affected sigh as she held the letter to her chest. "She's making one out of *cardboard*. Oh, you're just . . . just the *coolest!*" She'd said it as if literal tears were dripping from her voice.

My cheeks were burning. "Shut *up*," I grumbled, though it wasn't easy hiding how pleased I was. Someone thought I was cool. Maia Finley. Well, better late than never.

> *There's a fan convention coming up in August and I would love for you guys to show up! Please think about it!*

"That would be fun!" I said.

"All those neckbeards. No, thanks." Chae Rin tossed the letter, then the envelope, back to me. "Well, congrats, kid. You finally have a wittle fan! It's like you've come full circle: from an Effigy fan to an Effigy fan's soon-to-be disappointment!"

"Oh, just. *Quiet.*"

I could hear Lake giggling as she passed by us both. Shoving the letter back into my sweatshirt, I flopped onto the sofa as Chae Rin walked away.

I'd left my suitcase by the door, but Belle was already dragging hers up the stairs of our dorm. Our little home.

Home. I hadn't been home in two months. Sibyl's training regime denied us access to our homes and families to stay focused. Even Lake, who *lived* in London, was not allowed to venture into the city to see her mom and dad. I knew Uncle Nathan was alive, at least. But I hadn't had the chance to tell him with my own mouth that I'd become an Effigy. He certainly knew by now. After losing his brother, sister-in-law, and niece to a fire, he'd lost his other niece to destiny.

Uncle Nathan was the only family I had left. I should have told him right after I knew I'd become an Effigy. It was too late now.

Though maybe it was easier not having to face him.

In either case, I had a new home now, for the time being. Since I'd left New York in April, this round, two-story flat had become Effigy Central, and it was trashed accordingly: cookie crumbs on the carpet, dirty dishes in the sink, empty bottles overturned on the table next to a sticky television controller. Lake always tried to keep the place clean and Belle was very tidy, but these days, as the missions and stress piled up, not even Lake's nagging could keep the combined sloth of Chae Rin and me in check. I was sure half the dirty pairs of socks on the floor were mine.

As I picked one up and inspected it, Lake went straight for the fridge. It was all an open space with no walls separating the living room and kitchen, so I could hear her loud and clear when she said, "Okay, I'm hungry. I haven't eaten anything since that fried crap at the airport. You guys want something? Let's see what we have here."

Lake pulled out one of the many containers labeled with her name on it—not that it ever stopped me or Chae Rin stealing them. "Maia." She waved one container at me. "Plantains?"

Pulling myself up, I could see the banana-like fruit was already cut, but uncooked. Being Nigerian, Lake had a similar love for certain foods my Caribbean mother would cook back when she was alive. A few days ago we went on a supervised venture into town—supervised because Sibyl had to be sure Lake wouldn't try to escape and see her family in Woolwich. Little did Sibyl know, Lake's parents knew the owner of an Afro-Caribbean store in Southwark.

"Your parents are still in Nigeria right now, right?" I asked her. "For that wedding or something?"

"Yeah, that's what they told the store owner to tell me." Lake let out an overly dramatic sigh as she was predisposed to do. "They're off having fun while their daughter is trapped in this facility doing missions instead of joining in the festivities. They're so *cruel*. It's like they don't even *miss* me."

I doubted that was true. Mr. and Mrs. Soyinka had gone to great lengths to protect her in the past. The seventeen-year-old was as sheltered as you'd expect from a pampered only child. But it was fun going to the Afro-Caribbean store with Lake—a nice little connection between us. A decidedly more normal one than the cosmic link we already shared.

With Sibyl's ban on seeing our families, it was a connection we both needed.

As she poured the oil in the frying pan and turned on the heat, Chae Rin bent low and pulled some soda out of the fridge. "You know, I thought I'd be more tired, but weirdly it's like I'm wide-awake. Why is that?"

"You're a scary adrenaline junkie." I got onto my knees and dangled my arms over the couch.

Chae Rin walked over to the utensil drawer. "You could be right," she said.

Then she threw a knife at me.

"Hey!" I caught the tip inches away from my forehead. "Um, what the hell? Are you bored?" I added as Chae Rin laughed.

"Just keeping you on your toes, rookie." She leaned back against the fridge and took a big slurp of her soda. "Looks like all my training is really paying off. I'm impressed."

"So you're bored." I tossed the knife onto the kitchen table a few feet away. It clattered against the wood. There was a reason why Chae Rin had her own room. Same as Belle. There were only three to spare anyway, and Lake and I rooming together decreased the likeliness of a pillow suffocation happening.

The four of us were a team. It was what I kept telling myself. And on those long nights I couldn't sleep for fear I'd see Natalya, those nights I'd stayed awake trying not to think of Uncle Nathan or my dead family, it was the comfort of knowing there were three other girls with me that made life more bearable. But things weren't always easy, no matter how much I wanted them to be.

"Maybe instead of trying to kill me, save your energy for the next mission," I said.

"*Another* one." Lake slid slices of plantain into the pan. The thick, sickly sweet smell sizzled into the air. "Will I *ever* get a reprieve from all this blood and death?"

Chae Rin smirked. "Life was a lot easier back when you were still dodging the Sect's calls, huh, Victoria?"

I was so used to the stage name that I usually wasn't prepared to hear anyone use Lake's real name. Chae Rin only did it to piss her off.

Lake shot her a dirty look, grabbing the handle of the frying pan menacingly. "You're really asking for half a pint of hot oil in your face, aren't you?"

"In any case," I said loudly before this got ugly—as it often did, "now that we're all here, there's something I need to tell you. It's about what happened in Morocco."

Chae Rin sat at the table and crossed her legs. "So are you finally going to tell us what you saw in that dream of yours?"

My fingers gripped the sofa.

"You saw her, didn't you?" Lake said over the sizzle of her pan.

"Yeah. I saw Natalya. And she . . . she wasn't . . . right."

Chae Rin and Lake stared at me. But it was the shuffling upstairs that caught my attention. I swiveled around and looked up to see Belle peering down at us from the iron railing on the second floor, her hair loose over her shoulders. She'd shut the door to her room so quietly I hadn't even noticed she'd left it.

"What do you mean, she wasn't right?" Belle asked, looking down at me.

"Wow, it's like Bloody Mary," Chae Rin said in a low voice. "Say Natalya's name three times and Belle suddenly appears."

Belle usually ignored her snide comments, but this one earned Chae Rin a look so cold even *she* looked a bit shaken. Quietly, Chae Rin took another sip of soda while Belle started down the stairs.

"Maia, what do you mean?" Belle repeated, her eyes on me.

I always had to choose my words carefully when it came to Natalya. "What I mean is that she wasn't right. She was violent. Scary." I shuddered, thinking about the sword in Rhys's chest, but I didn't dare utter that detail. I couldn't. "She entered into my dreams."

"But that has happened to you before, has it not?" Belle stopped by the couch. "The only way to see former Effigies is to scry. Peeling back the layers of your own mind to access their memories. You would have to be in a trance—or else, you would have to be dreaming. You have seen her memories in your dreams before."

"But this time was different. Before, I'd just fall asleep and see her memories. This time, I was having a dream of my own and she appeared. In my dream, she ran around Marrakesh, telling me to catch her. That's when she led me into a new memory."

"*Led* you? Is she like your spirit guide now or something?" Chae Rin asked. "Telling you stuff, leading you places?"

"Well, I don't know about that. I mean, in the past, whenever I'd glimpse her memories, it'd be an involuntary thing. She'd only tried to directly communicate with me twice. Once when I took my oath at Ely Cathedral. And then in France, the first time I scried properly."

And then she'd tried to take my body.

I went rigid, my blood pumping faster as I thought of it. "I used to just dream my own dreams. And then suddenly one night, I began to dream Natalya's memories. But since France, I'd been hearing her more often in my head. And then this happened. I thought maybe it was because of the experiment messing around in there. But what if the true problem was that the barrier between my mind and hers was already deteriorating even before then?"

Then Natalya would have more freedom to play around in my head. It'd make taking my body all the easier. My throat tightened as I thought of the possibility. I rubbed the sweat beading off my flushed forehead.

"Well, we shouldn't jump to conclusions. Maybe it was something she could do all along and she's just decided to be more proactive," Lake said from the stove, her spatula dripping oil onto the counter. "If that's the case, then isn't it a good thing? We know the Sect lied about Natalya's death being a suicide. We know Vasily tried to kill you." She listed them off with her fingers. "We know he and some agents from Research and Development helped free Saul from Sect custody. I still think she wants us to know the whole story regardless of anything. She led us to the box in Belle's old foster home, but since then it's been radio silence. We've been waiting for her to beam another message to Maia."

But all I'd gotten from Natalya were taunts and hazy dreams of her death played on instant loop like a broken nightmare channel.

"Each time you've been in contact with Natalya's consciousness, you've learned something about her death," Belle said. "Her investigations of Saul, moving under the Sect's radar. It was because of all her efforts to find out the truth that she was . . ." The next words caught in Belle's throat, but she covered herself quickly, sweeping back her long hair. "If she's leading you somewhere, it's for a good reason."

Or she was messing with me. That was the problem. It's like Natalya herself couldn't decide if she wanted me to know the whole story behind her death and the mystery that she'd died for—or if she simply wanted to use her memories to lure me into a trap to take my body.

As if purposefully planning the cruel irony of her timing, Belle added, with utmost certainty, "It's Natalya. We can trust her."

I took the fan letter out of my pocket and turned it over. "The last time I trusted Natalya, she tried to take over my body," I reminded her quietly.

Belle stood frozen to the spot for a moment. "Yes, well," she said quickly. "I told you once before, scrying has its risks. Normally, you need to be calm. You need complete control of yourself. But at that time, you were in the middle of facing Saul. Such a high-stress situation would obviously compromise the barrier between your consciousness and hers. Given that, it *makes sense* that her mind would cross over involuntarily."

The letter crinkled in my hand. "Except it wasn't involuntarily." The words fell from my mouth, heavy like the stone sinking in the pit of my stomach. "She very, *very* purposefully chained me up in my own mind."

And I remembered every painful second. It was like being buried alive several feet underground. My mind was probably weaker for it now, which made it easier for her to scratch at the surface of my subconscious.

But did Belle understand that? From the awkward purse of her lips to her subtle attempts at avoiding my knife glare, her reluctance to accept the truth was obvious.

"We were *both* in danger." Belle raised her head almost in defiance. "I'd been captured by Saul. Chae Rin, Lake, and all the train passengers were the hostages of phantoms. You weren't enough to save us. She would have seen everything through your eyes." She met my gaze as if to challenge me. "She would have wanted to fight."

"Seemed to me like she just wanted to live."

"Wouldn't you?"

Belle's words evaporated into the silence that stretched out between us, unbroken but for the sizzling of Lake's frying pan.

There it was. That insidious, nagging suspicion that had bloomed the moment we'd spoken for the first time at La Charte hotel: that I was nothing more than a replacement borrowing Natalya. I lowered my head. That night in France, as she'd held Saul's ring in her hands, I really believed for a second that she'd do it: wish me away and Natalya back into my body. It would have been an easy wish to grant. Saul had said so himself. I wanted to believe in Belle. I wanted to believe in the tears she'd shed as she dropped the ring and collapsed to the ground. And though there were times it felt as if she were finally warming to the idea of us as a team and of me as the fire Effigy, other times I couldn't be sure.

Maybe she wanted Natalya back. Even if it meant I was gone forever.

"Wait." Chae Rin placed down her soda can and stood from the table. "You're excusing what Natalya did now?" She looked at her in disbelief. "Are you a body-snatcher apologist?"

But it was clear that Belle had realized her mistake. She was already shaking her head as each of us watched her. "That's not what I meant."

"Wow." Chae Rin let out an incredulous laugh. "That's kind of a new low."

"That's *not* what I *meant*." Her voice rang out over the room. Regret was clear in the pale blue of her eyes as she faced me again. "That's *not* what I meant."

Panic. Even if it was just a shadow, I wasn't used to seeing it sweep across her features. Suddenly, she looked sheepish, ashamed of herself. "That's not what I meant, Maia," she said, shaking her head. "Please don't take it that way. I would never." The regret in her eyes as she pleaded with me told me she remembered that moment in France as well as I did. "I wouldn't."

I played it off with a shrug. "I guess I'll just have to believe you, right?" I wanted to. I *had* to.

"My, what a well-adjusted, functional bunch we are." Chae Rin rolled her eyes. "Okay, look, we all know Natalya was your mentor and you and her were tight while she was still breathing or whatever, but we need to be realistic about our situation."

Nudging Lake out of the way, Chae Rin went over to the kitchen cabinet. When she reached under the pile of magazines in the bottom drawer, I knew what she was looking for. We had to put it in an unsuspecting spot after all.

She pulled it out: the cigar box Natalya had buried underneath Belle's old floorboards. A couple of weekends ago, Belle had cleaned off the moss and dirt that had clung to the dark wood, polishing the stunning handcrafted carvings in appreciation for their design. But it was what was inside that mattered. Lifting the lid, Chae Rin pulled out a small shard of white stone—the same mysterious stone that comprised Saul's rings.

"You said Saul wants the rest of this, right?" She squeezed the tip of the shard delicately between two fingers. "A death-powered stone that grants wishes. One of the dead fire Effigies in Maia's head knows how to find it. That's why he kept coming for Maia. Natalya led us to this thing. She clearly wants us to figure this whole mystery out, but given what happened to Maia, that doesn't mean we can trust her completely. It's possible that she wants two things at once."

She wanted us to solve the mystery she couldn't. But she also wanted to live again. No one knew which she wanted more. Maybe not even Natalya herself.

Placing the shard back in the box and shutting the lid, Chae Rin turned to me. "Kid, Natalya isn't going to stop talking to you. And that's fine. We need her. Listen to what she has to say, but keep two eyes open, you know? Not everything she says may be on the level."

No. No, it may *not* be, least of all Natalya's last living memory: Aidan Rhys, standing over her as she struggled to breathe from the poison he'd given her.

But was it really true?

And for the thousandth time I tried to justify my doubts, though it's not like they weren't already justified. If I, from the depths of my mind, could see her using my body to decimate Saul's phantoms in France, then Natalya could see everything *I* saw. She would have seen me with Rhys. She would have felt the way my chest tensed whenever he was close to me, the way my body flared to life when he smiled. She would have known—

I thought back to the way his head moved to follow me, almost involuntarily, as I passed him on the way out of the briefing room.

She would have known.

And Natalya hadn't wasted a single moment snatching my body the moment my mind crumbled at the thought that he might have killed her.

I knew how much it had meant to her, feeling the air rushing through her lungs again, feeling her muscles burning with adrenaline. More than needing me to find out *why* she died, she needed me to regain the life she'd lost. It was everything to her. But those memories had felt real. Too real to be lies. And—

And I didn't know what to think anymore.

"Maia." Belle's voice snapped me out of my desperate thoughts.

"Y-yes?"

A pause. "*Has* she shown you?"

There was a strange twinge in her voice as she spoke.

"Shown me what?"

"Who killed her?" Belle didn't even look at me as she asked it.

It took only a second for my whole body to flush, for my head to swirl in frenzy as I scrambled for the words I was now used to saying. "No, no. Not yet. Everything I see is choppy, you know? Hazy. Unfinished. You were right when you said scrying can be kinda unreliable when you're not super trained."

"Then we'll keep training." Belle turned for the stairs. "If we are going to take on Natalya's final mission, we need to know the whole story."

"Sure, for the mission," Chae Rin said under her breath. "Not like she wants to carve up whoever killed her."

Carve up whoever killed her. The thought of it chilled me to the bone.

Belle shut the door of her room behind her, leaving us in an awkward silence.

"Well, these are done!" Lake said suddenly, turning off the heat on the stove, her cheerful voice breaking the quiet dread that had settled over us. The hot, oily slices of fried plantain were already drying on a paper towel–covered plate. "Maia, you want some?"

She always tried hard, Lake. Whenever she noticed the mood taking a turn for the worse, she'd put in her best effort to lift it again. But with my heart squeezing against my rib cage, I could only manage a smile. "Thanks, but I'm not hungry. I'm going to bed."

After a few labored steps up the staircase, I disappeared into my room.

8

OUR TRAINING SESSION WAS OVER, BUT SOME-
thing restless in me still stirred. There were a couple of hours left in
the morning, so Belle went for a run. The other two returned to the
dorm to wash up. But I stayed behind in the gym staring down the
black punching bag mounted to the wall in the corner. With my unruly
hair tied at the base of my neck, I raised my arms, my hands nestled
carefully inside a pair of boxing gloves, wrapped up with bandages in
the way Chae Rin had shown me. And while I was not the pro she
was, I'd taken to this particular method of training over the weeks;
the sound of my glove-cushioned punches battering the leather-bound
sand was steady in its rhythm, the powerful impact offering me the
kind of release I craved as it shuttered up my bones. Saul on the loose.
Natalya plotting inside me. Secrets, lies, deception.

Yeah, the stress was there.

The creaking from the double-door entrance to the gym ricocheted
off the high, arched ceiling as someone slowly pushed the doors open.
I figured it was one of the girls come back for something. Maybe Chae
Rin—she'd forgotten her water bottle by the bench and it'd only cause

another blowup if she used Lake's without permission again. It was almost funny how comfortable we'd gotten around each other while still being so painfully dysfunctional in other ways.

My fists flew. I heard the footsteps behind me but didn't think to look back, not until I heard his voice.

"You've gotten better."

A sudden jolt in my chest made me miss the timing. The punching bag swung fast and hit me in the head just as I'd turned it. Stumbling, I fell back onto the floor at Rhys's feet.

"Or not."

Rhys knelt and gripped my arm softly, just above the elbow, while his other arm found my waist. I twitched at his touch but didn't pull back. His dark eyes caught the light that slipped in through the high windows.

"It's okay," he said softly. "It's just me."

Just me. The gentleness in his voice had returned, breaking down my defenses like it always did. Making me want to trust him.

"Sorry I startled you," he added as he helped me to my feet.

"No. It's okay."

He must have realized then that he was still holding on to me. Quickly, he withdrew his hands. I shifted awkwardly, looking down at my sneakers, my bare legs, before steadying my chest enough to look up at his sculpted face.

"Um, it's been a while," I said.

"Yeah." It was times like this I remembered that before he was a trained soldier of the Sect, he was also just a kid like me, a boy of eighteen. He looked as nervous as I did, his eyes focused on the punching bag instead of on me. "I hope you didn't think I was too short with you back there in the briefing room," he said. "It's just that we haven't talked in a while."

The side effect of dodging his calls for weeks. That was how I'd treated him. Even after he'd nearly died protecting me. Even when I wanted to know why he ever would.

"You didn't visit, either. At the hospital, I mean," he said, giving me a wry smile as he tilted his head sideways. I turned the moment I noticed my throat begin to tighten. "I thought maybe you forgot I existed. It's all right, I forgive you," he added jokingly.

I didn't tell him that I had visited him three times, but each time he was sleeping, and I begged the nurses not to let him know I'd been there. During every visit, I studied his face and watched the rise and fall of his chest, wondering to myself whether he was really a killer—and whether I'd really be able to turn him in if it was true. And to *whom*? The Sect? Or Belle.

Belle. My body froze up from the very thought of her murderous anger. If he had killed Natalya, and if she found out . . . if I said a word about it . . . Belle would kill him. There was no doubt about it. She would murder him in front of me.

Maybe it was better if I never knew.

I walked away from him back to the swinging punching bag. "Why are you here?" I steadied it with my gloved hands. "I thought you, Sibyl, and your dad were planning the next mission."

He paused. Maybe he wasn't used to me referring to his father. Well, he'd never even mentioned him in first place.

"I came to find Belle," he answered simply, and my hands froze before I could even ready my strike. "There are some things about her report on your last mission I wanted to clear up. You're boxing now?"

The thought of him and Belle interacting sent my blood pressure up. Sucking in and out a deep breath only marginally helped release the anxiety.

"Yeah, it's good stress relief." Which is what I needed right about now.

Rhys was much taller than me. When he stood next to me and rested his hand on the punching bag, he showed every bit of his six feet. "You've been working hard, huh?"

"That I have." Pride slipped into my voice as I said it, and I didn't know why, but the little boyish grin that followed made me glad I'd told him. "You should have seen me out there, Aidan. I'm a veritable badass these days."

"Show me."

"What?"

But Rhys was already taking off his jean jacket, showing the white short-sleeved undershirt he'd been wearing beneath it. His broad frame filled out the fabric almost deliciously.

"What are you doing?" I asked again, blushing as I kept my eyes on his toned arms.

Rhys scratched his eyebrows. "Take off your gloves. Let me see what you've got."

There was something still so unassuming about him even though I knew how long he'd trained for, how strong he was. How dangerous. And not just to phantoms.

I stepped back, unsure of whether to stay or go, or whether I could, even if I wanted to. My hairs were standing on end, my face continued to flush with heat, and while it didn't feel all that good, it didn't feel all that bad, either. This was crazy. This was why I'd gone through such great lengths to avoid him. Because being in his presence meant facing this dizzying, entangled mess of contradictory emotions. Stay or don't. Believe Natalya or don't. My hands were twitching.

I needed to punch something.

I threw off my gloves and lifted my arms in a ready stance. Rhys raised his eyebrows, but soon his surprise turned to excitement. He waved me over. I tried one strike, hard and fast. He dodged it easily, stepping to the side, but I went after him anyway. It's not like I wanted to hurt him. But somehow the drive of a good fight cut through the thick of emotions and, for that one moment, gave me the kind of peace I so sorely needed. I had just one thing to focus on. One goal: land a punch. Simple. Unlike my life.

But Rhys was too good. He never struck back at me, only dodged, ducking and weaving, tilting his head, tapping my arm away to tip me off balance. Fast. Precise.

Then he swiveled around me and tugged the back of my shirt almost playfully. I paused and stared at his grinning face in surprise, and before I knew it, my lips were spreading too. His smile was infectious. I launched at him again, my heart pounding, and not just from physical exertion. Despite his speed, I still noticed the way his forearm stretched and flexed as he moved, the slight strain in his long neck as he lifted his chin to avoid my strike. His body maneuvered fluidly, carefully. Gentle but powerful. It suited him.

"You're enjoying this way too much," I said when he let out an adorable little laugh.

"I mean, you've gotten better, but you're not exactly in the badass category yet." He caught my wrist and pulled me in to him. My breath hitched as he leaned over too close. "Unless you're going easy on me?"

I craned my neck up to meet his gaze. A catlike gleam turned his narrowed eyes wicked as he stared down at me. I could feel his breath against my face. We were both breathing heavily, our chests rising and falling in different rhythms. It almost made me forget.

Almost.

"Well, unlike you, I haven't trained all my life," I said, keenly aware of how close our bodies were now.

"The key is keeping up with your training." His hand was still on my wrist, my arm resting against his hip as he held it in place.

"Don't know how you managed over the years."

Rhys shrugged. "Well, I don't have many friends I hang out with."

"Friends . . ."

Friends.

By the way, are you interested in coming to see the dinosaur exhibit, by any chance? It's why I'm here. I even dragged a few of my friends along.

I straightened up. The question had already formed before I could stop it, but it wasn't until I peered up again into his quizzical face that I gave it words. "Have you . . . been to Prague?"

Rhys let go of my hand. "Prague?" He paused. "Maybe on a mission? I can't remember."

My arms felt heavy. "The museum," I said carefully. "Have you been to the museum?"

What little was left of Rhys's smile had disappeared. "Why would you ask something like that?"

"Why would you avoid a simple question?"

His unreadable expression was so fleeting, I couldn't be sure I'd seen it at all because in the next second he gave me a half-amused, half-incredulous look. "I'm not avoiding it, Maia. It's just a bit random is all. But if you're that curious . . ." He furrowed his brows and thought. "Prague . . . wait . . . actually, yeah. Yeah, I did once. I saw a dinosaur exhibit or something like that. Maybe earlier this year—I can't remember exactly when. Why?" With a teasing grin, he added, "You interested in going with me sometime?"

He'd admitted it. He'd gone to the museum. But . . . if he was trying to conceal what he'd done to Natalya, would he have admitted it so casually? Or maybe he was so casual exactly because he wanted to throw me off? I stepped back. What was I supposed to believe?

"You okay? Are you tired?" he asked, but the moment I saw his hand reach out for me, my body jerked away so violently that he withdrew it immediately, shocked. "Maia . . ."

"Sorry, I'm okay," I lied. And we stood there staring at each other.

Did he or didn't he kill Natalya? The truth was, I wasn't prepared for the consequences of knowing.

9

IT WAS EARLY IN THE EVENING WHEN I GOT A call from Cheryl, Sibyl's mousy assistant.

"The mission starts in sixteen hours," she said. "But before your briefing, Director Langley wants you to report to the Research and Development department. Fifth floor."

She sounded distracted, so I wasn't surprised to hear shuffling in the background. Probably another mountain of paperwork. She now had to deal with constant requests to set up photo shoots, radio interviews, and other frivolous marketing stuff superfluous to her actual job as an assistant. I guess when she suggested to Sibyl that we get pushed as the pretty and marketable faces of the Sect, she didn't expect to be the one taking on the brunt of the work.

"Just me?" I wasn't particularly feeling up to doing much of anything after what had happened this morning.

"Just you." Cheryl sounded annoyed over the phone, but then these days she was always a little irritated with someone. "You need to get fitted for your new equipment before the mission begins."

Effigies get equipment? I get equipment? I jumped off my bed.

Hopefully, it was something badass. I always thought it kind of sucked that agents got really high-tech weapons and gizmos while we Effigies just relied on our own natural ability to control the forces of nature and summon giant weapons out of nothing—

Actually, no, that was kinda cool too.

But having *actual* equipment certainly wouldn't take away from the cool; it could only *enhance* it. Like how you could equip Aki from the Metal Kolossos series with different armor and accessories. Hey, being an Effigy was dangerous and bloody and usually resulted in tragedy and death, but that didn't mean you couldn't have a little fun with it. I definitely could use a little fun right about now.

Chae Rin and Belle were off training again—separately. Not unexpected for the two in our team who were the least gung ho about being in one. My dear roommate, Lake, was still stomach-down on her bed, completely free other than anonymously writing malicious comments on pop forums about her old pop group.

"What?" she said. "I'm nervous about the mission and this helps me relax."

"Okay." I dragged her off her bed by the legs. "Let's get some fresh air."

It was better to go to R & D with someone else anyway. The long trek across the grounds was twisty and confusing, the directions taking us through the stone halls and the overhead walkways overlooking the grounds.

We reported to a giant, busy laboratory on the fifth floor of the department. While some scientists bustled up and down the long aisle, others were busy at their terminals, studying the metallic-blue specs projected onto translucent LCD screens so thin and wide the figures could have been twisting in the air all by themselves. Natural light sifted in through the army of blinded windows lining the walls. But the electric lighting fixtures on the ceiling would have been more than enough to illuminate the room.

My eyes followed down the aisle all the way to the huge monitor hanging on the wall at the front of the lab. There were other computer screens, much smaller, screwed into the wall, but this one showed a map of the world against a black screen. Some areas lit up with red spheres of different sizes, its color fading as it radiated outward.

"What's that?" I pointed at the monitor, walking ahead of Lake down the walkway.

"A map. Novel, isn't it?"

I stopped in my tracks. Behind one of the terminals to my right, just in front of a glass case filled with Sect-grade weaponry and Sect maroon suits, stood Rhys, dressed in a blue-gray baseball jacket and a pair of faded jeans just tight enough to showcase his long legs.

"Uh, I swear I'm not stalking you," he said, noticing my surprise.

As he started toward me, I thought back to the momentary silence that'd stretched between us in the gym and started shifting on the balls of my feet, my brain sputtering for some kind of excuse to leave.

"Those red circles represent cylithium-rich areas." He tossed his black hair with his long, delicate fingers. "Helps them anticipate phantom attacks."

"Right, right. Cylithium." I took a step back. "What are you doing here?"

I asked because I couldn't look at him without thinking of Natalya. It was difficult enough to approach the questions with a clear mind even when he wasn't around. But when he was . . .

"I said, why are you here?" I repeated a little too sharply.

Rhys stopped dead in his tracks. It could have been disappointment softening his eyes—or hurt.

"They made some upgrades to our suits." He pointed at the glass case. "I came to make sure everything was ready for the mission. That's all . . . really."

Maybe it was because of the accusatory sting in my tone that he sounded so insecure.

He started toward me again, but before I could run, he stopped at a terminal to his right by the wall, tapping someone on the shoulders. I couldn't see what the very short woman was welding at her desk, but I could see the smoke sizzling from the little pen she gripped gingerly in her hands. She jumped a bit at Rhys's touch, lifting up her safety glasses to glare at him, her sleeves pushed up past her elbows. But with an amused look, he pointed at me instead.

She whipped around, blinking when she caught sight of me. "Oh, you're finally here?" Grinning wide, she waved me over. "Oh, good, good. Get over here and take off your clothes."

"Excuse me?" Lake exclaimed behind me.

I could barely see the woman's face before she whipped around again.

"Dot, you're thinking of someone else." The blonde at the terminal next to her shook her head. "These are two of the Effigies." She nodded at me. "You're Maia, right?"

"Yeah," I said. "And I'm definitely not taking off my clothes."

"Oh, right!" The woman named Dot smacked her own forehead. That's when I finally took stock of her tiny face and nut-brown eyes, wide and bright like jewels against sallow, sickly skin. "Oh, I'm so sorry. Forget that, go away, I don't need you. Oh, wait, no . . ." A pause. "Sorry, the neck-band, right. I was working on that. Come here, come here."

Blindingly pink high heels clicked on the tiled floor as she adjusted her seat at the bench, her lab coat swishing behind her.

"Just working on a bit of tech for you. I'd explain, but I'm not quite done yet," she said, picking up her welding pen. "You're welcome to wait here while I work. Actually, I would have had this finished earlier, but there was a bit of a mix-up with the equipment storage down the hall. Luckily, Pete and Mellie over there were here to help me out with that."

At the terminal next to her, two young lab techs reacted to hearing their names, and the young blond woman who'd spoken earlier rolled her eyes.

"Yeah," Mellie said, peering up from her monitor. "You forgot your own code. Again."

"Even though you'd just reset it. *Again*," Pete said after rubbing the back of his brown neck, but he wasn't looking at Dot. He was leaning over the desk, fiddling with some wires linking up to one of the monitors. There was something beside him—some kind of box—but his tall frame blocked it from view.

"Yes, well, that's why you're my assistants." Dot rubbed her sunken cheek with a gloved hand, and it was only when I saw her cheekbones jutting out that I noticed how thin she really was. "You assist me."

"Yeah, we *assist* you in remembering what day it is," Mellie grumbled, her short blond bob bouncing as she shook her head.

"This is Dot Nguyen, by the way," Rhys told me, and I could tell he was suppressing a laugh. "Weapons and Tech expert. We got her from the facility outside Toronto a few weeks ago. She was the one who designed that inoculation device you used against Saul."

"Really?" Dot Nguyen. Director Chafik had mentioned her before. I certainly remembered that gadget, too. In Buenos Aires, I'd jammed the long tip into Saul's neck to temporarily disrupt his powers. It was brilliant. It saved my life.

Dot shook her welding pen as if it were out of ink, jumping back when she nearly dropped it on her knee.

"Uh." Rhys scratched his head. "All that matters is she's good at the things we pay her to do."

Dot scratched her scalp through her messy black hair. "Well, don't just stand there. Grab a seat while you wait. Don't mind the mess. I know my work space here is a bit . . ."

Chaotic. There were tools, design plans, beakers, and other equipment not exactly organized atop the white counter. Dot was pointing her metallic pen thing at a white chip the size of a cracker. Smoke had already begun to rise from the tips when she lowered her safety glasses.

Lake and I hesitated when Dot waved us over, but curiosity got the better of us. And Dot wasn't the only one busy. Pete and Mellie looked to be in the middle of some kind of experiment. When Pete finally moved out of the way, I could finally see what his body had been shielding from view: two glass cases no bigger than a box of tissues. The white shard inside one was just barely visible against the clear surface, but it was the long, twisted oddity placed delicately inside the other that caught my attention.

Once the two of us reached their terminal, Lake walked up to Pete. Pete noticed. The goofy grin never left his face as he stood up from his seat.

"What is that thing?" she asked as Pete adjusted one of the wires hooked into the cases.

Pete lifted off the cover. "Half a phantom's toe."

"What?" Lake spat as Rhys walked up to the desk next to me. Close.

"For real?" Rhys narrowed his eyes, peering through the glass. "It looks crystallized."

Indeed. Phantoms had the ability to harden their hides into an impenetrable shield. Saul had called it "petrification" during the battle in France, and using his ring, he'd forced the phantoms to demonstrate. I'd never forget the way their bodies cracked and crystallized in the night.

The toe looked like a curved tree branch with a sharp, hooked tip—a claw maybe.

Rhys leaned over the table for a better look, and I could feel his arm grazing mine as he touched the glass. My body reacted before I could stop it. I pulled myself away with an awkward spasm. It was only when I caught the shocked look in his eyes that I realized how it must have looked. Lake was watching me too. I said nothing as Rhys silently backed away from me.

"What's the other thing?" Lake asked slowly, though her quizzical eyes were still on me.

"A sample." Pete's silly grin came back. I figured it was probably related to the way he devoured the sight of Lake standing next to him. "Of the ring. We shaved off some of the stone. We've been doing different things to figure out the relationship between the stone and the phantoms, putting both through different stimuli. Particularly, we've been trying to figure out if both materials share certain chemical properties."

"See," Dot explained as Mellie stared at dark blue diagrams of the shard and toe on her monitor, "we've tried everything we could to figure out just what the heck the stone is. Where it came from, how it worked. If Saul were around, I'd ask him a few questions, but unfortunately for us, he's still in the wind. So we did experiments. Many, many experiments, which, by the way, took more time than necessary, considering a handful of our agents got arrested two months ago after that whole letting-Saul-go fiasco. Days and hours and seconds and charts and graphs and computers and looking at monitors—"

"They get it," Mellie said next to Pete.

"The stone isn't from this world." Dot whipped around so suddenly Rhys jumped back a bit, probably out of self-preservation. The woman jittered as if she survived on oxygen and espresso alone. "That's the conclusion we came to. It simply doesn't exist in the natural world—or we haven't discovered it yet." She ran her gloved hand through her messy black hair, yanking it out again when it got stuck in the knots. "It's either an alien ring or there's much more to this world we don't understand yet."

A world of shadows. Secrets veiled in darkness . . .

"We know that Saul used the ring to control phantoms and focus their attacks on targets of his choosing," Pete said as Mellie continued examining all the numbers and bars littered across the touch screen of her monitor. "But there could be more to it. Bystanders reported that Saul's phantoms petrified around that train when he attacked in France two months ago, and then unpetrified to attack you."

"He did it purposefully to hold the passengers hostage," I said.

"Willing it to happen by using the ring, I'm sure," Pete continued. "So not only can you use the stone to control phantoms, but you can also use it to force phantoms to transition between natural and petrified states. Whatever the ring is made of, it can control the phantom's biology down to a molecular level. The stone and the phantoms. There's definitely a deeper connection between them we don't know about."

Dot sighed. "What I wouldn't give to pick Saul's brain. You guys have no idea how much you screwed up by letting him go."

Lake scoffed. "*We* screwed up? The traitors that let him escape the facility in the first place were in *your* department."

Dot cocked her head to the side. "Oh, right," she said with a shrug. "Still, it would have been nice if you could have brought him back."

"Not exactly easy when you're being attacked by a bunch of phantoms, but whatever floats your boat," Lake said.

I would have shared Lake's indignation, but I was too busy contemplating what we'd heard from Director Chafik back at the Marrakesh facility. "You're the one who came up with the ether theory, right? That Saul represents a fifth element?"

Dot perked up. "Oh, so you've been reading up on me?"

"We heard about it in Morocco. Saul's powers—living forever, disappearing and appearing at will? It's like he can bend space-time."

"Well, it's just a theory I had. The four of you girls can manipulate different elements. For a time we thought that there were *only* four of you. But then Saul appeared—a fifth Effigy."

A fifth. And that dead soldier could be a sixth.

"For centuries," Dot continued, "scientists have theorized ether as a medium necessary for the very propagation of gravitational and electromagnetic force. The raw essence of all space . . . the mysterious foundation of the universe. Is this Saul's element? And is the ring tapping into the same force?"

Dot was lost in thought for a moment before heaving her shoulders with a sigh. "We need to learn more about him." The smoke drifted past Dot's safety glasses as she continued to solder. "What's more, we need to find the connection. Among the stone, the phantoms, and the Effigies. Those three very mysterious variables. If we had more information, we could find out where all three came from. Maia, I know you were debriefed after your mission in France, but sometimes we think of things after everything's settled. Are you sure Saul didn't tell you anything else about the ring when you faced him last?"

I placed my hands behind my back like a child who'd just been caught with her hand in a cookie jar. I wanted to help. And I could have. The ring controls the phantoms. The ring uses the deaths they cause to magnify its power. That was why Saul had been using the stone and its ability to control phantoms to go on a killing spree. Somehow, when he used the stone to force phantoms to kill, it added to the stone's ability.

Its ability to grant wishes.

All these facts would surely be of use to Dot and the R & D department. And if the Sect hadn't been involved in Natalya's death or Saul's escape, I would have told them happily.

Dot sighed when I shook my head. "Well, that's fine, I suppose. But anyway, that's not really why I called you here. Wait a second."

She opened one of the drawers at her bench and pulled out a small briefcase. As she unlocked it and lifted the lid, the glint of a silver steel band caught my eye. Using a screwdriver, she pried open a small section on the inside and began fitting in the chip she'd been soldering.

"What is that?" Lake asked.

"Maia, you've been having issues with scrying, haven't you?"

Rhys looked at me.

"Dr. Rachadi at the Marrakesh facility sent over the results of your earlier exam. Because of your encounter with Saul in New York leading to your premature summoning of your weapon," she said as she tinkered with the chip, "your mind is vulnerable to the consciousness of the other Effigies in your line. More than it should be. Case in point." Dot set down the bracelet. "You've seen Natalya a lot lately, haven't you?"

The intensity in her gaze froze me to the spot. I nodded before I could stop myself.

Rhys's back straightened a little. "You've seen her?" he asked.

"Well, I told you a long time ago I'd been dreaming of her," I said. "It's getting more frequent."

"Has she said anything?" A short silence followed after Rhys spoke. "Or done anything?"

"Why?"

The nonchalant shrug of his shoulders calmed me for the few seconds I believed it before the doubt began crawling back up my insides.

Rhys wasn't stupid. If he'd really killed Natalya, he would have known that I would find out eventually through Natalya's memories. Was he really innocent? Or was he just quietly waiting for the other shoe to drop?

Maybe we were both just trying to deny reality.

"I'm just worried about you." Looking suitably concerned, he folded his arms across his chest. "It's dangerous enough having past Effigies milling about in your head. You know that, Maia."

Why not turn him in?

Why not?

If he killed Natalya, he deserved to be punished.

My lips trembled as I thought of him rotting away in a Sect prison for the rest of his life. Or executed. Is that . . . is that what I wanted?

He looked convincing, natural. And why wouldn't he ask more about my scrying? It was the obvious question to ask considering everything that had happened to me. Right?

What do I do? I thought desperately, turning from him.

"Yes, it is dangerous," said Dot, picking up on Rhys's warning. "Hence the necklace."

Dot was finally finished. Standing, she carried the device in front of her as she approached. "Remember, Sibyl still wants you to scry to find this 'Marian.' That's who Saul is really after, right? But we don't want to hurt you in the process. This will help regulate your brain chemicals while using your powers to scry so you won't get any more surprise visits from previous Effigies. Let's see if this fits: Sweep back your hair for a bit?"

I did. "Ah!" My breath caught in my throat from the stinging cold of the steel. The effect was nearly imperceptible, slight enough for me to ignore it, but if I closed my eyes and concentrated, I could feel the cold vibrating softly through muscle.

"We can also inject her with a primer to help stabilize her cylithium levels," Mellie said.

"Oh, right, good idea," Dot answered. "You can handle that, Mellie."

"Won't that make it harder for her to scry?" Lake looked a bit worried. She knew how important my communication with Natalya was. But Dot was right. It was a dangerous game. I didn't want to lose myself playing it.

"Well, you won't be able to communicate as readily. It's like setting up a makeshift wall in your brain. The windows are still there—you'll just have to pull a bit harder to open them, but hey, it's better than the storm blowing in, you know?"

The neck-band was a bit clunky, but I could pass it off as a fashion statement if I needed to. It was better than being body-snatched by Natalya.

"I still don't understand how Natalya's mind is in me in the first place." I shook my head once Dot took the neck-band off again. "All this stuff about frequency and vibrations and chemicals and whatever, but at the end of the day, someone's mind is *in* my mind. I don't understand it."

"Welcome to our world." Dot gave me a pat on the shoulder. "Controlling the elements. Effigies passing on their consciousness, but only after they die. Magic. What you do is magic. Magic that shouldn't exist, but does. And the only thing we mere mortals can do is try to understand magic through science." With her bony hands, she propped herself against her assistants' table. "Because really, what else *can* we do? How can the ability to perform magic be created from inside the human body? Why can we also find it in phantoms?"

There was a wildness to her curiosity, smoldering as she pulled up her safety glasses and faced me. "How is the mind connected to the body? How is the mind connected to magic?" She tapped my forehead twice with her index finger. "How did Natalya's mind and magic travel into your physical body after she died? Mind, magic, body. One hundred years and we have more questions than answers. But we are trying our best. There's just so much we don't know yet."

"That's understandable, but it doesn't really help me," I said.

Dot rubbed the muscles in her neck as she moved back to her station. "It's like we're looking at the wall of a cave seeing only what we can see through our limited scope. Trying to grasp the universe into our hands using nothing but our flimsy, woefully insufficient technology." She picked up a screwdriver from her table. "But the real truth . . . the real truth, Maia, is always just out of sight."

10

SIBYL WORKED IN MYSTERIOUS WAYS. ORGA-
nizing a secret mission away from the prying eyes of the vast majority
of your highly skilled, perceptive agents must not have been an easy
feat. The few that were let into the loop were already in the expansive underground hangar by the time I arrived with Chae Rin and
Lake. I could see their tiny forms through the glass of my elevator as it
took us down. They were scurrying across the pavement, loading seven
white delivery vans. Belle had gone ahead of us. Maybe she was already
among them, helping to prepare the decoys.

It was part of the plan. Each van was inconspicuous enough to
pass under the average civilian's radar. Under Sibyl's orders, they would
drive off in different directions, forcing potential enemies to split their
forces to get to the cargo they wanted: the rings. Two rings, two vans,
two Effigies in each, waiting to strike like snakes in a gift box alongside a small crew of agents for backup. A city-wide shell game. It was
Sibyl's idea, but Rhys was the one who'd figured out the routes, the one
directing agents to their respective vans. In his maroon suit, Kevlar-
based like the one I was currently chafing in, he leaned against a wide

table set up next to one of the vans, a paper map spread across it.

"Howard?" I waved excitedly when Howard Day, the beefy, bald Sect agent I'd met in New York, lifted his shades to greet me.

"It's good to see you again, Maia." His voice was just as grave and his expression just as serious as ever. I was glad he was okay; he'd been in bad shape the last time I'd seen him. Cocking his head to the side, he narrowed his eyes. "What is that?"

He pointed at the leopard-patterned bandana around my neck. Lake had lent it to me to hide the steel neck-band keeping the little voices in my head in check.

"Neckwear is against mission dress code regulations," he started to say, suddenly reminding me how very stuffy he could be. "It can be a distraction on the battlefield and—"

"I think it's pretty. Howard, relax. We've talked about this." The beautiful woman standing next to him smiled at me through her long lashes, green eyes bright against her tawny skin, a similar shade to mine. "I'm Eveline. The wife."

She was shorter than I was, which made the height difference between the couple all the more noticeable, yet charming nonetheless. Her black hair was shaved close to her skull, pronouncing the square shape of her head. The three white studs at the corner of her left ear gleamed under the hangar lights.

"Didn't know you were married," I said as she greeted Chae Rin and Lake.

"Well, they say the family that slays together . . ." Rhys left his words unfinished as he flashed me a quick glance and an even quicker smile.

Keeping my face unreadable, I dodged both, looking at the map instead. "These are the routes we'll be taking, right?"

My evasion didn't go unnoticed. After a slight pause, Rhys

straightened up. "Yeah. The routes of the different vans are all here in marker." I could see the red streaks tracing lines through London and Essex, the two cities sandwiching us here in Epping. "Each will take different paths out of the facility, but, Maia, you and Belle will be in one of the vans going underground." He tapped the route with the tip of his covered marker. "Route L-9. It's an underground highway built during World War II. It was used for communications during the war, but since then, the Sect has revamped it and built new structures. There'll be Sect agents in stations along the way monitoring the route and keeping the tunnel APDs online."

"We're not headed to the same place, are we?" asked Chae Rin. I could hear the sound of music from her headphones as they dangled down her chest, her phone deep in her left pocket.

"You and Lake will be in Unit Two, heading out toward Dover Port with Unit Three following close behind as backup. Belle and Maia are heading northwest in Unit Seven with Unit Six as *their* backup. For security purposes, you won't be told the location until you get there."

"I'll be with you, Maia," said Eveline, picking up a gun off her table. "And a few other agents."

"Do I get one of those?" Chae Rin watched, far too interested, as Eveline fitted the gun inside the holster on the small of her back. "Hey," she added when Howard gave her a sidelong look, "unlike some of us, I can't generate my own weapon. It's for *protection*."

I peered around the hangar. "You really think we're going to need all these people?" Several agents were suiting up and equipping themselves. Preparing for Saul. Felt more like preparing for a war. My stomach lurched as I watched them pack into their respective vans.

"We know it's a possibility that Saul might launch some kind of attack to find the rings," said Howard. "He wouldn't come unless he had some trick up his sleeve. We want to be prepared."

"Don't worry." Rhys's tone was much lighter as he rolled up the map, sweet enough for my heart to speed up. The difference between his boy-next-door and boy-bred-for-battle personas was like night and day. But *both* were dangerous. "I'll be one of the agents in your van. And as I seem to remember, we've worked pretty well together in the past, right?"

I remembered too. "Okay, whatever," I said, avoiding his smile. "We should go get ready. Get in position or something."

I thought I'd be better prepared for the look on Rhys's face, the quiet but unmistakable pang of hurt in his eyes as he watched me. I pretended not to notice. It was better than dealing with the sudden twinge of pain I felt upon realizing that if he was really innocent, then I was hurting him unnecessarily.

But if this was a ruse and he was playing me . . .

"Good luck," I said to Howard with a quick nod before taking off.

The awful sensation corroding my insides was the same I felt every day I avoided telling Uncle Nathan that I'd become an Effigy. I would look in the mirror and wonder how I'd become so pathetic, or if I'd been like that from the beginning.

You're so annoying! Just confront him, I ordered myself, but I kept walking. The thought of confronting Rhys over what he *might* have done sent a fresh surge of panic through me. Because knowing the truth meant consequences I wasn't prepared for. Because I didn't want to believe he could hurt a friend in cold blood. Because I was a coward.

And because of that other thing.

You don't believe me . . . because of your crush? Pitiful. This body. This life. You don't deserve it.

I could still remember the way she'd laughed at me. Natalya . . . She was probably watching everything right now, more determined than ever to take me over.

That is, if sending me into a tailspin of doubt wasn't her plan all along.

"Oi, Maia." Lake tugged my sleeve as we walked side by side down the hangar, past the agents loading weapons. "Something going on between you and Aidan?"

I stopped. "No. Why? Who told you? What are you even talking about?"

"Relax!" Lake laughed in surprise before lowering her voice. "Wow, try a little harder to act less guilty, yeah? Seriously, you guys have been weird since he came back."

"What 'you guys'?" I could feel my mouth drying. "There's no 'you guys.' Since when has there been a 'you guys'?" Luckily, Chae Rin was already off somewhere hounding some agents to lend her a firearm "for protective purposes." Otherwise she'd have been picking apart my obvious insecurities like a barely healed scab.

Lake, on the other hand, only shrugged. "I dunno. A while ago you guys seemed to be getting along well." I hated the way her grin spread across her face as she added, "*Really* well. Especially on his part. It always seemed to me like he was a bit taken with—"

"That's not possible." The heat rose up from my cheeks.

"Not possible?" Lake made a face as she adjusted the tight black bun at the top of her head. "What does *that* mean?"

I struggled to find the words. "I mean, that can't happen."

"Why not? Goodness, you need to have a bit more self-esteem, yeah? There's nothing wrong with you." She patted me on the shoulder. "You're a bit neurotic and judgmental, but aren't we all?" She paused. "Actually, no, it's just you."

Self-esteem was probably one reason. Even before my family died and my introversion went into hyperdrive, I'd found the comfort of my own room and a good gaming console more reliable and relaxing to be around than the opposite sex. The other reason was something I didn't dare utter here, to anyone.

Not until I was sure of the truth about Rhys.

"I'm sorry. I'm not good with . . . romance feelings." My stilted delivery made that pretty clear. I couldn't blame Lake for laughing.

"Anyway, don't worry about that stuff. If it happens, it happens." And she gave me one last slap on the shoulder. "Nothing wrong with a little love on the battlefield, I always say. Plus, he's really hot. Pretty face, banging bod." She shrugged. "You could do worse."

"Duly noted," I mumbled, my toes curling in embarrassment as Chae Rin sauntered back to us, gunless.

"We're four minutes out from the start of the mission," Sibyl's voice came from the overhead. "Everyone get to your stations." She didn't have to be physically present to order us around. Communications was too public for a mission that was only supposed to involve part of her fighting force; she'd set up her own operations base from her office instead.

"Oh dear. I'm getting a bit nervous." For a few seconds, as Lake shifted uncomfortably on her feet, I could see the erratic rhythm of the rise and fall of her chest. Then suddenly, like a switch had been flipped, she snapped her head up. "Oh, by the way, Maia, speaking of Rhys—"

"We weren't," I said flatly.

"Since you two are in a bit of a rough spot, do you want me to help by getting him an invite to the TVCAs? I can ask my agent for tickets!"

Chae Rin laughed. "Of course you'd be worrying about some celebrity wankfest instead of the actual mission at hand. Why am I not surprised?"

"What?" Lake said as I distinctly heard Chae Rin mutter the word "airhead." "I'm just trying to lighten the mood a bit, *sorry*. I know you're all about blood, death, and destruction, but some of us aren't."

Lake tried to keep her voice measured, but I knew it wouldn't last. "Besides, this stuff is important too. We have other kinds of Sect duties, you know."

"*Other* kinds of Sect duties! I'm *dying*!"

"Yes, *other kinds of Sect duties*!" Lake's voice rose rapidly over the harsh dissonance of Chae Rin's laughter. "Going to this awards show is our *duty*. Cheryl and Sibyl okayed it—hell, they *want* us putting ourselves out there."

"Right, and this has nothing to do with your old girl group snagging their first number one. You really are completely, decidedly full of shit, Lake. I seriously—"

"I'm what? Say that again?"

It was never going to stop. It *didn't* stop even as the two stalked off to their vans.

Just as they left my sight, Belle turned around the corner of a van, her hair plaited down her head in a French braid. "There you are. You're with me," she said. "Come, it's time."

Sucking in a breath, I followed.

One o'clock. In the dead of night, the delivery vans drove out of the underground hangars through a network that took us up to the surface. Only when we were clear of the facility's reach did our silent procession break up as each van traveled down its prescribed route.

To the regular civilian passerby on the highway, our van would have looked almost too deceptively simple. But our boring, white moving cubicle skillfully hid from view the weapon cases strapped to the wall, the handheld blades and electromagnetic phantom-dispelling bombs tucked in the compartments beneath the black-cushioned benches.

And one of Saul's rings. It was in a black safe specially fitted against the division separating the driver and passenger seats from the cargo unit we were sitting in. Another van followed a few car lengths behind. The only way inside our compartment was sealed shut with an electronically locked door that could only be opened with a code.

With sweaty palms, I sat rigidly on my bench next to Belle, who laid her head against the wall, eyes closed. On the opposite bench, Rhys stayed alert, watching the several blinking red lights on the center screen of the monitor as the vans separated down different paths. The van floor rocked beneath my boots while I listened to the sound of cars rushing by.

The left and right screens of the monitor acted like a surveillance system showing us different angles outside the van. But they didn't show us every angle.

"Eveline, what do you see out there?" Rhys held a finger to his earpiece as the communication device picked up his voice.

"All clear so far."

I could only hear her; she was on the other side of the division in the passenger seat with another agent, Lock, who drove us along the highway.

"All units check in," came Sibyl's voice over the comm.

"Unit Seven, all clear," said Rhys.

"Unit Six, all clear."

"Unit Five, all clear."

And it continued like that.

"You don't think Saul would just ambush us out here, do you?" I asked quietly, shifting uncomfortably in my seat.

"Yes. That's why there are bombs in the bench, Maia."

It wasn't a tone I was used to from Rhys. He sounded annoyed. I heard the sting in his voice, but he kept his eyes away from mine as he continued to keep in contact with the other units. Not that I had a right to complain. But my throat still labored as I swallowed hard.

"Maia," came Belle's voice from beside me, and when I looked up, my lips almost parted in surprise. Her eyes weren't fully open as they looked at me, but the encouragement of her small smile, as fleeting as it was, had enough of an impact. "This is all just a precaution—you know that. Don't worry."

She wasn't as confident being warm. Her voice was softer, more fragile. It didn't come naturally to her. But she gave it a shot sometimes, as if she'd suddenly remembered during those odd moments that I wasn't just the girl whose destiny used to belong to her mentor. I was the girl struggling under the weight of it.

She was trying, Belle. Every once in a while, she'd set her grief aside and *try*. And I always appreciated it. But when her smile disappeared, the knit in her eyebrows returned quickly as if to make up lost ground.

"I'm sorry," Belle said. "I know I've been acting . . . strange lately." She said nothing else, but I already understood. As she brushed back some loose strands of hair streaming down her forehead, I stared at my knees.

"It's okay," I said as an insidious whisper of guilt taunted me. "And you're right about the mission. I guess I'm just nervous. I don't know if I'm really ready to face Saul again."

"You should be. This isn't your first mission," Rhys said flatly, watching the monitor as he twisted the sheathed tip of his favorite knife against his finger. "Haven't you been training? You should have toughened up by now."

That childishness was back, the same defiance masked as innocence while he pretended to be interested in his knife, twisting it against his finger. My hands clenched against my knees as we crossed through a Sect-controlled toll. I heard Eveline's voice from inside my comm.

"Entering the underground tunnel," she said. I could see that much on the monitor. The two-way highway stretched on in the darkness, speckled by the small lights lining the wall.

"Well, Rhys," I said finally with a bitter curl of my bottom lip. "Seems you've been reading some of my criticism online. Nice to know you found something to do back home for all those weeks."

"You mean aside from recovering?"

Recovering from his injuries—the injuries he'd gotten trying to protect me from Saul. I couldn't forget. A knife plunged into his chest close to his heart.

He'd done that for *me*.

He wasn't a bad guy. I knew that in my heart. He'd shown me as much while we were together. It was my head that needed convincing—not easy when there were other people living in it.

"Anyway, this is a mission, Maia." Rhys faced me with nonchalant eyes. "So let's stop this here, okay? No one's out to get you. Stop being ridiculous."

"Ridiculous?" I sat up straight on my bench. "How about you stop being a jerk?"

Rhys's jaw went rigid. His shoulders slumped. "Jerk," he repeated quietly. It seemed as though he wanted to say something else, but he thought better of it. Instead, he turned away with a pained expression that still didn't reveal his guilt one way or the other.

I heard Belle's quiet sigh before the road split off from the main highway down a closed-off path: Route L-9. The tunnel was available for commercial and civilian use, but the Sect's Route L-9 remained hidden from prying eyes. And it wasn't difficult to see how.

Our path was blocked. The wall stretched up from the paved road to the tunnel ceiling. For a moment, both delivery vans had to slow to a stop—that is before the solid wall smoothly shifted to the side, revealing the Sect's secret, expansive two-way network. It wasn't so much a tunnel as it was a miles-long underground bunker.

"We've reached the route without any issue," said Rhys in his usual, mission-fit tone as if he hadn't just sucker punched me.

"Good." The tension in Sibyl's voice was audible. "We haven't been able to detect any kind of dangerous frequencies on our end either. Checkpoint one, report."

Checkpoints. Sibyl must have meant the booth on the second-floor walkway above us, blocked off with a safety railing. It could have been either of the two agents standing at attention by the railing who answered, "No hostile sightings. Route is secure."

"There's a secret facility outside a small village in Oxfordshire," Rhys explained to us. "Only a select few agents know about it. Heavily fortified. This tunnel is a direct pipeline."

"And the ring will be safe there?" Belle crossed her legs, watching the monitor. "What of the other carrier?"

"On their way to another secret location," Rhys answered. "Everything seems all right on their end. Though their route is a little shorter than ours."

"Sounds like you missed out." It was lame, but I couldn't stop myself.

"Maia, look, I really don't know what's been up with you, and I don't know why you've been acting up around me or what I did to you that you can't stand to be around me. But whatever your deal is, it isn't my problem."

"Isn't your problem?" The dam broke. My voice rose several decibels. "Like hell it isn't. You of *all* people don't have the right to judge me. For *anything*."

Rhys's lips snapped shut as he looked at me in silence.

I could feel Belle's attention on me without looking. It was then that I realized the situation I was in. Rhys, a potential murderer. Belle, his potential executioner. With jittery hands, I clenched my teeth, thinking of a way out.

"Maia?" Belle leaned over when I turned my head and hid my expression with my thick bush of hair. "Are you okay?"

We crossed another checkpoint. Voices rang through our comms as various people reported in. Agents stood at attention as we passed, firearms ready at their sides.

With trembling fingers, I touched the scarf around my neck, hiding the neck-band keeping Natalya under control. All those weeks having the same nightmare tearing me apart every day and still no answers. No answer I wanted to believe, anyway.

"What I mean is . . ." I sucked in a long breath to still the rise and fall of my chest. "I may not be as calm as you are on a mission, Rhys. But not all of us were lucky enough to be battle-trained since childhood, so cut me some slack."

"Lucky." Rhys whispered the word as if it were poison. "You think I was *lucky*?"

We stared at each other, unspeakable words brimming beneath our heavy gazes. Rhys had told me once about his training at some facility in Greenland. He'd met Blackwell's right-hand man, Vasily, there as a child. Twisted, violent, vicious Vasily. But according to Rhys, not all of his malice could be blamed on nature.

Some training facilities are a little tougher than others, he'd said once.

"Forget it," I said more to myself than to anyone else.

"I agree," Belle said with a dangerous note of finality in her voice. "This is a mission."

Rhys gripped the handle on his knife. "Fine."

The agonizing minutes of silence that followed were mercifully broken by Eveline. "All's clear. We're approaching checkpoint three," she said.

"Good. We're getting close. Checkpoint three, report," Rhys almost mumbled.

He must have been distracted, stewing in his own anger, because it took him a while before he realized no one had responded. Blinking, he looked up at the monitor. So did I.

Two agents were there by their booths, standing behind the railing like they were supposed to be. Like the others we'd seen, they had their long, stalky firearms, similar to the one I'd seen Howard use to vaporize Saul's phantoms in New York. What I couldn't figure out was why their firearms were pointed at us, charging blue along the metal side strips stretching up the length of the guns.

Belle was already on her feet. Rhys had grabbed my hand before I knew what was happening, but it was too late. The deafening blast tore my eardrums, and all I could hear was a terrible ringing as our van launched into the air.

11

TWO BLASTS. OUR DELIVERY TRUCK FLIPPED and landed on the pavement with a crash. I felt my bones crushing against metal through my bruised, battered flesh. The sound of boots landing on the roof—no—the floor above us knocked me back into consciousness. I hadn't even realized I'd lost it in the first place.

"Rhys." With blood dripping down my eyelids, it was that much harder to pry them apart, but I managed to. Squinting, I felt around for him, my stomach pressed against the van's ceiling, my hands touching cold metal, until I felt strands of hair beneath my fingertips. "Belle?"

She stirred at the sound of my voice, her lips sputtering something I couldn't hear. Blood was streaming down the sides of her forehead, matting her hair, tracing a line down her ears. It was dark. Some of the weapons had burst out of their cases, a few phantom bombs rolling past my legs, hitting my twisted left foot. But they were still locked; none of them had gone off.

"Rhys!" Coughing, I looked around, lifting myself off my stomach to survey the inside of the delivery truck until I found him. He was out. Or dead? My heart rate suddenly sped up as I squirmed to him and felt for a pulse. No. He was still alive. Gingerly wiping some of the dirt and blood from his face, I sputtered out a grateful breath before shaking him. "Wake up. Wake up. Rhys!"

The pair of boots on the "roof" of the van stood still above us.

"U-unit Six," I said, trying to contact the van that had been behind us. No response. "Eveline? Lock?" I shook Rhys again. "All units, all units. Unit Seven is down. I repeat. Unit Seven is down! Help us! Someone. Anyone!"

I smelled the smoke before looking up and seeing the red line of a laser carving itself through the metal.

"Saul," I whispered. "Oh my god. All units, we're being attacked. I think it's Saul."

But Saul could vanish and appear anywhere he wanted. He didn't have to cut a hole into the van to get to us. Who was this?

"Hey!" I was yelling now, as much as my voice would allow. "Can't you hear me?"

"They cut the communications." Belle just barely managed to find her voice. "The mission is compromised."

The last thing I wanted to hear.

We were running out of time. I shook Rhys again and finally he began to rouse, but it wouldn't be fast enough. Whoever it was above us, he'd hopped down from the roof. The back doors of the van were already bent out of shape and half off their hinges, so I could see him approach. He needed only to push the metal doors to the side to find us squirming inside the van.

Or was it a "she"? The fitted bodysuit revealed an average-size feminine form, though her hair and face were sheathed inside a white metal helmet.

Metal helmet . . .

"It's the same," I whispered. The same helmet, the same suit. The same as the man we'd found in the Sahara hideout.

Whoever she was, she was blocking our way out and coming toward us. With a wave of her hand, Belle created a thick wall of ice to keep her from reaching us, but I knew the barrier wouldn't last; the mysterious soldier was already pounding against it. I had to do something. Dragging myself over to the side of the van, I placed my hand on the surface. My mind was still rattled by the impact, but I didn't have a choice. Summoning my will, I let the power flow into me, breathing it into my lungs. I felt it slide down my arms according to my will, my pulse quickening as it leaked out of my fingers.

Calm down, I told myself when my heart began beating out of whack. I saw my burning house in my mind's eye, but I banished the image. *Don't think about your family. You're not there; you're here.* The heat spread down half the length of the wall. Belle was pulling herself over to Rhys as the circle above us neared completion.

"Rhys, get up!" Belle gave him a hard slap just as the laser above us stopped.

One last kick sent the ice barrier crashing down. Belle knocked a block of it away with her arm, yelling out in pain. With a grunt, I let the fire explode out of my hands, closing my eyes from the blast. What was left of the van's wall soared off and skidded across the ground. Rhys was conscious enough to grab on to Belle as we jumped out after it.

I landed on my back, turning just in time to see the woman's boots clicking into the van, too late to reach us. She didn't seem to mind. Instead of coming after us, she stayed inside the van, busying herself as we dragged ourselves to our feet. Busying herself . . .

The ring. That must have been it.

"She's stealing the ring," I yelled as Rhys and Belle got to their feet. "We have to—"

The Sect agents by the checkpoint lowered their weapons only to pick up the guns in their holsters.

The bullets hailed. One flew past my head and another tore across my right arm as we ducked for cover behind the van. Effigies healed fast, but right now the stinging pain was hard to bear. Belle was breathing heavily, holding her stomach, still reeling from the explosion. Eveline and Lock, still alive, dragged themselves out of the van's window to take cover with us. But that woman remained inside the van. It was bulletproof, Sect-grade protection. With us occupied, she had plenty of time to take what she needed.

"This is insane." Rhys already had his knife in hand; the other held his head in pain. "Unit Six!" He'd yelled it instead, not bothering with his comm. "We need back—"

He couldn't finish, because he finally saw them through their windshield. They were dead, their heads rolled over at odd angles, blood dripping from the single bullet holes in their foreheads, shot through the window.

"Rachel!" Lock screamed in anguish as his hand dove into his holster.

Their murderer hopped down from the roof of Unit 6 onto the hood, crushing it a little. He had to be at least a foot taller than the woman and a hundred pounds heavier. Maybe more. He was huge, a bodybuilder on steroids. The man was armored from limb to limb, his head covered with the same sleek, robotic white helmet. But Big Guy's movements were strange, almost alien. His body seemed to convulse with each clunky step. It didn't stop him from raising his gun at us.

Lock charged past us, gun in hand.

"Wait!" Eveline cried, but Lock's sleeve slipped out of her grip. She ran after him.

Lock shot a hail of bullets, and every one of them found Big Guy's chest only to bounce off his armor with a loud *clink*. But did this thing even *need* armor? One of Lock's bullets shot through Big Guy's gloved hand as he raised it. He didn't even flinch. No blood oozed out of the hole.

One of the agent's bullets from the railings caught Lock's arm, and he cried out in pain. That distracted him long enough for the mysterious enemy to lurch forward and grab his neck. Eveline wasn't fast enough to reach him before the snap. Her hands weren't nimble enough to take her gun before Lock's murderer pointed his at her head. But Belle launched forward, wincing in pain, and with a swing of her hand, froze the gun in his hands before his bullet could leave the barrel. But something told me this guy didn't need a gun.

First, I had to get rid of the treacherous Sect agents. There was no other way. With a yell, I stretched my arm forward and a wall of a fire exploded from below the walkway, sending the agents into the air, shards of railing with it.

"Get back!" I told Rhys, and I tried the trick again, this time blowing our delivery van toward the wall and hopefully that woman with it. Better no ring than the ring being stolen by a couple of murderous cyborgs.

I was too late. While the van was sailing in the air, the woman jumped out through the busted back doors just as the van hit the wall. I had barely registered the crash when she rushed at me. Belle's sword was out before I could react, but the woman expertly dodged her swings.

Rhys grabbed his knife.

"Wait!" I said, clutching his shirt instinctively. "Are you okay? You're still injured."

"I'll be okay," he told me, though he couldn't hide his sudden wince. A fresh wave of fear shot through me as I watched him.

"But—"

With a gentle hand, Rhys wiped the blood staining my cheek. I fell silent at his touch. "Help Eveline," Rhys told me before tightening his grip on his knife and joining Belle's fight.

He was right. With great effort, I tore my eyes from him and followed the order. The other enemy was built like a fridge and moved like one. He didn't bother to dodge Eveline's gunshots, even when one bullet cracked his helmet. But that was good. It made him an easier target for me.

You can do this, Maia, I told myself. Well, it was either I did it or I died.

"Move back," I told Eveline, and, biting my lip, I forced my breath to calm. Fire erupted at my feet, the smooth pole forming in my hands. With the familiar weight balanced across my palms, I ran forward, flipping it around like I'd done so many times in training, bringing my blade down on him.

He didn't dodge. He didn't even try. I buried the sickled edge into the crook of his neck.

And yet he was still coming for me. Fear seized me. I let go of the handle and stepped back as he lumbered forward, undisturbed by the blade still in his muscle. With my mouth gaping, I did the only thing I could think of. A wall of fire, tall enough to keep him in place. Eveline jumped back from the flickering flames as it circled him.

"Is this thing human?" Eveline screamed, reaching into her pocket for new rounds, reloading her gun.

It couldn't have been. But his partner was. I could hear her laughing—a high-pitched voice, joyful and murderous as she dodged Rhys's and Belle's attacks. Still struggling against the aftereffects of the attack, neither fought at their full potential, but this girl's speed and agility would have been hard to guard against regardless. Blocking the swing of Belle's sword with her armored biceps, she ran for Rhys, dipping to the side to dodge his gunshot.

"What's wrong, Aidan? Nah, that's no good. You used to be a better shot, sweetie."

Rhys froze to the spot at the sound of her Australian voice, and in that one second, she was behind him, grabbing his hand, pointing his gun at Belle.

"Let me help you!"

The shot tore through Belle's leg, but it was Rhys I ran for, trying to make it before the woman, using Rhys's own hand to point his gun at his head, could fire the shot. Rhys overcame her himself, stretching his arm up just as the shot rang out into the air. She quickly snapped his wrist before maneuvering out of the way. Rhys doubled backward in pain.

"Rhys!" I said as he tripped on a spare wheel. I caught him before he could fall. "Rhys."

"Jessie . . . ," he whispered, his face pale. He couldn't see her face. But her voice was enough. "It's Jessie."

The woman he'd called Jessie was fast. Too fast. She dodged Eveline's shots until the agent's gun clicked empty, but she was already on Belle, whose sluggish ice attack couldn't land its target. As the ice spread across the ground a few feet away from us, Jessie grabbed Belle's wrist with one gloved hand and slammed her other hand into her neck. I didn't understand what had happened until I saw the frost forming at Belle's fingertips fizzle and die.

There must have been some device inside Jessie's glove. I could see a red spot of blood where Belle's neck had been pricked. And her powers . . . her powers were gone.

Jessie took advantage of Belle's shock to knock her out with a well-placed elbow to the temple. Next she came for me. Fast. Smoke sputtered from my hand erratically as I tried to control my equally erratic heartbeat. Calm down. I had to calm down. Jessie had already caught my wrist. A small circular metal device in the palm of her glove seized my attention, the tiny needle in the center of it glinting as she reached for my neck.

We heard the soft *clink* at the same time. My neck-band. I could almost picture Jessie's surprised expression behind her helmet as she paused, looking from her glove to my neck.

Taking advantage of her confusion, I kicked her away and summoned my weapon once more, but heavy footsteps behind me forced me around. It was the Big Guy. His armor was still smoking from the fire he'd just charged through.

With clumsy steps, he ran at me. From wild instinct alone, I swung my scythe at him, hoping that this time the blade would slice clean through his neck. But he dodged, catching the handle just underneath the sickle and lifting me off my feet. I swung my feet in the air, too shocked to react when the beast-like man rammed his other hand into Eveline's face as she made for him, swatting her away like a fly. Rhys was busy avoiding Jessie's hand-to-hand attacks. As Eveline hit the ground, unconscious, I knew I had to finish this guy off myself.

I grabbed his head and set it on fire, the force of the explosion pushing us back. I ripped his helmet off as I fell, and that's when I got my first look at him.

Oh, god.

The moment my boots hit the ground, I stumbled and landed on the floor, stunned. My stomach heaved as I saw the maggots—tiny, squirming things in the eye sockets of the rotted flesh where the Big Guy's head should be. Parts of his skull peeked through. I covered my mouth.

This was impossible.

"Ah, man," Jessie said. "You ruined the surprise. Still, it's impressive, right?" Flipping back to create enough space between herself and Rhys, Jessie took off one of her gloves, revealing a sickly pale, slender hand, and snapped her fingers.

The monster started to move. Lumbering. Lurching at her command.

But phantoms were the only monsters that were supposed to exist in this world.

Phantoms and Effigies.

"Take her, Dead Guy," Jessie commanded her slave. "Take the girl."

The girl. *Me.* My arms were lifeless at my sides as I stared at the maggots slipping in and out of his flesh. I couldn't move.

Suddenly, sirens echoed around us.

Sect vans sped down the tunnel from both ends. Encouraged, I whipped around to face my attackers again, but Jessie didn't waste any time. Without another word, she cut across the tunnel, grabbed something from her back pocket, and threw it against the wall. The small metal device latched on to the concrete with four metal arms spread out like a lucky clover, each arm lighting up with red bars down its length.

A second passed.

Then, the explosion.

Rhys and I shielded our eyes from the dust. And once it settled, Jessie was gone, her monstrous puppet falling to the ground with a dull *thud*.

A dead pile of flesh and bones on the pavement.

12

FAILURE. BETRAYAL. TWENTY-TWO HOURS
passed in disarray as Sibyl conducted an internal review of the London
facility's entire roster, though many agents had no idea what had even
happened in the underground tunnels.

But that wasn't enough for the Council. Apparently, after an emergency meeting, they'd called someone in from another facility to "aid
in operations." Whether that meant helping Sibyl or interrogating
her, I didn't know. Still, after what had happened, nobody could blame
them for taking action. Only two agents had helped those mysterious
soldiers attack us, but it was two too many. Lake's and Chae Rin's unit
had successfully delivered their ring to its new fortified hiding spot.
But Jessie had managed to make off with the one we were supposed
to deliver. If backup hadn't come when it did, she might have made off
with me, too.

Sibyl had told us to stay in our dorms, out of the way, while she
conducted the investigation, but that didn't last long.

"Open up! Open up, it's an emergency!" Rhys was pounding on the
door.

Chae Rin glanced up from her laptop. Lake and Belle burst out of their rooms on the second floor. Jumping up from the table, I ran to let him in.

"What is it?" I asked, taking in the sight of a blue cast on the arm Jessie had snapped. Dark circles caved in the skin around his eyes, his full lips cracked from dehydration. He looked like he'd been grilled all night.

"Bloemfontein's APD was hacked. Parts of the city have just been attacked by phantoms."

I sucked in a deep breath, my shoulders lifting with my chest as I let the dread sink in. Saul was back in business.

"Have agents been dispatched to the area?" Belle kept her eyes on Rhys as she walked down the stairs, her body mostly healed from her wounds thanks to her Effigy abilities.

"Yeah. It didn't look like it was a full-scale attack. The phantoms rampaged a farmers' market for a while before disappearing again."

"How do we know it was him?" asked Lake from behind the second-floor railing.

"It's his pattern," I said quietly, remembering New York. "Plus, phantoms wouldn't just target a specific area, then disappear."

Phantoms were forces of nature. They followed no will but chaos. So far, only the ring could channel that pandemonium into some instrumental purpose. It was him.

"We've been called to Communications." Rhys was already turning. "Dot's found something."

"Is it about that girl who attacked us?" I asked, following him through the door. "Jessie?"

Rhys's expression darkened as he tilted his head away from me. He rubbed his cast almost absently as he glared at something in the distance. "It'll come up. Let's get there first."

Under the night sky, we crossed the grounds to Communications, following Rhys up the elevator to the third floor. The room in which Sibyl, Dot, and Pete had been waiting for us overlooked the main floor, its front wall made entirely of glass.

I assumed it worked only one way. Though I could see the agents below clicking away at their keyboards, their monitors lighting up as they tracked disturbances around the globe, they surely, *hopefully*, couldn't see Sibyl pacing in front of a red-faced woman sputtering her usual anti-Sect rhetoric on the wide-screen television at the side of the wall. Tracy Ryan, Florida senator: the same woman leading the front on having us Effigies officially classified by international law as biological weapons of mass destruction so we could be quarantined accordingly.

"You can see the Sect's incompetence with your own eyes," she said as CNN split-screened her slim, pigeon-sharp face with live footage of the phantom attack in Bloemfontein.

My hands went cold as I saw large, spiderlike phantoms crash through streets with their clawlike legs. People screamed as they rushed past makeshift booths to save themselves from beasts almost half the size of buildings.

"I've said this before: The Greenwich Accords is nothing more than a locked and loaded gun holding the international community hostage while the Sect parades around, pretending to 'handle' these threats. But they're not doing that. What they're really doing is shoring up their arsenal and power while *pretending* to protect the rest of the world. They are waiting to strike."

"Well," said the host, "there's no evidence of them shoring up their power for any specific purpose."

"What more evidence do you need?" The big, blunt red headline beneath her face seemed to agree with her: TERROR IN BLOEMFONTEIN:

ANOTHER SECT FAILURE? "If we don't do something first, they will make their power known. It's time for the international community to come together to protect *ourselves*. More military spending and fortifying our borders is where we need to start domestically. But we need to unify against this dark threat."

"Threat," said the host, his head cocked. "Do you mean the phantoms? The terrorist Saul? Or the Sect?"

"At this point, is there even a difference anymore?"

"Idiot." Sibyl grabbed the remote from the round table in the center of the room and clicked the television off. "I wouldn't expect anything less than nonsensical fearmongering from that woman, especially when she's up for reelection. But this is really—"

She shook her head, staring at the black television screen for a moment, chewing her lip. Then, suddenly, she threw the remote to the floor.

"Uh . . ." Pete stared at the broken pieces of plastic on the ground before glancing up and seeing us. "Oh, hey!" he said, his voice a little too high. "Lake! And the others! Lake! Come here. Please." With a nervous grin, he waved us over frantically as he inched away from Sibyl.

Dot was bent over in front of one of two large monitors atop the long bench pressed up against the window. She clicked the screen twice and pictures popped up, each of the same white corpse laid out on a metal table. Lake gagged behind me, but after the guy I'd seen in the tunnels, this maggotless body was actually a nice change of pace as far as the grotesque went.

"No." Rhys spoke in a quiet whisper, his lips parted as he stared at the screen. Having been with the Sect for so long, he was certainly no stranger to death. Surely he'd seen bodies like this before, but the color drained from his skin the longer he looked at the corpse on the metal table. "It can't be. I can't . . . tell . . ."

"What is it?" I asked Rhys as he rushed up to Dot's side. "Who is this?"

"This," Dot said, pointing her pen at the screen, "this is another question. A question named Philip."

"*Philip.*" Rhys sounded each syllable as if it were a foreign language. "Is that him? Maybe it just looks like him?"

"Rhys, you know him?" I looked from him to the screen and back again. "I don't understand."

Pete scratched the back of his neck. "You know that dead guy you found in the desert?"

"That's him?" The mysterious young man we'd found in the Sahara hideout. Silently, I watched Rhys's face turn white as the body on the screen.

Lake covered her mouth. "Gosh. He's . . . really dead."

"Well, these pictures are from *before* he got dissected. You should see the 'after' pictures—there's loads more information to get from those!" Pete's tone was a little too flippant for Lake, as if he'd forgotten that dissections and autopsies were only delightfully interesting to a select group of people with very special interests. A group Lake didn't belong to. Her expression soured as if she was about to throw up.

"Rhys," I said carefully. "How do you know this guy?"

"Th-that's . . ." He stopped. Rhys was shaking a little, his eyes blinking rapidly, struggling to focus. He steadied his breath. "I think that's—"

"Philip Anglebart." When Dot tapped the screen, it went dark and what looked like a graduation photo appeared. There he was, the boy who'd died in Belle's arms, but with a few key differences. His blond hair was cut close to his skull in a buzz cut, his face not pale but rosy-cheeked. He was younger in this photo, as if he'd just entered his teens. But the downward slope of his close-set eyes was the same. "One of the seven chosen for the final cohort of the Fisk-Hoffman Training Facility in Greenland." She flipped her pen around between her fingers. "Along with Agent Rhys and Agent Volkov."

There must have been some kind of dark magic in those simple words Dot had spoken; at the very sound of the name, the life slipped and fell from Rhys's eyes. His neck muscles twitched as he clenched his teeth and nodded.

"Yeah. Yeah, that's him. I know him. We . . ." His eyes darted in my direction before he cleared his throat. "We trained together." He wouldn't look at me.

Rhys had told me before that he'd trained for a time in Greenland. *Some training facilities are a little tougher than others.* That's what he'd told me, though he'd never elaborated.

Rhys shook his head. "But he's dead. They're all supposed to be dead. Only Vasily and I survived the . . . the fire."

"What fire?" Walking up to him, I gripped his broad shoulder tightly, tilting my head low to catch his eyes. It slackened beneath my touch. "What are you talking about, Rhys?"

"The facility shut down four years ago," Sibyl answered instead, her piercing expression hardening as she stared at the picture of the young man. "Because of a wide-scale fire caused by an electrical fault."

My body stiffened involuntarily. A fire. Electrical fault. It sounded too familiar. But I couldn't let myself slip back into painful memories.

"It never reopened. Too many of the staff died, including all the doctors. And the students. Only Rhys and Agent Volkov survived and were relocated."

"I didn't know . . ." I trailed off as Rhys turned on his heel, pivoting out of my touch.

"Wait, so he's alive after all?" Lake asked, and thought about it.

"Well, I mean, *now* he's dead. But before, you know, *before*, how could he have been alive to die if he'd already died?" She sighed impatiently. "Ugh, you get what I mean, right?"

"The other five students were only presumed dead," Sibyl explained. "Their bodies were never recovered after the fire."

"Wait, let me draw up their profiles." A few series of clicks from Dot's fingers and the seven were on the screen.

Philip Anglebart. Talia Nassar. Gabriel Moore. Alexander Drywater. Jessie Stone. Aidan Rhys. Vasily Volkov. Each was young in their photo, barely into their teens, wearing the same blazer as if taking a school photo. Talia's long dark hair was split at the edges as it draped down her chest. Gabriel was very slight and handsome, his small eyes peering out from coal-dark skin. Alexander was the biggest of all of them by far, the size of a football player, his red hair as closely shaven to his skull as Philip's.

"Jessie . . . ," I whispered, and could sense Rhys reacting to the name. Jessie, in this picture, was very chubby with a hooked nose and a square jaw that turned her face into a box. Her brown hair fell around her face and her green eyes sparkled as she smiled cheerfully for the cameras. Innocent. Hard to believe it was the same girl who'd almost killed us in the tunnels.

"Wait. Alex?" I stared at the burly boy in the photo before turning to Belle by the round table behind me. "You remember, right?" I asked before shifting to Chae Rin, who was sitting on top of the table, swinging her legs. "Before he died, Philip told us to find Alex. Remember?"

Pete shuffled uncomfortably on his feet. "Yeah, I think we did. Well, you did. In the tunnels." When he saw that I wasn't following, he let out a weary sigh. "Um . . . we were able to identify the dead body that attacked you."

Oh. *Oh.* As my stomach lurched, Rhys whipped around. "You're kidding. You're . . ."

He turned to each of us as if hoping we would tell him this had all been some kind of cruel joke. Scrunching up his face from the torture of it, he took a few hurried steps toward the door and bent over. For a minute I thought he'd throw up, but he kept himself together. I couldn't blame him. That this young boy could have turned into the mass of dead flesh that murdered our comrades . . . It was too much for anyone to take.

"Care to explain what's happening?" Sibyl folded her arms. "These kids disappear from an old facility and reemerge as monsters?"

"Well, they're monsters, certainly. But of what sort? That's the question." Dot tapped the screen again, switching to a black-and-white diagnostic image of Philip's body. "The Marrakesh facility found cylithium-like particles all through his body."

"So he *is* an Effigy." With a grim frown, Belle folded her arms by the round table.

My heart sank. I wanted to believe it was Saul we'd tracked to that hideout before disappearing and leaving the other boy there to fend for himself. But Chafik was right. There was no reason why he'd have risked traveling through a Dead Zone of phantoms when he could simply appear and disappear at will. It was Philip all along. An Effigy.

"Effigy? Not quite," Dot answered, and at her urging, Pete brought up a diagram with a touch of his finger. "This chemical compound is certainly cylithium, but his body isn't producing it naturally."

"His body isn't producing it?" Chae Rin crossed her legs atop the table. "What do you mean? Was that guy an Effigy or was he not?"

"I can't tell yet." Dot straightened up, flipping back her sloppily braided ponytail. "Like I said, questions, questions, and more questions. But what I can tell you is that they found a network of electromechanical devices all down his spinal cord. We've just begun to study Alex's body in the lab, but we've noticed similar compounds. I would bet money that all the children have it—well, save for Vasily and Rhys, according to their recent physical exams."

"Nanomachine, we think. But this is really . . . advanced. Way advanced, even for us," Pete said, and as he touched the screen, a path down the back of the body lit up the dark diagnostic image. "There's a network down his spine. We think this may have been delivering the cylithium into his system. And then there's another one at the base of his neck, but it's too degraded to study."

The base of his neck. I remembered the red bruise on his skin.

"In fact, his whole body was dying long before you found him," Pete added, pointing at parts of the diagrams. "Cellular degradation, muscular atrophy. The cells couldn't maintain their integrity. It's as if his body couldn't handle the magic. Basically, he was burning out."

Maybe that was how Belle's attack had killed him so quickly. He'd already been dying.

"Mellie's still in the lab trying to figure out some of the structure," Pete said. "But Dot did say she recognized part of the chemical signature."

"What do you mean?" Sibyl's high heels clicked sharply as she stepped forward. "Do you know who might be behind this technology?"

Dot ran a hand through her unwashed black hair. Her dark eyes dimmed with fatigue. Someone else who probably hadn't gotten any sleep. "I'm not sure," she answered. "This kind of nanotechnology is still in its infancy. But this . . ." She shook her head. "I don't know for sure, but this reminds me of a lot of work that began in the sixties, after the Seattle Siege. A decade ago, they were making advancements in nanotechnology over at a university in Scandinavia before it was shut down. I read about this years before in a thesis that linked nano-technology to synthetic telepathy."

I blinked. "Synthetic what?"

"Synthetic telepathy," Dot repeated. "It's when you inject nano-technology inside someone's head. . . . The chip acts like a receiver that can channel someone's coded voice signal directly into the human brain."

"Brainwashing," added Pete.

Dot shrugged. "Yeah, that's what this work was on. But cylithium delivery has nothing to do with that. Meanwhile, this is more complex than I've seen. I'm not sure—"

"Find them," Sibyl said. "Find the other kids."

"Uh, about that . . ." Pete gave her a nervous grin. "It might be diffi-cult since the ones left seem to be off the grid."

"Find them *now*. Gather the research Dot read and figure out how they could be doing this. Whoever 'they' are. We need to find them." Sibyl had already turned from us, walking up to the bench against the glass window. Propping herself up, she peered out over the main floor. "Whoever could be involved, wherever they are, bring them in. If those . . . *soldiers* are any indication, that tech is out of its infancy stage."

"What are you saying?" Chae Rin asked slowly. "You're saying they're . . . making Effigies now?" One lone, incredulous chuckle escaped from her lips, dying the moment it touched air. Her shoulders slumped as she uncrossed her legs and leaned back. The expression on her face was the same as mine.

I studied the waves of particles on the computer screen. Soldiers. But I thought *we* were the soldiers.

"Rhys," I said. He stirred at the gentle inflection of my voice. "You really haven't seen either of them since the fire?"

"I thought they were dead." I could only see Rhys's back as he faced the door. "They were just . . . regular kids like me."

"Regular kids," Belle repeated with a grave expression. "Turned into Effigies after the fire."

Pete shook his head. "Well, we don't know. We can't even corroborate this yet."

"But that must be it," I said. "Whatever Jessie did to that dead soldier, Alex . . . controlling his corpse . . . ordering it to fight for her. That's . . . supernatural. She could never do that before. Someone must have done something to her."

I remembered her clearly: the cocky movement of her short, slender frame; the almost erotic pleasure she took in snapping Rhys's wrist. And how fast she was. This was someone who'd been taught to fight. A girl who reveled in hurting others.

"Communications couldn't trace her spectrographic signature, if she even had one," said Pete.

"Oh, she had one." Dot rolled up the sleeves of her lab coat. "She had to have had one with the cylithium in her system. Perhaps she could mask it. Like Saul."

Like Saul. "If they're making Effigies, then Saul could be a fake one too," I asked, "right?"

Dot didn't appear surprised to hear the question. "Ever since I saw the autopsy results, I've been wondering if that was the case. But we've already concluded that Saul—or rather Nick—was born in the nineteenth century, and they certainly didn't have nanotechnology back then. Given this simple fact, I still strongly believe in my fifth-element theory."

That was true, though the fact that both he and Jessie could hide their frequencies made it hard to let go of the idea that there could be another connection between them. Even so, the struggle between Nick and Alice was too like the struggle I faced with Natalya. Alice wasn't just some split personality. I'd seen her the first time I scried inside La

Charte hotel; she was real. No matter how good the technology was now, I doubted they could synthesize another life into someone's head. That was magic.

"Something else to think about," Dot continued, "is that Jessie came prepared to fight an Effigy." She picked something familiar off a table: an inoculation pen, the one I'd used against Saul in Argentina. She shuttled the long tube back and forth between her fingers. "It's the same technology, just a compact version fitted into her glove." She looked at Belle. "A temporary way to shut down an Effigy's magic. Don't know why I didn't come up with it," she added bitterly, before shaking her head. "This isn't something you just have lying around. Someone must have given this to her. Someone. Someone. Someone . . . or *someones* with access to high-powered tech."

"'Someones' isn't a word," mumbled Pete.

"Like the Sect." Sibyl straightened up. "It's Sect technology, after all. Sect technicians from our R & D department helped Saul escape our custody. Then those Sect agents who knew about our top-secret mission helped Jessie, an engineered Effigy with Sect technology, steal back the ring and hand it right to Saul, a terrorist who seemingly appeared out of nowhere and began attacking cities around the world."

"Seemingly?" I repeated.

"Where did Saul come from?" Sibyl's sharp gaze passed over each of us. "We know he's been alive since the nineteenth century. What has he been doing since then? Why did he surface only recently? How did he get linked up with Sect agents, scientists, and now these former students from one of our top training facilities?"

"In Greenland!" A burst of adrenaline rushed through my body as I made the connection. "Agent Chafik said you tracked Saul for a while after our fight in France, but his signal went dead in Greenland."

"Yes . . . another connection." Sibyl considered it. "We already sent a team there and found nothing. But perhaps it's worth another look. It's clear to me that there are those within the Sect who have forged some kind of partnership with Saul. We knew there were traitors in our organization, but this could be much larger than we ever expected."

"Much, much larger," Dot said. "It may not even be limited to the Sect. But whoever these traitors are, they're working with Saul. They're supporting him. Whether he's calling the shots or he's just one player in a larger team, I don't know."

Saul told me himself in Marrakesh that he wasn't the one I needed to worry about. They were his backup. His soldiers. But at least one of them had tried to escape. Why?

"So, how long do you think it'll be before the entire Sect collapses at our feet?" Dot tossed the pen into the air and caught it. "Shall we flip a coin?"

"Can someone just . . ." Hanging my head, I let out a haggard sigh. "Some freaks attacked us. They could do stuff. *Weird* stuff. And now Saul has a ring and he's attacking people again. That's what I care about. I just want to know what the hell we're supposed to be doing here."

The door burst open. Cheryl scurried into the room. "I'm sorry, Director," she said hurriedly, too flustered to hide her Cockney accent like she usually did. With a hand, she pushed up her glasses. "I would have warned you, but I didn't even know he'd be here—"

"That's quite fine, thanks. You can go."

A young man brushed by her, knocking her shoulder as he passed. His self-importance seemed to expand with his puffed-out chest, though his slender—well, scrawny—body didn't inspire much awe.

His dirty-blond hair appeared to have been slicked back with anti-frizz styling gel, keeping the wave of his combed-back bangs in exactly the angle and the direction he'd calculated. His prim dark suit and blue tie gave him the model student look, his silver-rimmed glasses perfectly perched on the ridge of his nose. He was at least attempting to project an air of confidence as he surveyed the room. Maybe it *was* confidence to him, though the smug lift in his chin as he straightened his tie screamed *false bravado*.

"Oh god." Rhys shook his head. "You're kidding me. Dad sent *you*? Is this a joke?"

The young man spared Rhys a quick glance but looked entirely unfazed when he responded with, "Oh good, Aidan, you're here too. It's been a while. Nice to see you."

Rhys didn't respond. They shared the same American accent, but the uptightness in the young man's voice made all the difference between them, as if he regulated his tone as staunchly as he did his appearance.

Chae Rin leaned sideways from the table. "Rhys, you know this guy?"

The young man straightened his back as he took his cue. "Assistant Director—"

"Brendan Prince." Sibyl kicked the broken pieces of controller away from her with a swift sweep of her shoe. "Formerly of the Munich facility. And the oldest son of the director of the North American Division."

Rhys squirmed, embarrassed as I stared at him with arched eyebrows.

"Rhys's brother?" Lake glanced from one to the other. "I guess . . . Yeah, I can see it. Oh, this might be fun."

Well, I didn't know about fun, but I could see the resemblance too. Brendan looked more like his father than Rhys did, but the straight nose, the high, handsome cheekbones—they were the same. But as Brendan preened in his well-cut suit, Rhys slouched in his baseball jacket, curling his fingers against his old jeans. Something told me their similarities ended with genetics.

"Prince." Chae Rin snorted and added under her breath, "Definitely acts like one."

"So, you're the one the Council called in. Interesting." If Sibyl was trying to mask the disdain in her voice and stay neutral, she failed. Her lips had already quirked into an amused grin as she took in the sight of him. "Prince's very ambitious son. And he criticized Blackwell for having a family position. Looks like he couldn't wait to put in a good word to upgrade his own son's career."

"Why not? He 'put in a good word' to give you *your* job," he said. "Or so I hear."

"But I didn't steal anyone's position," Sibyl retorted. "That's the difference between you and me, Brendan. I don't go behind people's backs."

"I'm not sure what you're implying." Brendan straightened his blazer. "My father may have recommended me, but it was the Council that brought me here because of the poor job you've done in handling things."

"Poor job," Sibyl spat, but Brendan had already passed by her.

"You've seen the news. You were instrumental in capturing Saul, but since then you've not only let him escape but botched the mission that led to his retrieval of the very weapon he used to slaughter innocents in the first place. It's only natural that the Council has lost faith in you." The pause he left after his last word was a dagger pointed at Sibyl. He gave her a meaningful look before stopping behind Pete, leaning over his shoulder as he looked up at the monitor. "This is the information you've received from the Marrakesh facility, right?"

He must have been leaning a little too closely to Pete, because the lab assistant scooted out of the way. "Uh, yeah. These are the autopsy reports, but, uh . . ." He turned to Dot for help, but she just shrugged.

"So what does the Council plan on doing with you here?" Sibyl folded her arms over her chest. "Are you here to investigate me?"

"Oh, no," he said. "I mean, you will be investigated—that goes without saying—but not by me. I've brought my own people for that."

Sibyl's eyes darkened by the second. "I've already submitted myself to the internal review."

"Submitted yourself to your own people?" He laughed. "Well, that's a comfort."

"Hey, relax," I said, frowning. I'd seen how hard Sibyl worked at her job, how desperately she tried to steer the ship even with new unimaginable threats popping up like a twisted game of whack-a-mole.

"Sibyl's been doing literally everything she could under insane circumstances," I insisted.

"Yes, that's all well and good," he replied. "It's clear there's an issue here at this facility that needs to be sorted out by outside agents. This is a drastic problem. Drastic problems require drastic solutions."

"And what solution did Daddy come up with?" said Rhys.

Brendan bristled at the word "daddy," especially with the mocking emphasis Rhys had placed on it. But while he shot his little brother a dirty expression, he managed himself nonetheless. "Sibyl is to be removed from leadership immediately until further notice," he said, letting the words fall to silence before he spoke again. "I will be assuming leadership for the time being. The Council voted on the recommendation. It's done. You'll be escorted back to your home in Philadelphia and looked after while the Sect conducts a more thorough investigation of you and your methods."

"Looked after." Sibyl rolled her eyes as she shook her head in disbelief. "That's what they're calling house arrest."

"They can't do that!" Cheryl cried. "This isn't Director Langley's fault."

"The APDs," said Belle, taking a seat on the bench by one of the monitors. "All over the world. Hacked. Who do you think is behind this?" She trained her sharp gaze on Brendan. "Now we have soldiers the like of which we've never seen before. They have power—the kind of mysterious power only we possess." She lifted her arm. Clouds of snow wafted up from her palm. "Who created them? Could it be just one person? Or one facility?" The snow dissipated into nothingness the moment she clenched her hand into a fist. "This issue is larger and more insidious then we ever thought possible. Suspending Director Langley is nothing more than an act for the public, to make it appear as if something is being done. But placing the blame squarely on her shoulders will not save the Sect from public scrutiny."

"She's right, Bren," Rhys said. "You really want to take charge of things, you've got to do more than take someone else's job."

Brendan obviously didn't like being challenged, but he stood his ground nonetheless. "The Council *voted*," he said as if this were the only argument he needed. He straightened his back. "I'm in charge now. If any of you are worried about my intentions or credentials, you're welcome to check my references."

"Yeah, your *dad*." Chae Rin snickered.

"I already figured that if I'm going to be convincing to you as command, I'm going to have to show a little more initiative. That's why, on top of bringing my own people to investigate this facility, I've brought in a specialist to deal with some of our more . . . difficult subjects."

Sibyl narrowed her eyes. "Specialist?"

"He's with Vasily Volkov in the holding cells as we speak," Brendan said. "I was just on my way there now—and actually, Aidan and Ms. Finley, I'd like you both to come with me."

Rhys and I exchanged wary glances. I hadn't seen that psycho since he'd tried to kill me in France. I wasn't exactly aching to see him again, but Rhys's brother was in charge now. That meant whatever he said was law.

"If it's who you're talking about, I'd ask you to reconsider," Sibyl said. "Even I could never approve of certain methods of investigation."

"Well, what you would approve or disapprove of doesn't really matter anymore, does it?" Brendan pressed the button by one of the monitors, and in just a few moments, five Sect agents marched through the door, their expressionless faces half hidden behind pairs of dark shades. "Don't worry," Brendan said. "They've been thoroughly vetted. *My* people are loyal."

My insides churned as I watched Sibyl, her head high, the defiance still burning from her eyes as she silently followed the agents out the door.

13

THE GUARDS IN THE LOBBY OF THE DETAIN-
ment ward swiped Brendan's ID card. I was about ready to take a swipe
at him myself if he wouldn't stop babbling about his accomplishments.
Graduated with honors from one of the Sect-run academies out of Virginia, specially trained since childhood, led his first mission in Zimba-
bwe before he was out of his teens, et cetera, et cetera. He gave us every
painful detail as if leaving anything out would mean losing the respect
and admiration he was clearly gunning for. The entire way there, he
kept peeking at me as if waiting for a reaction—awe, maybe—to yet
another amazing thing he'd done. I didn't give him anything. If he
was this insecure about proving himself, then he shouldn't have taken
someone else's job.

To be honest, I couldn't say I necessarily *liked* Sibyl, but I'd trusted
her this far, and she always did her utmost to keep us alive. I respected
her for that. Brendan preened like a peacock desperate for adulation.
Not my first pick for a replacement.

The guards looked tired of him too, watching Rhys's X-ray from
their desk with dull eyes as he passed through the body scanner last.

"He's clean," one guard said. "Okay, you're free to go inside, sir."

"Yes," his partner muttered so low I barely heard him. "Please go. Go now."

We went through the heavily bolted gates and began our trek down a network of long corridors, each plastered wall glinting pristine white. I had to quicken my pace to keep up with the businesslike stride of their long legs, though Rhys was the taller of the two.

"Did Aidan tell you he had a brother, Maia?" Brendan asked, straightening his suit.

"You literally haven't stopped talking since we left Communications," Rhys said before I could. "You want to give that a try next?"

"Come on, Aidan, don't act like that. We're brothers." Brendan patted Rhys on the shoulder, his smile wavering a bit when Rhys ignored the gesture. It was clear Brendan was genuinely enthused about this little family reunion. Rhys, not so much. "I'm four years older," he told me. "But we look alike, don't we? Though everyone always tells us that Aidan takes after our mother while I take after Father. How is Mother, by the way, Aidan?"

"Call her and ask."

Oh, boy. This was awkward. My shoulders slumped as I let out an imperceptible sigh. Why couldn't Sibyl stay?

"Wait," I said, suddenly remembering. "You two have different last names. But you have the same parents?"

"Rhys is my mother's maiden name," Rhys answered absently, rubbing the cast on his opposite arm. "So I'm not labeled as a director's son. It's just easier to be an agent that way."

Aidan Prince. I smirked. "Aren't you full of surprises," I said. "I learn more and more about you every day."

Rhys kept his eyes on me as he asked, "Is that a bad thing?"

"Not always," I said, my smile falling. "But sometimes."

Even from his side profile, I could see the vulnerability reflected in his soft eyes. He walked close to me, close enough for me to feel the heat from his body, or maybe I was imagining it. After I'd spoken, there was a slight uptick in his pace. The softness gone, he looked straight ahead.

"Well," Brendan said, "his taking our mother's name isn't *just* about living as an agent."

Rhys sent him an inscrutable glare as we turned a corner. There was a white, double-bolted door ahead of us. Brendan used his keycard, letting the red light from the scanner pass across the white plastic. The bolts unlocked with a *click* and the door released from its seal. Taking hold of the edge, Brendan pulled it back.

The door opened to a monotony of darkness broken only by some lamps lining a redbrick wall and a trail of steps spiraling downward into the unknown.

"The Hole is where we keep the worst criminals," Brendan explained as we began to step down the staircase. Brendan went first. Rhys followed after me.

The staircase was narrow, enclosed by two brick walls, narrowly spaced apart. It was as if we'd taken a wrong turn from the slick, high-tech enclave of the Sect and gotten lost inside an ancient castle dungeon. If it weren't for the electric lights in the walls, I would have believed this place had been built centuries ago.

Brendan was a step below me and Rhys a step above me. I descended carefully.

"The worst criminals. Like Vasily." Each creak of the steps beneath my feet sent jitters up my spine. They really could have spent more on maintenance down here.

"Vasily Volkov is dangerous. Well, you should know that. According to my briefings, you've had quite a few run-ins with him in the past."

"Quite a few." That Cheshire grin as he happily sliced off a man's finger would never leave my memories. "Yeah, I see why he'd be locked up in a place called the Hole."

"Not the first one he's been in," added Brendan, and with his hands tracing the wall for balance, he twisted around and looked up at his younger brother behind me. Rhys kept his eyes ahead, avoiding his meaningful glance.

"You mean the Devil's Hole," I said. The Greenland facility's *other* name. Rhys had mentioned it once before.

"Keep going," Rhys said, since his brother had stopped for just that second. I'd never seen Rhys so tense.

"Rhys, you once told me that some facilities are tougher than others. What happened there? What kind of place was it before it burned down?"

"It's not something we need to talk about, Maia."

Brendan looked at him sideways with narrowed, disbelieving eyes. "You're really still bitter about having had to train at Fisk-Hoffman. The very fact that you'd be bitter in the first place is just . . ." He scoffed, shaking his head incredulously. "Unbelievable. You really are something, aren't you? Like a spoiled child. Complaining about every opportunity you're given."

Rhys was very still.

"Maia, did you know that Fisk-Hoffman is—*was*—one of the most prestigious training facilities within the Sect?"

"Prestigious?" I frowned. That certainly wasn't how it'd sounded when Rhys had first told me about it in France.

"Not that I would expect a young civilian like yourself to know much about it," Brendan continued with a certain snooty upturn of his nose, "but since it opened in the sixties, only seven students from facilities around the world were selected as the cohort of a special program.

Training the leaders of the future. And leaders they *forged*. Like Father. And Grandfather. It made them heroes."

"Sounds like a family affair." A family of Sect-bound warriors, specially trained within carefully curated cohorts . . . until it was Rhys's turn. "Did *you* go?" I asked Brendan.

Brendan's expression turned sour for just a moment before his chin lifted a little higher, as if he were trying to save face. "No. Selections aren't made on the basis of family, but skill. Rhys was chosen when he was twelve, a year younger than the general recruiting age. Though technically he did have Father's recommendation. It's a great *honor*." He'd put emphasis on the word. It rang out into the darkness below. "Particularly for the youngest," he added under his breath, his jaw tightening afterward ever so subtly. "And yet he's angry just because training was a bit difficult. As if that weren't the whole point."

"Yeah, when I said it's not something we need to talk about, *I actually meant that*." Rhys's footsteps were getting heavier behind me. That menacing hint in his voice wouldn't stay buried forever. Even though I could breathe easy knowing it wasn't directed at me, it put me on edge nonetheless. This wasn't a subject he wanted broached.

Brendan didn't seem to notice that.

"I'm not even surprised he'd be like this." He was talking to me now, as if he'd already given up on talking to Rhys. "We haven't seen each other in a year. Barely talked. And yet the second he sees me, he doesn't even say hello. I mean, *I* said hello, because I'm the civil, responsible one. The *nice* one. But *he* just stood there." Brendan didn't seem to realize how ridiculous he sounded. "He's always like this. I bet he's told you nothing but the worst about me. Our father, too."

"He doesn't really talk about either of you that much," I said stiffly, because I could feel Rhys burning a hole through the back of my head.

"Because it's personal," Rhys said irritably. "How much have you told me about *your* family, Maia?"

"Everything there is to know about them was probably in whatever file you read before you met me," I coolly reminded him.

Well, he may have had a point nonetheless. I didn't offer up information about myself too willingly. But for me, learning more about Rhys wasn't about simple curiosity. Not with Natalya's screams echoing from the depths of me.

I touched the graveyard-cold steel contraption around my neck. Feeling the slight pinch at the back from Mellie's injection, I wondered silently when I would be free of it.

"It's not personal, Aidan. That's the thing," Brendan said. "It was never personal. Father chose you. You should be proud of that. He chose *you*." His voice wavered. "Fisk-Hoffman was notorious for being tough but fair. And when that rough patch was over, by the time it was Aidan's turn in the so-called Devil's Hole, the Council had gotten rid of the staff making a mess of things and the facility had been restored to its former glory. It was better than it'd ever been."

A mess of things? I would have prodded for more information, but Rhys's icy snickering cut me off before I could get the words out.

"Former *glory*?" That was all he said before falling silent.

Finally, Brendan stopped and looked up at him. "Precisely, but you seem to disagree. If I'm wrong, then tell me why."

Rhys didn't. He didn't say a word. He only stared off to the side, his gaze tracing a line up the wall. It may have been the way the whites of his eyes caught the light, but they seemed to be glimmering. Wet.

I didn't like seeing it. "Rhys . . ." I reached out to him, but he blinked very quickly and turned from me.

Brendan clucked his tongue impatiently. "I don't know if this is about those five—the ones we thought had died in the fire. Or maybe you're acting like this because the facility's training regime was harder than you'd expected. It may have been for a short time, but you received top training from the same facility Father did. Under Father's recommendation. And you can always trust Father's recommendation."

Rhys turned a glare upon him. "Don't *you* say that. You know how Dad was as well as I do."

Almost by instinct, Brendan's hand floated to his left arm. He rubbed it gently, as if to cradle it. It was still there when he answered his little brother. "Yes, I know how he was. A serious and dedicated man who wanted the best—"

"Who wanted perfection."

"—for not only his sons but for the Sect as a whole. He's never given anyone more than they can handle. And whether it's the Sect or his *family*, his every decision is always to make us stronger. Any objections to that, Aidan?"

In the silence that followed, Rhys shut his eyes. Brendan's self-satisfied smirk made it clear he interpreted that as a sign of little brother finally backing down. It was a power struggle that he was clearly desperate to win. His chest puffed out more when he figured he had.

"Good. I'm glad you finally see things my way, *little* brother." He'd probably emphasized the word "little" to knock him down a peg, but it came off as more of a self-assurance. He straightened his back. "Now, both of you can continue to follow me. And, Aidan, you'll do well to keep a more respectful tone from now on. Although we're family, I'm still in charge."

Rhys's laughter echoed off the wall. "Oh, shut *up*."

He hopped down to my level and grabbed Brendan's sleeve with his good hand.

"Hey!" I waved my hands wildly as Rhys yanked his brother close to him. "Wait, don't fight! Peace! Peace!" I hadn't expected things would get this messy quite this quickly.

But Rhys only flicked him in the head.

"Ow!" Brendan whined. His hands flew to his forehead, but with a smile, Rhys blocked them and flicked him again.

"*I'm the civil, responsible one,*" Rhys repeated in a mocking tone as he continued to keep the older boy from guarding against his flicks. "Aw, Bren, so all this is just because you wanted a little love from your baby bro, right? *Riiight?*" He gave the last word a childish swoon as if his older brother were a puppy he'd decided to tease.

"St-stop it!" Brendan struggled against Rhys as the younger boy tried to force a hug on him. "This is t-totally inappropriate!"

But Rhys succeeded, enveloping him in a bear hug with his good arm, so tight that Brendan's glasses skewed off his face.

"Look at you. You can't even fight me off, can you? Dude, I'm in a *cast.*" After waving his broken wrist, Rhys caught Brendan's neck by the crook of his elbow and didn't let go, even as his brother squirmed wildly against the steel cage that was his grip. "Looks like you could have spent a week or two in Greenland, eh? But Daddy gave me the recommendation, not you. I can see where the jealousy comes from. Guess you just weren't good enough to be the Chosen One."

"Jealous?" Brendan sputtered, indignant. "I was never— Who said I was—"

"*Please.* And since we're sharing, maybe I should tell Maia about how you wet your bed until you were twelve? Or how you locked yourself in your room writing crappy poetry for days after your girlfriend dumped you?"

"Enough!"

"Then performed it at a poetry slam competition and totally tanked. *Director* Prince."

I'd been expecting a real brawl when Rhys jumped down the stairs and grabbed him. Or a war of words. Not a litany of embarrassing anecdotes. But seeing Brendan's face redden and his eyes dart to me every few seconds made me realize that this may have been worse. The earlier tension had dissolved into something more playful. Rhys was laughing, after all, but there was a cold sting to his glee he couldn't quite hide from me.

"Okay, okay, break it up, guys." They stopped struggling with each other only after I began prying them apart. "Before someone's neck gets broken in all the fun and games."

The two straightened their clothes, breathing a little harder than before.

"You've got nothing to be jealous of, Brendan," Rhys said as resentment crept back into his features. "You didn't have to go to the facility. Trust me, if you had, your life would have turned out very differently."

Maybe he was referring to the other kids—Philip, Jessie, and the rest. That would make sense. But something told me there was more to his hostility that he didn't dare speak out loud. That hostility, even if it was just a flicker, had turned him into a very different Rhys—the one who made me think of that boyish smile of his and question everything.

14

FINALLY, WE CAME TO THE END OF THE STAIR-case, a seven-foot door of steel and bolts just ahead of us. Brendan's keycard brought us through the threshold and into a long path wedged between two rows of widely spaced holding cells. Each cell was sealed by solid red iron doors.

"It's like a refrigerator in here." Even beneath my long-sleeve shirt, I could feel the hairs on my arms stand on end. "It's dead quiet, too."

"By design." Brendan's glasses were once again neatly positioned on the bridge of his nose, his air of superiority back in full force. "The walls and the doors are all soundproof. The temperature is down in the cells too."

"To make the prisoners especially compliant," Rhys said. His grim expression had returned too. "Which cell is his?"

The only way I could differentiate between the identical cells were the tiny numbers carved out of black metal and nailed to the doors.

Without answering, Brendan set off down the hallway. Rhys and I followed after him silently until we reached the thirteenth cell on the right wall.

My chilled breaths disappeared into the air. "Why am I down here, anyway?"

Brendan looked at me. "He said he would speak only to you."

A swipe from his keycard across the security pad and the door opened. The cell was deeper than it looked from the outside. Blinding white. Several feet away, Vasily's blond hair, matted with sweat and blood, spilled over the table he'd been strapped onto. The brown leather latches pinned his emaciated body down so tightly I could see his ribs poking out through his white T-shirt. His eyes were closed, shut perhaps from the blood dripping over them.

"What is this?" I covered my mouth and stepped back as Vasily's hands began twitching over the table. A man stood over him, hunched, though maybe it was just the natural hump of his back. I couldn't tell if the white garment he wore was a technician's coat or a straitjacket.

This time when Rhys grabbed his brother's collar, anger flickered in his eyes. "You brought the Surgeon? You brought him here?"

The Surgeon. That would explain the navy-blue mask covering half his face, the same-colored cap tied around his small head, and the sharp, silver scalpel in his hands. Though judging from the jagged, bloody marks on Vasily's bare legs, it was obvious he wasn't trained.

"I suggested it, yes. But the Council voted," sputtered Brendan.

"Is that your excuse for everything?" Rhys looked livid. "Someone else said it was okay? This man's supposed to be in prison. I can't believe the Council *released* him! How long ago was it? How long ago did they sneak him out and put him back on the payroll?"

"He *was* a Sect agent. On an elite interrogation team with the North American Division."

"Yeah," Rhys said with a disgusted snarl. "Until he went rogue and started kidnapping and carving up the very civilians he was supposed to protect."

What? My blood chilled as I stared back at a man who'd used the skills the Sect had given him to mutilate innocents. We weren't that far away. He must have heard us speaking. But the Surgeon was more interested in carving the inside of Vasily's thigh, stopping just short of where his boxers began.

Cringing, I turned, stifling a gag behind my palm. Vasily wasn't anyone to cry about, but this was too much.

"The Council is desperate. We need someone with the interrogation skills—"

"*Torture* skills," Rhys spat.

"—to get Vasily to talk!" Brendan had had enough. With a burst of strength, he used both arms to push Rhys off of him. "Another city was just attacked by Saul," he hissed. "You saw them screaming, didn't you? And members of the Sect might be involved. You were almost *killed* last night because of it." His eyes snapped with fire. "So yes. I called in the Surgeon. He doesn't just use the physical. He's known for getting inside people's heads. Playing with their emotions. But with Vasily . . ."

As if on cue, Vasily started coughing, spitting out blood—or *was* it coughing? Those haggard breaths might have been laughter. Quiet laughter buried in pain. He might have been insane by now. I wouldn't have even blamed him.

"You should have known Vasily wouldn't crack," Rhys said. "You're so worried about leaks from the Sect, but you brought in someone we once *jailed* for going rogue."

"We don't have to worry about that with Agent Brighton. He's only ever wanted one thing."

Brendan let his grim words hang between us as he walked toward the gruesome scene. "Brighton. Give us a minute."

The Surgeon didn't speak, though he was clearly reluctant to tear himself away from his patient. I could see it in his tiny, deep black eyes, too close together—the only part of his face he'd left uncovered. Slowly, he stepped back as if the hump of his back made it difficult for him to move. Then Brendan waved me over.

I would rather have been anywhere but here. The sight of Vasily turned my stomach. Between the blood and torn flesh, it was all I could do to keep from throwing up. But Vasily would only talk to me. I didn't know why, but I intended to find out.

The moment I moved, Rhys grabbed my wrist and pulled me around. I was looking up at him, the hard lines on his strong face melted by a sudden rush of something delicate. The worry was clear in his eyes even as he held me resolutely in place.

"Maia, this is ridiculous. You shouldn't have to see this. You shouldn't have to be here."

The way he reeled me nearer to him made my heart contract for a painful second. He was scared for me. He wanted to protect me. *Me.*

"Please," he continued. "I don't want you to get hurt by this."

He loosened his grip, and his hand slid down my wrist until I could feel his fingers grazing my palm. "Come on. You don't have to do this. Let me take you out of here." His hand closed around mine as he silently pleaded with me.

This was the Rhys I'd come to know. Even with all the questions and mysteries, even with the ever-present fear of what he could be, *this* was the Rhys that made my pulse quicken. And I—the girl who barely had friends or family, the girl who'd never known how it felt to have someone like him, beautiful and strong, look at her with his deep gaze—had no idea how to resolve the warring impulses in me. Should I fear him or not? Should I believe Natalya or not?

"He's tied up," I told him quietly in lieu of an answer. "I'll be fine."

"It's Vasily," Rhys whispered. "That won't matter."

That was when I realized that I was close enough to hear his whisper. Willing myself calm, I pulled out of his grip.

"It's okay," I assured him.

Vasily seemed to stir as I approached. When I called his name, and only when I called his name, he pried open his bloodied eyes and grinned wide as if nothing had changed—as if he weren't strapped to an operating table with blood oozing out of his shallow wounds.

"You came." Vasily's light chuckles were overtaken by a coughing fit. "Let me have a look at you."

"Excuse me?" I scowled, my skin crawling as he lifted his head as much as pain would allow, his eyes sliding down my face before settling on my neck. "What are you doing?"

My neck. Something came alive in his eyes as he hungrily devoured the sight of it. In the next moment, he laid his head back down and closed his eyes, satisfied.

"Don't tell me you're into me," I said, disgusted at the thought. "I mean, you're not a bad-looking guy, but the sociopath thing is kind of a turnoff."

Vasily smirked. "Don't worry. I would never take what Aidan clearly wanted. We used to be such close friends, after all. I wonder if it's your innocence that intrigues him."

Both Rhys and I stiffened, but I didn't check to see if his face was flushing like mine. My skin was too hot. Otherwise I would have asked how he'd even surmised something so—

Ridiculous. Was it ridiculous? Or obvious?

I swallowed the lump in my throat and focused. This was supposed to be an interrogation.

"I brought her." Brendan folded his arms over his chest. "Now talk."

"No offense, but I was never that interested in her, to be honest." Vasily shrugged. "I just wanted to confirm . . . her *beauty* . . . with my own eyes." Opening one eye, he added, "You *are* beautiful, Maia. I understand now why Rhys almost murdered me to protect you."

I hadn't realized my shoulders were raised up so high. Without looking back at Rhys, I relaxed them. "You just wanted to *see* me? Why don't I believe you?"

Blood spurted out of his mouth with a cough. "I just like to confirm things myself is all."

"So do I." Brendan positioned himself on Vasily's right side, bearing down on him as if the blood didn't bother him at all. I stayed at the foot of the table. "Now tell me—or if you'd like to think of it this way, tell *her*—who ordered you to free Saul last April?"

A light, speckled mustache, darker than the strands on his head, lined the top of Vasily's thin upper lip. Both lips were pale and cracked, aching for water. Maybe they'd been starving him. "Saul did. Or haven't you figured that out?"

"But it's not just Saul, is it?" Rhys stalked up to us. "You take orders from Blackwell. Always have."

"Not always." Vasily let his head fall to the side, but his catlike eyes stayed on Rhys. "Once upon a time, I took orders from you, friend. Though I wasn't the only one."

I could feel Rhys go rigid behind me.

I had to fight the urge to react. Vasily was trying to take control of the interrogation, flip it to his favor. I wasn't about to let him win. "Did you know? We've been seeing your old friends around lately. From Fisk-Hoffman in Greenland. Some of them can do some pretty interesting things now."

Vasily's eyelid twitched from the blood slipping onto his long lashes. "Is that so?" he asked, but unlike Rhys, he was not in the least bit surprised that they hadn't died in the fire that took the facility. If they were Saul's soldiers, then even without the powers, so was he.

My frown deepened. "Was it Saul who ordered Jessie to attack us last night? Or someone within the Sect?"

Vasily stretched his pale lips as wide as they would go the second he heard the name. "Jessie?" Vasily rolled his head to the other side, his arms squirming just a little beneath the leather straps, as if her name had given them life again. "So you had a little reunion without me. I'm sorry I missed it. And she used to have such a crush on you too. Did she give you that?"

He flicked his chin up, and by the time I turned, Rhys's fingers had already instinctively gone to his cast.

"Classic Jessie." Vasily began coughing, but the fit didn't deter him from taunting his old friend. "You should have known how vicious she'd be, Aidan. You were the one who taught her how to survive down there. You taught us all." The saliva smearing Vasily's white teeth glinted underneath the overhead lights. "You should never feel ashamed of what you did, friend. You were wonderful."

"*Who* in the Sect is working with you? I need names!" As Brendan's voice rocketed across the walls and up the ceiling, Rhys and I froze, helplessly staring at each other for different reasons. For Rhys, the horror of a tightly woven secret beginning to unravel rooted him to the spot.

For me, it was the horror of the secret itself.

Brendan considered him silently. Then, with an impatient sigh, he pulled out his cell phone and began clicking.

"Who are you calling?" I hissed, but he answered by flipping over the phone and showing Vasily the face on the screen.

It was the ID photo of a young woman with sunken eyes, her sallow skin almost matching the pallor of her wispy, pale blond hair, which was tied in a strict ponytail at the base of her neck.

And for the first time since I'd met him in that little town in

Quebec, Vasily's features softened. His grin unraveled; his lips sagged as deeply as the woman's miserable expression.

"You recognize her, don't you?" Stepping closer, Brendan held the phone to his face so he wouldn't mistake her.

Vasily turned his head. The waver in his eyes was a foreign sight to me, all the malicious glee evaporating in that moment. The fading blue of his pupils mimicked the dead eyes of the woman he refused to look at.

"She was an agent of the Sect," Brendan continued. "A top agent. And yet even her superiors knew there was something not quite right with her. *Look* at her."

He grabbed Vasily's chin and forced him to see her, flinching only slightly when Vasily sputtered out blood in a series of angry hacks.

"Maybe it was the training regime back then that finally took its toll."

"Shut up," Vasily hissed, and his body gave a violent jerk. I couldn't tell if it was a spasm or if he was fighting against his binds.

"In the end, Irina Volkov took her own life that day eleven years ago," Brendan said, "leaving her seven-year-old son an orphan. It's a shame."

Vasily spat blood in his face. Brendan flinched from the impact, but he wouldn't lose this war of wills. He wiped the dripping blood and saliva off his cheek.

"Is that why you fought so hard to get recruited into Fisk-Hoffman like your mother did?" He slipped his phone into his pocket. "Did it make you feel closer to her?"

"Brendan."

Rhys had spoken up this time, a burst of concern that surprised even him. Vasily noticed. Silent words passed between them as they locked eyes.

It wasn't long before defiance returned to Vasily's voice. "Don't worry,

Aidan," he said, the corners of his mouth twitching. "You think Brighton never mentioned my mommy in all these days he's been fiddling with my flesh? Try a little harder, at *least*."

But I knew I hadn't imagined the waver in his voice.

"Vasily," Rhys started, his voice hollow. "Philip is dead. So is Alex. This isn't the time to play games."

At this, Vasily clenched his teeth. "I . . . didn't know that," he said after a period of silence. A few beats passed again. "That's a shame."

"But you *did* know about Jessie," I said. "You're working with Saul."

"And you're not the only Sect member," Brendan added. "Why? What's the end goal? What are you getting out of this?"

"What am *I* getting out of it?" Vasily's laughter had a bitter tinge, almost incredulous, as if the answer should have been obvious. "If you want to know that, you'll have to ask me another question. What happened in the Devil's Hole?" It was the question I didn't dare speak aloud. Rhys flinched at the name. "Come on, Maia. I know *you* want to know."

I could see Rhys's Adam's apple bob up and down his throat as he finally pulled away and stared down at the floor.

"Eyes here." With a quick snap, Brendan straightened his back. "I asked you a question."

"What happened?" Vasily's eyes were wild. "Ask me, Maia."

"Stop it. *Stop* it." I darted to Vasily's side, pushing away the table full of bloody tools, one of them a common industrial drill. The Surgeon didn't seem to mind. He stood at the side of room, quietly waiting his turn. I could see Rhys shaking. "Leave Rhys alone! Just answer our questions, damn it. Why are you working with Saul? Who else is involved in the Sect? *What are you planning?*"

"Whatever sins Saul has committed, it's nothing compared to those of the Sect." Vasily sounded calm, but his bloody hands had clenched into fists. "You remember, don't you, Aidan? All the people there with us. The staff, the doctors. Dr. Gladstone? You remember, right, Aidan?"

"That's *enough*." Rhys lowered his head, but I could see his unfocused eyes widen. Even as he caught his trembling left hand with the other, he didn't move from his spot. The name had frozen him to it.

Vasily let his head dangle awkwardly at one side, his lips creeping into a crooked grin when he added, almost wistfully, "Let's go, Aidan. One day, let's go back together."

"Enough!" Rhys charged past Brendan, nearly pushing him out of the way to grab Vasily's neck.

"If we ever did go back . . . I bet you we'd still find Gladstone's body down there." Vasily's raspy voice scraped up his throat as Rhys squeezed it. "But we both know she didn't die in that fire. A shame. She liked you too."

"*Stop lying.*" And Rhys turned to me, frantic, pleading. "He's lying. Don't believe him. Don't believe anything he says."

"Aidan! Let him *go*," Brendan warned, lifting his arms as if to stay a wild beast.

"Rhys," I said, more gently. "It's okay."

That's all I had to do. The sound of my voice was what snapped him back to reality. Rhys stared at me as if he'd woken from a dream, searching my worried eyes for answers. Then, finally noticing his own hand around Vasily's neck, he let out a gravelly breath and stumbled back in shock.

"I'm sorry," he said. Whether it was to Vasily, to his brother, or to me, I didn't know. Maybe it was to all three of us. Regardless, it didn't matter. Without raising his head, he strode out of the room.

"Now that you're here, I have something to tell you, Maia." Vasily swallowed painfully, as it seemed he'd overtaxed himself. He shifted uncomfortably beneath the straps as the blood started to ooze from his right wrist, adding to the dried stains on his shirt. "That day in France,

I was wrong to try to kill you. I acted on my own, but I was wrong, and I apologize."

He wasn't the first person to say that to me. But I wasn't buying it.

"So now you're sorry for trying to kill me, but you didn't have a problem setting Saul free and sending him right after me," I said.

"Saul doesn't want to kill you." He twitched beneath his straps. "We're not your enemies, Maia. The Sect . . ." His expression turned cold with a violent twitch. "It's the Sect that's wrong. Not me. Not Saul. Not Jessie. Yes, Jessie . . . Maia, when the time comes . . . make sure you listen to her. Listen well."

Listen? What did he mean? Was he reaching out to me? He sounded painfully sincere, *reasoning* with me to side with his team of psychopaths and murderers. No way. He was crazy.

"You think I'm just going to do what you people say?" My jaw was stiff as I said it, my teeth nearly grinding together. "Anyway, if Saul wants me, he can just pop in and take me whenever he wants, right?"

The thought chilled my blood as I suddenly realized it. I wasn't safe anywhere.

"He won't, no. That isn't the plan. There's timing to everything. When the time comes, you'll go with us yourself." Vasily rubbed the blood trickling down his hand between his fingers. "Maia, would it really be that bad if you left the Sect?" He shook his head. "Or have you gotten used to your prison? If so . . ." His eyes narrowed. "Then I truly pity you."

He was dead serious.

"That's enough. We're not getting anywhere." Brendan had finally realized it. "Maia, we're leaving. And you." He glared at Vasily. "We'll see if you're ready to tell us more in a few hours. Brighton."

The Surgeon began to stir from his place by the back wall. That was my cue. Life sprang to my legs, and I followed Brendan out of the room. The door shut against the sound of a drill whirring, but it was the crash of bone and flesh against concrete that stole my attention.

Rhys had just thrown Brendan to the floor.

"What were you thinking, Bren?" Bending over him, Rhys picked him up by the collar. "Was that an interrogation? Was that your plan? Are you satisfied with that?"

"Rhys!" I grabbed his arm from behind. "Stop!"

But Brendan wasn't even struggling. His glasses were askew on his nose as he looked at his little brother. All the pompous pretense and pride crumbled to pieces as his bottom lip began to tremble. "Aidan . . . don't . . ."

Cry. I could hear it before I saw the tears streaming down Rhys's cheeks. He turned from me quickly, but I didn't need to see his face. His whole body shook as he muffled his whimpering voice behind his one good hand.

I moved closer to him, pressing my hand gingerly against his face and pulling his head toward mine so he could see me, but he shook me off with a jerk of his head. "I'm sorry," he said. "I'm sorry, Maia. I can't."

And he turned to me, his beautiful features streaked wet. He trembled helplessly. "They weren't lies. I'm sorry. I . . . I wish you'd never met me."

15

I WISH YOU'D NEVER MET ME.

"Stop hesitating!" Chae Rin barked as her bō staff came for my head.

I hadn't even realized that I'd stopped moving. It was for a split second, but apparently that was enough for a hit to land. It wasn't Chae Rin's staff, though, but Belle's that swept me off my feet from behind. My own staff slipped out of my hands as my back hit the mat hard.

The morning sun filtered through the high windows of the training gym. We'd been training for hours; it was already a little past breakfast time, and yet I felt as if I were barely awake and functioning. I usually performed better than this during training. Once, I'd even earned an approving nod from Belle, who usually doled out her compliments with all the generosity of a miser.

Today, I was sluggish, falling to easy attacks. I was also careless, though having to block both Belle and Chae Rin at the same time wasn't exactly a walk in the park.

Harder still if your mind was elsewhere.

"You need to concentrate." Chae Rin stuck out a hand to help me up, but the moment I touched her fingers and began to pull myself off the ground, she snapped hers away, letting me fall back down. "And stop letting your guard down," she added, using her staff to hit my leg.

Belle nudged my head with her staff and flicked her chin up. "On your feet."

I got up, my bones burning as I picked my staff off the ground. The white bandages around my left arm, the ones I tied there to sop up the blood after one of Chae Rin's attacks, were starting to come unfurled. Lake probably wasn't having an easier time, having to climb the thick rope set up a few feet away from us all the way to the very high ceiling. She was halfway up, but I could hear her whimpering from down here as she climbed, inch by painful inch.

"What's wrong?" Chae Rin tapped her staff against the floor, forcing a flinch out of me. "You're distracted. What's going on in there?"

"Is it Natalya?" Belle suddenly launched an attack, twisting around to sweep me off my feet again. I jumped, dodging it this time, turning quickly to block Chae Rin's staff. The loud *crack* of wood against wood reverberated against the ceiling.

"No," I grunted, blocking Belle's next attack while leaning back to dodge Chae Rin. "This steel thingy is keeping the voices under control in there."

The neck-band was still around my neck like a dog collar. The back of my neck kept chafing from Mellie's stupid injection, and it was all I could do to keep my fingers from scratching the itch at the base of my neck, but it was doing its job.

"If that's the case, then maybe we should try scrying again." Belle lowered her staff. "We don't know when Saul will attack next. We have to get ahead of him. But with the existence of those soldiers and more rogues potentially within the Sect, the issue's getting more complicated. Last night, I tried searching the flash drive Philip gave us, but it's encrypted. Natalya might have an idea of what Saul's plan is."

"If she'd even tell me," I said, touching my neck. "She seems more interested in playing games—'Find the Keys to Maia's Body,' for one."

I caught myself. Belle couldn't help letting the displeasure show on her face whenever someone—anyone—said something negative about Natalya. It was understandable. Nobody would be cool with hearing someone crap on their hero. Even if there was a grain of truth to the smack.

Or a silo.

But truth and lies were dangerous, messy constructs, especially when they concerned Natalya. Even if this steel albatross around my neck stopped her from bleeding too heavily into my subconscious, I doubted it could keep her from leading me in the wrong direction.

"Look, I'm not crazy about having to go back in there, but since I'm your two-way radio, there's nothing I can really do about it," I said. "But, Belle, you'll have to help me."

Belle was about as easy to read as the Rosetta Stone. She said nothing as she stared back at me calmly, and I wondered, as I always did, which one of us she saw—the protégé or the mentor? But to her credit, over the past few weeks, Belle had legitimately tried to help me learn to scry properly, safely. She led our training, preparing us for the battles to come.

She was making an effort for us. For the team.

But when it came to scrying, the breathing techniques that worked for her didn't necessarily work for me. Belle was naturally calm; of course the process was easier for her.

"Scrying still isn't easy for me." I rubbed my chest as I remembered the way Natalya's mind had spread across mine like a virus, filling my body like too much air in a balloon. If I could get away with it, I'd never try to contact her again.

Belle thought for a moment. "There is a place we could go to."

"A place?"

"Here in London. They might be able to help with the process."

Suddenly, Chae Rin's staff hit my back, sending me flying to the floor.

"Hey!" I spat, flipping onto my back to see her standing over me.

"You're right; you should talk to Natalya again. Also, like I said." She set the staff against her shoulder. "Never let your guard down."

The double doors opened, the loud creak reverberating through the gym.

"Oh great, it's that guy." Chae Rin rolled her eyes as Brendan walked through the doors. He had the same prim suit on, though he'd changed his tie to match his new dress shirt.

"Good morning, girls. Good to see you keeping yourselves fighting ready."

I grimaced at the cheesiness, but Brendan didn't seem to notice. He kept his hands behind his back while he strolled toward us with a good-natured smile. There weren't any signs of last night's vulnerability, no sign of the boy whose eyes had welled up at the sight of his little brother crying in front of him.

"Usually I wouldn't come down here myself," Brendan started.

"Look at that, we're so blessed." Chae Rin turned from him. "God, I miss Sibyl," she added as she twisted her staff around and began to practice on her own.

Brendan coughed. "What I mean is, I'm here because I'd like to ask you something."

"What's up?" Lake grunted a bit as she let go of the rope and let herself drop from that great height, landing on the ground with a puff of air that blew up her training shorts. "Oh, no. Saul didn't do anything, did he?" Scurrying up to him, she grabbed him by the arm. "Was there an attack? Do we have to fight? We don't have to fight, do we?" She tugged at him childishly. "Please, *please*, no. I need a break. See? My skin is horrid, my eyes are sunken—it's all the stress."

Lake was starting to break out on her forehead, something I'd previously thought impossible with all the expensive skin-care products (one of which she endorsed) that she kept in our shared bathroom. But Brendan wasn't looking at her forehead. He was looking at her gorgeous face. That is, before his eyes, for a shameful second, slid down to the T-shirt tied around her stomach.

"Uh, *excuse* me." I leaned over and snapped my fingers.

Brendan jumped out of Lake's grip so quickly his glasses slid down his nose. "I'm sorry," he said. "Victoria—uh, everyone—no, Saul hasn't attacked." He gulped and inched away from her. Another fanboy. Perfect. "There's something I need to ask one of you to do."

"Get to it." Belle folded her arms as Lake went to pick up her water bottle by the side of the wall.

Brendan twitched under the pressure of Belle's intensity, but he kept his composure nonetheless. Impressive. "Blackwell is holding a black-tie fund-raiser this Thursday. Very exclusive. Nothing but the political elite."

"That's in three days," I said.

"What's he playing at, Blackwell?" Lake plucked off the cap of her water bottle. "I get that he's the Council representative, but that stunt he pulled with the press was sketchy. Whether or not someone from the facility gave him false information like he said, don't you think he's creepy enough to warrant an interview?"

"Believe me, I've done so," Brendan said. "He's been interviewed thoroughly, along with the other agents in the facility. The process is clearly ongoing, but for right now Blackwell checks out. And the Council has already approved of his event."

"Why?" I started to untie the rest of the bandages wrapped around my left arm. "What's it for?"

"At the outset? Press. Key members of the Sect's higher ranks will be seen with political leaders reaching out to victims of phantom attacks, donating to rebuild lives in places where the APDs aren't always sufficient to protect them. That's the overt purpose."

"And the covert purpose?" Belle plunked her staff onto the mat, hooking her elbow around the wood. "What's the Council planning?"

"Those key members of the Sect are going to be meeting with a few of the politicians that have been instrumental in fanning the flames against our operations—and against you."

"Inviting your enemies over for tea. Playing nice for the cameras." By the time Lake came back, she'd downed half the bottle. "Straight out of the diva playbook."

"The Sect can be seen as trying to build bridges," said Brendan. "While at the same time, they can exert their influence, make deals, do whatever they can to try to lessen the public and political heat on us right now. It's political maneuvering, but doing so under the guise of charity softens the edge."

"It's risky, though," Lake said. "I mean, you don't want to look fake while you're being fake. That's the first rule of PR."

"And it's actually because of the PR that I'd like you to be there—not all of you, mind," he said quickly because Chae Rin had already thrown her staff onto the matt. "You can't be seen as shirking your duties. I'd like one of you to go while the rest complete missions. Just one. For extra security and for the optics."

"Not it," said Chae Rin, splitting the air with the swift *crack* of her staff.

"Me! I'll go!" Lake waved her hand in the air enthusiastically. "I'm sick of being stuck in here anyway. Honestly, lately it's like we're either narrowly avoiding death or training up on *how* to narrowly avoid death."

"Sorry, but I think your image as a pop star might have the opposite effect," Brendan explained. "We need the charity and the Sect by extension to look genuine."

"What do you mean?" Lake pulled back. "You think I'm not genuine?"

Well, *I* certainly couldn't tell. Lake's big doe eyes were a weapon when they were trained at the right target. Brendan was already squirming with guilt.

"N-no, not at all. I was merely explaining the importance of framing and—don't get me wrong, Victoria, you've been an irreplaceable asset in humanizing the Sect through your activities. You're very . . . human." He covered his cough with his fist. "And certainly your appearance has been our asset—*appearances!*" he added fast, his face burning red. "Your *appearances*. Your appearances have been an asset . . . to us."

"I'm sure you've done a lot of thinking about her appearance." Without looking at him, Chae Rin spun her staff around her head and struck the air with one quick thrust. "And her assets."

"Maia!" Brendan blurted out my name, flustered, just as Lake began to consider him with a curious stare. "You, Maia. I think you would be good for this. You have the image of being somewhat of an ingénue. It would work."

"Great, another fund-raiser," I said. The last fund-raiser I went to in New York was a dud even before Saul started slaughtering everyone with phantoms. "All right, whatever. Let's just hope there isn't a death toll for this one."

"Good. I'll make sure they know to expect you." Without another word, he walked out the door.

"Oh, wait!" I stuffed my bloody bandages into the garbage and caught up with him outside.

"What is it?" Brendan said as I shut the door behind me.

"Uh. Well . . ." Now that I was out here, under the unfiltered glare of the morning sun, I didn't know how to start. The breeze lapped at my face, fluttering the curled hair across my forehead.

"It's about Aidan, right?"

Brendan looked at me like he understood. Of course he did. Aidan was his brother. They were family.

As I watched his brown eyes lighten, I suddenly felt bare, as if I'd just remembered that half of me was missing. It was the same phantom pain that always sprang up each time I thought of my sister.

"He'll be okay," he said before I could speak. "You're friends with him, right?"

I lowered my head. "Friends . . ." Was I?

"Girlfriend?"

Startled, I snapped my head back up, shaking my head resolutely.

"Well, whatever it is, thank you for caring about him." Brendan lifted his arm as if to touch my shoulder, but, overcome with awkwardness, settled on a curt nod. "He can be a lot to handle. He's always been mouthy, rebellious. Always talked back to Father." He paused. "Well, he used to before Greenland. . . ."

As he trailed off, I could tell the same questions screamed in the silence that stretched between us.

"Brendan," I started in a quiet voice. "What Vasily said back there in the Hole—"

"Vasily is a liar," Brendan snapped, cutting me off. Then, composing himself, he continued. "Vasily was merely trying to confuse us. It was my mistake bringing Aidan; I should have known something like that could happen."

But I wasn't satisfied with that answer. "Vasily made it seem like something went down, Brendan. Something beyond the fire."

"But nothing did," he said. "You can check the records yourself; it's all there for public viewing. Believe me, I've pored over them more than once. Was the facility tough? Of course. Was the training difficult? Historically so. But when the fire happened, there were so few survivors that the Council simply voted to keep it closed. That's it. No foul play. All the survivors of the fire were thoroughly interviewed. Even Aidan. He was only fourteen. The poor boy was traumatized. And he never wanted to go in the first place."

Brendan's lips trembled a bit as he closed them.

"He's not a bad person," Brendan said. "Really."

"Yeah." I'd felt it too. The warmth he'd shown me since he'd met me was genuine. But everything about Rhys seemed like a contradiction. The more I peeled, the more sweet parts fell away, revealing those black spots I wasn't sure I was ready to see.

"It's honestly not that complicated, when you think of it." Brendan shrugged. "He's a good kid. He has a soft heart, always had. Maybe that's why it was hard for him. . . ." He trailed off. "He had to go through things, sure—we all have. But he's fine now. There's no problem."

I let Brendan leave thinking I believed him.

Secrets piling up like bones in a graveyard. Natalya knew it too. She was probably mocking me in front of the red door, waiting. She had answers. And I had to know for sure.

I had to see Natalya.

Belle borrowed a vintage pink Beetle from the Sect lot—the same one she always took when she wanted to disappear for a while without telling us where she was going. The fully tinted windows made driving around the city a lot easier; she could peer at the outside, but the outside couldn't peer at her. It was a comforting thought as we drove through the outer gates, passed the warring crowds picketing and counterpicketing on the other side of the bars. Fans and Sect haters, newly spurred by the attacks in Bloemfontein.

I pressed my temple against the window as Belle drove. "Isn't there more we can do?"

"Agents are out trying to locate the remaining trainees of Fisk-Hoffman, assuming they're alive. Communications is still attempting to track Saul, but he's hidden his frequency. We don't know where he'll attack next. Of course, the usual method is to track phantom movements, looking for swells in activity, but we'll always be at least a little late. The only way to get ahead of him is to find out who he is and what his goals are."

Which meant we needed Natalya. Marian. Me.

"We know they'll be coming for me eventually." The dread I felt seemed the perfect reflection of the grim skies above. "Then again, Vasily seemed pretty confident that I'd go with them on my own. That I'd 'listen to Jessie,' whatever that means. Either way, I can't rest easy."

I shut my eyes, ignoring the cold sting of the window against my temple. It was hard to imagine there was once a time I woke up every morning and ate Uncle Nathan's pancakes. Being an Effigy had stolen the one connection from me I needed most right now. But worse still, it'd placed a target on my back.

"We'll be here with you." She'd said it simply, her stern gaze never leaving the road ahead of us. "The three of us."

"The three of you . . ." I let the words fall to silence, but they lingered between us nonetheless. *The three of us.* Yeah. Being an Effigy may have stolen one connection from me, but it had given me others in its place. I couldn't forget that. "Despite everything, we're in this together, right?"

Belle glanced at me and nodded. And with just that gesture, Natalya's haunting spirit had been banished, the two of us freed if only for that fleeting moment. We were what I always wanted us to be. Mentor and protégé. Part of the same team. I didn't know how long the feeling would last, but it was there, unmistakably. I smiled.

Belle drove us into London, through the winding streets. There was a church on the corner of Friary Road, its large sundial beneath the steeple carved into stone.

"A church?" I frowned as Belle parked by the side of the road.

"Natalya brought me here once to train me," Belle said, unbuckling her seat belt.

"This place will help me scry?" I considered it. "Well, scrying requires calm," I said. "I guess a church might make sense, but . . . I mean, I know you're Catholic and all, but I'm not particularly religious."

"Neither am I." Belle stepped outside. "And this is not a Catholic church," she added before shutting the door.

As I got out of the car, a scrawl of words written below the sundial caught my eye. *"Et in . . ."* I paused. *"In tenebris . . ."* I squinted, partly from the sun in my eyes. The Latin words were hard to read, chiseled too lightly on the plaque below the sundial. *"Invenies?"*

"'And among the shadows, you will find them.'"

Without saying more, Belle walked up the stone steps and entered the church. I understood the second I entered through the arched doorway and saw the solemn march of black robes down the long aisle. Rich, haunting chords from the church organ gave the procession its rhythm, and never once did they fall out of sync. Even their hands were sheathed in black gloves as they carried tall candles to the altar at the front of the church, where a man in flowing white robes spread out his arms, ready to receive them.

Phantoms painted black across the white walls . . . "Wait, this is . . . this is that death cult," I said, my voice hushed because the old man sitting in the last pew stirred and looked back at us once the door slammed shut behind us. "You're kidding me. They're *Scales*, Belle."

"The Deoscali," Belle said simply, using the "proper" term, as if we somehow needed to respect a group of psychos who thought getting eaten by phantoms was some kind of honor.

I'd heard they did rituals and worshipped phantoms in "churches" like these before going on pilgrimages into Dead Zones through illegal networks and letting phantoms kill them. They were probably in the middle of one now. Montreal's Cirque de Minuit may have had an unhealthy fascination with using phantoms for entertainment, but they did everything on the level and kept people safe. Then you had Scales, who took unhealthy fascination to a whole new level.

Not very many people out there bent the law in order to get killed.

Motioning me to follow her, Belle took her seat in the second-to-last pew. Disgusted, I trailed behind her nonetheless.

That was when the old man launched himself at me.

"Effigy!" he spat as he grabbed me by the collar and pushed me back out of the pew. "You're not welcome here. . . ."

He tried to push me again. Swiftly, I shoved him back into his pew and held my foot against his chest to pin him down.

"Okay," I said, no longer bothering to keep my voice low. "And you want to tell me why you took me to some den of phantom-worshipping death cult nutjobs? Especially when they *hate* us?" I added as the old man struggled against my foot.

"Not all of us," said the priest standing at the pulpit. Despite the commotion of the attack, the procession hadn't even stopped shuffling toward him until he put up his delicate hand. He'd tied his wavy brown hair in a ponytail behind his giraffe neck, showing the contours of his soft, small face. "Joseph, please escort Mr. Goffin out of the church."

A large man who'd been standing silently by one of the white pillars nodded at the order.

"Yeah, teach him some manners while you're at it," I said as Joseph grabbed the cursing man by the arm and began dragging him out.

"Pastor Charles," Belle said as the man came near us. "I thought you had made some progress with your teachings."

I straightened my blouse. "What teachings? Or do I want to know?"

The halted procession had turned to take a look at us and finally I could see each of their faces, all manners of shapes, sizes, and shades, but each with the same fear tinged in a slight hint of distrust. Scales were stupid enough to worship the monsters responsible for terrorizing mankind. Of course, this made Effigies the bad guys. We were like their Lucifer or something.

"Please sit," Pastor Charles told us. "Let us finish here. Then we'll speak."

When Pastor Charles asked the procession to continue, they did so, but only reluctantly. After prying their eyes from the two Effigies at the back of the church, they managed to complete their ritual, marching up the steps of the pulpit platform, circling the altar with their candles. I watched from my seat while their quiet chants rumbled low to the floor like the silent tremors of an earthquake. It was hard to concentrate for those ten minutes that they "gave thanks" to the beasts they called the spirits of life and death, "for where life begins, so too must death."

"The spirits, you see," Pastor Charles explained once the procession had ended and the worshippers had left, "are agents of both."

"Spirits." I stood up with Belle. "That's what you're calling them? Is that the politically correct term? Or are you trying to make phantoms more marketable and cult-friendly?"

"Phantoms are not spirits," he said. "Phantoms are *of* spirits. But they are not spirits. The spirits' existence is what allows for life and death to occur naturally in the world. In that way, they are also agents of fate."

Walking up the aisle, he spread open his arms as if the painted phantoms would tear themselves from the wall and fly to him.

"Life and death." Pastor Charles kept his hands behind his back as he spoke to us. "During our present lives, they maintain that balance, giving us the tools we need to live. They are in all things. They *are* our souls, the souls of nature, animals, the elements, the universe. They never leave us. They are with us always, even if we cannot see them. *Feel* them."

Closing his eyes, he breathed in the air as if he didn't look crazy enough.

"And when we die, our spirits leave our bodies and join the chorus before it's time to be reborn again. Maia, these spirits are not our enemies."

"Okay, I'll bite." I tilted my head. "You said phantoms weren't spirits. They were *of* spirits. Now, I have no idea what you mean, but all this weird crap just sounds to me like you're trying to let phantoms off the hook for what they do. If that's the case, then I've seen enough of their handiwork to respectfully disagree with you on that, sir," I told him.

I didn't dare close my eyes, even for a second, because if I did, I'd see the dead bodies of all the people I'd failed to save.

"The phantoms are not spirits," he insisted. "Indeed, phantoms are evil," he agreed, surprising me. "But the *spirits* are not. Neither are the Effigies. And that is what I've always tried to teach here."

"What do you—"

"Pastor Charles," Belle interrupted. "I called you earlier about a request."

"Ah, yes." He nodded. "And this is Maia Finley."

Despite his incredibly twisted point of view, he seemed nice enough. I shook his hand. "I don't agree with you at all, but it's nice to meet you."

"Come." He flicked his head toward the front of the church. "We'll take her to the cellar."

We followed him through a door at the rightmost corner of the church, which he opened with a key. He continued to explain his philosophy as he led us down the corridor.

"The common perception of the Deoscali is that we worship phantoms. And you're not wrong." His white robes skidded across the stone floor. "It's a common perception among the Deoscali as well. But this is only a corruption of the true teachings handed down to us—the teachings of Emilia Farlow, the originator of our church."

I raised an eyebrow. "Which are?"

"That it is the *spirits* who are agents of life, death, and fate. Not the phantoms. You see, we Deoscali are a relatively new religious group. The practice of worshipping phantoms began just shortly after the phantoms appeared themselves, but it quickly devolved into the blood-worshipping cult you've probably grown to disdain. I, too, once fell prey to this ideology." And he looked like he regretted it. He shook his head. "Many view Effigies as the enemy. Groff grew up believing this. He only recently joined us here at this church. An uncomfortable amount of Deoscali have even come to believe in the terrorist Saul as a kind of a prophet, an envoy of the phantoms."

Saul, a prophet. It really didn't take much to get people to believe in garbage.

"I've been trying to rehabilitate some of these wayward thoughts. One can only hate the Effigies if you worship the phantoms. But the phantoms are not the spirits. The spirits only exist in the world as silent shadows, protecting the world without ever being seen."

"A world of shadows . . . ," I whispered as Saul's words from that night in Marrakesh bubbled up in my memories.

"As I said, they are agents of life, death, and thus fate, existing all around us, existing *in* us, *connecting* us in a cosmic chain crossing space and time. They only become phantoms when something provokes them: a great sin, a great evil. The phantoms are a manifestation of that imbalance. Only then do they become beasts of nightmare."

It felt like semantics, a way to ease the guilt of worshipping monsters, but he was earnest enough as he spoke.

"Oh, yeah?" He was probably so into his own babble, he didn't notice the mocking edge I'd slipped into my voice. He didn't show one way or another. An eerie serenity possessed him as he spoke about his beliefs. Creepy, to say the least, but maybe all religious types were like that. "So then, what are we?"

"The Effigies." Pastor Charles breathed a sigh as he considered us as if we were the one puzzle he hadn't yet cracked. "Farlow's writings spoke at length about the spirits and the phantoms. But only one time did she ever refer to the four of you."

"And what did she say?"

"That you were blessed." Pastor Charles grinned down at me. "Perhaps it was the spirits that gave you your gifts. Perhaps you're more connected to them than any of us will ever be."

My family was never that religious. While many had taken to the refuge of the steeple to explain the existence of the phantoms, others like us chose to just take things as they were, but for me at least, I'd always figured there was a god. God. Magic. Spirits. Effigies and monsters. What was true? Or was it all true in this world where the impossible was possible?

I shook my head. "So what's in the cellar?" I asked as we turned a corner and started down a flight of stairs.

"I met Natalya, the fire Effigy before you, about a year before her unfortunate death," Pastor Charles said, and I felt Belle go rigid beside me. "She was curious about my views, about why my teachings differed from the usual discourse of the Deoscali. And one day, during our discussions, I showed her this."

The cellar looked more like a crypt. A small, square room, it was built entirely of gray slabs of stone, dark but for the sunlight streaming through one clover-shaped window.

But there was something else about this room, something I couldn't name. A silence hung in the air, so heavy I could feel it whispering against my skin. And when I breathed in, something primal in me lifted its head and groaned, a slight tremor stirring me from the inside.

"What is this place?" I asked, staring down at my tingling hands as if I'd never seen them before. At the far corner of the room, one of the stone slabs had writing etched into it, but I couldn't make out the words from here.

"It feels wonderful, doesn't it?" This time, when he lifted his head and closed his eyes, I understood why. There was something here, something that cast shadows of stillness over us. "Many years ago, when I was still young and misguided," Pastor Charles said, "I was fortunate enough to go on a spiritual pilgrimage with a traveling sect of the Deoscali. It's where I learned to return to the old teachings of Farlow. And where I learned there are many secrets in this world. Secrets beyond the old dichotomy of phantoms and Effigies."

"He calls this cellar the Listen," Belle told me, gesturing toward the chamber. "It's the same as I remember it. You can feel the cylithium here, can't you?"

I did. Cylithium existed in nature, and in some areas it was more concentrated than others. Those were the areas human populations stayed away from, the areas where phantoms sprang forth. But it was different here. The atmosphere seeped inside me, a targeted assault on my nerves, but strangely soothing all at once. Even though I knew London's antiphantom municipal defense was strong, I half expected phantoms would suddenly emerge in front of us, growing their limbs and bones and putrid flesh from thin air as they always did in cylithium-rich areas. But nothing happened. A strange sort of peace washed over me.

"Calm," I whispered. "I feel calm."

"*For only in the calm can you hear them speak,*" the pastor said as if reciting lines from a text. "The leader of that sect had a cellar like this built in an old chapel where she would rest every so often. She used it to meditate, to commune with the spirits."

When I breathed in deeply, my bones felt like liquid. "How did you draw so much cylithium here?" Like most cities, this wasn't a cylithium-rich area. "What did you do?"

"I didn't do anything," he answered. "The religious sect I told you about—*they* were kind enough to build one in my church, though they refused to share its secrets and I haven't been able to find them since. Natalya meditated in this place once or twice before, to do what you call scry, particularly when her mind was too perturbed to achieve meditation on her own. You Effigies have your own way of connecting with spirits of this world, it seems."

Spirits. No, not spirits; it was the cylithium resonating with what I had inside me. Had to have been.

"Go ahead," Belle said. "Find out as much as you can from Natalya. Try to reach Marian."

My body felt heavy, my heels tingling with each step toward the center of the room. The dense air dried me out inside. It was as if the warmth of my palms and the flush of my face had been sucked out through the skin. And my thoughts seeped out with it.

The secrets of the world.

Sighing, I sat quietly on the ground and closed my eyes.

Something shivered past my cheek, and I opened my eyes with a shudder, but there wasn't anything else here. *Concentrate. Ignore the presence of Charles and Belle. Keep everything out.* The breathing techniques Belle had taught me were useful enough to calm my nerves, but this was more intense: the rich energy in the air, the silence, the feeling of my sensations dying off inside me.

I listened and heard it: her humming. The same tune. Always the same tune. It was her song that carried me into the recesses of my own mind.

The water was still against my ankles. Ah, the white stream. I'd seen it many times before, ever since Saul had forced me into my own subconscious in New York. That's when I started to see their memories, the Effigies who'd fought before me. For a long time, I'd bumbled carelessly, recklessly through Natalya's thoughts, picking up only jagged pieces of a frame. But, as Belle had taught me, this was the proper route. Here in the white stream with the thick fog surrounding me. And the red door, large and magnificent, like the entrance to a palace. The door to her memories. The *first* door of many, perhaps.

But this time, Natalya was not guarding it.

I felt the tip of her sword against the bare skin of my neck, just above my neck-band.

"This . . . thing," Natalya said in her Russian accent, softly clinking her sword against the steel plate. "You let them cage you. You trust too easily."

"What's wrong?" I kept my voice as still as my breath. Losing my cool wasn't an option. My nerves were a latch Natalya could use to open the window into my body. "Mad because you can't go running around in *my* dreams anymore?"

"Your dreams. My memories." Natalya laughed lightly through closed lips. "We were becoming closer, you and I. The barrier between us isn't as solid as you would like to think. Who knows, we may become closer still."

"You'd love that, wouldn't you?" I hissed. "It would just make it easier for you to steal my body."

"It would make it easier for me to *lead* you. I am always trying to lead you, Maia. To the right memory. To the right path." Her blade tilted up and I could feel the added pressure against my skin. "You can trust me."

Finally, Natalya withdrew her sword and walked off to the side, letting the blade's tip trail the water.

"You just said I trust too easily."

"You do." Natalya pointed once more at my neck with her sword, but said nothing. I touched the steel brace, confused for just a moment before I snapped out of it. It was a trick. I couldn't let her distract me.

"That's why I don't believe you," I said, my chest tight.

"About what?"

"About Rhys."

"He killed me. Do you believe that, Maia?"

The question I couldn't escape, ghosting my every step, screaming at me from within every time I stared into his dark eyes. Rhys's secrets frightened me. But the dizzying feeling of meeting his gaze and the thrill of his touch was too real, as real as Natalya's will to live again. It didn't matter what I *reasoned*. It was what I *felt*, the way my heart clenched as his tears fell. He wasn't bad. I knew that. I believed it. The boy who fought beside me, protected me, teased me, laughed with me. That was the Rhys I was sure of. The only Rhys I wanted.

And so I decided.

"No," I whispered finally. "I *don't* believe that." My voice had started to rise dangerously, but when I saw the glint of readiness in Natalya's eyes, I held myself back. "Rhys is too kind, too gentle. He's not a murderer."

"He *is* kind," Natalya said, looking up at the sunless, cloudless sky. "He's too gentle, I agree. His heart is pure. And also . . ." Her scar-covered hand gripped the hilt of her sword more tightly than before. "He is a murderer."

"*I don't believe you,*" I repeated. I couldn't hide the strain in my voice.

"I can never lie to you, Maia." It was strange. Her grin felt as menacing as it did sincere. How was it possible? This woman I had once worshipped . . . that my sister, June, had once adored. The noble warrior. Looking at her smile now, I felt like retching.

No. I really *did* feel like retching. My body was beginning to buckle and bend. It was too difficult being here. It took too much energy, too much willpower. Every second I was here in the mist, I could feel my mind breaking down. I could feel something hooking me from the inside, pulling me back out.

"If you do not believe me, I will give you a sign of goodwill." Shutting her eyes, Natalya lowered her head. "Naomi."

"What?"

"Naomi will know. But, Maia . . ." A breeze swept over the strands of her short black hair as she looked at me. The nobility, the fierceness etched into her face, was as powerful in death it was in life. "Your enemies are all around you," she said. "Are you really not aware?"

"Maia!"

It was Belle. I'd fallen over and now was actually retching. Belle and Pastor Charles helped me back up to my feet.

"I'm sorry," he said. "I know that when Natalya was here, it was also an intense experience for her. Especially the last time she came." He shook his head. "I don't envy the burden you Effigies bear."

"What do you mean? What happened when Natalya came?" asked Belle as she propped my arm around her shoulder.

"Oh, she was just . . . distraught about many things. She never clearly mentioned why. She referred to a girl called Alice."

"Alice . . ." Wiping my mouth, I lifted my head.

"She asked me about Emilia Farlow's writings, about the leader of the traveling sect. Mentioned a man named Baldric."

"Baldric. Who is that?" Belle asked. "She never mentioned him before."

"I don't know. She never explained. She said so much—too many things to remember. But one thing I do remember clearly is the symbol she drew. She asked me if I recognized it, but I couldn't help her."

"Do you still have her drawing?" Belle asked.

"I can get it from my office."

After we returned to the main hall of the church, we only had to wait a few minutes before Pastor Charles returned with a torn piece of notepaper. Though my head was still swimming and my body still languid from scrying, I rose to my feet anyway, fast, holding the back of the pew for support as I stared at the picture of a bright, flickering flame.

"She didn't know what it was herself," said Charles. "She told me that she'd seen a glimpse of it while scrying into an earlier Effigy's memories: Marian, she called her."

"Marian," I whispered. The girl both Nick and Alice were really after. The girl inside me.

Belle took the paper. "I've seen this before . . . haven't I?" She searched the ink as if she'd find her answers there.

Yes, we had. It took me a minute to remember, but this was the same symbol I'd seen in the desert hideout. A symbol connected to Marian. Another clue into who she was. I looked around at the shadows scrawled against the wall.

The secrets of the world.

16

THE SYMBOL DIDN'T COME UP IN ANY ONLINE searches, and cross-checking it against Deoscali writings at the Sect's library turned up nothing. Belle tried a second time to crack the flash drive we'd taken from Philip, thinking it'd hold clues to the hideout we'd found him in, but she just didn't have the skills to get through its encryption. Nevertheless, she was sure she'd seen the symbol some-where else, not just in the hideout. She simply couldn't remember where.

Three days of searching yielded nothing, and by Thursday evening, I had a whole new problem to deal with: namely, Blackwell's fund-raiser. I, along with a few personnel from the London facility, were to join him in putting on a show for a host of select dignitaries at his estate near Henley-on-Thames, Oxfordshire. I guess I just had to accept that part of my job description as an Effigy entailed grinning like a trained monkey in front of the cameras.

By the time my Sect van pulled up to the nearly two hundred acres of parkland, ours was only one of a long list of expensive cars lined up along the lengthy driveway. I shouldn't have been surprised that

Blackwell's estate looked like a little palace perched on a high plateau overlooking the river, its rustic stone architecture and dark arches haunted by the French Renaissance. The pamphlet they handed us after we walked through the red-iron-rimmed double doors told us that the estate used to be a British king's country home before the Blackwell family bought it in the nineteenth century with the riches they'd accumulated through their rail and shipping empires.

"They seriously just handed me a pamphlet about the damn house." I rolled my eyes, trying not to make my uncomfortable tug at my frilly yellow dress too obvious. It was Lake's dress, which she'd managed to stuff me inside while screaming at her agent over the phone because the TVCAs were just around the corner and the single she'd recorded back in February had yet to see the light of day. It was because of her Herculean effort, and her arsenal of makeup and hair combs, that I looked halfway camera ready.

And, my, were there a lot of cameras.

Blackwell had let the photographers and reporters into the mansion, and they were certainly working. Flashes of light nearly blinded me as they snapped pictures of the important-looking men and women from different countries who drank wine under the high, arched ceiling.

So many dignitaries. So much power and wealth in one tiny space. Some individuals I recognized, and some I didn't. I thought I could just slip by them unseen like a trick of the light. What I wasn't prepared for were their eyes on *me* as I passed by, their hands reaching out to me and pulling me into their circle to say something, anything. To *me*. A British member of parliament, a Ghanaian diplomat, an Australian media tycoon. Congratulating me on successfully completed missions, asking me about our plan to take back Saul.

One asked me how school was going. This was insane.

I held my little black cross-body bag closer to me. "I'm being homeschooled right now," I explained with a nervous smile to a Mexican consul general stationed in Ottawa. Sibyl had hired an instructor to come in once or twice a week and, not surprisingly, I'd learned even less than when I was struggling to stay awake in Ashford High. "Th-thanks for asking, sir. . . ."

"My daughter is a big fan. Would you mind?"

Before I'd even decided on an answer, he whipped out his phone and snapped a picture of us both. I didn't even want to know what kind of bizarre shape my mouth had contorted into.

"Everyone, please," said someone by the door, presumably working for Blackwell. "If you'll follow us into the reception hall, Mr. Blackwell would like to give his welcome."

The reception hall was majestic with a high vaulted ceiling held in place by white marble columns. The tapestries stretching across the eggshell-white walls looked hundreds of years old. Some admired them, drinks in hand, while photographers snapped their photos. Busts of philosophers were perched atop dark oak tables, tucked into corners. That's where the servants stayed with their trays of food and drinks. The man by the grand piano at the head of the room was also sitting idly, waiting for word to continue his performance.

The not-so-subtly intimidating men and women standing at attention by entrances and around corners—they must have been Blackwell's security. They looked Sect-like in their shades and black suits, but they probably worked here full-time. Every once in a while, I saw them tilt their heads and open their mouths as if speaking to an invisible friend, so I knew they were probably communicating to each other through their inner earpieces. I guess with this many powerful people in one room, security had to be vigilant.

"Maia, you're here."

My heels halted against the marble floor. Brendan slipped out from the crowd and strode toward me in his finely cut Italian suit, his hair slicked into a preppy style, almost Rockwellian in its celebration of the cheesy fifties aesthetic.

"Hopefully not for long," I mumbled, wrapping my naked arms around my chest. "Hi, by the way," I added more loudly.

That, he heard. "Good to see you. Uh—are you okay?"

My neck was chafing from Dot's neck-band. Lake had given me a white crochet band to wear around it, and it worked pretty well against the steel. But the back of my neck was still burning, and since I was too afraid to take the collar off, I tried to rub it against the skin. Hence, Brendan's quizzical look.

"I'm okay," I answered, wincing. "This place is really something, isn't it?"

At the center of the room was a tall, white stone statue of a naked woman, her long hair wrapped around her body like robes, holding what looked like a white pearl high above her head. Blackwell certainly didn't skimp on extravagance.

"Well, now that you're here, there are a few people I want you to see—" Brendan started, but he was cut off by Blackwell's booming baritone voice reverberating down the room through the sound system in the walls.

"Everyone. I want to welcome you and thank you for coming as my guests this evening."

It was fitting for a man of Blackwell's means and ego that he would be addressing us from above. Though there were a few patrons on the first steps of the spiraling, kingly staircase off to the side, only Blackwell stood on the second floor above us, casting his gaze down at us from behind the gilt bronze and wrought-iron railings. His long, thick black hair draped over his white suit in lavish curls, and a row of rings climbed several of his fingers, catching the light of the nineteenth-century chandelier dangling high above him.

Blackwell didn't need a microphone, but he seemed to enjoy speaking into one. "This estate, as you may have read in your pamphlets, was purchased by my great-great-grandfather Bartholomäus Blackwell II more than a century ago. Since then, our doors have always been open for our colleagues in the Sect and our esteemed friends around the world. It has been our family pursuit to contribute our wealth, resources, and connections toward the higher purpose of ridding mankind of the mysterious demons plaguing us. And indeed, we have taken this duty seriously from the moment we were appointed to the high position of Council representative: a position of responsibility I, Bartholomäus Blackwell VI, take just as seriously as my predecessors did."

As Blackwell continued with his speech, Brendan scoffed next to me. "That's not what my father tells me."

"What do you mean?" I asked in a whisper so none of Blackwell's "esteemed friends" could hear us trash-talking him.

"Once the Sect got out from under the control of the British Crown and established itself as an independent agency, Blackwell II bribed and blackmailed his way into a prominent position—or at least as prominent a position as they were willing to give him."

How had Director Prince put it? Ah yes, the "ceremonial crust on the Sect's toe." It was good to know his oldest son shared his naked disdain.

"That's not part of the official canon, of course, but the relationship between the Blackwell family and the Sect certainly isn't as harmonious as Blackwell's trying to paint it. But the Sect benefits from his huge amount of wealth and resources. And I suppose *he* benefits from nepotism."

"Like your dad helping you snag Sibyl's job after the Council kicked her out?"

Brendan's ears flushed red, but before he could stutter a coherent response, the room broke out into applause. I hadn't even heard the rest of what Blackwell had to say, but it probably didn't matter anyway. He was rich and powerful, and so were the people here. It was a language they understood even without words.

I wondered how it felt to inherit so much wealth and power. Blackwell looked foreboding, looming high above us, framed, perhaps fittingly, by the large, golden-rimmed acrylic painting on the wall behind him: a painting of a medieval knight standing atop a mountain of bodies, sword tipped against the head of a pleading skeleton. A man conquering death.

"There's Director Prince with Senator Abrams of British Columbia," Brendan said, pointing toward the other side of the room once the crowd had dispersed.

I guess his father was one of the people he'd wanted me to see. I hadn't even known he was coming. One would think he'd have better things to do, but then this was all about optics. Arthur Prince looked much bigger in person, taller and brawnier in his gray suit than any of his sons. The other man, Senator Abrams, was practically dwarfed by his size, though his girth more than made up for it.

And next to them with a wineglass in hand . . .

"Is that Tracy Ryan? That crazy senator from Florida?"

Indeed it was, her pinched face unmistakable. She was tall too, but she looked like a scarecrow next to Prince. Her short brown hair bounced as she nodded good-bye to Senator Abrams after he answered his cell phone and left the two.

"Good, there are cameras," I heard Brendan say before he put his hand on my shoulder. "Maia, I want you to meet Senator Ryan and Director Prince Senior."

I blanched. "And say what?"

"Exchange pleasantries. Let them know you're working hard. We just need to appear to be getting along with the rest of the world here. It's why you came, remember? Wait here."

As he walked up to the pair, I wondered what the threads would be like on the Doll Soldiers forum. Maybe the title would be, *Maia Builds Bridges with Senator Tracy Ryan*, with a set of pictures of me shaking hands with the woman widely known for her xenophobic, anti-immigration rhetoric and misogynistic policies straight out of the Baroque period. Of course, it would more likely be, *Maia Selling Out to Political Trash*, or, *Self-Hating Daughter of an Immigrant Cosigns Racist.* Or maybe, *Maia Hangs with the Woman Who Once Suggested that She and Her Friends Be Locked Up and Tortured.*

I turned right around, the bag over my shoulder swinging by the chain, and almost ran straight into Rhys standing behind me in a gray suit tailored perfectly to his tall, lean body.

"Maia. I . . ." He reached out to steady me. "I thought that was you. Your hair . . ." He pointed to his head, and my hand unconsciously went to my thick, curly hair. Still, I said nothing.

He looked even better than he usually did. He filled his suit nicely, his physique sturdier than his brother's, his proportions cruelly phenomenal. I swallowed my greeting. It slid down painfully.

I'd already decided he couldn't have killed Natalya, so I should have been more comfortable around him. I should have already sorted out the conflicted mess that were my emotions, but they were still in turmoil. Was it because of how I felt about him? Or was it the shadow of his secrets refusing to be put at ease? I couldn't tell.

His long lashes fluttered as he blinked nervously before steeling himself with a cough. He kept a little amiable smile strapped to his face like a shield, but it wouldn't make me forget that night Vasily had picked him apart piece by piece from the inside with his words alone. Or the tears streaming down his cheekbones as he'd looked at me, ashamed.

He waited for me to say something, but whatever I *could* say fell limp on my tongue. I hadn't even known he'd be here. *Are you okay, Rhys?* I thought. I wanted to say at least that.

"Your . . ." The word came out timid, unsure. "Your wrist seems okay now," I said, pointing at his arm. His black wrist brace was noticeable, but his hand looked like it could move a lot more easily now.

"Yeah," he said. "The doctors did what they needed to. And I've been resting."

"That's good," I told him, and my little smile seemed to encourage him. His face brightened hopefully at the sight of it.

"Maia," he said finally, taking his chance. "I want to—"

"Maia—and Aidan, nice of you to come."

Damn it, I'd stayed still too long. I turned to find Brendan walking up to us with Prince and Tracy Ryan in tow. Prince was formidable up close, but I could smell the judgment on him, feel the air of superiority. Once he reached me, he stared down at me without a word, picking me apart, sizing me up, trying to quantify my worth with nothing but the power of his glare.

"Ms. Finley," Prince said finally. "It's good to see you in person."

"Yeah . . ." Then, catching myself, I added, "Um, yes, sir." I was supposed to call him "sir," right? There was something about him that made me feel like I had to add it.

He didn't greet Rhys. Looking at them both up close, it was clear that Prince shared most of his genes with his eldest son: the dark, dirty-blond hair, the square shape of his head. But the intensity in Rhys's and Prince's eyes was the same.

"Hello, Director," Rhys offered, only to be greeted with a curt nod.

"Maia, you know the director of the North American Division." Unlike Rhys, Brendan's voice swelled with pride as he formally introduced his father. "And this is Senator Tracy Ryan."

On cue, Ryan gave the photographers the practiced grin of a politician, even if she couldn't hide its insidiousness. "It's good to meet one of you in person, Maia."

I looked at the hand she offered me. "Does seeing me in person make it easier or harder to dehumanize and belittle me?"

"*Maia*," Brendan warned through gritted teeth, flicking his head not-so-subtly at a reporter talking to a dignitary nearby.

"Ryan has said some rather unfavorable things about the Sect," started Prince, his Adam's apple bulging in his throat. "But we welcome these opinions. The Sect has never been above critique or scrutiny. We are as accountable to the rest of the world and its citizens as any other agency, and we've always conducted ourselves as such."

He was great at hiding it, but I caught it anyway: the way his eyes scanned the reception hall as he spoke. He certainly made sure his voice was loud enough for others to hear.

"So you told me." Ryan swirled her wineglass. "Look, I'm not here to debate politics. Lord knows we can all use a break from that from time to time. I'm here in good faith as a public servant just like everyone else. I will say, though, that if you want to win the people over, you should try asking your girls to fix their attitudes a little."

I blinked, shaking my head because I wasn't quite sure what I'd heard. "If you have something to say, I'm standing right here."

"You see?" Ryan said to Prince again, who, to my fury, sighed almost in apology. It was only then that she turned to address me. "I know it's not your fault. That's just the trouble with young women. Despite all that, you've managed to keep things together so far, and I commend you." I glared at her as she sipped from her glass. She "commended" me as if I were a newly potty-trained child. "But can you blame good, honest people for being worried when you can't even behave yourself at a simple fund-raiser?"

"But where *are* the good, honest people?" I looked around. "Surely you don't mean yourself?"

"That's enough." Prince kept his voice low and menacing. "This isn't the time to make a scene. And you should know your place."

My place. It was like a gut punch I'd seen coming, but I reeled from it anyway, from Ryan's smug look of victory, from Brendan's docility as he avoided my eyes.

"Wow, this is really something, isn't it, Maia?" Rhys glared at his father. "So what, Director? We're surrounded by cameras, so you're going to pretend you can stand to be around someone you once called the political equivalent of a monkey on a tricycle?"

Ryan bristled. This was clearly the first time she'd heard this, but Rhys hadn't finished.

"The Sect has a bad image, so you're just gonna spread it for assholes like this and let them talk to *our* people any damn way they want?"

Brendan looked furious. "Watch your tone with the director," he hissed.

"No, *he's* the one who should watch *his* tone." His voice grew louder by the second, as if he couldn't control it. His eyes were blazing as he stared down his father. "Berating her like she's someone to *discipline*. Maia isn't your kid."

"But you are." Prince didn't need to raise his voice to be menacing. He painted the opposite picture to that of his son: chillingly calm. It was a frightening control that came only with age, the dominance of a man who knew just the amount of pressure to apply and where to break someone he'd already broken before. "Do *not* test me again."

He didn't. Rhys was boiling. But he didn't. Maybe he couldn't. His hands were trembling, and not just out of anger. He recoiled under the ominous weight of his father's glare. It may have been for just a second, but I saw the flash of fear in Rhys's eyes. It was in Brendan's, too.

As Prince and Ryan walked away from us, Rhys stayed rooted to the spot, staring at a target that had long since removed itself from his line of fire.

"You really don't know when to stop, do you?" Brendan was not nearly as menacing as their father, but the judgment was there in spades. He kept his voice low to avoid drawing attention. "There are cameras around, Aidan, but you just couldn't help yourself. You had to be a little brat anyway. I thought you'd learned better by now—hey, I'm *talking to you*," he added because Rhys wasn't even looking at him. Grabbing his little brother's shoulder, Brendan pulled him around to face him. "You know as well as I do it's stupid to test Father like that. You need to learn some respect."

Rhys shrugged him off. "You mean I need to learn obedience. That's what Dad said before he shipped me off to Greenland."

"Guys, come on, not here." I was scanning the room nervously because the last thing I wanted was for this spat to end up on national news. "Just relax, all right?"

But neither boy was listening to me. The muscles tensed in Brendan's neck. "There's nothing wrong with obedience," he said quietly. "We are part of the Sect. We come from a family of specially trained warriors. Obedience is just part of discipline."

"Dad's fists sure did their best to brainwash you to believe that, didn't they?"

Brendan froze.

"Oh, I forgot." Rhys gave him a lopsided smile. "He was only 'training' us."

Brendan couldn't respond. He was looking at me now, his face tense, his lips frozen in a part. He was terrified I'd understood what Rhys meant. And I had. I turned to Rhys, my throat tightening as I studied the fury in his eyes.

"Stop it. This isn't the time or place," Brendan whispered.

"You were jealous all these years because you thought he'd sent me to Fisk-Hoffman because I was . . . what? More worthy than you? No. He was pissed I didn't break. At least, not as fast as *you* did."

Brendan flinched as if he'd been spit on, his shoulders drooping, his head shaking as he struggled to keep his trembling body under control.

"But I . . . I did." Rhys rubbed his forehead. "In the end . . . I guess I did break after all."

"Aidan—"

"Forget it. I only came here because Mom asked me to." Rhys turned his back to his older brother.

"Rhys . . . Are you okay?" I asked. Without thinking, I pinched his sleeve around his elbow to pull him back, but the moment he looked at me, my heart jumped and I withdrew my hand. For another silent second, we were looking at each other, mouths agape with the words that seemed to come so much easier when we didn't have to speak them to each other.

"I'm sorry you had to see that," he said, giving my hand a gentle squeeze before slipping away.

Brendan and I stood in awkward silence.

"Um," I started. "Brendan—"

"Forget what you heard," he said shortly, and then following his brother's lead, he went off in the opposite direction.

"Great," I muttered.

I could still feel the touch of Rhys's hand against mine, which only made the ache in my chest that much more unbearable as I squeezed past dignitaries and ducked from the flashes of cameras. It was all too clear now why Rhys resented his father. When Dad was alive, the worst he ever did was ground me and June or take away our *television* privileges. I just couldn't imagine it. The thought of Rhys being hurt, and at such a young age . . .

A security guard watched me as I passed through the entrance of a corridor populated by yet more patrons. "Anderson, checkpoint four, all clear," I heard him say behind me, his comm scratching in that familiar way. I kept my head down, hoping nobody would recognize me, and it almost worked—that is, until I nearly crashed into one of the servers. We didn't connect, but in an attempt to avoid me, she slipped and fell back. The tray of food she'd been holding slid backward off her right palm and crashed against the white staircase behind her. Thankfully, we were both in a corner, away from any of the dignitaries and cameras.

"Oh no, I'm so sorry! Are you okay?" Her cell phone, tiny and black, had clattered against the floor near the food, but it looked okay. I bent down to help her pick it up, but she plucked it off the ground herself.

"Nah, nah. It's all right." Her American accent was somewhat bizarre. "Oh, and thank you for picking this up for me." She waved her phone before slipping it into her pocket. "I've been waiting for a call." She scratched the back of her neck.

She was average height and very pretty, though her green eyes were almost too big for her small, heart-shaped face. Her nose was pointed to a tip, and her hair was such a rich, deep shade of red, it was almost crimson; she kept it at the top of her head in a carefully crafted bun tied together with black string. She straightened her black pants and white tuxedo shirt.

"Are you sure you don't need any help?"

I moved to take the platter from her, but she waved me away. "Nah, it's fine." As she slipped her left hand into her pocket, I caught the glint of something between her fingers before they disappeared inside. "Don't worry about it, sweetie."

She grinned, scratching her neck again, just as *my* phone began ringing.

Nodding reluctantly, I stood and answered it. "Yeah?" I zipped up my bag with my other hand as I stepped away from the server.

"It's Belle."

"And me!" Lake piped up after her, though her voice sounded farther away.

"And me." Chae Rin this time. "Look, we don't have a lot of time—
hey, put it on *speaker*."

"What's up, you three? Where are you?"

"The elevator," Chae Rin said. "On our way to the hangar. We've
been called on a quick mission in Scotland. The Sect are anticipating
an attack—not a Saul mega-attack, mind you. More of a bite-size
phantom rumble in the countryside. It's just busywork."

There would be agents in the area for sure. There were always
agents stationed in areas that might not have the benefit of powerful
APDs. They'd probably be able to take care of it on their own, but then
I supposed this was more about the Sect worrying about optics again.

"More important, I think I remember where I saw that symbol,"
said Belle.

The symbol of the flame. Unconsciously, I looked around, waiting for the married couple to pass by me before I lowered my voice.
"Where?"

"The Castor Volumes. I read some sections of the first three volumes years ago when I started my training. I remember seeing it there."

"Which one?" I whispered.

"That's the problem. Whether it was the first or second book of the
twelve, I can't remember."

On the other end of the receiver, Lake sighed. "There's always
something, isn't there?"

The Castor Volumes. As one of the first Sect agents, Thomas
Castor had written about his early travels as he and his crew tried
to discover the secrets of the phantoms and gather together the first

Effigies. Each volume was hundreds of pages long, so "first or second book" didn't help narrow things down much.

"Well, I guess we can check the library when we get back," I said.

"We already went. They've both been checked out. We don't have time to track them down and get them back. You're at Blackwell's estate, are you not?" Belle asked. "He's boasted about his vast collection before. In his study. Take a look while you're there."

"But . . ." I looked around. There were security agents at nearly every entrance, waiting. "I mean, it'd look pretty suspicious if I went skulking around in his house, going through his stuff. There's lot of security around too."

"So don't get caught, stupid." Chae Rin was blunt, but right.

"Good luck," Belle said before clicking off the phone.

With a sigh, I shoved my phone back into my bag.

I thought of Vasily still in the Hole. Blackwell's former right-hand man. The Council's representative had already disavowed himself of Vasily, and, according to Brendan, all investigations had so far supported his innocence. But I still couldn't be sure. I couldn't risk tipping him off. I also couldn't just ask the security guards where the study was. Who *could* I ask?

I wandered around, through the corridors, past a kitchen full of busy cooks and frantic catering staff running in and out, no time to talk. I asked some dignitaries, but they didn't know either. I knew I was lost when I found myself in front of a set of glass doors leading outside.

On the other side of the glass, a woman sat alone, gazing out into the starry night through the wooden bars of her gazebo. Did she live here? Maybe she was related to Blackwell. Wife? I didn't see a ring on any of her fingers. Still, it wouldn't hurt to ask for some directions, as long as I made up a lie to cover myself.

I walked along the stone cobbled path leading to the center of the courtyard. It smelled like spring here—mint and jasmine and other fragrances I couldn't identify—they peppered the air, seeping in through the skin, calming my nerves.

"Hello?" I called, and when she looked at me, my breath caught in my throat. She was actually stunning. Her faded brown eyes had been watching the nearby fountain in quiet contemplation, but now they were trained on me. Her face was pale but for the blush of her cheeks. She was definitely older than me, but with the youthfulness of her face it was hard to pinpoint her age. The long, twisting hair draping down her slender back was dark as night.

"Are you lost?" She had an American accent. Her voice was as delicate as she looked.

Her voice. It felt so familiar. She looked almost frail, but regal, as much as the statue on the other side of the fountain—another white stone woman carrying a pearl in her hands to match the one in the reception hall. "Maia, are you lost?"

I blinked. "You know me? Oh, yeah." I winced with embarrassment. "'Course you do. Everyone does."

She laughed softly. An elegant and feminine sound. Her voice . . . I remembered its gentle strength. But from where?

"Actually," I said, trying to stay on track. "I'm here on duty. I was told by Director Prince that Blackwell needed something out of his study."

She tilted her head, curious. "Director Prince asked you to get that?"

"It's urgent," I lied. "Do you by chance know where I can find it? Do you live here?"

"I don't live here." Contemplatively, she rubbed the bare skin of her right middle finger. "But Blackwell's personal study is in the basement. If you go back to the reception hall and turn to the left, you'll find a set of stairs going down."

So I had to go all the way back. Great. But at least I was on the right track now.

"Thank you," I said, and turned to leave.

"Maia . . ."

I stopped. It's true that being a celebrity gave people a false sense of intimacy. They talked to you as if they knew you, as if you went bowling together every Sunday. But the way this woman called my name so easily unsettled me in a different way. "What is it that Blackwell is looking for?" she asked. "From his study?"

I cleared my throat to buy time while I thought. "Uh, that's classified. It's very important business." I nodded sturdily as if it made the lie sound somehow more official.

"Be careful."

"Oh, um. Yes."

Her eyes were deep, dark wells, the kind that hold too many secrets. Beautiful . . . but creepy. My muscles tensed and my feet were itching to take me in the opposite direction, but there was something nagging at me.

"By the way . . ." I leaned in and searched her face. "This is going to sound weird, but have we met?"

It wasn't just her voice. There was something about her face, its chiseled structure, about the way her deep brown eyes twinkled with mischief as she smiled. "Yes and no."

Not cryptic at all. "Okay . . . um . . ." I shook my head. This lady was clearly taking the whole mysterious-woman thing a little too seriously. As if she weren't being creepy enough. "I don't understand."

"You've done so well, Maia," she said. "Go now. Do what you need to do."

17

I RETRACED MY STEPS BACK TO THE RECEP-
tion hall and found the right set of plain pine stairs leading down into
the basement, which looked as majestic and well decorated as the main
floor. It was all hand-carved wood and oak, mahogany floors, golden
rims, Persian rugs, and silver doorknobs. There weren't as many people
down here—a few drifting patrons, a couple of catering staff. Even
asking one for directions, I wasn't sure if I'd find the right room until
I came to a set of double doors around a corner—guarded. A single
security guard had been stationed next to the doors. I ducked out of
his sight.

"Crane, checkpoint twelve, all clear," he said into his comm—that
is, until he saw me rounding the corner.

"What are you doing here?" He looked shocked to see me. Maybe a
little excited. He was a young guy, and he didn't quite have that stone-
cold security glare down like some of his colleagues. But whatever
excitement had flashed in his eyes passed quickly. He tilted his chin
to the side as if he were about to speak into his communication device
again.

"Wait!" I said, putting up a hand to stop him. "Um, this is Black-well's study, right?"

"It is." He adjusted the wire around his neck leading up to his ear.

Why guard the study? There wasn't anyone around. I checked behind me to make sure. This particular corridor was empty. I hadn't seen any other security guards except at major exits. The only reason Blackwell would keep someone here was to keep others out.

"Are . . . you lost, Ms. Finley?"

I fidgeted a bit at the sound of my name. I'd probably never get used to people just knowing it. "I was told to get something out of Blackwell's study."

"Sorry, no one's allowed in. Not even you."

"It's Sect orders," I pushed.

"Sorry," he said again. "But . . . now that you're here . . ." He scratched the back of his head sheepishly, trying to avoid my eyes until he reached into his pocket and pulled out a napkin. "I don't have a pen, but . . ."

He had to be joking. "You want my *autograph*?" I gaped at his expectant hands.

"It's not for me. It's for my little sister," he said quickly, shaking the napkin at me. "Please?"

"If I sign this, will you let me in?"

When he answered with an awkward, noncommittal shrug, I sighed and took a pen out of my bag. "Who do I make it out to?"

"Steven."

I looked at him.

"It's short for Stephanie."

"Of course it is." I signed my name, discreetly stealing a second look down the hallway to make sure it was clear. "Is this okay?" I handed it back to him.

His whole face lit up as he took it from me, holding it up as if he had to inspect the ink to make sure it was real. "This is lovely, thanks! Sorry, it's just that I've never really met a celebrity before."

"Oh, it's no problem! Glad to do it."

But the moment I started to move past him, he put up his hand to stop me again.

"Sorry, no one's allowed in."

"Are you *kidding* me?" I complained with a groan. Then I checked behind me one last time. "Fine, then. Plan B."

Plan B was hitting him really hard on the back of his neck. I was fast, too fast for him to react. He went down, but I grabbed him before he could make a sound and dragged him into the study. *Don't get caught*, Chae Rin had said. Well, that was out of the question now. Maybe I could bribe Crane into silence with another autograph once he woke up. At any rate, all the security guards would have to check in, which meant I didn't have much time in here.

The study was a musty, oval-shaped delicacy of books; one long mahogany case curved around about half the structure as if it'd been built especially for this room. Beautiful nineteenth-century portraits of old people hung around the room. A lavish rug lined the wooden floor, but there were only a few sitting chairs in the room: a couple by the left sections of bookcase, one behind the large desk where the bookcase ended, and a maroon-and-brown patterned settee in front of the fireplace by the right wall. But the main piece of the study had to be the statue at the room's center—another woman with a pearl, carved in white stone. The smooth groove representing her eyes felt somehow hollow and knowing. She was just like the other two.

No, not quite like the others. Each of the statues had been a little different, their hand positions and body poses slightly unique. This one curved her arms inward, hugging the pearl to her chest as if to protect what was hers. Blackwell sure had strange taste in décor.

Crane was out cold, but he wouldn't be forever. I'd have to think of some excuse once he did wake up, but for now I had to find that Castor Volume. The rest I'd figure out later.

After dragging his body inside a closet of smoking jackets, I put my phone on vibrate so no sudden rings would give me away. Then I started to search the books on the shelves.

"Okay, here we go." I scanned the bookshelf, tracing my fingers down the spines of first editions to check names. Blackwell did have the Volumes in his study. A couple of them were missing from the shelves, but thankfully, the first volume was here. The giant tome was as heavy as it looked, so big I had to carry it in the crook of my arms. The pages were thin and slippery. Hundreds of them. There was no way I'd get through all of this in time.

"Thanks, Belle." I rubbed the back of my neck because the band was never *not* itchy.

I set the book down on the desk. Then, dropping my bag to the floor, I plopped into Blackwell's chair with a heavy *thump* and a heavier sigh. Hard to believe Castor had originally written all this by hand. Where to start? My fingers touched the dark blue velvet binding gently before flipping through the first pages.

"Wait . . ." The red ribbon attached to the book set off where Blackwell had read last, right? Carefully, so as to not lose the exact page, I flipped pages until I reached the separation. "Okay, what's this about?"

Egbaland, 1878.
 One of the domestic servants, Omotola, the natives

*called her, stole a valuable jewel from one of the many
properties of Madam Tinubu, the Iyalode of this land. I
offered my services to the slave trader to retrieve her, but in
truth, I was more interested in the other properties the girl
possessed.*

*After hearing the stories of hurricanes tearing through
fields in one moment and disappearing the next, of a girl
dancing through the trees as if carried by the skies, I was
sure she was one of the special girls—like the one I found in
Beijing three years ago. Indeed, Tinubu surely had realized
as well that there was something magical about the girl.
She would never allow me to keep her. But, displaying the
inscrutable countenance of the shrewd businesswoman she
was, she offered me a trade instead: If I helped her to bring
her servant, she would reveal to me the secret methods
with which she has kept her home safe from the nightmares
plaguing the outskirts of her city. A treasure she has buried
somewhere deep under the earth.*

"A treasure buried in the earth," I repeated. What could she possibly bury that would keep phantoms away?

*Indeed, as my travels have long shown, the
nightmares stretched even as far as these lands. There
were not many of them yet—a needed morsel of comfort
in those days of uncertainty. It was the same as in
the other lands. The phantoms' sudden appearance on
English soil thirteen years ago was but a temporary
moment of terror. Then, after a year of recovery, they
began appearing again. I had thought, after witnessing*

*the horror in York, that the beasts would quickly overrun
the world, destroying mankind. However, according
to my observations, as well as the information I have
received from the colonies, the phantoms attack only
limitedly, at certain times, in certain areas. The attacks
I had documented never lasted more than one hour. They
would disappear. It was as if something was holding
them back. As if they were, despite their devastating
power, simply part of someone's monstrous experiment—
or the cruel game of a terrible god.*

It was similar to what I had learned in school. The phantoms only *appeared* in 1865, but there weren't too many attacks at first. They grew more frequent and widespread over time. It had given humanity a chance to survive in those early days when the technology wasn't so good, a chance to fight back, a chance to advance and to plan even as people were killed and uprooted. I remember June had to do some billboard project on Nikola Tesla's prototype antiphantom device for a science fair once. Super crude, but society had managed to build from it. Problem was that as the tech got better, the phantom attacks only grew more frequent, more widespread, until things became what they were now. And they weren't going away.

But those early devices were about electromagnetic impulses and other sciencey garbage I didn't get. This Tinubu woman had a "treasure" buried under the earth. How was that possible?

If it wasn't science, it was magic. But what *kind* of magic?

*The British Crown had exhausted many of her
resources learning about the dark beasts that roared death
into the wind. But the people here had found a curious*

thing: Tinubu's treasure. If I could bring both it and the
girl with me back to Britain to study, it would only be in
service to the Crown and the Sect.

I was surprised to see so many black markings on the page. I expected Blackwell would be the type to want to keep everything pristine and unblemished, but he'd circled the words "curious thing" and written the word "safe?" in the margins.

"What's safe?" I whispered, and kept reading.

But was it indeed some buried contraption protecting
Tinubu's people from the dangers that raged outside? In
my travels, I had found places such as these. Places of the
purest calm. Of silence. Places where the very air was rich
with the promise of heaven's blessings. Here in Egbaland,
I felt that same heavy air. The moment I stepped foot on
these lands I knew it was the same as before. The same as
those lands.

"Places of the purest calm." If I closed my eyes I could imagine it. No, I could *remember* it. Calm that felt like clean silence all around you. But what Castor was referring to couldn't have been the same as what I'd felt in Pastor Charles's cellar. Could it? Pastor Charles didn't know the cellar's secrets. It was the traveling religious sect that had created it, and they'd never told him how. Was I just jumping to conclusions?

His spiel about phantoms and spirits hadn't left my mind since we'd first met him in the church, but I still couldn't make heads or tails of it. The cellar itself simply felt like it had more cylithium in it than you'd expect. That was the simpler explanation, not all this craziness about the universe, cosmic connections, life, death, and fate. But still, it was incredibly strange. Feeling calm and safe in a cylithium-rich area. How?

Blackwell was curious about it too. He underlined "those lands," but wrote nothing next to it.

The door creaked. Oh god, did I not lock it? Ducking behind the desk was my first reflex, and a stupid one, because it wouldn't take much effort to find me crouched here. It was too late to change my mind, though, because whoever it was had already entered the room. I held my breath, flinching at each footstep. Poor Crane was still safely inside the closet. As long as whoever it was didn't come near this corner of the room, I wouldn't be stuck in the awkward position of having to explain why I was breaking, entering, snooping, and hiding.

But it looked like I wouldn't have to. I could hear the footsteps retreating, and the following soft *click* of the double doors.

Then . . . nothing. Whoever it was had left.

I waited for a minute more, listening until I was comforted enough by the silence to pop back out from under Blackwell's desk.

"Hi!" Rhys waved at me from the other side of the desk.

My heart jumped into my throat as I stumbled back and nearly fell over Blackwell's chair. Rhys leaned over the desk and, after catching me by the wrist, pulled me upright.

"Wh-what," I breathed, my throat still tight. "What—"

"—am I doing here?" Rhys held up his phone. "I've been trying to call you."

"I put my phone on vibrate." I picked up my bag. "Sorry, I guess I didn't hear it."

He'd clearly cooled off since the time I'd last seen him. Rhys looked around the study, then at the open book on the desk. "What are you doing here?" He slid the book around so he could read the words. "The Castor Volumes?"

"Just doing a little studying. Since I was bored."

"I don't believe you."

"Oh, come on." I leaned over the desk. "Is this the face of a liar?"

I figured he'd argue some more. I wasn't expecting him to grab my chin gently, turning my face left and right as he inspected it. His fingers were slightly calloused; I could feel them scratch delicately against my skin. Warm.

"All right, I believe you." He let me go with a little smile.

"Huh?"

He shrugged. "You're neurotic and adorable. How can I not believe you?"

"Oh . . . g-good," I said, trying to ignore the fluttering in my chest. I cleared my throat. "How did you even know I was here?"

"My mother told me."

"Your . . ." The beautiful woman I'd found outside with a strange penchant for cryptic behavior. "She's your *mother*?" No wonder her face was so familiar. Rhys certainly had some of the strong features I recognized in his father, but he'd received his gentle beauty from his mother. That was clear now.

"Yeah. She lost her wedding ring. I'm supposed to be looking for it. She's the director's wife, after all. Gotta have her ring, I guess." Though he looked a little annoyed, his face softened as he spoke about his mother. It was a stark contrast to how I'd seen him around his father; not too surprising given what I'd just learned about the man.

My heart dropped at the thought. I fidgeted awkwardly. "Did you . . . did you want something from me?"

Rhys slid a hand through his messy black hair as he looked away from me. "Well, first I thought I should apologize about what happened back there. Brendan and I . . . We have our issues, but it's not something you should have to worry about."

"No, it's okay."

He watched me self-consciously from the corner of his eye. I didn't know how to approach the subject of his father, or if he even wanted me to. It felt intrusive to bring it up.

"I also wanted to apologize for what my father said to you," he said, surprising me.

"It's all right." I shut the Castor Volume discreetly, making sure the red ribbon was in its original position between the thin pages. "You don't have to apologize for someone else's actions."

"I guess the problem is I have trouble apologizing for my own."

I lowered my head, clutching my bag closer to me. I knew there was a chance that the sadness in his eyes wasn't just because of his family. That he was haunted by more than just his past in Greenland. But I'd already chosen not to believe that he could have murdered his own friend. I just had to stick to that. My legs twitched as he came around the desk, but this time I didn't back away from him. And when he grabbed my hand, I didn't pull it away.

"Maia," he started, his voice strained as if the pressure of his words would break him, "about what Vasily said—"

"Before you say anything," I said quickly, "listen to me first."

The room was quiet. I let that moment of silence pass between us because I needed the time to steel my nerves, to decide whether or not I was going to ask the question that had been burning me from the inside since that night in France. "I don't know how I feel about you," I said instead. And it was true.

"Do you hate me?"

When Rhys suddenly asked, I looked up at him, shocked. "What?"

"I'm sure you've figured out that I'm not as . . . as entirely normal as I may have made myself seem when I met you."

"I never thought you were normal." When I noticed my lips had twisted into a wry grin, I hid it away guiltily. "And I . . . kind of like that. Not like I'm normal either."

Rhys's flicker of a sad grin told me he understood. "I've had a . . . weird life. Like you. It's like I told you that night on the train: Sometimes the Sect can feel like this unstoppable force. Once you're with them. All you have . . . all you *are* is because of them. Even when you're desperate to be more."

Desperate. I'd felt Natalya's agony as she scratched at the barriers of my mind, trying fiercely to climb back inside my body. The agents and the Effigies alike: We were all chained to the same wall.

"I understand," I offered, and that alone brought a tinge of wetness to his eyes. Someone understood him, even with the secrets he'd locked up inside himself so he could show the world his other face. Someone was willing to understand. I didn't think two words could mean so much to him, but it wasn't difficult to see why they did. We were both just kids, after all—kids struggling under the weight of impossible legacies.

"But you're innocent. Maybe that's why I . . ." He swallowed, lowering his eyes. "So if you don't know how to feel about me, I'd never blame you for that. But please don't hate me." He'd kept his voice as calm as he could, but he couldn't hide the anguish of his plea. "That's all I ask. You don't have to like me. You never have to fall for me either."

There was a strange twinge in his voice as he whispered it. I could see his eyes reddening, his lips curling into each other, trying to hold in whatever emotions threatened to spill out. I fidgeted. Rhys's grip held me in place, but I didn't try that hard to pull it away in the first place. Maybe I liked his touch a little too much.

"No matter what happens . . . please never hate me. Promise me you'll never hate me."

"I don't hate you," I whispered, and, pulling my wrist out of his grip, I pushed him gently against Blackwell's desk, cupped his face, and kissed him.

I hadn't actually kissed anyone before. Even before my family died and left me an orphan, I was a shut-in, preferring the sanctity of my laptop over other people. It scared me to feel his arms rough around my waist, but this kiss had been boiling up inside me for too long. Natalya could watch and seethe for all I cared as Rhys deepened the kiss. I needed to make things clear in my own mind.

It didn't.

I mean, it was wonderful. The warmth of his lips spread down the length of me from the inside, quickening my pulse, tightening my whole body, but it didn't give me clarity. It only made it that much harder to get. I pulled away from him, turning away quickly while I tried to calm the rise and fall of my chest.

"Maia . . . ," he whispered.

I had to be honest. I had to confront him. . . .

But I couldn't.

"I'm a coward," I said. To him. To myself. Or maybe to Natalya. "I'm seriously messed up. I really am." If it weren't for the neck-band, I was sure I'd be able to hear her yelling at me, furious. Or laughing. "I keep saying I want to know, but the truth is . . ."

The truth was I didn't. I didn't want to know. Because I liked him. I hated myself for it. I angled my body away from Rhys, my hand finding the table.

"I don't like how I feel around you." Shame crawled up my bones as I thought of Belle night after night on the terrace of our dorm, staring at her blank canvas with lost eyes. The first time I ever saw her there, she'd told me that none of us were heroes. Wouldn't she have thought differently if Natalya were still alive? It was Natalya's death that had broken her. "I don't understand what this is," I said. "I don't like that it's happening. I'm not here and I'm not there. I feel like I'm everywhere at once. You're wrong: I'm not innocent, Rhys. I'm totally messed up."

I looked at his large hand trembling at his side and thought back to all those painful days I spent buckling under the weight of a destiny I never asked for. Thrown into the chaos of a battle I didn't know how to fight. No uncle, no home.

"But you were always there." I gazed up at him. "Even when you didn't have to be. You were there for me."

And if I knew the truth, and it was what I feared, then he wouldn't be anymore.

"Maia . . ."

"I don't know what to do," I admitted with a helpless shrug. "I'm scared to do anything. I'm scared of what could happen. What . . . what should I do, Rhys?"

A shiver went through me as he touched the side of my face, lightly, in that vulnerable space just below my ear, his fingers brushing up against my thick curls. And as his fingers lingered there, I held my breath.

The door creaked. Rhys's hand dropped from my neck as Blackwell entered the study. His mild surprise gave way to amusement as he saw us standing behind his desk. He'd be more amused to find the security guard trapped in the closet. Poor Crane.

"Far be it from me to get in the way of a secret tryst between two lovers, but . . ."

My teeth glued shut as Blackwell's gaze trickled down to the book on the desk he'd left empty. Pressing my bag protectively against my hip, I started thinking up excuses.

"Sorry, I took her down here," Rhys said. "We needed a place to be alone."

My breath hitched as Rhys wrapped a strong arm around my waist and pulled me to his side, almost possessively. I was assuming that was supposed to be code for "a place to make out." Which we kind of had. Rhys really made sure to sell it too, his body curving toward me, his hand hard against my hip. I was *definitely* selling it with the way my face flushed and my head shyly dipped. Though that wasn't an act.

"Aidan, what would your father think?" Blackwell folded his arms and stepped slowly toward us. "It's not like you to do such things. Especially when you're here on duty."

"Not my fault your party's boring."

"Sorry, we won't do it again." Grabbing his wrist, I pulled him away from the desk. "We're going now."

Blackwell's eyes never left me as I scurried out of his study with Rhys in tow.

"Are you okay?" Rhys asked once we were back upstairs in the hallway with the other patrons. Probably because I was tugging at the stupid band around my itching neck.

"Yeah, sorry. Hey, do you think you can you get me out of here?"

Blackwell was going to find Crane in the closet tucked underneath all his smoking jackets. If he didn't, someone else would. I didn't have an excuse for that. "Like, can you drive me back to the facility?"

It didn't take Rhys more than a second to surmise the situation.

Without asking questions, he nodded. "We can take my brother's car. Just stay here while I get his keys."

He disappeared back into the reception hall. I waited in a corner, avoiding the stares of the patrons in their little circles, peering over one another's shoulders to make sure it was me before whispering to each other. Really. For a bunch of high-powered politicians and business-people, the way they conducted themselves was startlingly similar to the kind of stuff I saw at Ashford's last school dance.

"Ms. Finley," a reporter said, walking up to me. Damn it. I should have waited outside. "I'm Jonathan Headey from the *Sun*. Do you have a minute for a quick interview?"

"Well, I—"

"Sorry, but we'd like Ms. Finley to come with us."

The security guard had spoken politely enough, despite his intim-idating frame, but his partner had shoved the reporter aside rather roughly.

Crane's revenge. Blackwell had found me out. I was done for.

One grabbed my arm and pulled me along, though I shot one last frantic look toward the reception hall. I didn't suppose I could just set him on fire without anybody noticing.

"Blackwell sent you, right?" I asked as we squeezed through digni-taries. "Hey, stop!" I pulled myself out of his grip and stopped in my tracks. "I asked you a question."

"Blackwell didn't send us," said the taller one.

It was hard to gather anything from either of their faces since both guards were wearing shades.

"Then what's this about?"

"It's Mrs. Prince," one said. "The director's wife would like to see you inside Mr. Blackwell's office. It's an urgent matter. Please come with us."

Rhys's mom? Curious, I followed them through the corridors until the patrons and reporters thinned out and we were standing alone outside a lonely door at the end of a hall.

My phone vibrated against my hip. It was Rhys.

"Miss," a guard said before I could answer it, putting his hand on my phone. "If you please? We're here. This really is urgent."

I looked at the two men towering above me and wondered how much effort it would take to knock them both out if this turned out to be some kind of trap. If Blackwell really was waiting to try something behind the doors, I knew I could take him easily, but he wouldn't be stupid enough to try with all the people running around the house.

Discreetly, I answered the call, but only after I'd placed my phone back in my bag. "So this is Blackwell's office in the east wing?" I spoke loudly enough for Rhys to hear, but restrained myself so I still sounded natural. "Mrs. Prince is really waiting for me in here? Are you guys sure?"

"Yes," one replied after an annoyed grunt.

I slipped my hand back out without turning my phone off, leaving my bag slightly open so it could pick up any surrounding sound. It was a precaution—one they didn't notice.

The shorter security guard knocked on the door. "Ma'am, she's arrived."

"Maia?"

I heard the woman's voice call for me through the door, but something was wrong. It was less a call than a whimper, a pleading question suddenly muffled into silence.

Whipping around to glare at the security agents, I burst inside the room. Mrs. Prince was inside Blackwell's darkly lit office, standing behind the large wooden desk that shimmered in the moonlight streaming from the grand, arched window behind it.

And next to her was the tiny red-haired server girl I'd bumped into earlier, holding a gun to Mrs. Prince's temple. With her other hand, she held a finger to her lips.

"We're going to do this quietly, sweetie," she said in an accent she hadn't had before. Australian. This voice I recognized. "Or you'll see Mrs. Naomi's brains splattered across all this fine furniture."

18

NAOMI. *NATALYA'S* NAOMI? I LOOKED AT THE woman, who was deathly still, though her eyes screamed for help.

A rough push from one of the security guards sent me stumbling farther inside the room. The other shut and locked the door behind him with a soft *click*. Quickly, I lifted my arms, feeling the heat rush through them.

"Nuh-uh-*uh*! Hands down." The server waved her finger at me. "No powers. Neither of us wants things to get messy here."

"Jessie, right?" I said. She looked completely different from the picture I'd seen on the screen, but I couldn't forget that mocking, sing-song tone.

"Ooh? Did Aidan tell you about me? I'm touched that he remembers me."

"Aidan," Naomi hissed quickly. "Tell Aidan—"

Jessie's hand covered the woman's mouth. "Qui-*et*, please."

Discreetly, I lowered my gaze, checking my bag to make sure it was still open, picking up the sound.

"Jessie Stone, right?" I repeated as loudly as I could without arousing suspicion. "Yeah, I saw your picture once. Kind of a different girl when you were thirteen."

"I got a little work done in my off time. Wanted to look pretty for my big comeback, you know. I haven't seen Aidan in so long." She leaned in, pressing her gun closer to her victim's temple. "What else did he tell you about me?"

"That you're a psychopath."

"Really?"

"No, but I can gather. Otherwise, why would you have a gun to his mother's head?"

I shifted slightly, feeling my open bag swivel against my hips as Jessie giggled. "You talk tough. Ain't too bright, though." Her wild eyes traced a path down my face to my neck before rubbing the back of her own.

The security guards stood almost perfectly still, like soldiers waiting for orders. "Jessie, it's getting late, and they still haven't called," one said. "He should be out by now."

"Yeah, I *know* that, Anderson. Damn it," she cursed, glaring at her pants pocket. "What the hell is the holdup?"

"What exactly do you want from me?" I gripped the bag's chain around my shoulder. My feet itched to launch me forward, but Jessie's finger was too firmly on the trigger of her gun. "Just let Mrs. Prince go!"

"Can't do that. She's my insurance. See, you're supposed to come with us—me and Vasily, I mean. We're takin' you to Saul."

Back when they'd ambushed us the first time in the tunnels, Jessie had tried to get that giant monstrosity to capture me too—no, it wasn't a monstrosity. It was a person. Or it used to be. Alex. I felt a slight chill shudder through my bones.

"Even with the ring, he's very busy, you know. Prepping for

something hella big. Can't do everything himself. There's a plan in place. It's all about the *timing*, see? Now it's time for you to come with us."

"The problem with that plan," I said, my voice shaking, "is that Vasily's still in jail, currently being tortured by a crazy guy dressed like a doctor."

Jessie sighed. "Seems like. I thought I'd get confirmation by now. Once I did, it'd be easier to take you out of here."

"Confirmation of *what*?"

Jessie only shrugged. "But since I haven't heard anything, I'm taking matters into my own hands." She cocked the gun. "Now come with me. Very quiet. Or we'll both have fun watching Mommy's gray matter *fly*."

Rhys's mother gasped against Jessie's hand as the girl pushed the gun hard against her skull. Jessie's eyes were alight with joy and malice.

My trembling fingers curled around my dress. "You wouldn't."

The shot was muted thanks to the silencer on the barrel. I was frozen, my mind still working out what had happened, when one of the security guards behind me crumpled to the ground. The other guard looked horrified enough to retch as Jessie rather innocently shrugged and placed the gun back on Naomi's temple.

"Let's try this again," she said. "Come with me. Quietly. I won't say it again."

Naomi squeezed her eyes shut, breathing in slowly to keep herself calm. I couldn't stall anymore. But before I could get my foot off the floor, I heard something rolling into the room behind me.

"What the . . ." The guard stepped to the side to avoid them. They were three metal balls, tiny enough to slip underneath the door, like children's marbles.

Jessie tilted her head. "What's that?"

Click. The light that battered the room blinded me for a moment.

I covered my eyes, doubling over as the doors busted open. The crack of a fist against bone, the shudder of a body slamming against the wall.

"Hold it!"

It had taken only a moment. The flash was gone, and when my eyes readjusted, Rhys was next to me, holding his gun up at the unhinged girl still pointing a gun at his mother's head. Brendan shut the door, moving the other guard's limp body next to the one Jessie had killed.

"She's crazy," I hissed, rubbing my eyes.

Rhys kept his gun level. "Yeah, I know."

Jessie positively lit up at the sight of him. Her body twitched slightly as if she couldn't contain it. "Hi, Aidan!" She didn't seem to mind or even notice when Brendan cocked his gun in her direction. "I always said I wanted to meet your mom, remember?"

It was incredible. One minute she seemed determined to kill him and the next she looked as if she wanted to kiss him.

Rhys didn't move. "I remember."

"You promised you'd take me. But then, you promised a lot of dumb shit that didn't end up happening, didn't you?" Her hand clasped tighter around Naomi's mouth. "Well, I'm here now," she sang. "I'm *alive*, Aidan. Aren't you surprised? Don't I look pretty now? The surgeries turned out great, didn't they?"

"Let my mother go," Rhys ordered her calmly. "You're surrounded."

He nodded at the window behind her, and in the darkness I could see a figure moving, a gun glinting.

"Director Prince Senior is managing things outside. Nobody is any the wiser and we'd like to keep it that way." Brendan followed suit in training his revolver on Jessie. "It's over, Ms. Stone. Slide your gun to me and come with us—*quietly*. Let's not disturb the people here."

"It's over . . . ?" Jessie was enjoying this. She stifled a laugh. "Gonna take me in, huh?"

"Don't worry." Brendan smirked. "You'll be with your friend Vasily in the Hole."

A shadow passed over her porcelain face. "There's only one Devil's Hole."

It was slight, but I caught it: the twitch of Rhys's hand, just as Jessie's pants pocket vibrated.

"Oh, good!" Her eyes were back to shining again. "Finally!"

She lowered her gun, pushing Naomi forward with a shove to the back of her head.

"Mom!" Rhys and Brendan cried at the same time, though neither lowered his gun.

As Jessie began rubbing her neck again, I grabbed Naomi's trembling hand, pulling her behind me. "You can have this, too!" said Jessie. "You've been looking for it, right?"

She slipped her hand into her pocket and threw something small and glittering at the floor. A wedding band. Naomi's? I didn't know what she was up to, or how petty theft featured into Saul's grand plan, but whatever was going on ended now.

"Brendan's right." I lifted my right hand, ready to fight. "It's over. You're outgunned. And I'm not going anywhere."

"Well, you got one right. I *am* outgunned." In a show of surrender, Jessie bent low and slid the gun right to my feet. "We'll see about the other thing."

Shutting her eyes, Jessie breathed deeply, lowering her head.

"Mom, go," said Rhys, inching toward Jessie carefully. "Go find Dad."

"Wait, Aidan." Naomi lifted her hand up. "Something's not right. She's—"

Someone stirred behind us.

Someone dead.

"Oh my god," I breathed, my chest heaving. Rhys and Brendan whipped around, training the gun at the dead security agent with the tiny hole dripping blood out of his head. His corpse was suddenly rising to its feet, his eyes rolling back.

"What the hell?" Brendan yelled. "What . . . *what*?"

They shot at him, several rounds each splitting the air. The guard twitched and jerked but kept stumbling forward. The same as in the tunnels. Jessie . . . Jessie was—

"Maia. Look at me."

I turned back around to find Jessie holding up a tiny black phone—the one I'd almost picked up for her in that hallway. It stopped buzzing.

"Listen" was all she said before she clicked the button.

That noise . . . sounds like interference. . . .

That was the last thought I had. My mind went blank.

The door burst open.

"What's going on in here? Naomi?"

Blackwell. I didn't register the terror in his eyes as he saw the guns, the dead security guard lurching toward two freaked-out agents and their equally spooked mother. But then, I didn't register much of anything at all.

The interference. Its hellish screeching tore through my brain as I picked up the gun at my feet and shot Blackwell in the stomach.

"*Maia!*"

It was a bad shot, or maybe Blackwell didn't react quickly enough. It hit the left side of his gut. Gasping in pain, he fell back against the doorframe.

People were yelling various things I didn't care about. There was a shot through the window that shattered the glass and hit Jessie's shoulder. I took care of the agent who fired the bullet, swinging my arms fast, letting the flames dash across his face. Now he was screaming.

The back of my neck was burning. It was out of control now. But my feet carried me away nonetheless, as fast as I could run in heels, my gun still in my hands, even when Rhys yelled at me to stop. Jessie and I were out the broken window, my dress tearing a bit from the shards of glass. Together we ran down the grassy courtyard off the cobbled path.

"It's not so bad, right? You get used to it." As we trampled flowers underfoot, Jessie panted and giggled like the adrenaline had made her delirious. "Mine's Grunewald's very latest model."

Grune . . . wald . . . The name echoed in the vacant chamber of my mind.

"They put it in all us 'silent kids.' Doesn't need a trigger 'cause it's always working. It even helps me mask my frequency as long as it doesn't degrade. But yours is an earlier model, a one-shot activation. Doesn't work that good. It's definitely gonna crap out soon, so we gotta do this fast."

"Stop!" Rhys's voice, tense from the chase, called out to us in the night.

We were heading toward the river bordering the south end of the estate. A shot rang out. Jessie lost control of her body and crashed into mine, pushing us both down to the floor. She'd been hit. Her right leg was bleeding just above her knee.

Grabbing the gun from me, she rolled over onto her left hip and pointed the weapon at Rhys. I looked from one to the other, from Jessie to Rhys, both their guns trained on each other under the moonlight. But I felt nothing. My body was cold, hollow, my mind blissfully clean except for the lingering echo skidding across the surface of my consciousness: *Listen to Jessie. Escape with her at all costs.*

The command I'd been given.

"Maia, come with me." Rhys reached to me with his free hand still wrapped in its sling. "Please."

Despite the pain, Jessie laughed at him. "Nah, that ain't happening."

"Shut up," Rhys said. "Or next time, I'll take a kneecap."

"Mm, sexy." Jessy gave him a wry grin before turning to me. "We need to go. Vasily's waiting for us."

"Vasily?" Rhys spat. "What have you done? What the hell is going on?"

With her gun still aimed at him, Jessie pulled out her black phone. "I was waiting for a call and I got it. It's confirmed."

I barely twitched in response.

"He gave you a signal." Rhys inched closer to us, his feet making no noise against the dewy grass.

"You didn't think Vasily of all people would stay locked up for long, did you?"

"Who helped him?" Rhys crushed a posy underfoot.

"Who didn't?" Jessie laughed. "There's more of us than you realize. You really suck at picking sides."

The two stared each other down in the night, and something inside me was screaming for me to get ahold of myself, but my knees stayed helplessly pinned to the grass.

"Life really isn't fair, isn't it?" Jessie said. "All those years ago . . . we all went through it in that fucked-up facility—those insane training sessions, those 'psych evals' that felt more like torture. You were the one who said we could be free. *You* made me think we'd all escape *together*. Escape the Sect." Her voice, for the first time, swelled with a kind of childish hope, immature and fragile. It didn't last. "But everything went wrong. *We* followed *you*, but only *you* got to live. And what did you do but go right back to the Sect?" Her long red hair swept the air like a pendulum as she shook her head violently. "Unlike me and Vasily, you had Mommy and Daddy to go back to. People to protect you. You escaped one cage and dragged your *own* sorry ass right back into another. Ever the dutiful son." She smirked. "You'll never be free."

"And are you free, Jessie?"

Jessie rubbed the back of her neck with a trembling hand. I couldn't tell if she'd even meant to or not. "Maia," she said suddenly, and it was like my body shook awake. "Remember what the little voice in the phone told you. We gotta go."

Yes. At all costs.

I stood.

"Maia?" Rhys lowered his gun, his eyes narrowing as a hint of fear crawled into his features.

At all costs.

Balls of flame exploded at Rhys's feet like little bombs. Rhys jumped and dove to avoid them, rushing toward me every opportunity he got, but I didn't stop hurling fire at him. Jessie's unhinged laughter screeched over the chaos as she dragged herself up and balanced herself on her good leg.

"Kill him!" She goaded me, too excited at the mayhem of flames to bother shooting at him herself. "Kill him *now!*"

I was trying. The dull pain throbbed at the back of my neck, the steel band rubbing against my skin as if aching to crush my windpipe. *Listen to Jessie. Escape with her at all costs.* I was *trying.*

"Maia, wake up! Fight it!" Rhys cried before I sent a wall of flame crackling up at his feet. He jumped, but too late—he cried out in pain as the fire licked his leg.

A hard twinge in my chest, a sudden chill rushing through me. All these curious sensations my mind couldn't grasp as Rhys hit the ground hard, rolling on the grass to put the flame out.

Maia . . .

Maia . . .

Are you listening . . . ?

She was humming a melody I'd heard too many times before on those terrifying nights.

Her voice . . . Natalya's voice.

I told you. . . . You let them cage you. . . . You trust too easily. . . .

"What are you doing? Kill him! *Hurry*," Jessie ordered because my hands had frozen in the air.

My arms wavered, caught between falling limp and staying firm. My attacks stopped. What was I doing?

Its hold on you is getting weaker . . . If we work together . . . if we share this battle, we can overcome it completely. . . . For just today, for just a second . . . Maia, let me take you. . . .

There were too many voices in my head: one telling me to kill Rhys and the other telling me to kill myself.

I can't do it alone. Let me out. . . . Let us . . . help each other. . . .

"Maia." Rhys tried to struggle back to his feet, but his unwieldy legs collapsed beneath him and he fell back. He gripped the soil, dirt collecting in his fingernails as he let out a haggard sigh and looked up at me. "Please come back. Come back to me."

Painfully, slowly, my lips pried apart. "Rhys . . ." But that was all I could manage.

"Fuck, forget it!" Jessie raised her gun.

And that was the trigger. I released the mental defenses I'd desperately been holding on to, and just like that, a new power filled me. Natalya. Two energies connecting within one form. The power overwhelmed everything else in me, shorting out the command, the white noise that had been dulling my mind. With the force of two Effigies, I stomped on Jessie's hand, pinning it to the dirt. She gasped in pain, but she was strong too; she managed to slip her hand out from under the pressure. While she dragged herself away, my fingers curled around the steel band on my neck, and with a grunt, I tore it off.

"Shit," I heard Jessie swear. One could never underestimate the power of adrenaline. Despite the pain from her gunshot wound, Jessie dragged herself to her feet and began running as fast as she could to the river alone. And I was about to go after her. That was the plan. But . . .

It was as if a tidal wave had drowned me. Two energies suddenly torn out of balance.

I should have known.

This was never going to be a partnership.

"No, stop!" I doubled over, grabbing my head with both hands. "Stop . . . *stop!*"

I was . . .

I . . . I . . .

. . . . . . I . . . . . .

Air filled my lungs. Sweet and dense. I was alive again. Back into this body.

I was alive.

"Maia? Maia, what's going on?"

That voice.

Quietly, I turned my head.

And saw him.

Feeble. Burned.

Kneeling in front of me.

The hilt of my sword formed first from the elegant dance of flames, that cool, familiar grip. The tip was last, buried in the grass. The cold sensation that tingled through the skin. That horrid wildness I'd been taught to suppress my whole life now quivered through my bones.

"Aidan," I whispered.

Aidan heard the girl's voice but knew immediately that it wasn't Maia who'd spoken. For one passing moment, his arms were limp at his sides. He sat still, helpless—that is, until the panic finally settled in. His skin paled. His body shook. The fear of death gripped him.

"Oh god," he breathed. "Oh god."

What must it have felt like for him to see the large, beautiful eyes he loved wet with bloodlust? I could hear her screaming, fighting inside her own mind. It wouldn't take long for her to return.

But this wouldn't take long either.

Aidan was already leaning back, his wide, terrified eyes locked on my sword as I raised it high above my head. Zhar-Ptitsa. He knew its name.

"It's okay." Tears streamed down his cheeks—and strangely, tears streamed down mine as I aimed to murder the man I'd once called a friend. "It's okay. Do it. Do it, Natalya."

My hands shook above me.

"But . . . I didn't want to." The words trembled out of him as the tears wetted his lips. "I didn't—you have to know that. I'm so sorry. I'm so *sorry*."

I hesitated. Why was I hesitating? *Why?*

"Maia?"

"Agent Rhys! Ms. Finley!"

"Aidan!"

"Aidan! Oh god, Aidan!"

Figures were rushing toward us. Agents. I recognized some of them. Director Prince's eldest son, Brendan Prince, was among them and—Naomi. She was barefoot, running toward us with her high-heeled shoes in her hand, but she stopped the moment she saw me, saw the sword I lifted.

"I did everything I was asked," I called out over the noise. "I did everything, but you . . ." I lowered my arms, the tip of my sword touching softly against the ground before my hands started to shake. "You . . . Why didn't you protect me?"

I fell to my knees as Zhar-Ptitsa faded into embers that brushed past my body and fluttered with the wind into the moonlit night. My time was up. She was coming.

Closing my eyes, I let the darkness take me.

The story was that an anti-Sect gunman had infiltrated the estate looking to murder Blackwell. Blackwell's wounded body and the shattered windows were proof enough, though it didn't stop questions from being asked. Dignitaries left the fund-raiser quickly while journalists scurried to put together their news reports.

I sat on the front steps of Blackwell's estate, my dress torn in places, my body wet with sweat as I watched the ambulance take Rhys to the nearest hospital for his burns.

Rhys.

"Natalya," I whispered as the bright sirens disappeared into the night. "You . . . weren't lying to me after all."

Each word plummeted to the floor like a stone. I had to fight to keep from following them. My limbs felt weak, my mind blank but for the memory of Rhys pleading for death at Natalya's hand.

I was wrong about everything.

I touched my lips, lips that had touched his, my fingers trembling. Liars and traitors were everywhere. I was surrounded by them. Brendan had taken the shattered steel neck-band in as evidence, and I was to be sent to the London facility immediately to check out the back of my neck. But even though I needed to know what had happened to me, I couldn't trust them. I couldn't run away either. I couldn't hide. What *could* I do?

I lowered my head into my hands as soon as I felt the tears budding.

"Maia."

Lifting it again, I looked down the line of parked cars in front of the estate. Naomi called me from the back of a sleek black Rolls-Royce. She waved at me to come over.

"Are you okay, Mrs. Prince?" I asked once I finally reached her.

The window was down, but she kept the door open. That didn't mean I felt welcome coming forward. Naomi sat rigidly in the backseat, her long, sleek black hair draping down her chest like a blanket.

"Somewhat. I'm still shaken."

I could see that. Her pale hands trembled against her lap.

Did she know? About Rhys?

"Mrs. Prince . . ." I looked around, making sure nobody could hear me, and lowered my voice. "The last time I scried, Natalya told me to talk to you. She gave me your name specifically."

"She did." It was something between a statement and a question.

"What Natalya said to you earlier . . ."

Naomi's bottom lip curled inward. "Yes. Come inside."

I hesitated but eventually listened. Whatever Natalya blamed her for, she'd sent me to Naomi for a reason. The woman shifted over to make room. Once I was inside, she rolled up the tinted windows. We were alone.

"Please tell me you know something." I gripped the back of the passenger seat. "What the hell is going on here? Saul is out there. Jessie said something big is gonna happen. And he's got people helping him, soldiers with abilities like him, like *us*, but I don't know who the hell I'm supposed to trust anymore." My eyes watered as I thought about Rhys, our kiss. The burning sensation still hadn't quite disappeared from the back of my neck. "The Sect—"

"Can't be trusted," Naomi finished quietly. She kept her expression calm as she looked up at me, but she couldn't bury the urgency in her eyes.

I frowned, studying her carefully. "Who are you?"

Her features were stone as she answered. "A member of the High Council of the Sect," she said. "From one of the so-called Seven Houses."

"Seven Houses . . ." I pressed my back against the door. A member of the Council. Suddenly, I realized why her voice sounded familiar. She'd spoken that day in the cathedral when Blackwell had made me pledge allegiance to a broken institution on my knees like a servant. Hers was the only voice of reason, of kindness, among those that filled the hall with jeers.

"So your husband's the director of a Sect division while you're from some family dynasty of Council members?" With one director son and another son who was a murderer. A derisive laugh almost escaped my throat. Interesting family.

"No. There's no dynasty," Naomi corrected. "The 'Seven Houses' moniker is a red herring for secrecy's sake. Council members are elected into their positions, though there are some—very few—exceptions. . . ."

Naomi twisted her wedding band around her middle finger as if by habit. "Something is happening . . . within the Council and within the Sect. Saul, the terrorist. Those soldiers. They're all a part of it. That woman Jessie was right. Something terrible is going to happen. I can feel it." She looked at me. "And you girls, you Effigies. You have to help me stop it."

My mouth dried, and my body began trembling. I didn't want to show how scared I was, but I couldn't stop my voice from shaking when I asked, "How?"

"Not here." She flicked her head toward the window behind me. An agent had just walked out of the front doors of Blackwell's mansion holding a set of car keys. "We can't use phones, either. It's too danger-ous. I bought Natalya's home in Madrid. Nobody knows, not even my husband. In exactly four days at sundown, meet me there, but make sure you're alone. I'll tell you everything. I'm sure you've been waiting too, haven't you? For the truth."

The truth. Yes. Ever since I first saw Natalya die in front of me. Ever since her parents warned me against the Sect in Argentina. If I had any chance in hell of stopping Saul for good, I needed to know how. But remembering the anguish crushing Natalya from the inside, remembering her pain as she stared at the woman through my eyes. It was the pain of betrayal.

"How do I know I can trust *you*?"

"I understand your hesitation." Naomi must have seen my hesitation. "And it's up to you to decide one way or another. I'm just afraid this will all go too far before we can stop it. But before you go"—her hand firmly seized mine the moment I moved for the door—"there's one thing I need to tell you. I want to be honest with you before you choose to move forward with this."

"What is it?"

The driver came closer.

"Natalya's death . . . My son was just the gun. And he . . . he is who he is because of the sins of his parents. Because I was too weak to protect him." Naomi's features pinched as she struggled against a sudden well of tears that never fell. She blinked them away. "He was the gun. But a trigger can't pull itself."

There was no hesitation as she stared back at me, as she held me in place with little more than a confession.

"Though I didn't order her death, Natalya's blood is on my hands." Her words hung in the silent air. I hadn't realized my mouth was open until I heard my own breath shuddering out of me. "Knowing that, if you still want to stop Saul, come and find me in Madrid."

I opened my door the moment the driver arrived. And I watched quietly as Naomi's car took her from the estate into the dead of night.

PART TWO

All around the house is the jet-black night;
It stares through the window-pane;
It crawls in the corners, hiding from the light,
And it moves with the moving flame.

Now my little heart goes a-beating like a drum,
With the breath of the Bogie in my hair;
And all around the candle and the crooked shadows come,
And go marching along up the stair.

The shadow of the balusters, the shadow of the lamp,
The shadow of the child that goes to bed—
All the wicked shadows coming tramp, tramp, tramp,
With the black night overhead.

—Robert Louis Stevenson, "Shadow March"

19

VASILY HAD ESCAPED. WITH THE LOOMING threat of his father's disappointment hanging over his head, Brendan dispatched several units to find him, but I knew it wouldn't do any good. He'd escaped through the tiniest cracks in the Sect's defense structure with the help of several agents who were now missing. Of course, no one was more displeased than the Surgeon, who'd lost one of his favorite toys. It was everything Cheryl could do to keep this mess a secret from the press.

Meanwhile, I had other worries.

"Okay, Maia, we're all done." The technician spoke through an intercom from the other side of the glass. With an angry mechanical whir, my flat white bed slid back out of the hole in the CT scanner.

"Did you find anything?" I asked as one tech came into the room and started removing the straps from my neck.

"Well," she said, helping me up, "you know, we need to go over it further—"

"Please." It was cold in the room and the hospital gown was too big, so I felt the chill brush up my bare legs. I reached out with the arm they'd punctured with an IV line and tugged at his shirt. "Can't you tell me anything? I need to know what they did to me."

He turned to the other technicians waiting behind the glass.

"Well, in vivo CT molecular imaging can only give us so much," one said through the intercom, "but from what we can see so far, our targeted probes did detect the presence of a similar molecular structure to the one in the dead soldier you found in the desert."

The dead soldier. Philip. Thinking back, he'd said someone was forcing him to do something . . . before he broke free and ran to the hideout. He wanted us to find him. To help Alex, maybe the others too . . .

"Pete and Dot told us it was a nano . . . thing," I said. "Nanomachine?"

Jessie had it at the base of her neck. She said it hid her frequency for as long as it didn't degrade. That guy we'd found in the desert. Once his degraded, the Sect could track him.

But maybe that was what he wanted. A defector.

I rubbed the back of my neck. "So it wasn't the neck-band Dot and Pete gave me. . . . Wait!" My head snapped up. "Mellie. Mellie injected me with something before I put it on. We should question them!"

"They're questioning Mellie Beasley as we speak, as well as other personnel. Though Beasley is cooperating."

"What about Dot and Pete?"

"Those two fled not long after Vasily escaped."

My stomach gave a painful little lurch. You didn't run unless you were guilty. The band was a front—even if it'd done its job in dulling Natalya's consciousness, it still gave them a convenient excuse to plant something in me. Not to mention Mellie was the one who'd done the deed, so even if she was cooperating with the Sect, I wasn't ready to believe she was innocent. Dot, Pete, and Mellie . . . They'd seemed nice too. . . .

"The good news is that it's mostly degraded—so degraded it's lost its functionality," said the tech. "That's why we couldn't quite tell what it was at first."

Jessie had called it an earlier, weaker model; she knew its sway over me wouldn't hold for long. That's why she was so desperate. She only had the one shot, all or nothing, but they couldn't get me. The combined strength of Natalya and me had shorted out the machine's effects before it was too late. I guess the two of us made a pretty powerful team. That is, when she wasn't trying to hijack my body. I'd buried her deep now, very deep. She was too weak after her last stint to try anything again. But how long would that last?

"Jessie used a phone that sent out a signal," I said. "It sounded like radio interference."

"That could have been the trigger. We have to let R & D figure that out, except they're under investigation now too." The tech sighed. "This whole thing is a mess."

"That seems to be the common theme these days," I said, getting off the table.

At least my neck was free and a little less sore. But I couldn't relax.

Mind control. The very thought made me shake my head, incredulous. Well, they'd tried and failed, but I knew that wasn't the end of it. I could only imagine what they'd come up with next, especially after regrouping with Vasily. I was supposed to meet Naomi in a few days. But in the meantime, I had to be prepared.

I needed the other girls.

"Sounds like a rough night," said Chae Rin back at the dorm. She was still sweaty from training, sitting cross-legged on the chair at the right side of the coffee table. Perhaps in a show of support, she slid the open pizza box on the table closer to me. "Now I feel kind of guilty for having such an easy time during that boring mission in Glasgow. Have you even eaten since you got back? Here, have some. It's only like a day or two old; it's still good."

Everyone was treating me rather nicely after they'd heard what had happened to me. I didn't hate it. It was like being with friends. I had a feeling that Chae Rin, at least, would throw something at me if I ever used the term out loud, but it was a comforting thought nonetheless. A team. Friends. Didn't have much of those even before my family died. It was nice to finally gain some after I'd lost so much already.

Why was that? Why was it that no matter what I did, I just end up losing something else?

"Maia, you okay?" Lake said, and the weight of her body plopping onto the long couch next to me snapped me back to reality. "You don't look too good."

"I'm okay," I lied. "As okay as I'll ever be."

Lake grimaced at the stale pepperoni and flipped the lid closed. "How's Rhys?"

I tried to pass off my flinch as an awkward stretch. "He's at the hospital."

"You didn't go see him?"

I did, once. Just like all those other times, I went while he was sleeping because after that night, I couldn't handle facing him. Couldn't bear it.

That night in Blackwell's courtyard had turned my hopeless suspicions to reality. I thought once I knew for sure, everything would become clear. But everything was worse.

I thought of Belle, my insides churning. *What do I do?*

He'd begged me not to hate him, just as he'd begged Natalya for death. There had to be more to the story. Why did I want to believe that so badly?

Ignoring Lake's question, I rubbed the back of my neck. "Is my neck still red?"

Lake rolled onto her knees and brushed my hair back to check. "Yeah, a bit. They really did a number on you, didn't they?" She plopped back down. "I can't believe Pete's a bad guy," she said, sinking deeper into the couch. "He's a bit odd, but really quite good-looking. I was even thinking of asking him out after the TVCAs. Oh, well." She started fiddling with her phone.

"We don't know for sure," I said. "The investigation's still ongoing."

I flinched, surprised when Belle suddenly placed a bowl of fresh fruit in front of me, pushing away the pizza box.

"Right now we have to treat everyone as a potential enemy," she said, her long French braid sliding across her back as she took the chair opposite Chae Rin. "You said that this Jessie Stone is one of Saul's soldiers. We haven't located the others from Fisk-Hoffman, but we have to assume they're like her. And there could be more."

It took me a while to answer her. I wiped my clammy hands on my legs but didn't know where to put them. Quickly, silently, I buried the thought of Rhys deep within me. Only then could I answer.

"There are two from that facility still unaccounted for." Two left like Philip and Jessie. And *Alex*. The memory of his dead, rotting face hitting the pavement still made me shudder. "But they're *not* Effigies. Right?"

"Dot said they found an entire 'electromechanical network' down the spine of that dead guy. The *first* dead guy," Chae Rin clarified. "Philip. Not the undead one that tried to eat you."

"Got that." I plucked a cherry out of the mix of fruit and tossed it into my mouth.

"Dot and Pete definitely made it seem like we could be looking at the possibility of something man-made," Chae Rin continued. "And, hey, it's not like there wouldn't be a basis for it. Some people out there already think Effigies are government experiments. There was a whole special about it on the Conspiracy Channel."

Lake snorted as she tapped away at her phone. "Watching the Conspiracy Channel. Sounds like a rousing Saturday night."

"It's interesting, okay?" Chae Rin glared at her. "Anyway, people have been trying to figure us out and re-create what we can do for so long. You heard about all that illegal research in Europe decades ago, right?"

"Wait." I sat up, my mouth sticky and sweet as I chewed another cherry. "When I was under control, Jessie mentioned some-one. Grune . . ." I frowned, waiting for the name to come to me. "Grundewall. No, Grune*wald*? She said the mind-control tech was his. Ever heard the name?"

"Grunewald." Belle folded her arms. "No. I don't recognize it."

Grunewald. Was he a scientist working for Saul? Was he part of the Sect?

"Ugh, this is confusing." Lake flopped sideways, kicking her bare legs onto my lap and curling her toes as she rested her head against the arm of the couch. A bit intrusive, but I didn't mind. It was the kind of familiarity that came more easily with her. "What about the Castor Volume? Did you find anything about the symbol that Natalya drew?"

"No, but I didn't have the chance to search long."

"Of course not." Groaning, Chae Rin jumped to her feet and wan-dered behind the couch.

"We have this." From her pocket, Belle slipped out the white flash drive she'd pried out of Philip's hand. "I've been trying to fiddle with it with no luck."

"We just have to find a way to crack it, then," Lake said. "Belle said it herself: We have to get ahead of Saul, right?"

"Yeah? How?" challenged Chae Rin from behind the couch. "None of us can do it. We're not about to take this to the Sect after they tried to fry Maia's brain. And if I'm being perfectly honest, I don't even think we're safe here anymore. We need to run the next chance we get."

"Run where?" Lake mumbled.

Belle turned the drive around in her hand, considering it carefully. "We have to give this to someone. Someone we can trust."

"No shit," said Chae Rin. "But do you know anyone who can do it?"

"Wait, yes!" I stood up so fast, Lake's legs slid off my lap, her left heel banging the coffee table. "Sorry," I said when she started cursing in pain, "but I know. I know someone!"

I wasn't sure why I didn't think of it before. Just thinking of him now, of the possibility of seeing him again, made the weight on my chest lighten for the first time in what felt like forever.

"Uncle Nathan!" I said.

Chae Rin cocked her head to the side. "Who?"

"My uncle Nathan! He's supersmart. He's one of those tech geniuses that work New York's Needle at the MDCC—the Municipal Defense Control Center." I said all this with a kind of breathless urgency that sent the words flying out of my mouth in rapid-fire succession. "Hell, he *chose* to work at the MDCC. He had people in the government practically throwing jobs at him, but he said he wanted to stay in New York and 'take it easy.' If anyone can do it, he—*ow!*"

Chae Rin slapped me in the back of my head. And just when my neck was starting to heal. "Okay, you were waiting until *now* to mention this?"

"Well, I've had a lot on my mind," I answered, my teeth clenched. "Besides, with Sibyl's family ban, I didn't think I could contact him even if I wanted to. I mean, despite everything, I'm technically still in the middle of my training period."

"Well, Sibyl's not the director anymore," Lake said.

"No . . . ," I said. "No, she's not."

It'd been two months since I'd seen him: my only tether to the life I used to live before monsters swallowed it whole. After everything that'd happened, if I could find any excuse to see him—it didn't matter what it was.

But soon the corners of my mouth sagged, my hands slowly lowering. The thought of Uncle Nathan filled me with the kind of hope that these days wasn't easy to come by. There was only one problem.

"If we walk right up to him and hand him this flash drive, we're putting him in danger," I said, sitting back down. "I mean, let's say he cracks it and the Sect or Saul or whoever finds out. What if it traces back to him? Saul is after me. What if I lead him right to my uncle?"

"Well, obviously we can't just walk up to your place and hand it to him." Chae Rin thought. "We have to meet him somewhere secret."

A rendezvous at a secret location. Well, Uncle Nathan was obsessed with spy movies, so I suspected he wouldn't mind temporarily living in one.

With one sharp jolt, Lake sat up from her slouch and excitedly shook my shoulders. "The TVCAs! They're this Sunday!"

"Oh god, not *that* again." Chae Rin rolled her eyes. "*Yes,* Lake, we *still* remember, and sadly, we're *still* going. But we're kind of in the middle of talking about something here."

"Yeah, and I'm talking about the same thing." Lake flashed us her phone displaying the main website of the awards show. The sleek black-and-red logo popped out at me first, but underneath it in white letters: 299 QUEEN STREET WEST, TORONTO, ONTARIO. "I'll ask my agent to get him a reservation at our hotel under a pseudonym. He's too busy ironing out the details to my single promo to ask questions one way or another. He won't think twice about it."

"Thank you, Lake," I said. "Really."

I looked at my phone lying flat on the table, wedged between the pizza box and the bowl of fruit. All the times I thought about calling his number, knowing that he wouldn't pick up under the Sect's orders. Sibyl had said it was supposed to make me stronger, more focused. But right now, I needed him.

I just had to make sure I didn't get him killed in the process.

20

WE ARRIVED IN TORONTO FOR THE TEEN Viewers' Choice Awards at noon, just seven hours before the street party–style event was supposed to start. They had already blocked off Queen Street and were setting up the barricades behind which all those shrieking fans would be having camera-friendly meltdowns.

Me and June had watched (well, streamed) the party every year as the mostly American pop stars, models, and anyone with a semi-popular social media account marched down the red carpet–covered street and begged for attention. Always amusing.

But now that I would be joining the parade of self-absorbed celebrities basking in the adulation, I was too preoccupied and para-noid to let any of it sink in. Under the unforgiving sun, I kept peering around as we hopped out of the Sect van and entered the expensive hotel, scanning the crowds of Effigy fans that had gathered there for Jessie and her personal army of zombies. All I saw were signs, tears, and flashing camera phones.

Which introduced another set of problems. There wasn't a single moment I wasn't surrounded by people: hotel staff begging for autographs, coordinators for the event explaining where we needed to go and when, and Lake's agent—a slightly flabby, mousy British man with a black goatee to match the color of his suit and pants—running around yelling at everyone, trying to make sure Lake had the best press to cover up the fact that her single had been delayed again and her fans were starting online petitions.

"It's not my fault!" Lake whined at her phone as we entered our hotel suite, not that there was anyone on the other end. She was glaring at the disgruntled comments from Swans because they'd just started a thread on the Doll Soldiers forum for the sole purpose of utterly dragging her to the ends of the Earth. "*You* wankers try to promote a single when you're fighting monsters and terrorists at the same bloody time!"

Admittedly, she was probably just on edge because the four members of GBD, her old girl group, had already arrived at their hotel a few blocks away surrounded by a crowd of rabid fans. The videos were all over the internet.

I cast a wary glance at our hair and makeup team setting up shop in our hotel suite before pulling Lake into the empty bedroom. "He's here, right? Uncle Nathan?"

"What? Oh, yeah. Room four thirty-two. And he's Mr. *Caldwell* now." Laughing, she called Belle over.

"And you got the drive?" I asked Belle after she shut the door.

Belle nodded, patting her jeans pocket.

"While we're being skull and bones, take a look at this." Lake slid off her brown knapsack and pulled out the cigar box we'd found under Belle's floorboard.

I peeked around her shoulder to take a closer look. "You brought that here?"

"Yeah . . . well, you know, with everything happening, I've been a bit antsy about keeping stuff like that in the dorm."

"Good to see you've come prepared," I said, impressed.

"Bloody right, I'm prepared." Lake pulled a pair of shades out of her bag and gave it to me, then plucked the ones from the top of her head and passed them to Belle. "Now, you two be careful once you leave this room. There are probably fans and reporters sneaking about."

Belle and I nodded and started off.

"Oi, where are you lot going?" Lake's agent lowered his phone and stopped yelling into it for long enough to see us leaving. "You're supposed to be getting your makeup done—"

"Never you mind, Henry. They'll be back. Just going for a short walk," said Lake.

"Yes. Walk. I like walking. I want to go too." Chae Rin rose out of her chair like a ghost, but the hairdresser pushed her back down again.

I shut the door behind me, the commotion muffled behind wood. Belle and I donned our shades as we entered the elevator. I had my hood up covering my hair, pulling the strings so it covered a good portion of my face. Belle was less obvious, letting her uncombed hair loose as if she looked somehow less glamorous and recognizable in a pair of jeans and a gray sweatshirt.

"This will be your first time seeing your uncle in a while, yes?" she said as she pressed the fourth-floor button. We'd have to go down from the twentieth.

"Yeah."

It was the first time he would see me as Maia Finley, the fire Effigy. He'd learned about it on the news with everyone else because I couldn't muster up enough courage to tell him before I was thrown into battle. I should have faced him. But I was a coward then.

And now.

I looked up at Belle, who leaned against the elevator wall, her arms folded as she waited.

"Maia." Belle's quizzical eyes narrowed as she noticed the slight trembling of my hands, even when I clasped them together and buried them behind my back. "What's going on?"

A few days ago, when I was at the hospital, watching Rhys, I'd noticed certain sights that were now etched into my memory. Like the sliver of light escaping through the curtains kissing his face. The quiet innocence softening his features, as if sleep had mercifully taken from them all the guilt and grief. He'd rested as if he were finally at peace, the peace he'd begged Natalya to give him. Natalya, whom he'd betrayed.

Both mother and son.

"Naomi Prince, Rhys's mother, is a member of the Council."

At this, Belle's eyebrows rose. "What?"

"Not only that, but she asked me to meet her alone in Madrid in four days, which was three days ago, so, like, tomorrow. At sundown. Natalya's old apartment. I wasn't sure if I should tell you guys because she asked me to come alone."

Belle pulled off her shades, and I wished she hadn't. She could never hide the vulnerability in her eyes when it came to her mentor. "Why there? What does she want to tell you?"

"The truth. About Natalya's death."

The elevator's gears shifted in the walls behind us. A silent shadow passed over Belle's face, though she made no change of expression. "Why would she know?"

My lips felt heavy as I parted them to speak, but before I could, the elevator door opened at the fourth floor. The bellboy looked impatient as he waited for us to scurry out. Dipping our heads low, we left.

"Room four thirty-two," Belle said when we stopped at the door. The moment stretched out, long and painful, as she knocked. What was I going to say to my uncle? What could I—

The door opened. I didn't need to see more than a few strands of his limp brown hair before I slammed the door the rest of the way open and jumped on him. With my arms wrapped around his scrawny neck, I was bawling before his back hit the ground.

"Maia." My uncle's voice. My family. My blood.

He was *laughing*. Teary-eyed, I lifted my head off his chest just to make sure of it. His youthful face flowered into a grin too childish for his thirty years.

"It's only been two months." He showed all his teeth as he laughed, sweetly, happily, because he was just as ecstatic to see me. It was just the two of us, after all, since the day his dead older brother's only surviving daughter had arrived at his New York apartment looking for a place to sleep.

My body shook as we both sat up, and a fresh wave of tears spilled out as both his hands crushed my cheeks together. I could feel Belle awkwardly maneuvering around us, trying to shut the door. "Sorry," I said, and moved. We weren't exactly being stealthy.

Uncle Nathan let go of me. "After the hotel was attacked in New York—"

"I know, I know. I wanted to call you, but—"

"Yeah, the Sect. Don't worry, I'm up to date. Well, on most of it. I've read enough headlines to fill in the rest."

We stared at each other, and that's when I noticed what I didn't before: the weight he'd lost. He'd already been a thin guy, but though his face had kept most of its vibrancy, it'd slimmed down too much for me to ignore, his skin matte and dry. And the circles under his eyes . . .

"You haven't been sleeping." Just like after Dad died.

Uncle Nathan's hands stayed around my face, but his grip had slacked to the point where I could only feel the rough touch of his fingers. "I'm so sorry" was all he said.

It was his turn. The tears began to leak out one by one before he swiped his face quickly. "Maia, I'm sorry I couldn't protect you from this."

A thousand words passed between us in silence. His hands fell onto his lap as we considered which to speak out loud.

"Hey!" I tapped his shoulder. "Look what I can do!"

I sat back, sliding from him a little in case something went wrong. Then I snapped my fingers. The tiniest flame erupted at the tip of my thumb, flickering gently in the air.

Uncle Nathan laughed in amazement. "Look at you! You're a little lighter!"

"There's other stuff too!" I stood up excitedly, but Belle gripped my shoulder before I could get too carried away.

"We don't have a lot of time," she said. "Mr. Finley, my name is—"

"Belle Rousseau. Of course I know." He jumped to his feet to shake her hand, a little too fast like he always did when he was nervous. "It's an honor to meet you. Wow, Maia, you've really upgraded your list of friends."

"Yeah, from zero to a positive whole number."

Belle seemed a little taken aback and—maybe? Was it my imagination?—shy. *Shy* at the word "friend." Her cheeks were a little redder, but it might have been a trick of the light.

"We've asked you here for a specific purpose," she said.

"Yeah, the agent of one of the other Effigies—Lake? He called me and said you guys would explain. I don't know, I could barely understand what he was saying—he just kind of barked stuff at me and hung up."

Grabbing his hand, I helped him up. "I'll fill in everything now."

It took some time to put everything out there. Saul being at large, he knew about. But he didn't know about the mysterious soldier with the mark at the back of his neck. Jessie, who could control the dead with her thoughts. The mind control. The flash drive. When I told him about that, Belle handed it to him.

"Are you okay?" Urgently, he pulled me by the arm and swept back my hair to check my neck. "It's still red. God. Maia, if I'd known you were going through all this . . ."

"You couldn't have done anything anyway," I said with a shrug.

Running his hand through his hair, he turned and started across the room. "I've never heard of nanotechnology that advanced." He sat in a chair by the curtain-drawn window and set up his laptop on the table, pushing away a little tray of milk and sugar for coffee. "But none of this surprises me. Development firms around the world have been looking for a way to reproduce Effigy-like abilities. And I suppose they'd also need to come up with a method to control them."

I walked behind him. "Why?"

"Why else? For defense. For *war*." He looked at the drive. "When I was at Caltech, I heard whispers of a program jointly developed by DARPA and another defense subcontractor. That guy you mentioned, Grunewald? His name definitely came up."

"DARPA?" I furrowed my brows, confused.

"The Defense Advanced Research Projects Agency." He pushed up the lid of his laptop and clicked it on. "An agency within America's Department of Defense."

"What are they working on?" asked Belle.

"*Were*," Uncle Nathan corrected. "I mean, it was years ago, after the Seattle Siege. An entire American city reduced to ashes by phantoms—of course the government was spooked enough to try different things. A black project. But the Senate axed it, I guess."

He shoved the flash drive into his laptop and, for a moment, only stared very seriously at the empty black screen that popped up, sitting back in his chair with his fingers clasped.

"If this is even close to being similar to what I think this could be . . . then, Maia, you've stepped into some serious crap here." He sighed. "Well, I guess I'm right in it with you."

"Sorry." My hand tightened its grip on the back of his chair. "Effigy or not, I'm still just some dumb kid asking you to do my homework for me."

As he turned to look up at me, his lips quirked into a lopsided grin. "Well, the stakes are a bit higher this time around. There are worse things than getting a call from your principal."

I watched him get out of his chair, stretching his arms above his head. "I didn't want you to get roped into this."

"No, you did the right thing coming to me." His expression darkened as he lowered his voice almost instinctively. "If what you're saying about the Sect is true, then you can't trust them with this. We don't know how many people inside *and outside* the organization are working with Saul. We don't know how big this could really be, or how many people like Jessie are out there. Maia . . ." He grabbed my hand. "I strongly suggest you don't go back to London."

My phone buzzed in my pocket. Lake had sent me a text to hurry back, because apparently it was getting harder to keep her agent from sending out a search-and-rescue team.

"Well, I'll leave you to break into the Sect's or the American government's or whoever's secrets. Hopefully, you can find something out about those freaks who keep trying to kidnap me. Meanwhile, I have to go get ready so we can present the award for Male Hottie of the Year." I paused. "My life is weird."

"No kidding." Uncle Nathan smirked. "You guys go ahead. I'll stay here, pour myself some coffee, and work on this." He cracked his knuckles. "Though, to be honest, I haven't done any serious hacking since college."

"Make sure you keep out of sight," warned Belle.

"Sure." He reached for the empty coffeepot next to his laptop and paused. "Heh. It's kinda like a spy movie, isn't it?"

I rolled my eyes. "Yes, Uncle. Just like a spy movie."

"Good luck," Belle said, and we left him to the drive.

21

LAKE WOULD NOT ALLOW US TO ARRIVE AT
the red carpet too early. "You know who shows up early to red carpets?"
she asked once our limo finally started toward the venue. "*Has-beens*
and D-list reality TV show *wankers*. We are the *Effigies*. We hold the
security of the *world* in the palm of our hands. Now pass me my phone.
I need to take some selfies."

The windows were tinted so none of the Torontonians jaywalking
across the street could see how ridiculous I looked squirming into
Lake's photo, or the terrible kissy face I made with my lips because
she said it was a popular pop-star pose. Chae Rin and Belle stayed
resolutely out of the picture, a comfortable distance away from us and
each other. The series of pictures that Lake uploaded was on the Doll
Soldiers forum in under a minute.

Soon, we were on Queen Street. My nerves were shot as the
screams bombarded us from all sides. Under the gray, sunless sky,
fans stretched their hands out at our limo from behind a set of barricades glowing neon blue, almost like the metallic lights that skidded
up a fully powered American Needle. Maybe it was antiphantom

technology. Toronto was well protected because of the extra security they had around the city as well as the rail system protecting most of Canada's small population. At least I knew I didn't have to deal with phantoms tonight, but as our driver parked our limo right on the red carpet and we stepped out into the chaos, I almost wished I'd been sent on another mission.

"And look who just pulled up to our red carpet!" I heard the woman's voice speaking into a microphone, but I had no idea who she was. "Looking as badass as ever—I'm about to be joined by the always-hella-epic *Effigies*. Make some noise for the Effigies!"

The crowd did. We were immediately swarmed by giant video cameras, staff, and security. Lake had stepped out first and she was already waving to the crowd, posing with her best angles in a short, off-the-shoulder red dress that matched her earthen skin tone. Lake had ordered us all the same one in the correct sizes and colors—peach for me, silver for Belle, black for Chae Rin. Had to look unified but distinct, she'd said. I hadn't actually realized how much work and effort she'd put into this event in the midst of all the Saul chaos until this moment as I watched her confirm with event staff where we needed to go. She had the poise and control of someone who'd done this before, someone who fed off the energy like a willowy, starving plant soaking in the sunlight.

"Here we go—we've got the Effigies with us!"

Oh, so she was the interviewer. She was tall and busty with a beige dress on and her blond hair slicked back behind her ears. Lake ushered us forward, but my heels were too high and thin for a straight, smooth walk, so the second I tried to twist around to face the right way, I stumbled and nearly fell over.

"Oops, looks like she's having a little bit of trouble there!"

Chae Rin grabbed my arm and helped me walk. I was sure that the one-second gaffe was already online, but what could I do about it?

I had to keep smiling even as my cheeks hurt, even as I continued to scan the crowds for any sign of trouble.

"Hi!" the interviewer said, and only Lake and I bothered to respond as jovially as we could. "Ladies, hi! Wait a second, let's turn around here and face the camera."

We did. It felt strange being herded like sheep, but that was probably the normal condition of a celebrity on a red carpet.

"What an entrance," she said as Lake stood closest to her. "A limo. Very classy. You girls seem to have gotten used to luxury!"

"Well, Kacey, they don't call us warrior princesses for nothing," Lake said into the mic, and I was sure the camera caught my cringe. I tried quickly to warp it into a mangled smile.

"Absolutely! Who else could make world security look so glamorous?" There was something so glassy and cheesy about Kacey's grin; she probably wasn't even half as excited to see us as she looked. "Awesome, awesome. Now, you guys are not only presenting today, but you've been nominated for Favorite Badass Role Model, and with all that fighting evil you guys do, I bet you're not surprised."

"Oh, we were surprised!" Lake said genuinely. "I mean, it's really an honor to be recognized by people who look up to you—right, girls?"

"Yes! Absolutely! It's so exciting!" I bobbed my head up and down, my eyes wide-open with that deer-in-headlights look that made me wonder suddenly why I had any fans at all. Belle and Chae Rin already looked over it, but they smiled serenely for the sake of the cameras.

"And, Maia, how's your training going?"

"Good." I tried not to make my fidgeting too noticeable. "It's being put to good use."

"Yeah? You were just at a fund-raiser over in the UK and now you've been whisked off to Canada for the TVCAs—where do you have the time to do any actual *battling* these days?"

That was a strange jab. The quiver in Lake's expression told me she thought so too. Was it a trap?

"Well," Lake said, recuperating, "we've just gotten back from a mission outside Glasgow. And we've been hard at work doing other stuff that unfortunately the cameras aren't always privy to. But we're always happy to come to events like these for the sake of anyone who looks up to us. You know, we want to show girls that anyone can be heroes, and—"

"Wait!" The interviewer was already looking past us. "Is that—is that who I think it is?"

We turned. Four of the biggest, loudest Harley-Davidsons, each painted pure neon pink, drove up to the red carpet like a motorcade. Each driver was muscled and topless as if they'd been dragged out of a bachelorette party in the middle of performing. And behind each man was a member of Britain's current top girl group, GBD.

Kacey was beside herself. "What an entrance! Cameras, can we get a closer look at those motorcycles?"

Lake looked furious as the crowd went wild and Kacey started calling the girls over. Joanna, Hailey, Misha, and Cara. Their latest brand change had finally taken off when they started this latest "Scandalous" era with their heavy *chola* makeup, tank tops, high-waisted jeans, high ponytails, and the heavy spray tans concealing their originally pale skin. It was certainly a far cry from the cutesy, teenybopper, kids-next-door image they'd originally been given by their label back when Lake was part of the group. I guess some music exec figured Girls by Day was more fit for made-for-TV movies targeting the middle school market. Well, the rebranding had done wonders. "Scandalous" was now number one on the Billboard Hot 100—a point Kacey would surely bring up when she invited them to join our interview.

"Kacey, hi!" Jo was as tall as Lake, but built like a linebacker. She bumped her broad shoulders into Lake, maybe purposefully, as we all shuffled to make room for one another and yet still catch the camera. Chae Rin and Belle certainly didn't mind stepping out of the frame. "Oh, Victoria, how are you, love? When's that single dropping? Any day now?"

Lake's lips thinned into a straight line, her brown eyes dripping with malice as she laughed cutely enough for the cameras to believe it. She tapped Jo a bit too hard on the shoulder.

"Wow, look at this: ex-groupmates meeting again for the first time in years—are you getting this, guys?" Kacey needn't have worried; two more cameras swarmed us. "Lake, how does it feel seeing your old group again after so long?"

"I'm shocked, to be quite honest." Lake tilted her head and made a show of staring at Jo's outfit. "So much has changed. You're almost as dark as I am now. Bit too long in the tanning bed, then? Strange, considering how you always used to manage your *real* skin tone by avoiding the sun." Lake giggled into her hand. "Like a vampire."

"Yes, love, I avoided the sun like your singles avoided the charts. But anyway!" Jo said as Lake bristled. "So excited to be here."

"Yes, I know, so you've got *several* nominations," Kacey said, and I could see Lake flinching at her emphasis. "And you're performing 'Scandalous,' which has been number one on Billboard for, like, three weeks straight."

"They're saying it's totally going to be the song of the summer!" chimed one short, stalky member, her black hair tied in a huge bun with a blue ribbon. Misha? Maybe Cara. One of them.

"And since you two are finally here, together on the red carpet for the first time in years, Jo, what do you think of your old group member getting nominated for Favorite Badass Role Model?"

Another trap—a barely concealed one. Lake kept her smile plastered on her face as she waited for the attack.

Jo's light brown ponytail swished as she tilted her neck and considered it. "Well," she said, "personally, I'm just excited for her. And to be honest, I'm a bit surprised, too. I mean, little Vicky being nominated as a role model?" Her "friendly" laughter had a knife-sharp edge to it. "She's really come a long way from faking injuries and illnesses to get out of fighting as an Effigy. I like to think of her as a little butterfly that finally spread her wings after years of being . . . well, whatever butterflies are first. Worms?" She smiled.

"Lake," Kacey said, "we all know you had some kind of breakdown in Milan. Is it true you faked all that just to get put on leave?"

The veil fell. Lake looked terrified. Even with all the constant screaming, there were some members of the crowd watching the interview intently. Kacey must have gotten word from her producer through her earpiece, because she suddenly shifted.

"Okay, I see I've kept you for too long—well, enjoy the night, ladies! And, GBD, I have a few more questions to ask about your hit single!"

Lake composed herself as we continued down the red carpet, but I could tell from the creeping redness in her eyes that she hadn't been prepared for that particular attack. Showbiz cattiness was all about the dog whistles and low-key shady remarks. But this was live, and regardless of what the truth was, the idea that Lake had purposefully wrangled herself out of her cosmic duty in favor of embracing what many called a failed celebrity life had now been televised.

"Lake, are you okay?" I held her hand when she stumbled a bit over her high heels—something I'd never seen her do.

"It's true. So what? My parents didn't want me to fight," she said in a low whisper. "They still don't. They don't want me to die. What's so wrong with that? Jo . . . She couldn't possibly understand."

I squeezed her hand as we continued down the red carpet through the glaring flashes. Lake tried to recover by taking selfies with fans and signing autographs. I followed suit the best I could.

"Chae Rin! Chae Rin!"

We looked for the voice. It was faint, but soon we could see someone pushing her way through the crowd to the barricade. Chae Rin's whole body seized up, her lips parting as soon as the girl broke free from the rest, her hand touching the glowing metal bars.

"Unnie?" Chae Rin dropped her clutch purse and rushed to the metal bars. "Oh my god!"

The girl looked very much like Chae Rin, though her sleek black hair was longer and rather limp over her buttoned-up blue blouse—a little stuffy for an event like this. She was only slightly taller, and a bit chubbier, her round cheeks as rosy as the girl whose fingers she clasped. I'd seen her face before in Chae Rin's electronic file, which Rhys had shown me on the way to Montreal. She was one of four faces on Rhys's tablet screen as he told me all about Chae Rin's family.

Her sister?

"Unnie!" I'd never heard Chae Rin's voice like this, almost childish as she jumped up and down and hugged her big sister. "What are you doing here?"

"I know I'm not supposed to contact you, but I saw that you were nominated and I had to try to get here."

She had a slight accent, which I could only assume came from living in Daegu for longer than Chae Rin had. She looked at us, her eyes stretching into beautiful crescents as she grinned. "You're the other Effigies, right? I'm Ha Rin, big sis. Thanks for keeping my little sister in check."

"Hey, *nobody* keeps me in check." Chae Rin folded her arms brattily as her sister rubbed her head, messing up her hair.

The only thing I knew about Ha Rin was that she was studying to be meteorologist at the University of British Columbia. She certainly looked the part with her professional dress blouse, thin white sweater, and black dress pants—an odd combo in the middle of sweaty, screaming children in rocker T-shirts.

"Seriously, though, what are you doing here? Did something happen?" Chae Rin looked suddenly concerned when her sister's smile fell. "Mom. Mom's okay, isn't she? Or did she have another—"

"I can't explain here—I'll meet you in your hotel room after the show, okay? Text me when you're done. Don't worry, it's nothing really bad . . . ," she added, though unconvincingly, when she saw Chae Rin's expression begin to twist with worry. "You'll be up onstage, right?" she added quickly. "I'll try to work my way there."

"How?" I said. "I'm sure the pit's already completely occupied."

"I have my ways. Okay, kids, *move* it!" What her mousy blouse didn't show was the sheer brutality of the sharp elbows concealed within the fabric.

I laughed, hoping Chae Rin would follow suit, but she stayed quiet down the rest of the length of the red carpet.

The rest of the evening passed by like a dream. Backstage, celebrities I'd only seen before on television came up to me, asking me what it was like fighting monsters, telling me how cute my dress was, though obviously there were others who didn't seem that willing to share the spotlight even if there were no cameras around. That clique of willowy socialites-turned-models every girl at Ashford High was obsessed with completely ignored me when I said hello. And that one British blue-eyed soul singer was too busy throwing his half-empty coffee cup at a volunteer's face to even notice me trying to talk to him. At least pop sensation Aaron Jacobs spared me a minute. He'd gotten much nicer after coming back from rehab.

It was all well and good. Belle was off being chatted up by a young actor who'd once professed to be her fan, not that she seemed very engaged in the conversation. Chae Rin was off by herself, eating half the tray of tiny sandwiches left on a table full of food platters. It was a little bit of respite from everything I'd been through in the past few weeks. Taking pictures with celebrities, watching people go crazy online. For a few blissful hours, I could forget that there were monsters chasing me. I could go back to being just a fan again.

Maybe it was all the noise, but my head was suddenly throbbing. I grimaced and bent low. GBD had just returned backstage from performing "Scandalous," and in the midst of glaring at Jo, Lake noticed me wincing.

"You okay?" Lake asked when I pressed my hand against my forehead.

"Yeah, I'm fine." I'd have been more worried if it were the back of my neck again. This was probably just the aftereffect of the mind control. "I think I'm just tired."

"Well, it's almost over." Lake seemed relieved at the thought as the mechanical female voice called out the nominee list over the sound system. The crowd went wild after every name, but they gave a resounding cheer when the Effigies were listed. Even though I was backstage, I was still streaming the show on my phone—I could see images of us fighting phantoms spliced together in an awesome montage they showed on the jumbotron.

"And the winner is . . ." The presenter of our award paused for effect. "The Effigies!"

"Yes!" Lake pumped her fist in the air. "*Yes!* I told you, bitches!" she said, turning and giving Jo the finger before grabbing me and pulling me up the stairs.

Everything hit me at once. The lights. The biting cold. The herd of fans, the sound of their screams echoing in the night sky. The jumbo-tron behind us had a split screen of our profiles, our faces plastered against different-colored backdrops with our names scrawled under each one. The host handed Lake some kind of strange silver trophy as Belle, Chae Rin, and I lined up beside her.

Lake was babbling her thanks as the rest of us posed and just tried our best to look good. That's why we were here, at the end of the day. Be pretty. Be a role model. Be a celebrity. Gather your fans and make the Sect look less menacing. That was the task we'd been given, and even knowing what we knew about the Sect, it was too late to skip out on the event Sibyl had okayed. Lake wouldn't have let us, anyway. I could see how much holding the trophy and waving to her fans meant to her. She clung to the moment as tightly as she clung to her new award.

"Ugh." My head was throbbing again. Even in front of so many cameras, I couldn't stop myself from wincing.

Maia . . .

No. My hands fell at my sides. I could hear her. Natalya. I thought I'd buried her deep after that last time she'd tried to take me.

Maia . . . Don't be fooled. . . . Pay attention. . . .

Panic seized me as another wave of pain crashed against my skull from the inside, like she was pounding against the bone with her knuckles.

"Stop." I winced again, shutting my eyes. Next to me, Belle shifted her head, confused as she watched me struggle.

Don't be fooled. . . . Pay attention!

My eyes snapped open. Quickly, I looked at the crowd. Something was wrong. I scanned the army of bodies until I found Ha Rin close to the front of the pit behind the glowing barricades. She was waving at us, trying to get our attention. But no, something was wrong. What was this feeling? What was Natalya—

A rush of cold slipped down my body, freezing me to the bone. Vasily.

His stringy, unwashed blond hair draped over half his face from beneath a black hoodie. He looked at me and smiled.

My heart thumped so painfully it was difficult to breathe. In that moment, he'd slipped out from between a pair of screaming fans to stand behind Ha Rin. She didn't notice. Nobody noticed. Nobody could see because nobody was paying attention—not the fans, not the staff, not the celebrities, not the other girls.

His skin was sallow and bruised, but I knew he was hiding worse injuries beneath his clothes. He looked wired and ready, like a rabid dog that had been starved too long.

He looked *hungry*.

Ha Rin was still trying to get her sister's attention, but Chae Rin was distracted by Lake, who'd shoved the microphone in her face to get her to say a few words. She didn't see Vasily float his two fingers near her sister's temple without touching it, his index and middle finger pressed together and his thumb in the air in the shape of a gun as his eyes locked with mine.

No, no, no. The blinding lights, the shrieking crowd. In that moment, my senses were off-kilter, panic surging through me. Vasily's emaciated face sparked with malice. And through it all, Natalya was screaming.

Don't be fooled. . . . Pay attention! Pay attention!

Vasily's hands, quick as a flash, flew into his left pocket.

"Stop!" I screamed suddenly, and, as the music began playing us off the stage, I erupted into flame, the pole of my scythe forming in my hands, its blade glinting in the night. Everyone onstage jumped back to avoid being touched by the flickering fire.

"What are you doing?" cried Lake after tripping and falling to the ground. "Stop it!"

Camera phones were flashing, and while some gasped in fear, there were more excited screams echoing in the night as if I were showing off my power for their amusement. Vasily's hand was out of his pocket, but it took me a moment to realize that he wasn't holding a weapon—it was a remote control. He fiddled with a few of the buttons before slipping it back inside his pocket and, with a wink, disappearing into the crowd.

The screen of the jumbotron behind us fizzled out, our image replaced by static snow. The scythe dissipated in my hands as we turned and watched.

"What the hell is going on here?" Another host looked around for help, but the staff was too busy running around trying to get the jumbotron working. With a frustrated shrug, he brought his mic up to his mouth, pasting a phony smile back onto his face. "Okay, folks, we're having a little bit of technical difficulty, but hey, it's live TV! You know what that means, right? Despite our best efforts, anything can happen."

He was trying to spin this as some kind of wild ride typical for teenager-targeted TV, but I could see the beads of sweat dripping from his face. He was worried. He was right to be.

A few staff members in black clothes rushed up to us. "Ladies, please come with us. We need to get you offstage," one said.

But before we could move, the screen turned to darkness.

The crowd fell silent.

"Good evening, everyone," called a voice from the screen. My breath hitched.

Saul's voice.

The darkness receded to show bright lights shining from the ceiling before the camera panned around the room. From what I could tell, it was a cabin: The walls and floors were made of logs. As the camera panned, I saw first a chair, then a tall standing lamp. But the camera didn't linger. A hung oil painting of an old man eating soup with Death. Boarded-up windows. A potted plant . . .

Then the camera panned around to the desk, where Saul sat with his legs crossed on the chair in front of it. He was surrounded by phantoms in the shape of wolves, snapping at his feet. Those wolves . . . It'd been a long time since I'd seen them. Like the ones he'd used to attack me in New York and Argentina, their mouths frothed as they snarled. His metal hand tapped the armrest in a steady rhythm. The knife in his other hand glinted underneath the ceiling lights.

So did the white stone of the ring he wore.

An old man in a respectable suit lay bound and gagged at Saul's feet, his chest heaving, his gray hair shaking with the rest of his body. His eyes bulged as he watched the black wolves leave Saul's side and circle him silently.

"Oh my god!" The host dropped his mic, and the sound interference split my ears.

Lake scrambled back to her feet. "What's happening?" She tugged my arm. "What's going on?"

"I recognize that man," whispered Belle. "I think . . . Is he not . . . the Ontario premier?"

I had no idea one way or the other. Belle paid more attention to politics than I did. I could see her hands twitching, aching for her sword, aching to fight, but she couldn't fight an image on-screen and she knew it. Frustration crinkled the skin around her eyes.

Chae Rin immediately turned to us. "We can catch him. We should try to figure out where he is. We can save him, can't we?" She grabbed Belle's arm and a little too violently yanked her around to face her. "Come on! We have to do something!"

Belle didn't appreciate being manhandled, or maybe it was the tension of the situation itself. She pulled her arm out of Chae Rin's grip and shoved her back.

"What?" Chae Rin spat, once her feet stabilized onstage. "We're just going to stand here looking like morons? Oh, I guess if it's not about *Natalya*, you don't give a shit, right?"

Belle responded to Chae Rin with a livid glare, which Chae Rin matched.

"You know me. My name," Saul said, grabbing our attention once more, "is Saul."

His voice, though forceful, carried with it the kind of well-mannered, gentlemanly lilt I'd associated with Nick. But this brutality . . . The premier's face had been bludgeoned; his saliva was dripping over the white binds in his mouth. That was Alice.

The last time I'd faced Saul in France, he'd made it clear that the drives of both were the same: to find the rest of the stone from which the rings had been made. To find Marian. To make a wish. Even if their wishes were different, both personalities, the body and the Effigy ghost inhabiting it, had proven well enough that they were willing to do whatever it took to achieve their goal. A relationship that had started out with antagonism now seemed to have become a begrudging partnership—the kind Natalya and I had shared, for a fleeting moment, before she'd tried to take me over again. Nick's calm, calculating personality with Alice's vicious bloodthirst.

"My name is Saul," he declared again. "I am an Effigy." He shoved the point of the knife into the desk behind him, his eyes never leaving the camera. "And you should fear me."

In that moment he raised his arms. Black smoke dripped up from the floor, limbs forming before our eyes. More shadow wolves shivered into existence, their dead flesh clinging to their bones, the smoke curling off of their black furry hides into the air over the trembling body of the poor man I knew we wouldn't be able to save.

"I come to tell you that I am not acting alone. I come to give you a message."

I clenched my hands into fists.

"And that message is this." Saul sat back in his chair and folded his arms. "The pain and terror you've experienced thus far is only a shade of what lies ahead of you. And the people you've foolishly trusted to protect you can't save you. No. They *won't* save you. They'll betray you." He flicked a hand and his wolves descended on the senator.

His screams rattled the walls as the wolves tore apart his flesh.

No. I looked away, my heart rattling, my body limp and heavy as his screams joined that of the crowd. And through it all I could hear Saul's promise. It was unmistakable. "You'll see. In seven days, we'll come. And death will follow."

22

"LOOK, I DON'T BLOODY KNOW WHAT HAP-
pened, Henry. Just try to *spin this*." Lake paused. "I don't care if you
don't work for the other girls; the press is killing us. Do something,
yeah?"

In our hotel room, she wasn't the only one yelling into her phone.
Belle was by the heavy, drawn window curtains shouting angrily at
Brendan on the other end of the line. Chae Rin sat with her feet on
the couch and her knees to her chest, picking the skin on her lips dis-
tractedly. Next to her, Ha Rin watched the news with bloodshot eyes,
listening limply to terrified pundits collectively implode while they
tried to make sense of what had just happened.

What was there to make sense of? John Walsh, a Canadian premier, had just been torn to shreds, his death streamed internationally.
There was no news of any city's antiphantom defense systems being
compromised, so Saul must have taken him to a Dead Zone. It had
already been declared an act of terrorism. And while it was happening, the four Effigies whose duty it was to protect the world had been
standing onstage at a teen awards show, collecting a spray-painted

trophy for being role models. The headlines wrote themselves.

I was pacing back and forth by the door, unable to calm myself. Natalya's voice had receded back into my mind, but I was still disturbed, still on edge, which is why I jumped at the sound of a few swift knocks at the door.

"It's me," came Uncle Nathan's voice from the other side of the door. I let him in.

"What are you doing here?" I shut the door fast as he stalked inside with his laptop underneath his arm. "Nobody can see you here."

"It's okay—nobody saw me." He set his laptop down on the table a few feet away from the minifridge. The sounds of pundits screaming over one another drew his attention, and after mere seconds of watching the television, he shook his head. "This is bad. Very bad."

"You saw it, right?" I said.

"Yeah. I don't drink much, but I definitely felt like knocking back a couple of those complimentary mini-scotches in the fridge."

"Seven days," I said.

"Seven days. Giving a timeline only ramps up global hysteria, fear, and anger. Anger at the Sect." He looked at me with worried eyes. "At you."

Belle clicked off her phone. "The top officials from the Sect are already planning on conferencing with the world's leaders. But many of them are refusing to meet. They're furious."

"We should have done something." Chae Rin gripped her knees, her chin pressed against them. Then, lifting her head, she glared at Belle. "We should have *done* something."

"Done what?" Belle shot back. "We couldn't do anything from where we were."

"Exactly!" Chae Rin jumped to her feet, staying rooted to the spot only because her sister had climbed up after her and grabbed her arm to calm her. "We're *Effigies*, damn it. We're supposed to be out there *fighting*, not playing dress-up like clowns on TV. We're not supposed to be looking pretty. We're supposed to be making people feel *safe*. That's what I . . ." She looked back at her sister before lowering her head. "Saul told the world he was an Effigy. I can't even imagine what my parents think right now. What must be going through their heads."

"I'm sure they're all right," Ha Rin said. "Well . . ." She paused.

Chae Rin became anxious, her lips parting as she looked back at her sister. "Well, what?"

"No," Ha Rin said. "It's nothing. I—"

"They're slaughtering us out there and there's barely anything my agent and my marketing team can even do about it." Lake groaned, pressing her phone against her head as she walked over to the table. "What the hell are we supposed to do? How do we get Saul?"

"Brendan wants us to return to the London facility immediately," said Belle.

"No!" Uncle Nathan stepped forward, waving his hand in protest. "No, no, no. Don't do that. Trust me."

"Why?" I asked.

He answered by pulling up a chair, plunking himself down, and lifting up his laptop screen. "Uh," he said, turning to peek over at Ha Rin. "This is kind of sensitive."

Chae Rin sat up quickly and tapped her sister's shoulder, taking the hint. "Unnie, I'm glad you're here, but, uh, I hope you don't mind." And she pressed her hands over her sister's ears. "It's for your own protection."

"Okay." Ha Rin let out an incredulous laugh as her sister kept her head facing forward. "This isn't weird at all."

I came around Uncle Nathan's shoulder as he plugged in the flash drive. "Did you find something?" Belle and Lake gathered around me.

"I've only been able to get through the first few layers of defense on this thing," Uncle Nathan said. A series of *click*s on his keyboard brought up a black screen, but soon several dark, metallic-green letters appeared at the top left-hand corner.

Project X19.

Four large square icons materialized in a line, filling up the entire screen. Computer files. And each icon came with a label underneath.

Phase I: Research

Phase II: Silent Children Program

Phase III: Minerva

Phase IV: Consolidation

"'Project X19.'" I stared at the cursor blinking next to the last number.

"What is that?" Lake asked, leaning over my shoulder. "What are those files?"

"I don't know." Uncle Nathan clicked on the first icon, an error screen appeared, and the screen blinked off. "That keeps happening."

"The Silent Children Program." I squeezed my eyes shut, trying to remember Jessie's frenzied babbling as we rushed through Blackwell's courtyard. "Silent . . . yeah. That's what she called herself back then. Jessie. She said Grunewald put devices in all the 'silent kids.'"

"I told you before about firms that have been trying to reproduce Effigy-like abilities. And you told me about the nanotechnology detected in that dead soldier, Philip. Creating empowered soldiers." Uncle Nathan tapped his fingers on the surface of his laptop, his expression grim. "Looks like Phase II was successful."

"But there's more," I said, my pulse quickening at the thought. "More phases. What's Phase III? What's Minerva? Do I even want to know?"

"I don't know," he answered. "But I do know that X19 was part of a code of communications between city defense control centers, like the one I work at, and the Sect. The APD technology was originally developed and fronted by Sect research, and if there were any issues, the communication between the two bodies would usually be encrypted to protect sensitive information. X19 is like a kind of Sect signature."

"The Sect?" Lake repeated. "There you go. They really *are* evil."

The Fisk-Hoffman kids could have been chosen for the project by people within the Sect. Those children, the traitors in the R & D department, the agents who helped Jessie ambush us in the tunnel, and now "X19," a Sect signature. There were too many connections between the organization and Saul, but when had they begun working together? Had they recruited Saul recently, or had they been working with him since he appeared? They could have even linked up with him before he started his attacks all those months ago. This was insane.

I gripped the back of Uncle Nathan's chair. It couldn't be the entire Sect working with Saul. But for an operation this big, the network of traitors would have to have been extensive. An organization within an organization. Naomi had said herself that something was happening within the Sect.

"It makes sense," I said. "The Fisk-Hoffman kids were reported dead and suddenly show up now. Higher-ups in the Sect could have faked their death records. And maybe they're just the start."

The Fisk-Hoffman kids. Jessie, Philip, and Alex were all connected to Saul. Vasily may not have had powers, but he was working with them too. And Rhys—

Rhys. My fingers felt numb, my stomach fluttering painfully as I thought of him looking up at me in Blackwell's courtyard, at Natalya's rage glinting through the whites of my eyes. He'd gone to that facility. He was there when the fire happened. Did he have something to do with this too? But unlike Vasily, he was just as surprised as I was when we were attacked in the tunnels—I know it. How far did this go? I buried my head in my hands.

"It's the next phases that worry me," Belle said. "Minerva. Consolidation. Saul's stunt might mean that we've already entered into the next stages."

"You . . ." Lake's breath hitched. "You think it could be worse than fake Effigies?" The stiff quirk of her body told me she was terrified of the answer.

"I don't know," Belle answered, though the steady inflection of her voice told me she'd already made up her mind to the affirmative. "We need to know more. Nathan, can you crack these files?"

Uncle Nathan rubbed his neck. "I mean, usually, given the asymmetric algorithm, you can't break into the locks by just guessing the key. So I was surprised to get even this far, but now that I've come to this screen, I'm just facing a wall. The real goods are through the veil. Peeking through it is gonna take me a while. But what I do know is that I won't be able to figure out anything from here."

I watched him take out the drive and stand up. "Where are you going?"

"New York," he said, shutting his laptop. "If I'm going to crack this, I'm going to need stronger tech to mess around with it. The MDCC has far more powerful computers and other stuff I can use. There are some . . . issues I want to check out there as well."

Like how had it gotten hacked all those months ago? I grabbed his arm, his black sleeve crinkling in my fingers. "Isn't that dangerous? What if you get caught? What if you get—"

"Thrown in a Russian gulag?" He gave me a wry grin. "Well, I'll just have to try not to let that happen. Don't worry about me. You guys have other things to focus on."

"Seven days," I said, Saul's promise echoing in my thoughts. "The clock is ticking."

"What Saul did will only galvanize support *against* the Sect—and you. Not just among the people, but among world governments. But you can't exactly go back to the Sect and do what they say anymore. There's no telling what might happen. Whatever you do from now on, you'll have to move carefully. And stick together."

"We'll go see Naomi," Belle said. "In Madrid. All four of us."

Lake and Chae Rin exchanged a puzzled glance as Belle moved toward the bedroom where all our suitcases had been stacked.

"Madrid?" Lake repeated. "Why? Who's Naomi?"

"Rhys's mother," Belle said. "She has some information that can help us. At least that's what she told Maia."

"What if she won't tell us anything?" I asked, thinking back to our conversation at Blackwell's estate. "She asked me to come alone."

"You'll have to take that chance," said Uncle Nathan. "It's too dangerous for you to be alone right now."

"If push comes to shove, I guess we can always just force her to give up the information," Chae Rin added with a shrug. I could only imagine what she meant by "force." As badly as I needed answers, I wasn't sure I was prepared to beat it out of anyone. "I agree. The four of us should go together."

"But how do we get there without the Sect knowing?" Lake prodded.

"Maybe we don't have to," Belle called back without turning. As she disappeared into the bedroom, Chae Rin finally released her sister's ears.

"Looks like I'm heading off again," she told her. "Give Mom and Dad my love. Make sure you keep them safe."

"But that's why I'm here." Ha Rin shifted onto the couch, her weight on her right knee. "It's Mom."

I could see Chae Rin's face fall from here. "Is she all right? She didn't have another . . ." With a self-conscious glance at us, she lowered her voice. "Another episode, did she?"

Ha Rin looked very uncomfortable, her anxious gaze flickering between the rest of us and her sister. "No. Well . . . she just wants to see you and— Ah!" After an exasperated sigh she gave her sister a pained smile. "It'd be better if I could actually speak with you in Korean."

"Like that's my fault." Despite the sharp note of defensiveness in her words, Chae Rin shrank back. "We can talk about it outside."

They got up to leave. A few minutes after they shut the door, Belle came out of the bedroom again with her suitcase packed and ready, holding her cell phone to her ear. I didn't pay any mind until I heard her say Rhys's name. My heart skipped.

"Rhys? Why are you talking to Rhys?" I rushed forward before stopping suddenly. "Is . . . is he okay?" I asked timidly, but Belle put up a finger to silence me.

"You're sure you can do this for us? Okay. Thank you, Rhys. I appreciate it."

With a relieved sigh, she clicked the phone off. "I asked Rhys about the possibility of securing us a Sect jet under pretense. Remember, Communications can track our cylithium frequency—we can't mask it like Saul. But Rhys said he can convince Brendan to issue an order to send us to Spain on a lead. It's the best he can do."

That he was willing to help us didn't make the truth about him any easier to swallow. Especially when I still hadn't figured out what to do about it. "What did you tell him?"

"Nothing about his mother," she said, rolling her suitcase to the side of the door. "I only said it was important. He seemed to understand."

"But—"

"Don't worry, Maia." Belle turned to me. "It's Rhys. We can trust him."

I stayed quiet as Lake went to pack her things, calling me to follow her when she'd noticed I'd stayed rooted to the spot for too long. Uncle Nathan went back to his hotel room to get ready to leave himself, but it was only in the prospect of his leaving that I realized how much I needed someone to talk to. I followed him to his room.

"What's wrong?" Uncle Nathan said as he shut the door behind me. I kept my head low, so he couldn't see my face behind my mess of hair, but he must have seen my shaking. "Maia? Are you . . . are you crying?"

He must have heard me whimpering too. I lifted my head, revealing the tears dripping off my eyelashes.

"Tell me everything," he said.

I did. And by the end of it, I could have sworn his blue eyes were reddening too.

"God, Maia." Calming himself with a sigh, he placed his hands delicately on my shoulders. "I had no idea you were going through this. I'm so sorry."

I thought the weight of finally telling someone would make me feel better, but I only felt more lost. "I just don't know what to do. If I tell Belle that Rhys killed Natalya, she will kill him. That's not even a question. Depending on what his mom says, she might kill her, too. Belle had no one," I explained. "No, it was worse than that." I thought back to that day in France when we visited her old foster home. The simple, pragmatic way she asked the children living there, in front of their foster mother, if they'd been beaten. "Natalya was like the only family she'd ever had. Her mentor, her hero. She was like . . ." I shook my head. Natalya had meant the world to Belle.

And I understood. After my family died, there would be those quiet moments when I would lie awake in my bed, staring up at the ceiling, *feeling* that deafening silence of loneliness, that silence I'd felt that night after the funeral, the kind you feel in your bones when you truly have no one.

But then Saul appeared. I left my home, left my uncle, and yet despite the chaos, there were now people in my life, and suddenly it didn't feel so barren. Running from city to city, completing missions, fighting monsters, escaping death. Always with them by my side.

And I . . .

"I don't want to lose anyone." I hastily wiped the tears dripping down my cheeks as Uncle Nathan looked on. "Not Belle. Not Rhys. Not anyone. I don't want anything to change."

"But, Maia." Uncle Nathan held my hands to stop their shaking. "If this boy really did murder Natalya, even if it was because of impossible circumstances . . . it's going to come out eventually. You can't keep that a secret forever. The longer you hide it from Belle, the worse it'll be when she finds out."

"I *know*." I gritted my teeth as the tears continued to fall. "I know that. But I . . . I just can't. I hate myself."

"There's something else, isn't there?" Uncle Nathan tilted his head, staring at me. "You have feelings for him too, right?"

My tears silently dripped onto his hands.

"I'm so sorry." Uncle Nathan hugged me.

"Just judge me, please." I shifted my head off his chest to free my voice. "Tell me I'm dumb, weak, stupid, selfish, delusional, a terrible role model, a terrible person, neurotic, overemotional, hysterical, whatever. Everything and anything you can think of."

"That's a lot of adjectives." Uncle Nathan laughed softly. "But no, I won't. This isn't something I can judge. It's not like I've ever been in your shoes. And to be honest, I wouldn't wish your shoes on anyone."

When I gazed up at him, the sight of his kind smile did give me a little comfort. I relaxed my shoulders with a quiet exhale.

"I don't envy your burden, Maia. And I'm . . ." His voice broke. "I'm sorry that I can't help you. You're my brother's kid, and I'm practically useless to you."

"Never say that," I told him. "Because it's really very false."

"Even still. This is a burden I can't take from you. But I can tell you this." Letting me go, he gently placed a hand on my head. "Secrets never stay buried. They always find a way to the light. Don't let yourself be caught off guard. Soon, Maia. Even if it's not today. Try to tell them."

Two roads diverged. But neither path would lead me where I wished I could be. The whisper of dread passing through me, the quiet chill settling in my skin, told me as much. I was trapped either way.

"Please be careful," I whispered before leaving him alone in his room.

23

IT WAS A LITTLE JET AND A BUMPY RIDE. IT dropped us off just inside the city, but we refused a Sect van even though, technically, we were here on official duty.

Being on official duty, of course, had its constraints. Rhys had only bought us a few hours in Madrid, and even in the state the Sect was in now, it was still pretty strict when it came to loaning out its aircraft. That meant that we were on borrowed time; we were to complete our investigation by the end of the day and return to London immediately. The jet wasn't even going to leave the tarmac.

Naomi wanted to see me by sundown, so as long as she kept it short, we could make the deadline, though I still wasn't keen on having to go back to the facility. Disguised in the same ball cap and shades we all had, Belle rented us a car and we set off down the Spanish streets.

"Who knew you spoke Spanish?" said Chae Rin from the backseat, though it was one of the few comments any of us had made the entire trip. None of us was much in the mood for talking.

Belle had been in Madrid before and knew the way to Natalya's apartment. She drove us through the city, the skies clear, the sun pleasantly biting. Madrid had not gone untouched by the influence of modernity and globalization. Popular brand-name coffee shops, stores, and restaurants were on every corner. But there were sights I wasn't as used to. We drove past the Plaza de Cibeles square, the castle-like white marble structure stretching up into the morning. Gazing out the window, I watched the street vendors and performers pass in and out of view. People skated under the sun and under the safety of the APD outside the city: a tower at the top of which a giant kinetic structure of moving metal plates reflected a frequency that spanned over a hundred miles. It was too far away for me to see it from here, but I'd seen it from above when our jet had begun to descend.

Natalya's apartment was close to a gigantic park, tucked away in the Salamanca neighborhood, packed with chic restaurants and outdoor bars. Belle knew someone who ran a rooftop bar nearby—not her friend, per se, but certainly Natalya's. It was still morning, and the bar hadn't opened yet. He was willing to let us stay in secrecy for a few hours while the bar was closed, but he warned us that we'd have to leave before the clients started streaming in at sundown. Well, that was our timeline to begin with.

"Are you okay?" I asked Chae Rin after following her to the roof. She was sitting at one of the many empty tables with a glass of water in her hands. Water. Huh. I'd expected she'd have taken advantage of the setting and gotten some alcohol. But Chae Rin didn't seem like herself. She was slouched over the table, worry aging her soft, pale features as she stared into her half-empty glass.

When she saw me coming, her expression hardened. "What's it to you?"

"Whoa." I stopped, holding up my hands in a sign of placation. "I'm just asking if you're okay. No ulterior motives. I'm just a bit worried, that's all. You've been weirdly quiet for a while."

"You're worried about me, huh?" I couldn't tell if Chae Rin's laugh was a jab at me or herself. But she waved me over and I took the invitation, sitting next to her.

"Hey, kid, you remember when we first met in Quebec? You were whining at me endlessly about joining this ridiculous fight, which, by the way, we still haven't won because shit just keeps getting crazier and crazier?"

"Yeah." A sudden surge of shame made me look away from her. "I said some really messed-up stuff too. I'm so sorry."

But Chae Rin shook her head with a little smile. "No, it's okay. I already beat you up for that, so it's all good. But . . . you remember when I said that being an Effigy is hardest on families?"

I did. And after seeing Uncle Nathan, his worry and shame, I knew exactly what she meant.

"After the awards show, my sister told me that my mom had another . . . um."

She hesitated and quickly looked at me. As she squeezed her hands against her glass, the normally confident Effigy seemed at once like a timid child scared of sharing her secrets.

"Sorry," she said. "It's not something that's easy for us to talk about. My family never discusses it and my mom never sees a doctor because they're all against it. I don't know, I can't explain."

"No, I get you." Back then, on the grounds of Le Cirque de Minuit, Chae Rin had been more fixated on her family than on the prospect of Saul attacking more cities. And I'd never even bothered to consider why that would be.

"She's just not well, you know. She stays at home a lot. My dad takes care of her. But she gets so much anxiety normally, and it's just gotten worse since I became an Effigy." Lying back, Chae Rin looked up at the clear sky, squinting under the glare of the sun. "She's so worried and paranoid all the time. And me being who I am, getting in the news for screwing up some mission, getting suspended, beating someone up, destroying a car or several—it doesn't help."

"But you save people too," I said hopefully. "They won't just see the bad, you know. They'll see the good. And the good far outweighs the bad."

Chae Rin didn't look convinced. "I don't know. The thing is . . ." She went quiet, fiddling with her fingers. It took her a while to speak again. "Even with all the crap we deal with on a daily basis and all the times I screw up . . . I'd rather be here than at home taking care of her like my sister. My sister can handle it. But I . . . Sometimes my mom's anxiety is scarier to me than chasing monsters." She let out a sigh, shaking her head. "Gross, right? I'm totally awful, *right*? I mean, I *want* to see her. I love her. And I was happy that last day at the circus when I thought she'd come to watch me perform, but maybe that was because I knew she'd just be there for a day or two. How could I be more comfortable out here than at home with my own mother? I mean, look where we are!"

Chae Rin gestured at the Madrid skyline, at the shopping boutiques and Spanish markets around the corner down below, at the tiny specter of the magnificent APD tower we could now see, somewhat, in distance. "It's one mess after another. Since Saul appeared, we've basically been nomads, hopping around the world trying to stop him. I feel like a sprite in a role-playing game."

"I once had this dream that we were in the Metal Kolossos MMORPG and my player didn't equip me with the right defense accessory and I ended up getting killed by a dark elf. Which is weird because there are no dark elves in the game." But before I could go too far, I noticed Chae Rin staring at me. I stopped, pursing my lips together sheepishly.

"This may never end. But I . . . At some point, I *should* go home. I should do it. Right, Maia?"

Hearing her speak my name was more jarring than I'd anticipated. She usually called me "kid," or maybe "moron." A flush of surprise rose up my chest, but Chae Rin was serious. As she looked back at me, she had the world-weariness of someone who'd lived much longer than her eighteen years.

"Right now going home is only going to put our families in danger. So we'll just have to work hard and end this thing as soon as possible. I know it's difficult, but . . ." I breathed deeply, summoning what I needed for the hopeful smile I gave her. "I think if we stick together, it'll be all right. Don't worry, Chae Rin. We're a team."

Chae Rin raised an eyebrow, amused, before sipping her water and staring out over the terrace. That's right. As insane as everything got, we could count only on each other. I had to admit that as dangerous as it was, traveling the world trying to stop Saul had given me something important: a purpose. Comrades. That became all too clear whenever I thought back to how things were just a year ago, those nights alone in my room, that terrible loneliness after my sister and parents were gone.

I wasn't alone so much these days. It was a good feeling.

"Thanks, Chae Rin," I whispered.

"Huh?" She set down her glass. "For what?"

But I was already feeling too embarrassed to elaborate. I got to my feet. "Come on—there are a lot of people on the streets now. Even if we're all the way up here, we might get recognized."

I tugged at her sleeve annoyingly, until she got up with a groan and followed me back to the door. For all of our sakes, we had to stop Saul. It was the only way we could go back to our families without looking over our shoulders—or theirs. But as long as we were in this battle, we had to rely on one another. It wasn't only what I wanted; it was what I *needed*—the four of us together.

I didn't want to lose anyone.

We left the bar just before sundown. Our suitcases were still there; the man who ran the bar said he'd keep them in the storage room for us, though Lake had had the good sense to take a few things she said we might need and stuff them into her knapsack. Strapping on our caps and black shades, we did some reconnaissance of the area, scanning bodies as they made their way to nightclubs and the restaurants surrounding the apartment building. No Jessie or Vasily. But we couldn't be sure how many soldiers Saul had on his roster or who else knew we were in Madrid other than that handful of Sect agents. We'd have to be careful.

We were buzzed in almost the moment we got to the door. Naomi must have been there already. There wasn't anyone in the narrow hallways, but we moved quickly, going up to the twelfth floor. Belle knew the way. She stood in front of Natalya's door silently for a moment too long, her hands hovering close to the solid peach wood. I knocked for her.

A man in a black suit opened the door. A Sect agent? I could see his female partner standing by the wall silently, her shades covering her face.

The man nodded to his partner before stepping aside. His broad shoulders nearly bumped against the wall as he moved to let us through.

It was exactly the same as Natalya's memories. The treelike coatrack on the far left-hand side. The steel fridge next to a little coffee table and a clear sink. Glamorous pop art hanging from the eggshell walls.

Something in me stirred when I saw the familiar sights, the narrow hall that opened up into an expansive living room.

The living room.

A sudden vertigo hit me, my head spinning. The crystal decanter on the shelf that I knew was always filled with scotch. The stylish bookshelves and modern furniture, the ceiling that sloped down at one angle. And the chair. The one Natalya had been sitting in the night she'd died. It was in the same place, at the center of the room. *Everything* was in the same place. A memory, a former life. A crime scene.

"Maia, are you okay?" Lake had her knapsack dangling off one shoulder. Sliding it back up, she hooked my arm with hers so I wouldn't fall over.

"Were you followed?"

Sucking in a sharp breath of air, I turned and saw her. Naomi. Still beautiful with her clean, youthful skin and long black hair that veiled her chest. In a plain mauve dress, she sat in a chair—not *the* chair, but a lonely settee by the tall set of windows that spanned almost the entire length of the wall. The nighttime city lights crept through slivers in the blinds, casting a glow across her. The lights in the living room were dim, but I could see her bright brown eyes.

"*Were you followed?*" she repeated, the urgency quiet but palpable in her voice.

"No," Belle said.

Naomi paused and took in the sight of us all. "Maia." She moved the shawl over her dress. "I expected you'd come alone." Her eyes flicked fearfully toward Belle, and I instantly understood.

"Yeah, that's not happening." Chae Rin folded her arms. "You're Rhys's mom, right?"

"Maia said you were a member of the Council," said Lake, still holding on to me.

Naomi shifted uncomfortably in her seat, turning her wedding ring around her middle finger. "Ah, is that so? What else did she tell you, I wonder?"

"Don't get salty about it," Chae Rin barked. "It's not like we were going to let her come here alone, so you might as well spill what you know."

I could stand up straight now, though Lake continued to link arms just in case. The place had the musty smell of an apartment that hadn't been lived in for some time. I could feel traces of her here.

"Why here?" I asked her. "Why did you want to meet me here? And just me?"

Naomi stood up and walked to the window to look out over the city. "You feel her, don't you?" she said without turning around. "Like a ghost in the shadows."

I brought up a hand to my chest, my fingers curling around the fabric of my shirt. "You want me to scry."

"It's Marian we need, Maia, not Natalya. The other Effigy in your line. The first."

First? I could feel Lake and Chae Rin glance at me, surprised. Belle's gaze never wavered from Naomi.

"Why Marian?" I asked, but Naomi was too distracted to hear me, peering through the blinds, searching the streets below.

"We don't have much time. I'm supposed to be back at home in Virginia by morning. I told my husband I wanted to stay in England for a little while longer, so he left without me. Nobody but James and Rosa know I'm here." With a shift of her head, she indicated the two agents who stayed vigilant by the front door. "And I can't be sure I wasn't followed. So I'll get through this quickly."

"Yeah, talk, please." Chae Rin tapped her foot impatiently. "Saul is out there planning something big; we can't afford to stand around anymore."

"But it's not just Saul," Naomi said, and I noticed her voice had dipped in volume. "There are members of the Sect helping him. Even members of the Council. This is much bigger than just him. You must have realized it. How could Saul alone have taken down the APDs of all those different cities?"

Even after what Uncle Nathan had told me about his job in the MDCC, I may not have known exactly how it all worked, but I knew that the city's system was complex enough that it required networks of very smart technicians with very expensive computers to play with. Unless Saul could shut off complicated technology with the power of his mind, he'd need people from within the center, or maybe a special group from the outside hacking into multiple ones. It was the only explanation.

"It's why Baldric fled," Naomi said.

"Baldric." Belle stepped around the coffee table. I watched each step she took toward the woman with anxious eyes. "Natalya mentioned him to a priest we know. Madame, who is this man?"

Naomi brought her hands up to her chest, her thumb caressing the ring around her finger. A nervous tic. "Baldric Haas. He's also a member of the Council. Like my family, he's been in service of the Sect since its inception. They are the only ones who knew about the last volume: the one Castor had written in secret."

"A secret volume?" I looked at the other girls. "A thirteenth volume?"

Naomi nodded. "It's said to carry the most dangerous secrets Castor couldn't divulge even to the Sect. But as dangerous as it was, Castor wouldn't destroy it. Instead, he entrusted it to the Haas family. They've been guarding it since, but eventually Baldric grew anxious."

"What secrets?" Lake asked. "Like . . . like about us?"

"About you. About the phantoms. About the beginning of

everything," she said, her eyelids fluttering shut as she remembered. "Or so he told me. I can't know for sure. He's probably the only human alive who knows what's inside those pages. But he's always been a paranoid man, and he only trusted me to a point. He was the one who first told me at the beginning of this year that there were rumblings of treason within the Sect. That Saul appeared not long afterward isn't a coincidence. Baldric was sure that the secrets in the volume were central to the happenings in the Sect, to Saul, to the attacks around the world. But he wouldn't tell me how until he was sure the volume was safe in his hands."

"You said you know how Natalya died." Belle stopped by the chair Naomi had been sitting in, her hands brushing the top. "Can you tell me?"

It was only for a fleeting second—Naomi's line of vision crossing with mine. Her eyes dimmed as she held her hands close to her sides to hide their slight tremble.

"Every generation of the Haas family places the volume in a new location to keep it safe. Baldric wanted to retrieve the volume from where he'd been hiding it—in Prague's National Museum. But he'd fallen sick. Though he asked me to help him, if he really was being watched, it would be dangerous for me to go alone. On his behalf, I sent Natalya." She watched Belle's expression carefully as she spoke. "By then Natalya had already become suspicious about things. Around half a year ago, she came to me. After the Frankfurt attacks."

"Frankfurt," Belle said. "Sibyl told us. She confronted Saul then. Yes . . . just before the attack. Though he disappeared before she understood who or what he was."

"I needed someone on my side," explained Naomi. "I told her about the volume and asked her to bring it to me secretly, without the Sect knowing. But Natalya was a soldier. She was anxious about going against them . . . so I promised her what Baldric promised me—that with the volume, we'd know the truth. And that I would protect her from the Sect."

She lowered her head.

"But you couldn't," Belle finished for her.

"She was intercepted and couldn't retrieve it. Afterward, it was too risky to move. Baldric became jittery and finally fled Britain. Natalya would have tried again once the heat was off of her, but . . ."

"That's when she was killed, right?" Chae Rin said. "She didn't get a chance."

Naomi took a shaky step forward. "I'm sorry, Belle. I know she was close to you. Like family." Her eyes were glistening. "I'm sorry."

"Do you know who killed her?"

Silence. Though Belle had sounded calm, I knew better than to take that stone mask as truth. Naomi said nothing, but I couldn't keep this secret for much longer.

No. It wasn't right. I had to confess.

My fingers clasped together, my body shivering from the stinging pain of my teeth biting into the corner of my lip. I couldn't stay silent. No matter what my feelings were. No matter the consequences. I didn't want to be a coward anymore. I had to trust Belle.

But when I opened my lips, the confession passed through Naomi's instead.

"I did," she said. Simple, bitter words.

The room went quiet. Seconds passed in silence.

An unbearable cold suddenly crashed into me as if I'd been caught in a torrent of wind. I closed my eyes, and when I opened them again, frost lined the bookshelves, clinging to the ceiling. Snow gathered on the furniture, the marble counters. And Belle's sword was already at Naomi's throat.

"Stop!" We all ran to Belle, but I got there first. My hand hooked her elbow, though it did nothing to deter the girl's murderous gaze. Naomi's bodyguards, who'd heard the commotion, were rushing through the narrow hallway, but before they could reach the living room, Belle covered the entrance with a barricade of ice to keep them out.

"Yes, I did it." Naomi pressed her head back against the blinds, her lips trembling. "I sent her to Prague. I put her in danger. She died because of me."

"Did you or did you not kill her?" Belle pressed her sword against Naomi's neck just hard enough for a line of blood to form. It dripped down the edge of her blade. "Tell me. You either killed her or you know who did."

"Oh my god, oh my god, oh my god." Lake was bobbing up and down on her feet, freaking out. "Is Belle going to kill her? Please don't kill anyone!"

"Belle, please stop!" I cried. "Natalya's killer—"

"Doesn't matter." Naomi was looking at me now. "*I* killed her. *My* actions set her death in motion. It didn't begin with Prague. It began years ago." She was shaking. Tears started to dribble down her cheeks, mingling with the blood slipping down Belle's sword. "Everything that happened . . . It's because of my weakness. Because I can't protect anyone. I never could. Not *then*. And not now."

Did she mean Rhys? I frowned, my grip on Belle's elbow failing. I tried to speak again, to fill in the blanks Naomi kept hidden. But as much as Naomi could against Belle's blade, she shook her head.

"Please. Please don't," she said. She was talking to me. "It's my fault. The sin is mine from beginning to end."

"That's not good enough," Belle hissed.

"Stop." Chae Rin stepped forward and grabbed the edge of Belle's blade with barely a wince. "Stop, Belle. *Enough* with this crap."

But despite her warning glare, Belle wouldn't back down. "I promised myself that I would find Natalya's killer. And murder them. No
matter the cost. I will *murder* them."

I took a stumbling step back, my feet heavy. So I was right.

"Well, that wouldn't be productive, would it?" Chae Rin said. But
they were at a stalemate. Neither would budge to the other. "Lady," she
said without looking at Naomi. "You said you sent Natalya to Prague.
That's where the secret volume is, right? What if we get it?"

Naomi spoke very carefully. "Baldric told me that the information
in it could help us fight whatever is coming. And that we couldn't
allow the Council to get their hands on it. Baldric is gone. Off the grid.
I can't just ask him. We need the volume or—"

Chae Rin kept a firm grip on the blade. "Or?"

"Marian. Baldric mentioned it, that Marian knows the secrets
that even he does not. I would have asked Natalya, but—" Her breath
hitched as Belle's grip tightened around her sword. "Maia . . . Maia
could scry right here."

"That would take too long!" Lake said. "You said Marian was the
first fire Effigy, right?"

Belle had told me once during training that I would have to go
through each Effigy. But I couldn't even get past Natalya, not when
she was still plotting to take me over. I held my head in my hands.

"Belle, let's get the special volume," Chae Rin said.

"No."

"Damn it!" In one quick movement, Chae Rin pushed Naomi
out of the way with her elbow and with her great strength broke the
sword's blade. It dissipated—cold frost into the air. She'd pushed
Naomi so hard, the woman had tripped and fallen to the floor, her
hand grasping the window ledge as she tried to reorient herself, but
Belle was already stalking toward her.

"I said *stop*." With her bloody hand, Chae Rin grabbed Belle's collar and pushed her against the window, but Belle's fingers were already curled around her shirt. The tension was palpable, as chilling as the air around us. My feet wouldn't move. I was too scared to even tell them to.

"Oh, come *on!*" Lake gripped the straps of her knapsack, her voice trembling with fear.

"You know what, Belle? I'm getting real tired of your crap," Chae Rin spat. "You want to kill a woman because she blames herself for someone's death. Clearly she didn't murder anyone, but you *still* want to cut her open. What the hell is wrong with you? It's not like you—"

"To be this cold?" Belle's lips curved into a small smile. Not a nice one. "Surely you of all people know better than that."

"Yeah, you're a bitch," Chae Rin said. "And that's usually fine. But you're not a murderer. You've been acting freaking bizarre since we got back from France—no, since Natalya's death. Like what you did in that desert hideout? And that wasn't the only mission where you jumped the gun. You've been good at hiding it so far, but you're slipping, Belle. I know it. *They* know it too."

She flicked her head toward us. It was true. Belle had been off since Natalya's death—especially once she found out her mentor's suicide was a murder.

I thought back to that night in France by the river. Belle had taught me to scry, but it wasn't to reach Marian. The way she'd shaken me, pleaded with me. The desperation.

She was *still* desperate.

"So what are you going to do?" Chae Rin tightened her grip. "You're going to kill a director's wife? And then we all get stuck in a jail cell while the Sect continues to fall apart when we have less than seven days to stop whatever Saul is planning?"

"Why not?"

"I want to go *home*." The word sounded as if it'd been somehow mangled coming up Chae Rin's throat. She was shaking. "I want to see my family. My mother."

"Me too," Lake whispered. "I'm an only child. I'm all my parents have, and they've been so patient this whole time." She sounded close to tears.

"We can't do that until we get Saul once and for all," Chae Rin continued. "And your selfish shit is going to get in the way of that."

"But you all have families," Belle whispered. "That woman took mine. She *admitted* it."

Naomi held in her sobs. She couldn't speak. So I did.

"Belle . . ." I swallowed hard, glancing at Naomi, who shook her head ever so slightly. She was begging me. I balled my hands into fists. "I know what it's like to lose people. My family died, remember?"

But even I had Uncle Nathan. Most of my grandparents were still alive. I wasn't completely alone. But Belle was. She didn't even know where she'd come from.

"Getting revenge isn't going to change anything. Please. I hate this." Tears trickled down my cheeks. "We're supposed to stick together. You guys are the only friends I have. My sister's gone. . . ."

I felt Lake's comforting hand on my shoulder. The thought of June made me suddenly feel faint and weak. It was that phantom pain again, like I just found out I was missing an arm. "Don't fight. We *have* to stay together. I . . ." I inhaled. "I don't want to lose anyone else."

That was enough. It felt like the tension was finally starting to dissolve. Belle's body relaxed, and Chae Rin let her go. We stood awkwardly in silence, pairs of eyes avoiding each other. I walked over to Naomi and helped her stand.

"Belle," Naomi started.

"Quiet," Belle hissed, brushing herself off and stalking away from the window.

"No, I need to say this." Naomi kept her hand firmly around my wrist. "As a member of the Council, I watched Natalya, I've watched you—all of you—swear allegiance to the Sect. And then I'd sit in my ivory tower and let you all fight and die for the cause *we* gave to you."

It was hard to forget the vast emptiness I felt as I knelt before Blackwell and the seven members of the Council in Ely Cathedral. Naomi's had been the only soothing voice among the cacophony of judgments. Maybe this was how she'd felt that day, when she alone had tried to give me something to hold on to.

"I never understood just how heavy that burden was until I learned of the death of one Effigy, Jemma Moretti. One of the Effigies of wind before you, Victoria. Suicide." Naomi gripped my wrist tighter. "Perhaps it was the funeral. I can still hear her mother's wailing. And since then I've wanted to do right by you. By all of you. When Natalya first became an Effigy, she used her power to kill a mobster who'd held her family in debt."

"What? I didn't know that," I said. And by the way Belle frowned, it didn't look like she did either.

"I covered it up. I thought doing little things like this would help ease my guilt . . . help me feel useful again. Maybe that's why, when Baldric suggested that there could be corruption in the Sect, the very organization that marched little girls to their deaths, I wanted to do what I could. But in the end, nothing's changed. I sent Natalya to her death like all the others. And now I could be sending you straight into danger."

Finally, she let go of my wrist and moved toward the other set of windows, her black hair glimmering under the moonlight streaming through the blinds.

"I may never be able to atone for anything I've done," Naomi said. "But there's nothing I can do on my own other than this. I have to lean on you again, Effigies. I'm sorry, but please . . . *please* find the volume. There's a secret passageway beyond the museum that only Baldric knows, but he told Natalya, which means he's told *you*, Maia." Naomi looked at me meaningfully. "Get it before the Sect does. If what Baldric said is true, it could be the key to stopping all of this. I have to believe that. I just—"

She was looking at Belle, the pain of too many lives lost sinking into the wells of her eyes. "My only wish is that we could find a way to stop this painful cycle. Girls being trained and sent to the slaughter. Fighting and dying. Pain and revenge. If only it would end."

"End . . . ," Belle said as if the word were foreign to her.

Naomi closed her eyes. "It needs to change," she said. "All of it. Baldric said so himself before he disappeared. The Sect. Humanity." Her lips trembled. "Our world needs a revival. If only . . . if only we were . . . *free.*"

A deafening round of shots exploded through the window, but only three pierced Naomi's body. None of us moved. None of us could figure out what was happening. Not until Naomi hit the ground.

24

I WAS ALREADY ON THE FLOOR, THE BLINDS falling, glass shattering around my head. Lake was shrieking something. Naomi. I had to get to Naomi. Heart racing, I pulled myself up to my knees swiftly, keeping myself low to avoid the next barrage of bullets. Carefully, painfully, I crawled on my knees atop the broken glass until I reached Naomi's twitching body. One in the shoulder. Two in the chest. Her eyes were fluttering, rolling to the back of her head.

I scooped her up and made a run for it. My heart pounded in my ears as I tried to stop myself from slipping on the ice. I managed to get past the couch just as a group of men in pitch-black strike-team gear swung through the broken windows from ropes.

As she crouched on the ground, Belle melted the ice wall closing off the hallway with a sweep of her hand. Naomi's bodyguards, James and Rosa, ran into the room shooting.

"Give her to me!" Rosa said, diving to the ground.

James ran past me, still shooting, just as I felt a bullet pierce my leg. Screaming out in pain, I doubled over and nearly dropped Naomi, but Rosa caught both of us.

The shots and yells pounded my senses. My head screaming, I turned and saw Chae Rin grabbing a soldier's gun and swiveling it around so it could shoot one of his comrades instead. Lake blew a group of them away with a torrent of wind as Belle sliced across a man's chest with her sword, melting the ice around the living room to make it easier to move.

Rosa pulled me into the hallway. "Are they Sect?" I grunted in pain as I passed Naomi to her, the weight of her body lifting a bit of pressure off my bleeding leg.

"I can't tell," she answered. "Those aren't Sect uniforms."

They covered their faces with helmets, like police in riot gear. Black fatigues. Concealed identities.

"We did a perimeter sweep and even checked the room for bugs," Rosa said. "We weren't followed. Nobody could have known Naomi would be here. How did they find us?"

The Sect knew we'd be in Prague, but they didn't know we were meeting Naomi, not even Rhys. And yet Naomi was clearly the target. They'd wasted no time taking her down.

Whoever they were, it was Naomi they wanted dead. And they'd come prepared. The assailants were down, but it wasn't the end. One last attacker, before he fell, threw a metal ball across the room. It landed hard against the wet floor before I realized Belle was yelling at us to run.

A few seconds of silence, of shoes splashing and scrambling across the ground. The explosion that followed was just big enough to take out the living room. Belle's warning and the others' quick senses had saved them; they jumped with the blast, diving to the ground and avoiding the worst of it. Everyone made it out of the living room and into the entrance hallway safely, though Lake's head was bleeding badly. She still clung to her knapsack's strap as she sat against the wall we'd found shelter behind.

"Ugh . . ." My ears hadn't stopped ringing. I could hear screaming and commotion on the other side of the door in front of us. "What do we do?" Getting on my knees, I pressed my hands down on Naomi's chest, but the blood was swelling up too much. "We have to get her to a hospital."

"No," Belle said.

"She's *dying*," I yelled, staring at her incredulously.

"She needs medical attention, but we can't be seen here," she clarified. "It'll raise too many questions. And it'll make it harder for us to move."

"Belle's right," said Chae Rin. "Whether they were Sect or not, they obviously wanted to kill Naomi before she could tell us anything important. If that doesn't say we're on the right track, I don't know what else could." Breathing heavily, she stared at Naomi, wincing from the sight of her quivering in her bodyguard's arms. "Best thing we can do now is get to Prague before they do. But like Belle said, we can't be seen here."

Belle stood. "We can leave quickly. Cover our faces. But we have to find another way out of the city. We can't take the jet that brought us here. The Sect will never let us stray from their sight the moment they find us."

"No, you can't." Naomi's second bodyguard, James, stood, his left arm bleeding from a gunshot wound. "But I can fly you out on the helicopter I used to bring Mrs. Prince here."

"What about Naomi?" I said.

"There're two of us," he said, flicking his head toward his partner. "Rosa will get Mrs. Prince to the hospital."

We didn't have another choice, and time was running out. I took one last look at Rhys's mother dying in Rosa's arms before tearing myself away, my lips concealing a sob as we ran through the front door and into the chaos of bodies in the hallway.

Everyone was too busy fleeing for their lives to notice that there were four Effigies among them. We kept our heads low, navigating down the stairs and through the emergency exit with the rest. Cop cars already lined the street. James took us around the back of the building, through the narrow alleyways until we came to the car he'd driven Naomi in.

"Get in," he said quickly, and we did. Lake was moaning beside me, still dizzy from the blast. I tore off my sleeve and made a bandage out of it, tying it around her head as we zipped through the streets. The helicopter he'd flown Naomi in was at a private heliport at the edge of the city. Fully fueled. We hopped inside and strapped ourselves in.

"EMA activated," came the feminine voice from somewhere inside my headset. The ringing in my ears got worse as the helicopter lifted off, as the gravity shifted around me. This would usually be around the time when I wanted to throw up. But my body had become so numb, I could barely feel the helicopter rocking from the turbulence. I let my head sink back against the chair.

I was squished between Lake and Chae Rin, with Belle in the front next to James. Lake was sleeping; her head dangled awkwardly as her languid body leaned forward against her seat belt. Her neck looked like it was going to break off, so I pushed her back up against the seat and positioned her head properly against it before settling back into my own stupor.

"No way this thing can take us all the way to Prague," Chae Rin said, though with the intense helicopter noise, I could only really listen to her voice through the headset.

"We'll need to refuel en route," James said. "I know it's not as ideal as taking the Sect jet, but it's faster than driving and less easily followed."

"Thank you for helping us," I said. My sleeveless arm was chilly, but we'd left our suitcases at the rooftop bar. Lake was the only one who'd had the sense to take her knapsack with her. All my clothes were back in Madrid.

"It's what Mrs. Prince wanted. . . ." James's voice tapered out as the question no one wanted to ask hung in the air. Rosa must have gotten Naomi to a hospital by now. I had to believe that. But when I closed my eyes, I pictured the look of devastation on Rhys's face and my fingers curled on my lap.

"They're going to know we had something to do with it," I said. "They knew we were in the city when it happened. Then we suddenly disappear without telling anyone?"

"And they'll track us." I could see the knit in Belle's eyebrows as she looked out the window. "We need to work quickly." She looked at James. "And rely on whomever we can trust."

There had to be a way to mask our frequencies like Saul could. If the Sect could just track us wherever we went, what would be the point? We didn't know for sure who'd attacked us in Naomi's apartment, but it had to be them. If they caught us, even if they didn't kill us, best-case scenario would be that they'd lock us up and question us over Naomi's attempted murder. Considering Saul was working on a timetable, both options were inconvenient.

We flew in silence, each of us lost in the dark of our thoughts. We were out of the comfort of the APD tower protecting Madrid and the satellite cities. We were low enough in altitude for me to see a Spanish mountain range. Darkened earth covered in thin sheets of snow at the highest peaks, everything blanketed in night. Even in the dark, I could see something shifting and scuttling across the rocky domain, too fast to be human. Phantoms. It'd be impossible to describe them; it was too dark and we were too high. But there were enough of the tiny specks climbing up the rock for me to feel their menace.

"Dead Zone," I said as we flew over them. "Down below."

"From what I know, some of these mountains are protected by the mining industry," James said. "But there's one prominent barrier to expanding their territo—"

His word cut off with a grunt as the helicopter began to struggle with turbulence.

Or maybe it wasn't turbulence.

I could see it out of the window to my right: the beginnings of a snarl forming out of the cloud in front of us. The white mist shivered and sank into a gaping hole, black as the night around us; round, soulless eyes shimmered bright like white jewels as the rest of the phantom's face shook itself free from the cloud. A demon snout, black steam smoking through its long, jagged jaws and off its scaly, leathery hide. A single horn stretched back from the crown of its head. This one had wings, tiny ones, on its back, and short little arms that dangled uselessly from its torso. Its long tail flitted behind it as it began slipping through the air toward us.

"It's okay," said James, though he clearly looked more spooked than we did. "Our electromagnetic armor is still operational."

"Better be," Chae Rin whispered as the phantom swooped under the helicopter and then curved itself around until its long, spindly body was parallel with us. For an uncomfortable few minutes, it followed beside us. My eyes tracked its body's mesmerizing undulations, its form silhouetted in the night. It was shadowing us like a faithful pet, waiting for its chance.

Four more descended from the sky and sank below us; they were making their way toward the mountains instead. Something else had caught their attention.

I gasped and held my seat belt to keep myself stable from the sudden convulsions of the helicopter.

"Ugh," James grunted. There really *was* turbulence. "Hold on." He gripped his controls even tighter. The helicopter shook so violently, Lake shuddered awake. "Just let me get this under control."

He didn't get the chance. Two shots were fired from below, and they were too close for comfort. The helicopter swerved dangerously, tilting us over with a violent jerk. I held on to my seat belt for dear life, my body half raised out of my seat as James tried to get the helicopter level.

"What's happening?" I screamed. "What was that?"

James shook his head, his jaws clenched. "I don't know!"

Belle was trying to see where the shots had come from, but soon another two rang out. The haunting, whalelike cries of a phantom pierced the air as one of the bright flares blasted into the sky in front of the cockpit.

"It got hit!" Chae Rin looked out her window, eyes wide as the phantom that had been following alongside us barreled high into the sky, screeching with agitation, its tail burned off. "The phantom! The phantoms are being attacked, not us!"

But we were, even if not intentionally. Just as one blast shot off the head of a phantom, another one blasted off the helicopter's tail rotor. The helicopter shuddered and shrieked out its warning, the loud, dull sound bleating against my eardrums. We were going down.

James was clicking buttons desperately, but we were spinning out of control too quickly.

Gulping in air with short, desperate inhales, I grabbed Lake. "Get us out of here!"

Lake could barely breathe; she tried lifting her arms up to still the air, but that required concentration she didn't have with the helicopter flinging out of control.

"Jump!" she screamed. "Jump *now!*" Grabbing her bag, she started unbuckling her seat belt. "Trust me!"

There was no time for debate. Belle pulled a petrified James out with her into the night, Chae Rin, Lake, and I following close behind. Holding my breath, I plummeted through the sky, the cold wind biting my skin. Below us, two halves of a smoking, bloodied phantom crashed into the mountainside, but I was too far up to see who'd hit them.

Another phantom went down with a well-aimed shot, but there were more circling back toward us with gaping jaws. Belle and I attacked at the same time, one phantom bursting into flames and the other falling back down to the earth, encapsulated in ice. The wind rushed past my ears as I continued to fall to the mountainside.

"Lake!" I heard Chae Rin scream, but we were already starting to slow down. The wind rushed up to meet me but softened to a caress as it pillowed my body. The farther we descended, the clearer the figures below became. For the first time, I could see the people who'd killed the phantoms. There were three of them bundled up in thick jackets and climbing boots: a woman and two men—no, not two men, but one man and one kid. I couldn't see their faces properly, but I did see the smoking barrels of their giant, body-length guns flashing with blue electricity.

Guns aimed at us.

"Stop!" I cried, but they weren't looking at us. One last phantom. I could hear its screeching drawing closer to us from above. Our feet touched the ground just as two more shots were fired, but they both missed their target. Belle already had her sword out, but it was Chae Rin who rushed forward and, leaping, caught the phantom's thick neck in her arms with her incredible strength. It pushed her back, but as she slid across the rocky terrain, she held the phantom's gaping jaw in place. With her magic, the earth caved in and snatched the phantom's tail, pulling him in like a sinkhole. She had to let go of its snapping jaw and jump out of the way so that the stone and soil could do their work, swallowing it up and crushing its body. By the time the earth had finished shifting, the phantom's horn was all that was left peeking out of the soil. Chae Rin kicked it off.

That's when I heard the *click* behind my head.

"Who are you?" a female voice, deeply inflected with a Spanish accent, rumbled in a low and throaty tone as the gun pressed against the back of my head.

"I thought that would be obvious," I answered coolly, even as I raised my hands in the air. "Seeing as we just smoked a few phantoms for you."

"Abril, enough," said the man to my right. His face was hidden behind a blue scarf, but from his Scottish-inflected voice I could tell he was young, maybe a bit older than us. I recognized the huge, long-range weapon he'd used to fire at the phantoms in the sky. The metal covering, the electric blue bars that slid up the sides as it powered up— it was the same weapon Howard had used to fight off the phantoms in New York. A Sect weapon. The design was exactly the same.

The man rested it against the ground while his hands fumbled in his bag, searching for something. He took out a metal stick that, when he tugged at it, stretched out in new sections. "We need to set up protection or we'll get eaten out here. Put your gun down. This isn't over."

He was right. I could feel the rumbling beneath my feet.

"They're coming!"

The kid. He'd pulled his scarf down long enough for me to see his olive-skinned face before he turned around again and aimed his weapon at the mountain peaks. Several phantoms, as black, rotted, and smoking as the rest, crawled over the hills on thin, towering spider legs. They were moving too rapidly toward us, even despite the weight of their giant, cicada-like torsos.

I batted Abril's gun away with my hand, and though her face was covered with a red scarf and a thick hood, I could see her eyes rounding in fear at the sight of the phantoms. Shoving her gun back into her holster, she dove for her Sect weapon on the ground.

As big as the phantoms were, they were fast enough to dodge the blasts, scuttling back and forth. The kid jumped out of the way, narrowly avoiding the sharp edge of a phantom's leg as they came for us.

One leapt out from behind us so quickly, Lake and James didn't have time to react. Lake screamed as the phantom smashed its leg into James hard and he flew back, landing on the ground with a heavy *thud*, out cold. I couldn't see if he was breathing or not.

Belle ran, ducking to avoid Abril's hectic blast, and slid, cutting off two legs in one go. Chae Rin created another sinkhole in the mountain, which took a phantom down, but she had to be careful—the Scottish boy had to run and duck out of the way to avoid being taken with it.

It was chaos. With a great yell, Lake managed to push one of the phantoms back, but there were two more coming around the corner. Rushing forward, I summoned every bit of strength I had to set them on fire. I managed to burn off some legs, though there were so many trees nearby, I had to be careful not to start a wildfire.

Off to the side somewhere, the Scottish boy was busy fiddling with that stick he'd pulled out of his bag while his partners shot blue electricity from their Sect weapons. But one phantom slipped through the perimeter just as I heard a weapon jam with a series of frustrated *clicks*. Spinning around, I saw the boy a few feet away eyeing his weapon in terror, desperately trying to shake it awake. As a phantom lurched toward him, I was already running for him.

"Derrek!" Abril yelled, but she was too busy fighting off her own phantom to go to him.

Derrek screamed and dropped his weapon, falling back and covering his head with his arm. I threw a wave of flame at it, but it brushed it off with a shake of its shelled head. It raised its needle-sharp leg and brought it down on Derrek's head so fast I barely had time to think. On instinct alone, I slipped underneath it, blocking its attack with my arm and crying out in pain as the thin point pierced through my flesh.

My blood dripped down the needle onto the forehead of a terrified Derrek, who lay flat on his back looking up with wide, blue eyes at the two of us monsters, Effigy and phantom, struggling over the fate of his life. Grabbing the leg with my other arm, I sent a tunnel of fire scorching up its length until the torso was aflame. Then, with a heave, I pushed it over and hit the ground even before it did, grasping my bloodied arm.

"Are you okay?" Derrek sounded Eastern European somehow. He had that harsh lilt to his voice, but it felt mixed with many things, as if he'd been moved around too much before his voice could settle anywhere. When he pulled down his scarf, I could see his thick pink lips and his rounded cheeks. He took his cap off, revealing the pincer-straight black hair covering his ears. "You . . . you saved me." He looked at me in utter awe.

"I need a bandage," I told him, but there wouldn't be any time for first aid, not when there were more phantoms coming.

"It's done!"

The Scottish man. He was finished setting up his trinket: a tripod that glowed from the metal feet to the glowing tip that reached just above his head. A few swift *click*s and it was operational.

"Take this, you little fuckers," he swore. The moment he turned it on, a wave of blue light flashed out in a circle, evaporating the phantoms in the area as far as I could see.

We were safe, but it didn't seem like there'd be any time to rest. The Scottish man pulled down his scarf and pushed off his hood with a flick of his head. His brown eyes matched the dark chestnut hair curling over his forehead in ringlets. His jaw was square and straight, his jawline defined as he surveyed the mountains.

"All right, everyone move your arses. This isn't going to hold forever." He looked at me and grinned. "That is, unless you Effigies come with APD systems built into those indestructible little bodies."

"Not indestructible," I said, holding up my bloodied arm.

"And not little." Chae Rin approached him slowly, looking him up and down. He didn't seem to mind. Seeing a disheveled Chae Rin approach him menacingly only made his grin turn wicked. "Who are you?"

"Traffickers." It was Belle who'd answered, though her gaze was on the weapons they held. "Sect grade. You've stolen these." She looked at the three of them. "Is this what you trade in?"

"Sharp eyes," said the Scottish boy.

Traffickers. They usually weren't any of the Sect's business—we battled monsters, not humans, as sick as those humans may be. But they were criminals nonetheless, setting up hubs for their networks through Dead Zones, smuggling and transporting anything from drugs to people—but I didn't see either.

"We're not bad guys, you know," the man said, putting up his hands as a sign of peace.

"You shot at us," Chae Rin said.

"By accident!" he insisted. "We were shooting at the phantoms. Come on, seriously, we're not bad people. Believe me, we're not your run-of-the-mill group of villains and criminals, and we're not out here hurting anyone. Never would. Our wares—"

"Sect wares," Belle interrupted.

"—this *antiphantom technology*," he tried again, "is going to places and people that need it. And we're not a threat to you, obviously. I didn't get in this to fight any damn Effigies." He straightened his back. "But since we did just save one another's lives, let's all of us calm down and clear things up on the way, yeah? Derrek, Abril. You okay?"

"Yeah, Lucas." Derrek stood up. "This girl saved me. But she's bleeding bad."

"Ah, she can handle it. Don't you Effigies heal fast?" Lucas laughed.

"Yeah, but as you can see, despite that, I'm still bleeding." I doubled over. "Actually, I think I'm going to faint."

"Sorry 'bout that." Lucas picked up the tripod. "But I'm sure you'll be fine. You gals can take care of yourselves." He turned from us, waving Abril over before giving us a quick farewell salute. "Well, we'll be off now."

He took several steps before pausing and looking back. "Don't suppose you're just going to let us go, are you?"

"We have to go with you," Belle said. "Not only for medical attention. There's somewhere we're heading and we can't get through these mountains alone."

Lucas cocked his head to the side. "Sorry, but I don't believe I asked you to come along."

"I don't believe I was asking for your permission," Belle answered flatly.

Abril's hand looked like it was itching to fly to her gun.

"You think we're going to come down on you for selling Sect stuff, right?" I said, wincing from the pain of my wound. "We won't. Seriously, we don't care. We're just trying to get out of here. And you could use the extra muscle, right?" I said this as mine felt like it was about to burst apart like an overheated sausage.

Lucas, Derrek, and Abril exchanged glances. "Fine." Lucas threw his arms up in exasperation. "I'll take your word for it, though it's my arse on the line if you go back." He shook his tripod. "We're taking this with us until we get to the campsite. Actually, now that I think of it, our leader, Jin, is probably going to be interested to see you guys."

"We need to get him medical attention too," said Chae Rin, flicking her head at James. Lake had already gone to pick him up.

Lucas sighed. "Well, come along, then. We'll patch your friend up, too."

He walked ahead of us, Abril and Derrek picking up the equipment and bags and following. Exchanging wary glances, the four of us followed the traffickers down the rocky mountain path.

Out of the three of them, only Abril was from around the area, but she didn't speak much, merely grunted every once in a while, whenever her name came up. I suspected she was more comfortable with barking threats and pointing guns at people.

Lucas was the chatty one. And flirty. Didn't matter which girl. I caught him checking me out a couple of times, and I doubt it was to make sure my arm was any better after Derrek had tied it up with one of the bandages he'd found inside his bag. I couldn't imagine why a thirteen-year-old would be out in the mountains as part of a criminal gang, but I'd seen stranger things.

As they explained on our way down the mountain, they, like so many others, were an insular, nomadic group that sometimes picked up strays as they traveled—like Abril. She was an orphan and an escapee of a pretty vicious gang herself.

Usually these smaller groups were part of bigger organizations that transported illegal wares through these networks. But some groups, like this one, worked alone, setting up their own pathways, making their own money at the risk of their own lives. The three of them had been sent out by their leader, Jin, to scout a new route through the mountains, but their APDs crapped out at the wrong time. Dangerous life.

It got warmer as we descended, though the air around me was still just chilly enough to keep me alert. Then again, with my lack of sleep, I couldn't be sure how long that would last.

"We're almost at camp. Now, maybe you girls can tell me what you're doing here?" Lucas hoisted the tripod up as it started slipping down his hands. The field it generated was still going strong. I could only see a slight blue tinge of the waving particles spreading out from around us in a perfect sphere, blanketing the night. The leaves of the trees around us shimmered from its hue: a beautiful sight marred by the foreboding scuttles of phantoms off in the distance.

"Four Effigies lost in the Urbión Peaks. And I was just looking at your pictures at an awards show not too long ago. Get around fast, don't you? 'Round the world in eighty damn days." Lucas's laughter was as light and rosy as the natural flush of his face. "You each looked quite gorgeous in your photos, by the way."

"Thanks!" Lake said very genuinely, her hands gripped around both straps of the knapsack she carried on her back.

"Yeah, *thanks*," Chae Rin grunted while hoisting James higher up her back. Of course, with her strength, she could carry him just fine. But he was a considerably unappealing accessory, especially when he kept unconsciously murmuring delirious nothings in her ear.

"We're trying to get somewhere," answered Belle. "We have to get there as quickly as possible."

"You're on a schedule, huh? Well, aren't we all. I saw the video that terrorist sent out yesterday. Saul, right?"

My teeth naturally clenched at his name.

"He's given us all seven days to live or some'n like that." He shrugged his broad shoulders.

I kept my hand pressed around the bloodied bandage as we descended through the thick of mountain trees. One wrong step and I'd trip over the gray slabs of rock, so I watched every step carefully. "Well, that's why we need to hurry," I said. "We need transportation."

"To do what?" Lucas said. "You gonna stop Saul?"

"Yes." I pushed the word out with a little more force than necessary, probably in defiance to the way his eyebrow arched in amusement. "Of course we are. We're Effigies."

Abril led the pack carrying one of the Sect's long-range guns on her back. It got warmer as we descended, so she took off her hood and let her shaved, slender head cool off with the slight chill in the air. She was already a few paces ahead of us, but even from where I was, I could hear her stifling a derisive chuckle under her breath.

"You have something to say?" Chae Rin barked as she tightened her elbow grip around James's knees. Abril, predictably, didn't respond, though little Derrek nudged her warningly.

"Come on, you can't blame her if she's a bit skeptical, can ya?" Lucas answered for her with a shrug. "Not sure if you're aware of this or not, but since that video was broadcast around the world, everyone's been wondering where the hell you are and what you've been up to. Hell, last anyone seen of you, you were at some awards show like a bloody girl group."

I could feel the warm, wet blood from my bandage seep into my fingernails as I gripped it. "You're saying people are losing faith?" I asked quietly.

"People have *been* losing faith for a while out there. Well, for me it's not really a problem. We do what we do, never needed an Effigy to solve things for us. But you had Saul and you lost him and now he's out here killing politicians and doing as he pleases. Isn't he an Effigy too? Not hard to see why your fan club's getting a little smaller by the day."

The four of us fell silent. The stinging pain of my arm was enough to bear. This was salt in an already festering wound.

"I'm not," said Derrek ahead of us. "Losing faith. If it weren't for you, we'd be dead. *I'd* be dead." He turned around so I could see his smile. "If they're out here, it's for a good reason."

"I wonder about that." Lucas gave us a sidelong look.

"There's a lot going on," I said as Naomi's limp body crawled back into my memories. "But we're doing what we can under the circumstances."

"Do you even know what Saul's planning?"

Belle narrowed her eyes, her expression graver than usual. "That's what we need to figure out."

The note of finality in her voice made it very clear that the interrogation was over. Except for Lucas, who switched to chatting easily about the mountains, the rest of our party stayed quiet. We ventured down the mountain in silence until we could hear voices.

"They're just beyond those trees," Lucas said. "Wonder how they'll react."

The cacophony of voices grew louder, but it wasn't until we made it through the forest that I could see them: a small camp of people packing Sect equipment into small trucks and vans, or sitting on logs smoking food by a campfire. They were lined up all around the circumference of a beautiful lake, its obsidian surface rippling gently under the slightest caress of wind. A few feet away from us was a metal ball snuggled between the protruding roots of a tree—the same as the one we'd used in the Sahara. If I squinted, I could probably find more of them lined up around the perimeter. This is how they lived, these nomads, day to day, trying to escape the wrath of phantoms as they lived among them.

"Welcome to Black Lagoon, girls." Lucas whistled as we entered the camp space, drawing all eyes to us. It was inevitable; they recognized us right away. I saw one person reach for his gun, but Lucas waved a hand to stop him. "'S all right. They're not here about what we do. They're only looking for a ride into town." He gave me a friendly pat on the back. "They're Effigies in transit. Fell from the sky just as we were getting attacked by a particularly vicious group o' phantoms, didn't they?" He smirked. "Four falling stars."

"What do you mean attacked?" A large man who'd been standing with his back to us by the lake turned around, his long brown coat sweeping the rocky earth. His thin, pink lips almost disappeared inside his thick hickory beard, which had annexed the bottom half of his face. His eyes peeked out from behind some rather familiar flat black hair—familiar because it was the same as Derrek's. The boy jogged up to him, flinching a bit when the man patted his head. "Derrek, what happened?"

"Dad, our tech malfunctioned. We would've been dead if it weren't for those girls." He gestured toward the four of us as we carefully entered the camp. "That one with the bushy hair protected me."

That one with the bushy hair must have meant me. The man's eyes traced a line from my face to the blood dripping down my arm.

"She needs to be stitched. Abril, help patch her up."

Abril clearly didn't want to. But even though she shot me a withering look, she didn't protest. With a bitter scowl, she strode over to one of the vans nearby, gesturing me to follow with a curt wave of her hand. There was a first aid kit over by some coolers. Sitting on one of the coolers, she swept off her jacket, revealing her thin, bony form, and picked up the first aid kit, rummaging around until she found some disinfectant and a needle.

"You'll be gentle, right?" I smiled. She didn't. This was gonna hurt.

As Abril went to work, Chae Rin passed James's unconscious body to a couple of men, who set him down rather roughly by a log. I tried not to look at Abril's needle as it pierced my arm, stitching my flesh together with the exact amount of finesse I expected from someone who didn't even bother to flinch at my whimpers. Wincing, I watched the busy men and women instead as they packed loaded weapons and APDs into vans already weighed down with cargo.

Vans. "Sir," I called, jolting a bit once I felt the tip of the needle in my flesh.

"Jin," he corrected. "My name is Jin. And thank you for saving my son."

"You're welcome." I looked at the other girls, who nodded. "We really need help. We were actually flying overhead in a helicopter when we got attacked and crashed here."

"By *accident*," said Lucas as he stopped over by Abril and took a beer out of one of the coolers. "That shot wasn't mine, by the way. That was all her." Abril rolled her eyes.

"That's all right, but we need to get out of these mountains. We *also* need a car. Or a van?" Grunting from the pain of Abril's handiwork, I not-so-subtly hinted at one of the several that were camped around the lagoon, most of them old and rickety vintage models.

"They're going to fight to Saul, Dad," Derrek said. "You know, the terrorist?"

"Saul." As he stroked his bushy chin, I had no idea how his fingers didn't just get caught in the wilderness of his beard. Walking away from his son, he sat on a nearby log and stretched out his towering frame. "He's been moving in networks like these."

"Saul has? He's really been—*ow!*" My arm gave a violent twitch as I cried out. Abril didn't care.

Belle's eyes narrowed as she walked past me, approaching Jin. "How do you know this?"

"We move around." Jin's voice was a low grumble, the kind you listened to in the subways before it slid to the back of your subconscious as white noise. "You hear things. If you're paying attention."

"Oh, yeah?" said Chae Rin. "And what have you heard?"

"Trafficking rings being attacked." Jin propped his elbows up on his knees and leaned over, resting his chin on intertwined fingers. "Around Europe, mostly. Though I heard of some attacks in Northern Africa. Lots of high-powered weapons being stolen. And people."

"People?" Lake wiped the sweat from the mountain trek off her forehead. "Stolen people?"

"Or maybe they left on their own." Jin's haunting gaze was on her, bottomless and black as the lagoon. "Not too long ago, I heard of an empty camp in the forests of Romania. We'd dealt with the people there before—turf war. You can't escape that kind of conflict when stepping into another gang's territory. But if what they say is true, it's not something we'd have to worry about again. The camp was torched. No bodies. Just footsteps and ashes . . . and ghosts."

"Come on, you don't actually believe that, do you?" Lucas laughed, but he couldn't hide his shiver even from underneath his heavy mountain jacket.

"He appeared with the wind and left no trace when he was gone," Jin said. "That's what I heard."

"Yeah." I looked at the other girls, my expression grim. "We know someone like that."

"So what?" Chae Rin folded her arms. "In the middle of attacking trafficking gangs, he took a bit of time off to kill a Canadian politician? Well, he's been busy."

"The only camps I've heard of being attacked were those who move high-powered weapons, like ourselves. These weapons aren't just from the Sect, either. Some are military-grade, new models." Jin looked at me when he added, "And luckily for us, there are even some newer weapons that would be a danger to you Effigies."

My body tensed, but he shook his head. "Some of that is for sale and some of that is for our own protection. If we need to fight Saul, we're prepared. But knowing what he can do, I'm not sure even we'd win if he ever strode into our camp like he did all the others."

"Are you sure he's really doing all that?" Lake gripped the straps of her knapsack.

"I've been doing this long enough to know there's a grain of truth in every story out here." Jin lowered his arms, letting his hands dangle in the space between his thighs. "We do what we do and stay under the radar. But if even we can't stay out of Saul's way . . ." He looked at his son. "If you say you can stop him, then do it. I'll do what I can to help." He nodded to a group of men lugging silver cases to the vehicles. "Unload one of the smaller vans—we can spare one."

"Thanks, but even if we can get to where we need to go, we can still be tracked by the Sect," Chae Rin reminded us. "As long as they can track our cylithium."

"Wait." Lucas almost dropped the beer in his hand. "The Sect can track you?"

He wasn't the only one staring at us. It was a good thing Abril had just finished stitching me and bandaging up my throbbing arm, because I could sense our time here running out.

Jin was already on his feet. "You should have told us from the beginning. Everyone, finishing loading. We're heading farther west."

"Well," Lake started, twisting quickly to avoid the bodies rushing by her, "it's not like the Sect cares about illegal activity out here."

"They'll care about it if it has to do with their stolen shit, miss." Lucas nodded to Abril, who got up from the cooler and joined the rest, though not without giving us one last glare.

"Stolen . . ." The light bulb went off. "Inoculation!" Rubbing my sore arm, I stood from the ground. "Jin, you said you guys have weapons that could be used against us Effigies. What about an inoculation device?"

Chae Rin narrowed her eyes. "Are you crazy?"

"If our powers go dead, they may not be able to track us."

"You may be right," Belle said.

Jin ordered his people to unload some of the silver cases, and after some frenzied checking, they managed to find a case with five long black tubes lined up on the inside. They were a little smaller than the one I'd used against Saul. That one had been disguised as a pen, but it was too bulky; these were streamlined and sleek. It fit into my palm when I picked it up, and if I ignored the little silver pump at the top, I might have thought it was a pen shooting out ink instead of Effigy poison or whatever it was that jammed our powers.

"I didn't know they'd made more of these," Lake whispered, peering over my shoulder as I studied it against my palm. "Maybe because of Saul?"

"Yeah. Maybe." Chae Rin didn't sound convinced. "Put that back. Hey, we're taking this. Anyone got a problem?"

If they did, I doubted anyone wanted to fight her over it.

"You can take the van at the far end of the line." Stopping next to Derrek, Jin pointed toward the rusty-looking old one at the curvature of the restful lagoon. "You'll have to head north to get into town. Lucas will give you a map."

"Thanks," said Belle. "We'll take our friend and drop him off there."

Naomi had still given us a mission. Find the secret volume. Maybe find out the truth about Saul while we were at it. With the counter running down, we'd have to move quickly.

"Girls." Jin stopped us just as we began toward the van. "Saul's hand reaches far. Not even we here in the mountains are safe."

Nobody in Jin's group stopped moving and loading long enough to say so, but their uneasy gazes told me as much.

"We're all counting on you." He gripped the shoulders of his son. "*All* of us."

That was the burden Effigies couldn't escape. But we weren't running away. We nodded our silent promise before setting off.

Baldric hadn't done much to decorate. Who knew how long he'd even spent here.

"You don't have to do this," Natalya said as Baldric beat his hand against her long legs so she would move out of his way. His wheelchair arm brushed against her skinny jeans on his way to the table. "You don't have to run away. I can go back to Prague and try again."

"You said you had to leave the Little Room quickly because you were followed." His voice was low and raspy, his proper British accent mangled by barely concealed panic. "Followed by Sect."

"Not followed." Natalya picked up a book that had fallen off the bed. "I bumped into Aidan Rhys."

Rhys. Like the dream I'd had in Marrakesh. My heart sped up, but I knew the consequences if I couldn't calm myself here. Natalya's will was growing. Whatever I heard, I'd have to deal with it if I was going to make it out of this memory in one piece.

"Followed." He snatched the book out of her hands. "By the Sect."

Natalya shook her head incredulously. "Aidan is my friend—"

"He is no friend of yours. He's the son of Director Prince, and believe me, he's had loyalty beaten into him, the poor boy. It's in his bones now."

"He was there with a few others visiting."

"Visiting? Just happened to be there at the same time, did he? You fool." The cantankerous man looked like he could throw the book at her, but he dropped it into a suitcase. "He is Sect. Probably an Informer, sent by the Sect to watch you. Which means they're already onto you. They're already onto *me*." A shadow of fear passed over his face as he considered the implications. "If what I suspect about the Sect is true, then I need to leave. Now. And we must leave the volume where it is. It would be too dangerous to go back there now. You would only lead the Sect right to it."

25

NATALYA STOOD BY THE FOOT OF THE BED watching as the old man rushed his wheelchair back and forth in his cubicle-like bedroom carrying handfuls of clothes and shoving them into one of several suitcases. I'd slipped into this memory comparatively easily this time, maybe because Natalya was still reeling from her previous banishment. I knew it wouldn't last long. I could sense her will getting stronger. But Baldric had told only her the way to the secret volume. Whatever I needed to see here, I'd need to see it fast.

Actually, when Naomi had said his name, I hadn't been expecting the gray hair and small eyes sinking into a bed of wrinkled skin. A black bowler hat obscured most of his head, but his large white mustache covered his lips as it drooped down like a fishtail from his large, bulbous nose—a nose that twitched every time he sneezed from the dust in his room. Natalya was stealthily covering hers, and I didn't blame her. I couldn't feel much of anything in this memory, not even my own body. But I could see the particles of dust as they caught the light trickling past the curtains. That was the only distinguishing aspect of this bare-bones space. Besides a bed, a chair, and a table,

"The thirteenth volume." Natalya narrowed her eyes. "You said that it contained secrets not even the Sect knew. Secrets about us."

"Among many things. It doesn't matter. We keep the volume where it is. But to truly keep those secrets out of the Sect's hands, I need to disappear. Mr. Boones!"

A few moments later a man younger than he, though not by many years considering the gray tinge of his hair, appeared in the doorframe.

"Please proceed to bring the car around," Baldric ordered. "We're leaving within the hour."

"Very well, Mr. Haas." The man bowed forty-five degrees, his black butler suit crinkling on his way back up, and then left.

"You promised you'd tell me," Natalya said. "That's why I helped you in the first place."

"*Helped.*" Baldric snorted as he rested an artifact on his gray flannel trousers. It looked like a statue.

"I *tried*," Natalya said. "I tried because I wanted to know, and you promised you'd tell me."

"However you look at it, the Sect's secrets aren't for you to know."

"Not for me to know?" I could see Natalya's fingers curling into fists. "Baldric, by chance, do you know what my number is?"

Absently, Baldric grabbed another book off of his bed. "Number—"

"Fourteen. Fourteen years I've fought for the Sect. And I will probably die for the Sect. I've given everything to them. I let them turn me into a child soldier because they taught me to believe it was the right thing to do. And I tried to trust them. I tried. But then Naomi tells me that the Sect could be corrupt. And I— *Listen* to me."

Natalya stood in front of him, blocking his path. Baldric strained his neck to look up at her, but he matched the power of her stare nonetheless.

"I deserve to know. I deserve to know if everything I've been fighting for has been a lie. I deserve to know what I am. No matter the cost."

Baldric cast his gaze to the floor. Silence stretched between them until his mustache twitched again, his lips parting to speak. "And among the shadows," he said, "you will find them."

Natalya narrowed her eyes. ". . . Deoscali? What does this have to do with that foolish cult?"

"The cult may be foolish, as is anyone who worships the phantoms. However, there's more to Emilia Farlow's old teachings than you would expect. The secrets of the shadows . . . and the secrets of the beings who dwell among the shadows."

"What do you *mean*?"

Baldric rolled his wheelchair back away from her and over to the open door. With a swift movement, he reached for the knob as if to shut the door quickly, but unexpectedly, his hand rested there.

"Have you heard of *Allegory of the Cave*, my dear?"

Natalya nodded. "Plato. Of course."

"Yes, Plato." Baldric's fingers tightened around the doorknob. "The unlearned men and women chained in a cave, unable to turn their heads to see the puppeteers behind them. All they can see are the shadows dancing across the cave walls."

"The shadows are lies," said Natalya.

"But these shadows are all they've ever known. How can they know that the shadows have been cast by the puppeteers under the light of a fire burning behind them? How can they not help but think the shadows real?"

"I don't take well to riddles." Natalya scowled. "Tell me plainly."

"The Haas family has had to speak in tongues since the day the phantoms appeared." Baldric let go of the knob. "1865 . . . perhaps the skeletons of those days cannot stay buried forever. The sins of those little girls . . ."

He must have lost himself in the riddles of his thoughts, because he trailed off for a moment before snapping himself back to reality. "Don't go there again," Baldric told her. "And forget what I've told you. When the true battle begins, you will not find me."

Natalya had just begun to speak again when I felt her hands wrap around my mouth and pull me out of the memory with a violent tug. Baldric's room ripped away from my sight as I fell into a black void. I should have known she'd take her chance when I least expected it. No matter how hard I struggled, Natalya wasn't letting me go. We struggled and sank deeper into the ever-expanding darkness. Scenes stretched past my vision as I sank deeper into the depths. Natalya fighting. Natalya speaking to news reporters. Her duties to the Sect. The empty bottles of alcohol around her apartment living room.

And then I saw Belle. Little Belle. Couldn't have been more than thirteen, though still lanky for her age. Her legs were bent at odd angles as she crouched near a dirty toilet, barely conscious. She was losing too much blood. It was Natalya who'd found her, but it was all she could do to keep pressure on her bleeding wrists. Her phone was on the ground, the paramedic still trying to speak with her on the other end of the receiver. Natalya, whose tears did the speaking for her.

"It's my fault." Belle slurred her words. "I killed the phantoms but I couldn't save them. The agents tell me every night when I close my eyes. They say, what good are you? What good are you? I don't want to hear them anymore. . . . Please let me die. . . ."

"Let go of me!" I struggled against Natalya until finally my eyes snapped open and the bright white overwhelmed my sight.

"You okay, kid?" Chae Rin asked from the backseat of our van. I was back in the land of the living, my body jolting to life in the passenger seat. But I could only answer her by rubbing the sweat off my face with both hands.

The old, rusty van Jin had given us was a vintage sixties Volkswagen. It was a classic, but barely maintained. There was rust around the edges. The paint job—white for the top half, red for the bottom—was dull and peeling, and the flannel curtains covering the windows smelled like cat. I guess they couldn't have given us their best, but they could have spared us one that didn't give me the jitters with each sudden shake. At least the gas tank was full.

It was going to be a long trip, an almost twenty-hour drive—and we'd just started it. Naomi had wanted us to get to the museum fast before the Sect, but "fast" was a luxury when you were driving across countries in a crappy car. We'd already given ourselves the inoculations so the Sect couldn't track us. We'd also dropped James off at the first town out of the mountains. It'd actually taken him a while to come to, but after he had, despite still being a bit shaky, he'd scrounged up some money we'd need on the road and promised to let us know if he heard any rumblings from the Sect—or from Naomi. If she was even still alive. For Rhys's sake, I hoped she was.

"I think inoculating myself made me weaker in there." I held a hand against my head. "I guess it's good that I was still able to get there in the first place, but I don't know if it helped. I know we're supposed to get into a place in the museum called the Little Room, but I didn't get a sense of what we're supposed to do once we get there."

"It's okay." Lake had a whole bench to herself, lying down with her knapsack on the floor of the car beside her. "James told us Naomi already has a guy there waiting for us. He worked for Baldric. He'll help us get in after hours."

My phone buzzed with a text: **Where are you?**

I sucked in a breath. It was from Rhys.

"What is that?" Through my mirror, I could see Chae Rin gripping Lake's seat to get a look. "Is that your phone?"

Another text: Are you hurt? Are you okay? Mom is in bad shape.

Naomi. I bit my lip as another one came in succession: Tell me where you are and I'll come help you.

"Turn it off!" Chae Rin threw one of the dirty pillows that came with the van at my head. "We inoculated ourselves to make sure we *didn't* get tracked, stupid."

True. James had even given us a burner phone to use.

"She's right, Maia," Belle said. "They can track through Wi-Fi and GPS."

Belle. She looked rigid in the driver's seat, her knuckles white as she gripped the steering wheel.

My eyes lingered on her wrist until another pillow hurled by Chae Rin had me turning my cell phone off.

"Did he mention something specifically?" Lake asked, her sneakers pushing the old window curtains back and forth. "Baldric, I mean?"

"A lot of what he said didn't make much sense." I laid my head back against my seat. "He talked about shadows on the wall. . . ."

"Like in that desert hideout?"

I blinked. *Yes.* And that church in London. Shadows that looked like phantoms. But Pastor Charles had been adamant that they weren't really shadows at all.

There's more to Emilia Farlow's old teachings than you would expect, Baldric had said. *The secrets of the shadows . . . and the secrets of the beings who dwell among the shadows.*

"He also said something about the sins of *those little girls,*" I repeated, sitting up quickly. "Back in the nineteenth century."

"Wait!" Lake dove into her knapsack and pulled out the cigar box—the one we'd kept in our dorm back at the London facility.

Chae Rin's eyebrow arched as she peered down at the box from behind Lake's shoulder. "You had that in there?"

"Yep, brought it with me. I showed the other two in Toronto." She cracked the lid open. "It's just something you said, Maia. I've been try-ing to figure out what's up with this doll." Lake didn't want to touch it, so Chae Rin did. Dried mud still painted its face brown. Chae Rin's fingers pinned down its maid dress, and when she showed it to me I could see, once again, the torn-out eyes.

Chae Rin shook her head. "Freaky as hell," she said, tugging gently at its disheveled hair made of black yarn.

"Exactly." Lake shivered. "Gives you creepy little-girl vibes, doesn't it? Alice and Nick. Weren't they around back then?"

"Wait." I stuck out my hand. "Show me the letter."

Lake gave it to me, and I scanned it. I'd read it enough times this past month, but there was something nagging at me. I was missing something obvious. . . .

"There it is!" I tapped the paper. "Emilia!"

Chae Rin blinked. "Who?"

"'Two years, my dear friend, my sister,'" I read, "'since you passed away, and I find my thoughts are still attached to you, to Patricia, to Emilia, and yes, even to Abigail. Perhaps it is guilt.'"

"Emilia?" Lake repeated.

"In Natalya's memories, Baldric mentioned Emilia Farlow."

Belle quickly glanced down at the letter in my hands before direct-ing her attention back to the road. "Emilia Farlow. The original creator of the Deoscali cult."

"The cult that worships phantoms. But her teachings were dif-ferent." I remembered the serenity in Pastor Charles's eyes as he'd explained it. "That the phantoms aren't really phantoms at all—or that they're not bad? Or maybe they're bad under certain circumstances? I don't know." I pressed a hand against my forehead. "He said they control life and death. And fate."

"Well, it can't be a coincidence," Chae Rin said.

"I agree." Belle's eyes were stern as she gazed into the horizon. "The secret volume has to tell us more. We should hurry."

She pressed on the gas. Belle didn't say much as he drove down the highway, the antiphantom nets, much like those in Britain, lining the roads as we traveled. It was only in the seventh hour, when the other two had fallen asleep, when my own eyelids were starting to feel heavy, that I felt comfortable saying anything to her.

"Belle . . . when I was scrying, I saw another of Natalya's memories. Not just the one with Baldric."

Belle seemed to understand what I was insinuating, probably from the guilt written all over my face—the guilt of prying into someone else's darkest moments.

"You weren't concentrating hard enough, then. Remember that scrying is dangerous, Maia. You should be careful."

"Is that what you really want?" I mumbled under my breath before I caught myself. But strangely, knowing how horrid it felt to have another person claw at your mind to drag you into the dark with them, I didn't feel too guilty over that one.

Belle let an almost imperceptible sigh pass through her lips. "I had thought, originally, that Natalya went to Prague in order to leave me a message . . . because she knew I'd be there. Really, I had only wanted to go in the first place because a few weeks earlier, Natalya had begun talking about the museum so suddenly. How could I have known the real reason she was there?"

"I thought you guys would have shared everything."

Belle laughed sadly. "Natalya shared only what she wished to share.

She always kept me at arm's length. Maybe because she knew she could not live up to the esteem I held her in."

"Well, I certainly don't know what that feels like." I gave her a playful smile and sank deeper into my seat. If I squinted, I might have been able to see the beginnings of a smile playing on Belle's lips, but it was gone in the next second.

"Perhaps. I know you've had a difficult life as well, Maia. And I identify with that. I understand your pain—I truly do."

I couldn't respond right away. It was rare to hear her refer to us as *sharing* something—something other than a destiny and the weight of Natalya's life and death. The pain of severed connections. It was a pain that cut through the magic and mystery of our Effigy bond and tapped into something frail and human in us. A twisted connection. And though I wasn't quite the same girl who'd waited for her that day outside Lincoln Center in New York, it was still a connection I strangely craved.

"Still," Belle continued, "Natalya was the only family I had. And if it weren't for her, I would have died long ago."

I lowered my head but stayed silent.

"You must know as well as I do: When you have no family, when you have nothing, the longing you feel is more painful than whatever you could think of," she said. "You search for anything, anyone to fill the loneliness. Natalya may not have been perfect, but because of her, I wasn't alone anymore. She helped me. Guided me. Made me something. *Someone.* I owe her everything."

"That's all I wanted too," I whispered. Sleep was coming fast, but there was still so much to say. "I have my uncle, but it's not the same. Losing my dad and mom was awful enough. But losing my sister, June . . ."

I didn't even know how I survived those first few days with Uncle

Nathan. Or how he survived my shutting myself off, deadening myself to the world.

"But then this whole thing happened and you guys came along." I turned, my gaze passing over Chae Rin's and Lake's sleeping forms. "That's why . . ."

That was why, even though holding this secret in my heart was the biggest of betrayals, I knew I couldn't give it voice. And it wasn't just about my feelings for Rhys. It wasn't just that Naomi had begged me not to give up her son. What would happen when Belle turned her sword on Rhys? When she crossed a line she couldn't come back from? Everything would fall to pieces. *We* would fall to pieces. All four of us Effigies.

Holding that secret was for Belle. It was for all of us.

Maybe it was for me.

I pressed my head against the window. Finally giving in to the heaviness of my eyes, I let them flutter shut. "I don't want us to change. I don't want to lose anyone either. Belle, you won't hate me, will you?"

I didn't hear Belle's answer before I fell asleep.

26

PRAGUE'S ANTIPHANTOM TECHNOLOGY RAN
through pipelines underground that stretched beyond the limits of the
city. An expensive network, to be sure, so Belle told us; its construction
began after the split of Czechoslovakia, replacing older models as part
of a national campaign, its might signaling the beginning of a new
republic.

Keeping the systems underground may have had its strategic, sci-
entific purposes. But aesthetically, they kept the scape unmarred by
the very technology that every day served as a reminder of humanity's
captivity. Prague was untouched—the romantic labyrinth of narrow streets, the cobblestone painstakingly paved over centuries. The
Gothic spires and domes howling ancient secrets into the skies, the
curved cupolas of Baroque churches. The traditional red roofs of the
tall houses in the old square and the modern apartments we passed by
as we drove up the streets in the afternoon. There was no trace of the
electric field protecting the beauty of the city and the people inside of
it. No trace of the gilded bars protecting us from our own destruction.

Our first order of business was to scope out the National Museum, the grand Neo-Renaissance icon of the city. Rows of windows stretched across the building; there must have been dozens of them, maybe more, arched and straight-edged, decorating the brown stone. The deceptive simplicity of the museum's rectangular layout belied the detail etched into the surface, the careful brickwork, and the imposing design of the four quadrilateral tours stretching upward, the spear tips on each of their domes piercing the skies. The winged stone statues along the main tower rising above the frontage guarded the central dome and lantern, though they'd no doubt look even more majestic under the night sky.

I was sure our vintage van would stand out as we parked near the upper end of the square, but the patrons were none the wiser, walking around the planted flowers and trees, passing by the stone statue of a man mounted on a horse—the Wenceslas from the carol, Belle told us.

There couldn't be a secret section buried deep in a prominent museum without someone among the staff knowing about it. The museum's director had long worked with the Haas family to keep their secrets safe; even if he didn't and couldn't know them himself. According to James, he was willing to help out of loyalty to the Haas family. Naomi had already told him to expect our arrival, but we couldn't just walk inside the museum in the middle of the day right as it was beginning to open; there were too many people around, people who knew our names and faces. We'd have to wait until nightfall, when the museum was closed, but even then, to avoid the people milling about the square, the front door wasn't exactly an option. But we'd thought of that, too.

"Climb?" Lake exclaimed.

Belle nodded. "The museum's director will help disable the security to make things easier."

"*Climbing.*" Lake collapsed against her seat. "Never gets any easier, does it? I should have just stayed in the bloody dorms."

"Stop whining. That's nothing," Chae Rin said. "The scaffolding at the back of the building'll make it easy. Just a couple of stories."

"A couple of stories!" Lake whipped around as the sleek, black burner phone began to ring from the backseat. After flicking Lake's forehead with her finger, Chae Rin picked it up.

"James? Yeah, what's up?" Then, covering the receiver, she whispered to us: "It's an update on Naomi."

An update, finally. It had been around a day and a half since the attack, with no news. Each of us watched her expression carefully as she nodded and listened. I almost wished I hadn't. My chest ached as I saw her face fall. "Still in critical condition," she said.

"Damn," Lake whispered, drawing up a knee to rest her foot upon the bench.

"Wait, *what*?" Chae Rin's back popped into a straight line, her eyes wide as she listened. "What did you say?"

"What's going on?" I asked quickly, but she wouldn't tell us until she finally clicked the phone off.

"The Sect is investigating the hit on Naomi. But someone saw us escaping from her apartment. Someone saw *you*, Maia."

My body responded with a deep shiver, my fingers cold. "They saw me?"

"It's all over the news." Chae Rin shook her head. "The Sect is looking for us. Director Prince is on the warpath."

But I'd covered my face so well. How could they have spotted me? I swallowed, clasping my hands together. "So we have to get into the museum fast. Grab the volume. Find out the truth."

"And then what?" Chae Rin said. "We can't avoid the Sect forever."

"But we can't work with them either," I pressed. "You heard what my uncle said."

"This whole thing is turning into a damn mess." She flung the phone down onto the bench in frustration. "I mean, what is this? Are we fugitives now? Effigies wanted in connection for attempted murder of a Sect director's wife?"

"Oh my god, we're criminals," Lake cried. "My name is ruined. My fans will leave me! What will my parents think?"

"Calm down," Belle said quietly.

"*You* calm down, Ice Queen. This whole thing is going to hell!" Chae Rin snapped.

"What if they capture us?" Lake was breathing heavily. "I can't release a single from prison; I don't have the connections!"

"I *said* calm down." Belle didn't turn, but surely Chae Rin could see her features turn to stone through the rearview mirror. "We also have to consider that the Sect may have been responsible for the attack in the first place. Someone tried to kill a director's wife and an Effigy just happened to be at the scene?" Belle tapped her fingernails against the wheel as she thought. "Under normal circumstances, the Sect would have done everything they could to control the narrative. They would have gotten to that witness first and made sure she never spoke to the press. Allowing this to reach the airwaves could just be an attempt to make us panic and draw us out. We have to stay *calm*."

Ironically, *Belle* would have been the one to kill a director's wife if it weren't for us holding her back. Nevertheless, she was right. Keeping our heads on straight was a tall order, but we did our best as Belle drove us somewhere we could park until nightfall. It was a place Natalya had always told her about: less than a half hour away from the square on the northwest side of the city was a natural reserve they called Wild Šárka, named so after a legend Natalya had once cherished. We parked off the curb of Evropská Street. I stared at the thick of trees, holding the old window curtains open a sliver with a gentle brush of my finger.

Šárka was a fierce warrior maiden who met her tragic end off the cliffs of these very reserves, according to the myth. I could see why Natalya would hold a certain fascination for the tale, but I couldn't drum up the same kind of enthusiasm. There was nothing beautiful about tragedy. Not for someone like me, who'd already lost everything once, who was about to have everything taken away again. I'd tried to stay calm like Belle had said, but she wasn't the one whose name was being mentioned in connection to the possible murder of a prominent official.

Rhys's mother. I could only imagine what he'd be thinking watching the news. Or Uncle Nathan. Or my classmates and teachers back in New York. Chae Rin was right. Everything was going to hell. We were betting everything on some book whose contents were a mystery to everyone except a jittery old man who'd long fallen off the grid. And in the meantime, Saul's clock ticked ever still.

Hours passed inside the van until I couldn't take it anymore. I had to get out of the car. It'd been several hours since I'd even stood on my own two feet. I needed to stretch my legs and breathe in fresh air that didn't carry with it the hint of stale curtain. And maybe go to the bathroom.

"No way," Chae Rin said. "It's dark now; we should be heading back to the museum."

"Please, just for one second! I'll be in the trees, out of sight!"

"Ew." Lake scrunched up her nose, but I was already tying my hair and wrapping it up in one of Lake's scarfs she'd kept in her knapsack.

"Nobody will see me out here, I promise."

Lake peered through the windows on either side of her, making sure the coast was clear before passing me a pair of shades.

"Ten minutes," Belle ordered.

I answered with a quick nod and hopped out of the car. My legs felt like noodles the second my feet touched the ground. I wobbled into the trees, finding my footing only as I soaked in the solace of nature under the cloak of the ever-encroaching dark. The night weaved through the sturdy trees, concealing secrets of ancient lives told only through fairy tales. Tales of love and suicide, the bloodied bodies of warriors left in their wake. It was more June's thing than mine—how she would have loved to come here, to see the world the way I'd gotten to as I breezed here and there. June had always planned to take a year off after high school to travel. The moonlight dancing across the leaves was just another reminder that I was living her life.

I walked a little bit deeper into the trees, stepping over the roots and mushrooms sprouting out of the bark of fallen logs. I inhaled in the clean air, hoping the calming breath would give me a moment's peace.

But the hand around my wrist trapped the breath in my lungs as it yanked me behind another tree.

My first instinct was to summon my magic to fight, but the magic was dead, at least temporarily—by my own hand. I prepared for a struggle nonetheless, whipping around, squeezing my hands into fists, but my strength left the moment I looked up and saw his face.

Rhys.

Maybe my eyes were tricking me, but he'd pulled me close enough that I could see the outline of his defined jaw, his soft, focused eyes. His black hair fluttered, ruffled, across his forehead, though the majority of it was hidden underneath a baseball cap.

My chest swelled, and for that moment I looked up at him, my mind was blank. That was until I remembered Naomi, the blood oozing out from the bullet holes in her battered body.

My name in connection to the attack.

He wasn't here on duty. In his waist-long corduroy jacket and jeans, I couldn't see a weapon, though I knew he was trained enough that he didn't need to carry one to do harm. I was ready again, ready to fight, but when Rhys grabbed my shoulders it was only to shift me this way and that. He was checking for wounds.

"Are you okay?" he asked.

"How did you find me?" was all I could say.

"Are you *okay*?"

"I didn't hurt your mother."

He straightened his back almost immediately and took off his cap, his lips flattening as he tensed at the mere mention of her.

"I didn't hurt your mother, so . . ." I exhaled, steeling myself. "Are you here to turn me in?"

Rhys tossed his cap against the protruding roots, and then his hands were on my shoulders again. But it was a gentle grip. His hands were soft as he pushed me back against the tree and kissed me. Short, sweet. So quickly, I could barely register the moistness of his lips as they separated from mine. I was still in shock when he answered.

"No," he said simply. "No, I'm not."

He let me go, picking his cap up again before turning his back. If he was confident I wouldn't take the opportunity to run away, he was right to be. My legs were practically petrified against the solid earth. I wasn't going anywhere.

"When I heard about my mom, I convinced my brother to lend me a jet to go see her, but I flew to Prague instead," he said. "Rosa told me you'd be coming here. And not long ago, James told me what car to find you in. That crappily painted Volkswagen, right? You girls sure travel in style." He turned and smiled.

Rosa and James. Well, I shouldn't have been surprised. It was his mother. Of course they'd know him. Trust him. Why wouldn't they? They didn't know what I knew.

Rhys must have noticed my features crease with concern. "You're scared." He paused. "You're scared that I'm here."

"Yeah."

"I told you I'm not going to turn you in."

"The Sect is looking for me. Your dad. They think what happened to your mom is our fault."

"Yes, they do. But they can't track you. And I'm not going to turn you in."

I looked up at him. "But you're loyal to the Sect."

"I'm not going to turn you in." Rhys's voice was hushed, but I could hear the desperation in his words—the desperation to be heard. "I'd never hurt you."

"But you killed Natalya."

Silence fell. The kind of silence that held the secrets of a thousand years. The symphony of cicadas receded into the recesses of my consciousness, insignificant. I thought Rhys's eyes would grow wide, but they remained steady. I thought he'd stumble back or turn to escape the judgment barely concealed in my stare. But he remained still.

"Even so," he said, "I'd never hurt you."

I didn't have the energy for any of the emotions I'd thought would stir in me once this moment came. I was tired. I kept my back against the rough bark as I shook my head and searched him. "Why did you do it?"

Rhys fitted his cap back onto his head and looked up at the sky, his broad shoulders limp. "Does Belle know?"

"I haven't told her."

"She's going to kill me."

"That's why I haven't told her."

He shifted a little, surprised. "You're protecting me from her."

"I'm protecting *both of you* from her. But maybe I should have told her." The anger rose in my chest, corroding me from the inside as the words formed on my tongue. "Do you know how awful it's been, not saying anything to anyone? How much this hurts me?"

Rhys lowered his head. "I'm sorry. You didn't deserve that . . . and I don't deserve your protection."

"You *don't!*" I agreed, stepping closer, my hands shaking at my sides. "Why did you do it? What happened?"

Rhys was quiet for too long before finally letting a sigh escape his lips. "I got my orders through an encrypted line. Scrambled voice, so I didn't know who the order had come from. But these kinds of orders come from very high up. They're orders from the Council. They said Natalya was becoming a danger to the Sect and that I had to watch her."

"A danger to the Sect . . ."

"Someone like Natalya could do a lot of damage if she ever went rogue. She could easily kill a lot of people. It's happened before. In the fifties, Mary Lou Russell went from training at a Sect facility to trying to start a genocide in an effort to 'purify her race.' And she was taken out the same way. These kinds of orders don't come every day and they don't come lightly. But when you get them . . ."

"Why did they ask you?"

"Because we were friends." Rhys choked up at the word and swallowed quickly, keeping his face turned from me. "I didn't want to. I ignored the order for as long as I could, but they called again, telling me lives were at stake, reminding me what happened to traitors. The Sect would never kill their greatest asset if they didn't have a good reason. I had to do it. No one else would have been able to get close enough to manage it. Natalya was a powerful warrior. One of the greatest Effigies to ever live. How else do you stop her?"

"By betraying her? Rhys . . ."

Tears filled our eyes at the same time, though only his fell. Neither of us could speak.

"Are you *our* Informer?" I asked quietly.

He shook his head. "I'm here because I genuinely want to help. This is not for the Sect. For once, it's not. It's for me. My life isn't . . . just another chip for them to play. That's what I decided, but . . ."

"If that's the case, then you need to know what's happening in the Sect," I said. "And what Natalya died for. Why they asked you to kill her." I paused, watching his eyebrows furrow slowly in confusion. "You really don't know, do you?"

He couldn't hide it; the horror of the unknown was stripped bare and staring me in the face. "What's happening?"

I told him what I could. About the mysterious Project X19, the second phase of which had transformed his friends into monsters. The mind control. The unidentified assailants who'd attacked Naomi just as she'd told us about the book she and Baldric had sent Natalya to get all those months ago.

"Wait," he interrupted me. "*Mom?* Mom's a member of the Council?"

He looked genuinely shocked. I searched his face. "You didn't know?"

"No . . ." He fell silent for a moment, staring into the distance as he considered it. "The identity of all the Council members is a secret to all outside the Council, though I'm sure Dad would have known about Mom even if Brendan and I didn't. I can't imagine she wouldn't tell him—or that he wouldn't notice."

"Naomi's the one who sent us here. We are all just trying to figure out who Saul is," I said. "Who the phantoms are. Who we are. Where we come from. If we do, we can get ahead of Saul. Find a way to stop him. Obviously, there's someone who doesn't want that. That's why your mother was shot. That's why you were told to kill Natalya."

Rhys took a few steps away from me, his feet coming to a rest against an arched root that blocked his path.

"I mean, you said those orders come from high up. Was it someone else in the Council? Or maybe one of the directors? Even your—"

I caught myself, but Rhys had already crouched down to the ground.

"Sorry," I said quickly. "I didn't mean to suggest—"

"But you're right," Rhys said. "Dad could be involved. How can I know for sure he wouldn't do something like that to his own family? He's not above it, what with the way he fed me to that place."

"The Greenland facility . . ."

Rhys sucked in a haggard breath, his body shaking as he did. "Brendan was right. It used to be prestigious. But then things started getting out of control. Fisk-Hoffman died and the facility was left in the hands of his sadistic son. Training got more brutal. People didn't even start to notice until they could see the effects on its graduates. Andrew Brighton, for one."

The Surgeon. The Sect agent who'd turned his well-honed interrogation skills into a method of serial killing. *That's* what Brendan meant by Fisk-Hoffman's "rough patch." Understatement of the century.

"Vasily's mom, too," I said, remembering Vasily's face screwed up in pain as Brendan forced him to look at the picture of his dead mother.

Rhys nodded. "They weren't from the same cohort, so they wouldn't have known each other. But they graduated from the same cruel system. Brighton's murders finally brought what was happening at the facility to the Sect's attention, and the Council took it over. It was supposed to be a new leaf. That's what they told everyone, anyway. My cohort was supposed to be different, but . . ." He exhaled, shaking his head. "It wasn't. They taught us not to think. To be cruel. To do what was necessary."

I wondered what memories Rhys saw when he closed his eyes. But he didn't have to tell me for me to understand. Vasily, Jessie, himself. Their deeds spoke volumes. I knew all too well the legacies of that place.

"After the fire, the few of us who survived signed nondisclosure agreements to never speak about what had happened, and by then I was too broken to disobey anymore. Brendan doesn't even know. Dad never let on one way or another, but maybe he did. Maybe Mom knew all along too what that place did to me."

"I don't know," I said quickly, because Rhys looked shattered at the thought of his mother hurting him. "Your mom said there are members in the Council helping Saul. She only found out about that recently. They were probably the ones who knew. What if they kept it open on purpose? And grabbing some of those kids was part of the plan? What if they started the fire?"

I knew I was getting ahead of myself, but I was still surprised to see Rhys react so strongly. His body went rigid at the mere suggestion.

"Yeah," he said, his voice hollow. "Look, I don't know. If that's true, I don't know if they would have chosen Jessie and the rest for their project. I don't know if Dad was in on it. The only thing I know is that Dad wanted me broken and he got his wish. He said it was the way it should be. Loyalty. It's in our family's blood. Mom believed that too. We lived for the Sect. The facility burned it into me and my dad made sure I didn't forget."

A trigger can't pull itself. That's what Naomi had told me. Neither parent had ended the suffering their philosophies and actions had caused their son.

"But now," Rhys said, standing up, "I'm here for you. To help you."

That was when I remembered I was talking to Natalya's murderer. A chill seeped into my voice. "The four of us are fine. We don't need your help."

"You do," Rhys said. "Rosa didn't tell anyone but me."

"Tell you what?"

Rhys held up his hand. "My mother's wedding ring. She had a hunch, so she took it off and examined it. It was bugged."

Bugged. The heat rushed from my head as I considered the consequences. "You mean . . . someone was listening to our conversation?" When Rhys nodded, I inhaled sharply and turned. "So they already know we're here. I have to hurry."

It'd been way past ten minutes, and I'd gone far deeper into the trees than I'd meant to. The other girls were probably searching for me. And if Rhys could find me, we didn't have any more time to spare.

"I'm coming with you."

He reached for me, but I jerked my hand away before he could touch it. "No. I told you we don't need you."

"I can help. Let me prove myself to you."

"Forget it." I was determined to ignore the way his wounded expression shook me. I kept my hands curled into fists and pressed against my side, to keep them still. "I appreciate you telling me about what happened. But it doesn't change the fact that you killed Natalya. No matter how I . . ." I caught myself, the words catching in my throat despite my efforts to submerge my ache beneath a slab of ice. "Regardless of anything, you deserve to be in jail."

"No. I deserve to die." He said it simply as if talking about the weather. "But I still want to help you. When I know you're safe and it's all over, I'll turn myself in. I already decided that a long time ago."

I fought to keep my trembling lips steady. "If they tell you to kill me, will you do it?"

"I already told you I wouldn't hurt you."

"What makes me so special? Why do you care?"

For the first time, his lips cracked into a sad smile, hesitant and unsure. "I'm in love with you," he told me. "Maybe because you make me feel like the man I should have been."

My body felt numb. I didn't know how to respond.

He stood before me, broken, and it was then I realized that he'd been in pieces long before I'd even met him. He'd just been so very good at hiding it. And I couldn't forgive him. But I couldn't ignore the soft longing in my heart. I couldn't ignore his pleading eyes or the tears they must have shed during each terrible night in the Devil's Hole.

He deserved to be in jail. I didn't want him near me and I couldn't stand him being apart from me. It was an infuriating contradiction. My chest throbbed from the pain of it. So I compromised instead.

"Here's the number of our burner phone." I gave him the digits. He only needed to hear it once before nodding to confirm he'd memorized it. "You can be our lookout. Let us know if trouble's coming."

"You mean the Sect," he said.

He moved toward me, and I stepped back quickly, turning away. "I'm trusting you," I said, my back to him. "Don't betray me like you did Natalya."

And without waiting for a response, I left him speechless among the trees.

27

AT NIGHT, THE STREET LAMPS ILLUMINATED
the narrow cobbled streets and tall buildings in a romantic golden hue.
The National Museum stood proud like a castle of the ancient world of
Eastern Europe, its dome lit up white, its brick splashed red and gold
from the tall lamps in the front court. We parked far enough away to
not draw attention and began our trek around the back of the building.
After hopping the fence, we scuttled past the moss-covered brick to
the metal scaffolding stretching up the building.

"Lake, you have the cigar box in there, right?" I pointed at the
knapsack she carried on her back.

She nodded. "Although it's going to weigh me down while I climb.
You all should thank me for sacrificing myself."

"Oh, stop whining," said Chae Rin as Lake pouted.

"All right." After silently staring up at the scaffold, Belle cracked
her neck side to side. "Let's go."

The director of the museum confirmed through James that he'd
disabled the security and left a window open, but only for the time
being. We wouldn't have too much time. Grabbing the metal bars, I

began hoisting myself up, finding footing wherever there were metal surfaces to stand on. Chae Rin was the best at this, unsurprisingly, her circus-trained equilibrium and deftness helping her zip and flip up the scaffold. It was all I could do to keep pace.

Once we squeezed ourselves deeper into the labyrinth of metal poles, we came to a section of the scaffold blocked off by a wall of netting. The net, at least, made it harder for us to be seen, though I doubted at this point that anyone could even see us. Maybe Rhys was somewhere below, out of sight, watching for trouble. Looking out for us like I'd asked him to.

It got colder the higher we climbed, but I shook it off with a shiver. Looking over the edge of the metal poles, we could see the entirety of Wenceslas Square, the streets lit up gold, the white blinding lights of cars scuttling up and down their length. It was a breathtaking sight. But soon we found the old square window the museum's director had told us about. Third one on the west end. Belle pounded it open with a fist, and it swung with a labored creak. One by one, the four of us dropped into a room of paintings—paintings of clowns.

"Why *clowns*?" Lake cringed as she scanned the oil and colors etching out, in an exaggerated, avant-garde style, a rather pessimistic portrayal of their work endlessly entertaining insatiable crowds of ravenous spectators. Creepy. *Depressing.*

"Brings back memories," Chae Rin said with a wistful sigh. "Anyway, we've got to get down to the first floor. Let's go."

Shadows of this place remained in my memories from the time I'd watched Natalya in my dreams. Down the flight of stairs, slipping through the golden arched doorways, I scanned the black marble walls and columns, white streaks scribbling beautiful patterns across their length. It was because of Natalya's memories that I knew right away where I needed to go—the shadowed archway in the forgotten corner of the building still, maybe always, blocked off by yellow tape. We rushed through the long, dark hallway until we reached the security pad at the end of the path.

"Wait," Lake said, "the code—"

"I know it." Indeed, I did. My fingers were quick, pressing in each key. The metal door next to it shuddered and slid open with a groan.

The Little Room, Baldric had called it. Well, it was certainly higher than it was wide. I remembered these bookshelves spanning the two semicircular stories. Tomes of texts. Unhung portraits on the floor, propped up against the walls. We were in. This was as far as the director could help us. Now I'd have to rely on Natalya. If she was up for it.

We spread out. It was dark. I had to search around for the light switches, but when I found them, strange lamps ahead snapped on. Lamps of different shapes, dangling from thin wires, cast an orange, red, and yellow wash over the marble floor, like glowing pendants.

"Who the hell designed this place?" Chae Rin shielded her eyes from one pendant directly above her.

"Maia, what do we do?" Lake asked.

She weaved between two globes that have been knocked off their stands and stopped at a display blocked off by chains. The fossilized phantom. Yes, I remembered this all too well. Natalya had been mesmerized by this too, this phantom crystallized—no, "petrified" was the official term, though it certainly glittered like crystal. The phantom was like a dragon about to take flight, its wings spread out, its jaw gaping as if prepared to swallow any of us whole.

"This is all well and good," Lake said, "but how do we find the volume? There're two stories of wall-to-wall books here."

Belle was staring up at the portrait hanging above the fireplace at the west end of the room. *Bartholomäus Blackwell II: 1849–1910.* Blackwell's ancestor. He had the same wild, long, dark curls and the same ridiculous, elaborate sense of fashion. The moment I saw him, something stirred inside me. Natalya.

I pressed a hand against my forehead. There was something there. Something I was missing.

"You okay?" Chae Rin walked up to me and shook my shoulder.

I'd seen the memory through Natalya's eyes. It wasn't the right way of scrying. It left you vulnerable to someone else's emotions and feelings . . . but at the same time, the chaotic nature of intertwining your mind too tightly with someone else's made the process unwieldy, untrustworthy. I may have felt emotions that were wrong, or not felt emotions I should have. The thoughts I'd heard could have been heard incorrectly. I had to think back to it. Back to that dream.

I closed my eyes. It was months ago, so I knew I wouldn't be able to remember it completely, but shadows of old feelings crept back inside me. Natalya's fear and urgency as she walked through the room to leave her message for Belle. She'd walked over to the shelves on the first floor to get to the Castor Volumes, the first ever printed, preserved in this secret space. But there were only twelve of them, each bound in velvet. What was I missing? And why did my eyes keep slipping back to the portrait?

Natalya had stared at the portrait too for a moment before moving on.

It doesn't matter.

That's what she'd thought to herself. Natalya was being chased. She'd only had a moment's worth of time, but the portrait had still managed to capture her attention.

It doesn't matter. . . . It doesn't matter now. . . . It doesn't matter anymore.

But it did matter. Something in me screamed it.

"Help me take this down," I told Belle.

Belle had to raise me above her head so I could reach the portrait and bring it back down. The black letters written in cursive on the wall behind it were so tiny I had to squint to read them. But I recognized the Latin immediately.

"*Et in tenebris invenies*," I finished slowly. "And among the shadows, you will find them."

"What does that mean?" asked Lake as I hopped down from Belle's shoulders.

"Among the shadows." I remembered the paintings of phantoms all along Pastor Charles's church: shadows dancing across the walls, bathing only in the light of the stained glass windows. "The shadows are phantoms."

I pivoted on my feet, my focus on the petrified phantom at the center of the room. "I think this is it."

I joined Lake by the phantom. She eyed me as I hopped over the chains and began sweeping my hands across the hard crystal. "What exactly are you looking for?" she asked.

I didn't know. All I knew was that the thirteenth volume wasn't here. No way would Baldric just place it, handily available, among the other books. There was something I was missing.

"Wait." I stepped onto the platform itself and lifted myself up on my tiptoes. "What's that? There something in its mouth?"

Carefully, I climbed up its bent knees, jutting out just far enough to make a pretty good foothold. As I came almost eye to eye with the phantom, I remembered, looking into their hollow, black depths behind the sheen of crystal, that this thing was not a "fossil" at all. It was *alive*. Its flesh and exoskeleton may have transformed into a different substance, but like Pete and Mellie had demonstrated in the

London facility, with the right material it could be called back to life. It was an unsettling thought. More unsettling when I stuck my hand up its exposed throat, my arm avoiding its long teeth, sharper now inside the crystal coating.

My hunch was right. Deep inside its mouth, jammed neatly into the roof of its mouth, was a key. I grimaced, trying to yank it out without impaling my arm on its jaw.

"Yes," I whispered when it finally came loose, but the deep rumbling behind the bookcase caught me by surprise. Startled, I turned too quickly, slipping off the phantom's knee and falling off the platform.

"What's going on?" Lake said, helping me up from the other side of the chains. "Is the bookcase *moving*?"

Chae Rin scoffed. "You've got to be kidding me," she said, shaking her head in disbelief as an invisible force dragged the shelf out at an angle, revealing a black space behind it.

There was nowhere else to go but into the passageway. It had opened only a sliver, so we had to slide ourselves through one by one. The girls followed me down a set of creaking stairs, deeper and deeper, and then into a dimly lit corridor of red brick until we came to a locked iron door. The key fit perfectly. The lock clicked, and after swinging the door open, we entered a vast space that could have been another exhibition area anywhere else in the museum.

It was a little dusty in here, but otherwise, the area was well kept. Perhaps Baldric visited from time to time during his tenure as the secret volume keeper. The elaborate white border stretching across the four corners of the ceiling had beautiful patterns in the plaster: rose vines twisting and sprouting blooms across the wide strips. On each side of this secret area were three tall suits of armor carrying real spears, standing guard in their rows. I walked across the marble floor, marveling at the two crystallized phantoms on display at the front of the room with only a velvet rope separating them from the rest of the hall. Dragons, like the one upstairs, though these were even bigger, their outstretched wings almost touching the ceiling. And in the middle of the wall between them hung a beautiful painting—a portrait, rather—of a plump, rosy-cheeked girl in a lavender Victorian dress, her charcoal hair swept up at the top of her head. At the bottom of the frame read a dedication:

For Patricia Haas: 1848–1865.

"Patricia Haas," I whispered as the other girls spread to different corners of the hall. Naomi had said that Baldric's family had kept the secret volume safe through generations. But the girl's first name caught my attention also. "Emilia, Abigail, and Patricia . . ." The three girls Alice had mentioned in her letter to Marian.

"Guys, come look at this!" Lake said excitedly, disappearing behind one of the two open doors. We followed her inside.

"Okay, I think we can agree this place is hella weird," Chae Rin said as Lake motioned to the three stone statues in the center of the room.

I'd seen them before. These women, their bodies carved out of white stone, naked but for their hair wrapped around them like ancient robes. They were exact replicas of the statues stationed around Blackwell's mansion. And like Blackwell's statues, each held a pearl in her hands, their bodies only slightly different in position. The mysterious "knowing" in the hollow grooves meant to represent their eyes was the same for each of them. As if they saw us. As if they'd known we would be coming here.

It was like the statues were just another exhibit. Well, secret room or not, we were still in a museum. The three statues faced each other in a triangle on top of a wide, circular platform at the center of the room. And next to the platform was another golden stand with a plaque telling its visitors the name of this exhibit. This time it was only one word: FĀTUM.

"'*Fātum*'... does that mean 'fate'?" I asked.

Belle walked up to the velvet rope surrounding the platform. "Fate. Destiny. Sometimes 'death.' Though other times it refers to the words uttered by gods. Their words . . . their will . . ." Belle went silent, but her eyes never left the statues. "What are these? Why are they here? Who are you three supposed to be . . . ?"

"We tried to get into the other room, but it was locked," said Chae Rin. "I have no idea what these statues are. Or that." She pointed at the digital clock screwed into the front of the room behind the statues: 20:00. Twenty-four-hour time. But that couldn't have been right; we'd left after midnight.

Belle stepped over the velvet rope and knelt down next to the platform. "These depressions . . ." At the foot of each statue was a straight, sunken path that stopped just at the edge of the platform. "It's leading the statues away from one another."

After a long moment of considering the pathways, she hopped onto the platform and tried to push one of the statues.

"This is so weird." Lake shook her head and snapped her photos.

Chae Rin walked up to the rope. "What are you doing?"

Belle gave her best effort, but they didn't budge. They were a little taller than us and made of marble. Heavy. Too heavy to move yet. "It's no use," she said, righting herself. "The inoculation is wearing off, but I'm still not strong enough to move these on my own. Chae Rin, what about you? You could use your power to move the stone."

It was true that it had been a while since we'd inoculated ourselves. I could start to feel the beginnings of magic struggling awake deep within my body. It must have been the same for Chae Rin, who sighed.

"I don't know what you think is going to happen, but all right. Why not?" She lifted her hands, grimacing as she struggled to channel the power through her body. Gradually, one statue began to move, dragging along the depressed path in the stone platform with a terrible screech. Our powers were coming back, but that also meant we had to finish up here and get out fast. It was hard to tell how long we had until the Sect could track us again, and with Naomi's ring bugged during our conversation with her in Madrid, we couldn't be sure who was already on our tail.

Still, Belle was serious about this, so Chae Rin pushed herself despite the strain it caused her. She heaved each statue until they'd reached the edge of the platform. The moment the third statue clicked into place, a buzz rang out softly from outside our room, but it was the clock that took my attention.

"It's counting down," I said. Nineteen minutes and fifty-nine seconds, fifty-eight seconds . . .

It wasn't a clock at all, but a timer.

"Okay, counting down to what, exactly?" Lake looked from one statue to the other. "Should we be worried?"

"What was that sound back there?" Chae Rin nodded toward the door, breathing heavily as she recovered. "Did anybody else hear that?"

Jumping off the platform and stepping over the rope, I ran back out of the room. Just as I thought—the second door. Directly across the hall, it was open just wide enough for a soft light to slide through the crack. Whatever we'd done to the statues must have triggered the door. But if the countdown was any indication, we wouldn't have much time to inspect it. Calling the girls over, I strode across the floor and entered the room.

I felt the change in the air immediately. The way gravity suddenly weighed my body down the moment I crossed the threshold. Each step felt alien atop the stone floor tiles. The air was rich with an unspeakable energy. Familiar. I'd felt this before.

"What is this?" Shutting the door behind her, Lake drew her hand to her chest. "I feel really . . ."

"Calm." Closing her eyes, Belle raised her chin and soaked it in. "I feel calm."

"Belle, it's the same as the chamber at that church," I told her.

Pastor Charles's cellar. A place of pure calm.

This room was a cellar too, the walls, the floors, the ceilings, all stone. But when I closed my eyes and listened to the quiet, when I let the thoughts slip out of me, I could almost feel something slithering by my arms, my legs—a whisper of a touch. It'd happened in the church, but I couldn't ignore it this time. No, it wouldn't *let me* ignore it. Whatever they were, the air was dense with them, and I was connected to them. Or maybe we were connected to the same force, the same energy flowing through us, sparking the magic in me that began swelling up from the depths of my soul. I lifted my hand, considering the fingers that curled inward, twitching whenever one of them glided by. It didn't take any effort: a little flame burst from my fingertips.

"Woah, okay." Lake shivered. "Something just grazed my cheek. This room isn't haunted, is it?"

"Haunted" was one word for it. The cellar was cylithium-rich, but it was more potent than what I'd felt in Pastor Charles's cellar. Still, it couldn't have just been the cylithium I felt.

Spirits? Pastor Charles's ramblings suddenly didn't seem so unreasonable.

"There's something there." Chae Rin walked up to one of the tiles at the very center of the room. A longer slab, it stood out from the rest, with its larger concrete frame, its clearly defined edges, and the handle protruding from the surface. "Looks like a trapdoor."

But the etchings made it look more like a grave—not only words but also a symbol was carved deep into the gray concrete. I could only make out the drawing's pointed talons, but I could tell it was a drawing of a beast. Of a phantom.

"What does it say?" I asked, but as we drew closer to it, we could read for ourselves the words written above the symbol.

Belle bent down by the door, brushing off the dust that had settled on the surface. "'Summon calm,'" she read.

Calm. Castor had mentioned it too, in his first volume, that there were places like this. The door looked heavy, but the four of us were brimming with power here in this mysterious room. Gripping the handle, Belle lifted the door up with ease.

The secret volume. Placed only two feet beneath the door in a darkened pit, it sat atop another solid surface. There was nothing ceremonial about its burial, nothing to signal its importance. It looked the same as any of the other Castor Volumes—same binding, same silver engravings. I bent down and picked it up, running my hand along the Roman numeral on the cover. XIII.

And something else.

"'And among the shadows, you will find them,'" I read. It was in English, written in small plain letters toward the bottom of the cover, just below another strange symbol—the flame I saw in Saul's bunker, the symbol Natalya drew.

"For only in calm," Belle said, "can you hear them speak."

She was reading too, but not the volume. This time, the words were etched upon the floor on the very space the book had rested. And below the single line lay a symbol of three swirls, three energies, joining together to make the whole.

Only in calm. I felt another sudden chill whisper along my skin. Like eels in a tank, they fluttered past us, saying nothing, saying everything. Were they really spirits? The sensation was overwhelming, making every cell flare to life inside of me. Belle, Lake, Chae Rin, and I were moving toward one another. No words passed between us. Nothing told us to stand in a circle, and I didn't know why I stretched the volume in my hand out into the center. One by one, the other girls placed both hands on the book as if fate compelled them. Whispers only our souls could hear, secret truths binding us together. My hand was last.

It happened so suddenly, I barely had a chance to breathe before my soul ripped out of my body, away from the girls, away from the room, through many doors, through infinite space. Scenes flashing one after another, faces blurred as they whipped past my face like the wind.

I'd felt this before. Yes, La Charte hotel, that night Saul attacked New York. The night he kissed me. The touch of his lips had forced me away from myself, and now here I was again, flying, but to where? I was in my own consciousness. I knew that much. But I glimpsed the shallow stream only once as I rocketed past too many red doors too quickly, each of them blowing open for me so fast, I hadn't a chance to see the girls guarding them. I was skipping the line. Going back, back, back. Back through memories, back through fire, through tragedy, through death. Back to the beginning. I closed my eyes.

And I . . .

I . . .

And when I opened them, I was standing on a grassy field with the world burning down around me. The heat was unbearable. It was from the flaming mansion behind me, its smoke and embers reaching into the sunset sky—a sky raining chaos upon us.

I could see them off in the distance, monsters of nightmare barreling down to Earth in a cloak of black fire burning from their bodies.

Beasts like dragons and serpents from the old tales Alice's father had collected all those years he traveled around the world searching for its secrets. But these were not creatures of myth; they were terror made flesh—black, rotting flesh, their white eyes glowing ominously, emptily, at their prey below.

We were safe here. Alice had made sure of it. But we were the only ones to be met with such a fate. Beyond the trees bordering her family's estate, I could hear the screaming of the townspeople off in the distance, hear buildings coming down. The death and destruction. I'd narrowly escaped it myself. The tears in my dress and cuts on my body were proof of such.

None of this had moved dear Alice. She was focused on me alone as she stood at a distance, her chest heaving, the half stone clenched in her pale hand.

I couldn't breathe from the smoke. The soot darkened the white of my servant's clothes, graying Alice's sapphire dress. The flames would destroy the whole city soon. Even I hadn't the power to banish them all. The fire of death would engulf everything.

"Is this the world you wanted?" I asked her. "Is this what you dreamed about when you began your game? Look around us!" The white bonnet was already slipping from the crown of my head, so with a bloodied hand, I grabbed the straps and pulled it off, letting it fall to the grass. "The world is ending. The *world* is *ending!*"

"The world is *beginning.*" Alice's countenance had always been praised by those around us despite concerns over the sickly hue of her skin. Her blond hair, freed from its bindings, whipped around her pointed features. Her blue eyes, usually dark with secrets, were now bright and wild as she stretched out her arms as if to encompass the whole of the world. "Don't presume to judge me when you are just as guilty as the rest of us."

"The rest . . ." I shuddered as I remembered that young mistress's eyes, hollow with despair. "Because of what we did, Miss Patricia is dead. I do not even know where Miss Abigail and Miss Emilia are."

Alice's smile disappeared.

"Do you truly feel nothing?" My dressed flapped in the heavy wind. "How many more lives have to be sacrificed, Miss Alice?"

But these words only seemed to enrage her. "Do *not* presume to know what I feel and don't feel, you mud wench. That you dare speak to me as an equal is the biggest shock of all."

She was gone. The Alice I knew had disappeared into the ether of memory, her soul twisted and mangled into the sad, empty vessel I saw before me.

Maybe I never knew her at all. Maybe I was a fool for once thinking I did. The throbbing pain in my chest was enough to tell me so.

"Miss Alice," I started, my tongue heavy. "If you had seen what I have seen . . . would you feel remorse? Or are you beyond even that?"

"I told you to watch your words." Her hands were shaking in anger; she must have cut her palm against the sharp edge of the stone she held, because blood began to drip from it. "Never forget that it was my father who took you from the mud. From the *jungles. My* father who saved you from a life among the savages and allowed you to live here in the *civilized* world."

"Your father told me where *they* are." I spoke quickly as if every word could be my last. "'For only in calm can you hear them speak.' Miss Alice, we can *go* to those lands. We can ask them for one last wish! I can take you! Let us go together! If we do, we can finally end this!"

"But my dear *poupée*. What if I don't wish to end anything?"

My fingers curled against my dress, crumpling the fabric. The slightly mad look in her eyes used to send terrors through me. I would hide behind corners to avoid their gaze. But I couldn't hide anymore. I couldn't cower. "Then I will have stop you."

"Stop me? You?" Alice lifted her chin, her lips stretching into an amused grin. "*My* Nicholas would never have looked at you if it were not for the training I gave you, the civilized words I taught you to speak. You should never have doubted me, Marian, when I told you that I would change everything. I changed *your* destiny. I dressed you. I raised you. I made you *whole*. My little doll."

The sound of her giggles chilled me from the inside.

"And, *poupée*, I will not stop," she said. "You will not stop me."

Slowly and silently through breaths of flame, the handle formed in my hand. "My dear Miss Alice," I said as the steel blade stretched out from the handle, born and forged from fire. The sword of the legends I'd learned of. "I was already whole before you met me."

I brought up the sword, and in the reflection of its blade, I could see my own dark face, chestnut eyes narrowed in determination. In a blink, Alice disappeared and she was behind me, a knife raised above her head—

"Maia!"

It sounded like Lake's voice.

Yes, I was Maia. I was *Maia*.

With a deep shudder, my soul started flying again. The sound of my name crashed through the surface of the memory, sucking my consciousness out of the apocalyptic scene, back into my own body in the museum. Breathing heavily, I dropped to the floor, though it wasn't until my head had stopped spinning that I realized I wasn't the only one down here. Lake was struggling to get onto her knees. Chae Rin was sitting, her legs flat against the stone, her body hunched over. Belle was the only one still standing, though she pressed a hand against her head as if to keep it from spinning.

"What was that?" I squeezed my eyes shut and opened them again just to make sure I was me. The special volume was on the floor. "Did you all see that? Did you see Alice?"

"What?" Chae Rin looked genuinely confused. "No . . ."

"You didn't?" I drew my knees up, gripping them with trembling hands. "Was it just me?"

"I saw her die," whispered Lake, finally on her knees though she kept her hands against the floor to keep herself steady. "Patricia . . . She . . . she killed herself." Her voice choked with emotion, and she covered her mouth with her hand to stifle her sob.

"We saw different memories." Belle looked at us. "Of different Effigies. The first."

We were silent.

"*Links in a chain. A dangerous game,*" Chae Rin said suddenly. "That's what Abigail said. She was crouched in a dark room somewhere rocking back and forth. She just kept repeating it."

"For me it was Emilia," said Belle. "She was trying to save as many people as she could in York, but throughout it all she had a single focus—to find Castor. To tell him something. But what?" She shook her head. "It wasn't clear."

"In mine, Marian and Alice were fighting," I said, narrowing my eyes as I recalled the memory. "The phantoms had filled the sky. They were on an estate, but the mansion was burning. She said they had to end things."

I didn't know how the pieces fit, but I knew they were involved. The five of them together. The ones whose supernatural burden so many girls had inherited after them.

"How?" Chae Rin asked. "How did we just scry them like that?"

The volume. Back at La Charte, it was Saul's kiss that had forced me into Marian's memories before. Both Nick and Alice were intimately connected to the girl. This volume . . . The secrets in this book were intimately connected to each of us.

"Let's take this back with us." With sure steps, Belle walked over to the book and picked it up. "Hurry. Our powers are in full effect. The Sect is probably tracking us as we speak."

I helped Lake to her feet, but took one last look at the open trap-door. The words written there. *For only in calm can you hear them speak.*

Who are "they"? Where were those lands Marian spoke of? That Castor spoke of? The more I learned, the less I knew.

"Maia, come on!" Chae Rin said, jolting me out of my thoughts, and I turned to follow.

The others disappeared quickly through the door before me.

That's why they were hit first.

I ducked back behind the doorframe fast enough to miss the dart, but the others had struck their target. From around the frame, I saw Chae Rin stumbling forward, Lake falling to the ground, and Belle leaning against the statue for support. Belle's hands shook as she pulled the large needle out from her neck. The one meant for me was still lodged into the doorframe.

"Come out, Maia."

Vasily. My heart pounded against my chest as my head starting spinning. How did he get here? What was going on?

Pulling out the dart from her neck, Chae Rin raised her hands, and though the earth trembled beneath us, it was nothing but a whisper that died off the second it'd started.

"Maia, are you going to leave your friends here to rot? Do come out," he said, and I could hear the smile in his voice.

"Yeah, bitch!" Jessie. She was already laughing. "We've got something for ya."

I couldn't hide here forever. Steeling myself, I stepped out from the doorframe, ready to launch an attack, but my hands froze the second I saw Jessie's arm around Rhys's neck and her gun to his head, her menacing grip squeezing his trachea to the extent that he could barely speak. Even captured, he remained stoic, but I couldn't. My pulse was already racing, my eyes wide. I'd just begun to say his name when I felt the needle sink into my neck.

28

I STUMBLED FORWARD AND TRIPPED, HITTING one suit of armor on my way down. As its spear clattered onto the ground next to me, I looked up. The other girls were huddled together in front of me, dizzily trying to regain their bearings. Vasily and Jessie stood just beyond the iron gates with Rhys as their hostage. Though they wore their regular street clothes, they looked menacing nonetheless, both with their fingers on their respective triggers.

"You may feel a little dazed after the inoculation. This model's a bit more powerful than the others." Vasily slipped his dart gun back into his jacket, his hair tied up in a ponytail at the back of his head. "Just a protective measure."

Jessie's sneakers squeaked against the marble floor as she shifted her position to peer at the four of us over Rhys's left shoulder.

"Now you're all here!" Her manic laughter bounced off the high ceiling. "Great! Now you all get to see pretty Aidan's brains fly out of his—"

Vasily put his hand up to silence her. He was clearly the more measured of the two, and that was saying something. But even without a gun, he was the one who frightened me the most.

"Maia," he said as Jessie bit her lip moodily. He stretched his hand out to me next. "It's time. Come with me. I know you don't want Aidan to die."

After pushing myself onto my knees, I let myself fall back, my dizziness blurring my vision. When my back hit the suit of armor, I hoped it wouldn't topple over. "How did you get here?"

But I already knew. Naomi's ring. Rhys had told me it'd been bugged. Jessie had been fiddling with it during Blackwell's party days ago before throwing it back to her. They would have known we were meeting in Madrid. . . .

"Your prints on the keypad." Vasily still showed a little sign of the torture he'd endured earlier under the cruel hand of the Surgeon. There were scars all over his face, and his skin looked swallow and dry, like he'd aged several years. But that Cheshire grin hadn't changed. He showed just a taste of it to me. "You should have used gloves. Rookie mistake."

"Besides," Jessie added wildly, "Vasily followed Natalya around months ago. You think we wouldn't find this place? You think we're that *stupid*? Huh?"

Behind me, Belle stirred, her hand twitching against the floor.

"Calm down." It was Rhys who spoke, saying words he'd probably said thousands of times before. He didn't need to be able to see her face to feel her sudden frenzy. For a moment, it seemed as if Jessie had listened, her hand relaxing due to habit alone before she steeled herself and pressed her gun harder against Rhys's skull.

"He's right, Jessie. There's no need to worry. *This* time, Maia will come with us."

"Come with you where?" Chae Rin said. The other four were starting to come out of their dizzy spell, but I knew they couldn't fight because *I* couldn't fight. Whatever surge of power we'd felt in that mysterious room had once again disappeared under the influence of the inoculation dart Vasily and Jessie had hit us with. Our strength and our magic were gone for now.

"To Saul. The preparations are almost done. But we need you, Maia. You're the last piece of the puzzle. There's something you know that nobody else does. Even if you don't know you know it yet."

Marian's frantic plea to Alice played back in my memories, her soft cries just an echo deep in my consciousness: *"For only in calm can you hear them speak." Miss Alice, we can go to those lands. We can ask them for one last wish! I can take you! Let us go together! If we do, we can finally end this!*

"And what exactly is he preparing for?" Shakily, I got to my feet. "Is it Project X19?"

Vasily hid his shock much better than Jessie, who gritted her teeth and tightened her grip on Rhys's neck in retaliation.

"For you to ask that question means you know a little, but not enough," Vasily answered.

"I know the Sect is fractured. So is the Council. I know whichever part Baldric was terrified of is the part working with Saul—and working with you two."

The flash drive we'd given Uncle Nathan—the one we'd taken from Philip—pointed to the Sect. The nanotech Mellie had injected into my neck was a similar model to the one in Jessie's own. Baldric was right in thinking there was a connection between Saul's soldiers and the Sect.

But why would Saul work with them? During our battle in France, Nick had told me that both he and Alice wanted the same thing: the rest of the stone so he could grant some wish. Marian knew where to find it. But that couldn't have been all. What else did he have in store?

"How did they recruit you, Vasily?" I stared him down. "You don't have any powers, so you weren't in the Silent Children Program. Neither was Rhys."

"The job was offered to me one day by a close associate," Vasily said simply. "I didn't think twice."

"Because you wanted to help Saul?"

"This is much bigger than Saul. It's not about the Sect, either. It's about the whole world, Maia. It's about *changing* the world." Vasily slipped both of his hands into his pockets. "We're making a world where poor girls like you don't have to fight anymore. You can throw away your 'duty' and live your lives. Don't you want that?"

Vasily was sincere, as sincere as when he'd stared pale-faced at the image of his mother, broken by the same cruel system that had abused him.

"The only way you can do that," Rhys said, struggling against the pressure of Jessie's arm, "is if you destroy the Sect."

"The Sect *should* be destroyed, Aidan," Vasily said, his voice rising dangerously, his face alight with quiet anger. "After everything they did to you. To me. To . . ." He swallowed his next words, but I already knew what he wanted to say. His mother. "We're nothing to them, agents and Effigies alike. We have to build something greater. This is the only way to do it."

Silently, he walked through the rows of suited armor, his gaze as sharp as the towering crystallized phantoms watching over us with their slitted eyes.

My feet felt weighted as I stepped out to the middle of the hall, directly in front of him, my back facing Patricia's portrait. I had no magic, not enough training to go up against a monster like Vasily. But I wasn't going with him without a fight.

Neither was Belle. I hadn't seen her pick up the spear that had fallen next to me, but she had it firmly gripped in her hand as she stepped out from behind the suits of armor.

"Vasily." She let the tip of the spear drag against the marble floor with a loud scratch as she walked. "Tell me again. That you followed Natalya."

Rhys's eyes met mine, secrets whispering silently between us. Belle still had the special volume in her hand, but not for long. She threw it to the side and it skidded across the floor until it came to a stop against the suit of armor. Belle was readying herself for battle.

Vasily laughed. "Who? Sorry, did somebody mention her?"

"Tell me." She pivoted on her feet, facing the trio.

"Belle!" Lake got up, though she stayed where she was, her eyes nervously darting between both poles of the room. "Calm down!"

"Did nobody tell you?" He gave Rhys a sidelong look, delighting in the way Rhys's jaw set. "She's nobody. You should know that by now. Important to no one. I can't even remember what I did or didn't do to her."

The spear shook in Belle's hand. But out of the corner of my eye, I could see the digital wall clock ticking down from inside the opposite room. I could see the red numbers flashing just above the heads of the three stone statues. *Ten seconds . . . nine seconds . . .*

"Guys . . ." I grabbed Belle's arm, but she shrugged me off without even looking back. Her breaths labored, her hands trembling, she raised the spear, pointing its blade at him.

"Did you kill Natalya?"

Four seconds . . . three seconds . . .

"Maybe." Vasily smiled. "What a pity that you're the only one who still seems to care."

Belle raised her arm, ready to let her spear fly, when a buzzing noise sounded behind us. Two small square hatches in the wall burst open on either side of Patricia's portrait.

Chae Rin rose swiftly to her feet, her eyes wide. "What . . . the hell . . . is that?"

That was a machine gun. Two, one in each hatch, their barrels pointed into the room.

And they started firing.

Belle and I ducked to the floor, covering our heads while Chae Rin and Lake found cover behind separate suits of armor. Rhys had used the moment of confusion to free himself from Jessie's grip. I could barely hear her gunshot above the rattling of the machine gun, but I saw the gun sliding out of her grip onto the floor as they both ran and dove out of the way. The bullets riddled the floor, turning right to left almost as if to make sure no life escaped its reach. The Haas family had truly spared no expense in the security of their secrets.

It stopped, maybe just for a moment, maybe forever. I didn't know. Belle didn't care. Once the coast was clear, she ran down the hall, crossing diagonally to the opposite end of the room to where Vasily was hiding. He came out to meet her, dodging the swipe of her spear, punching her in the stomach. Chae Rin ran to help but was intercepted by Jessie, who tried to catch the nimble Effigy with her fists. That wasn't so easy with Rhys striking her from behind. Yet while Jessie fought her battle, I could see the clock reset. *Ten seconds . . . nine seconds . . .*

"Guys! Take cover!" I found a suit to hide behind. "Take cover!"

The rattling began again and everyone dove out of the way. It would go on like this forever if we let it. We were all going to die unless we figured out a way to stop it. But just in front of me, Jessie, taking advantage of Chae Rin's distraction, leapt onto her, her head staying well below the rain of bullets even as they clinked against the metal suit they hid behind.

After a swift punch, Jessie started choking her.

"Stop!" I cried. Rhys tugged at Jessie's leg, but he couldn't do much while he tried to avoid the machine guns' attack. Chae Rin was dying.

On my other side, Lake flung off her knapsack, searching for the cigar box while the bullets wailed overhead. She flung open the lid and grabbed some of the shards of stone strewn about the paraphernalia. Was she making a wish? But there was no black sliver in the stone she picked. It wasn't powered up for a wish—

Then I saw the crystal phantoms stirring.

"Lake . . ." Slowly, the phantoms stretched their necks out with a shiver, the crystal crackling and melting off of their flesh. "What did you just do?"

"I just told it . . . *willed* it to . . ." Lake's trembling hand dropped the shards. "It was the only thing I could think of." The whimper in her voice begged me to understand.

Just like Saul who'd used the stone to force his phantoms to harden their bodies around the train in France. Lake must have remembered Pete discussing the stone's power. It could control a phantom's biology. It could make a phantom petrify.

And it could do the reverse, too.

If Lake's plan was to distract Jessie, it worked. The girl had stopped choking Chae Rin just long enough for the Effigy to push her off her body with as much strength as she could muster. The crystal hides of dragon-like phantoms began to shift and shatter.

"Change them back!" I yelled, but Lake's shaking, sweaty hand couldn't grasp the shards of stone before the phantoms roared, their unpetrified wings crashing into the machine guns, breaking them to pieces. A hunk of metal flew at our heads. Lake and I left the shards behind to dive out of the way before the debris could crush us. The guns were out of commission, but we'd only replaced one weapon with another. The phantoms hadn't fully shed their crystal skin when they spotted us and began rushing forward.

"Run!" Lake screeched. Leaving her bag behind, she took off, pulling me along with her. Chae Rin was on her feet too, and Rhys. Jessie, Belle, Vasily—friend and enemy alike made for the gates as the phantoms charged after us, destroying everything in their path. I could hear their cries echoing behind us, too close for comfort as we ran through the corridor that led back out of the hall. It was mayhem behind us. Bricks crashing, walls crumbling as the half-petrified phantoms stampeded after us. I was the last one up the stairs, and I could feel half of it bursting into pieces below me as the monsters smashed it. I managed to just barely squeeze past the open bookshelf and back into the Little Room, but the phantoms held no such courtesy. They crashed through the bookshelf itself, sending spines and covers and wood flying into the air. I stumbled over a globe rolling across the floor, but before I could recover my footing, a phantom's wing slammed into my side, sending me flying back. I felt my left ribs crack against the door from the impact.

"Maia!" Rhys cried, but he paused and turned, staring at the phantom. Wincing in pain, I looked long enough to catch it too. The phantoms—their bodies were starting to dissolve. Maybe they already had been from the beginning, but it was more noticeable now. The parts of their bodies that had unpetrified disappeared first, but I was sure the rest of them would follow eventually. I could see the black mist sizzling off their bodies, their bones wafting off into black mists.

"It's the effects of the city's APD," said Rhys.

The phantoms slowed down, but with parts of them still petrified, they wouldn't be stopped that easily. With a roar, they smashed what was left of their wings into the wall and stomped forward menacingly.

"Yeah, time to go," Chae Rin said.

I couldn't move. The pain from my cracked ribs was nearly debili-
tating. Rhys scooped me up into his arms and, punching in the code
he must have glimpsed from Vasily, carried me out of the room.
Rhys and I ran across the museum with the other Effigies following
close behind. But Vasily still had his gun—I could see one dart fly
past Rhys's ear as we neared the entrance. The phantoms did whatever damage they could before they disappeared, the floor rumbling
beneath their feet. It didn't take long. The last of the phantoms finally
disappeared, their faint cries echoing into the air, but we were far
from free. I knew it the moment we crossed the doors of the National
Museum and into the open air.

We saw them lined up along both staircases leading down from the
front entrance. The national police force. Sect agents. Some were on
the ground, hiding behind the doors of their police cars. Some were
standing in front of the Wenceslas statue.

And all had their guns pointed at us.

"Effigies! You are under arrest!" one agent said. I couldn't tell who.
But I was sure I'd hear all the juicy details on the news later on, if the
helicopters above were any indication. "Put your hands up and surrender yourselves into Sect custody!"

I peeked back over Rhys's shoulders. Vasily held Jessie back, both
of them concealed behind the doors. Wordlessly, he parted his jacket,
and what he showed me made my heart stop. The thirteenth volume.
I'd been so concerned with running for my life from the phantoms and
guns, I hadn't kept track of my *human* enemies; I hadn't noticed Vasily
snake the book for himself. He smiled. But I couldn't do anything.
They knew it too. The pain in my sides was so horrible, I couldn't even
speak.

Jessie stuck out her tongue at me as they disappeared back inside
the museum, leaving us to be captured.

29

WE ARRIVED BACK IN LONDON IN CHAINS. Well, at least they'd given us a bit of hospital time in Prague first. I heard they'd kept me sedated for about twenty-four hours, letting my cylithium levels rise to heal me enough for transportation before inoculating me again. They'd inoculated all of us, so they had nothing to fear while they hauled us through the front gates of the London facility in the back of a transportation van. They gave us the strong stuff. Top-grade.

What could we have done anyway, in front of the crowd of horrified protestors and fans alike begging us for an explanation or else just calling us murderers? The agents kept burlap sacks over our heads so that the news couldn't capture our faces, but if the Sect truly wanted secrecy, they could have taken us back through one of the secret paths.

Rhys wasn't with us. Since he was technically an agent of the North American Division, Director Prince had stepped in to negotiate his "freedom" in Prague. The son was to be released into the father's custody. For Rhys, that was probably worse. But as for us, we were going in the Hole.

Brendan himself led our grim procession through the same path he'd taken me before. Director Prince had apparently flown to London to advise him as they coordinated the Sect's next steps. I tried to get Brendan's attention without words, to signal to him that I hadn't been responsible for the current state of his mother, but there was a wall of agents between us. I saw only a glimpse of his face before they threw me into my cell. I don't think he meant to show me his confusion, his hurt. But when I grabbed hold of his pants cuff with my hands and spoke Rhys's name, his expression turned cold.

"The Sect—maybe the people here—they're responsible for what happened to your mother, not me," I blurted out. I didn't care how many agents were glaring down at me with narrowed eyes.

"Yeah," said Chae Rin, who was fighting with her own group of agents as they tried to shove her into a separate cell. "The Sect's corrupt, and yet *we're* the ones being thrown into jail? What bullshit!"

"Stop," Belle hissed at us.

We shouldn't reveal our hand; we shouldn't let on what we knew. I figured as much, but I needed to get through to someone. Saul's clock was ticking down and time was almost out. Less than a day left. We couldn't be locked up in here.

"You'll be readied for interrogation soon," Brendan said, his back still facing me. "Save your conspiracy theories for them."

"Please. You saw Saul's video, the message he sent all of us. Whatever he has planned is going to happen soon. We need to fight him." When Brendan didn't answer, I let out a frustrated cry. "Please! I'm not lying! Ask Rhys. He'll tell you!"

Brendan jerked his foot out of my grasp. "Rhys," he said, his voice hoarse and deep. "Rhys is my mother's maiden name."

He didn't look at me when he left. I had to move my hand out of the way to protect my fingers when the agents shut the heavy iron door in my face. Three more such slams echoed against the cold hallway. The four of us were in our cages.

Time ticked away. Minutes. Hours. I was alone and shivering in this cold, tiny room, its walls of red clay different from the deep, blinding white cell Brendan had taken me to—the cell Vasily had been tortured in. Though Brendan had called that an interrogation too. Was that what we were in for?

There was no bed, only a dirty toilet I was never going to touch no matter how many days they locked me in here. The walls were sound-proof, so I couldn't know how the other girls were doing, couldn't even ask them as I curled up against the wall, wrapping my arms around my knees. Vasily had already promised that Saul's plan would launch soon. We couldn't be here.

Hours passed. I didn't know how many. I had just begun to fall asleep when the door creaked open.

"Howard," I said. Or tried. My voice scratched painfully against the inside of my throat. I had just enough energy to lift my head. Howard kept his eyes concealed behind a pair of shades; maybe it was better. That way I wouldn't have to see the distrust in them. In his standard agent black suit and tie, he held a tray of food. Beans, corn, and a slab of meat—who knew what kind?

"Howard," I whispered just as he approached. "There's something happening inside the Sect. Howard . . ." When I looked past his body, I could see five other agents, fully armed, including his wife, Eveline. She was in Lake's room, directly opposite mine, giving her a similar tray of food. From what I could see, Lake looked worse for wear, and when she wiped her face and thanked Eveline, I knew she'd been cry-ing.

"Ask Rhys," I tried again. "Wh-where is he? If you ask him—"

"Agent Rhys is otherwise disposed," Howard answered coldly. He didn't get too close, but he was near enough that I could hear him speak even as he lowered his tone. "On a mission."

"What mission?"

He looked behind him with a slight shift of his head and knelt down a few steps away. "Director Prince Senior sent him to Oslo." He placed the tray on the floor. "To help stop Saul."

The tray clattered against the cold floor. The terrible sound battered my shot senses as I stared up at Howard. "Saul attacked." The words limped off my tongue.

"It's none of your concern."

I launched at him, desperately clinging to his jacket, but with a hand he pushed me back against the wall.

"I said it's none of your concern," he said. "In four hours, some people from the R & D department will come down to record your vitals and administer another inoculation. Until then, I suggest you eat. Unless you're planning on starving yourself in here."

"Saul's finally attacked, and you're keeping your best weapons drugged and locked up in a hole underground," I whispered just as he turned his back. "Or are you another traitor, Howard?"

Howard didn't answer.

"If Oslo's APD went down, then there must be a ton of phantoms already."

"It hasn't gone down," Howard said, so suddenly it gave me a start. "Not yet. It's the most fortified city on Earth. Maybe that's why Saul chose it. He's sending a message."

Through the door, one agent stared at the two of us with narrowed eyes. "Quiet down in there. Agent Day, if you're done—"

"I'm done." Howard got up, dusting off his hands. "Like I said, Finley, this is no longer your concern." He turned his back. "The only thing you can do now is eat. *Eat*, Maia."

Only my own reflection stared back at me from his dark lenses as he turned around one last time. Stroking the stubble on his chin, he left the room, slamming the door behind him.

The food looked sickly and dehydrated, as if it'd come from cans with expiration dates several years past. But my body was weak and my head was throbbing. I needed something. I pulled the tray toward me with a finger and picked up the disposable spoon, the only utensil they'd given me. Saul attacked. Oslo—that was in Norway, wasn't it? But before, Saul had only attacked cities after their APD had fallen. How in the world did he manage to subdue the most protected metropolis on his own without the help of phantoms?

The food was ash in my mouth. It went down in lumps like coal. I had to do something. We had to figure something out, not stay locked here like rats, but for some here in the Sect, that was obviously the plan.

I prodded the mysterious slab of meat with my spoon—veal, maybe? I'd staved off eating it all this time because it smelled a bit funky, though maybe it was my imagination. I lifted it up to make sure.

Wait, what?

Furrowing my brows in disbelief, I leaned in for a closer look at the device that had been tucked underneath the meat—an earpiece. Dropping my spoon, I plucked it off the tray quickly and examined it. A little tawny-colored piece of plastic shaped to the curvature of the inner ear—it couldn't have been anything else but one of the Sect's communication devices, the same I'd used in so many of the missions they'd given me. Howard did this.

After rubbing the grease off carefully, I stuck the device in my ear. "Hello? Hello?"

"Finally, you're on." It was Chae Rin. "I wondered whether she'd ever figure it out."

"Well, Eveline could have been clearer about it," Lake said. "I almost ate mine."

"Lake, are you okay?" I asked because I could hear the weakness in her voice.

"Thanks for asking, love. I think we've all been better," she answered. "Even still, we need to figure a way out of here."

"They're coming in four hours." Belle kept her voice quiet, controlled. "We'll need help if we're going to escape."

"We know."

I sucked in a sharp breath. It was Eveline's voice this time.

"That's why we took the risk." Howard.

"Howard," I said, "you—"

"Don't worry," he said. "We're speaking on a secure line. Though—" He stopped to greet someone. My earpiece caught the sound of his footsteps and those of others. He must have been in transit.

"We're going to have to be careful," finished Eveline.

"How many of you are there?" Belle asked.

"This is a delicate operation," she answered. "We had to keep the circle small. But we need to get you out. Saul attacked Oslo only an hour ago. But we didn't anticipate *how* he would infiltrate."

I was almost afraid to ask, but I did anyway. "How?"

"With an army," Howard said. "Traffickers, gang members, criminals. People on the outskirts with access to powerful military and Sect-grade weaponry."

Jin was right. Saul really had been attacking and gathering up all those groups.

"Not just them." It was almost imperceptible, but I could hear Eveline's breath coming out of her in a shudder. "There was one . . . with powers. That girl, the one we met in the tunnels. There are dead bodies attacking with Saul's army, and she is the one controlling them."

"Jessie Stone." My fingers naturally curled into fists as I spoke her name. "She's one of the special soldiers helping Saul. We think she was created as part of the second phase of Project X19."

"Project X19?" Howard repeated.

"Some secret project of doom we've been looking into. Saul and part of the Sect are involved. Phase II was called the Silent Children Program. There're supposed to be two more like Jessie—the rest of the Fisk-Hoffman kids that supposedly died in that fire. Engineered Effigies."

"They really engineered . . ." Howard caught his words.

"Gabriel and Talia are the names of the other two," I said. "They could be there too. If you managed to capture one of them, you could interrogate—"

"We have to focus on the chaos in Oslo," Howard said. "People are already dying, Maia."

Rhys. My throat closed up as I thought of him struggling in that nightmare thanks to the orders of his father.

"Saul infiltrated the city and took over the defense center," Howard continued. "It won't be long until their APD is down. The place is a war zone now, but once the phantoms come in, there won't be much we can do. We need the *real* Effigies."

"And I'm betting that's exactly why we've been locked up here without so much as a word," Chae Rin said. "Damn it!" I heard the slam from her fist against the wall and the grunt of pain immediately following. "Okay," she said. "I really need my powers back."

"We're working on that. Your next inoculation is coming in just under four hours. Once you cross the four-hour mark, you'll start to feel your powers return rapidly. There'll be one, at most two people coming to your cell. Check underneath your tray."

There was another surface underneath the bottom of the tray. I lifted off the first layer. A small syringe.

"It'll knock them out temporarily," Howard said. "But you'll have to be fast. And you're only going to have one shot. After that, one of us will tell you where to go."

We had a plan. In four hours, we'd strike. I just hoped it wouldn't be too late. Howard and Eveline couldn't use even a secure connection for too long at the facility when you never knew who could be around the corner. But the girls and I could talk. Belle explained how to hold the syringe while concealing it, which tissue to hit for maximum effect.

"It's a bit creepy that you know this," Chae Rin said.

"It was part of my training," Belle answered, annoyed. "It's small enough to fit inside your palm. You can use a napkin to hold it."

"Then what? We force them to take us to Saul?" Lake sounded skeptical. "I don't see how that would even work."

I picked up the syringe and inspected it closely, turning it every which way. "Have a little faith, I guess."

But only one hour had passed when my earpiece picked up the sound of a door opening to one of the cells.

"What's happening?" I said. "Are you guys—"

"What is it that you want?" I heard Belle ask whoever had entered her room. "My inoculation isn't scheduled for another three hours."

"Director Prince Senior's orders. Your interrogation over the attempted murder of Naomi Prince starts now," said one agent, and though his voice grew farther away, I could still hear him when he said, "Congratulations. You're first. Take her to the interrogation cell. And prep her for the Surgeon."

First I was on my feet. Then I was at the door pounding it with my fists. There was no point; it was soundproof. I knew they couldn't hear me yell, but Belle could. Her earpiece would have picked it up.

"Belle, fight them! Use the syringe!"

She didn't. She couldn't. First, from the sound of their voices, it was clear there were more than two of them. If she attacked, she'd give us all away, and we'd never see the other side of these cells—until it was our turn to be "interrogated." But I was well aware of how liberally the Princes interpreted that word. And I knew all too well the horrors the Surgeon was capable of.

"Belle, it's okay!" I cried, and the other two girls agreed with me. "Save yourself!"

"Quiet," she said suddenly. "You think I can't take this?"

Her words were followed promptly by a slap to the face. I heard the impact crisp and clear over the comm.

"This one's got a mouth. The little uppity French bitch," the agent said. I was sure she'd made them think she was talking to them. She wasn't.

I kicked the door in frustration as I heard Belle's tray skid across the floor.

"Take her!"

Belle waited for the agents to leave and the door of the interrogation room to slam behind her. I could hear her earpiece moving, muffling between her fingers, then inside her palm.

"Welcome." A deep, chilling voice. One I remembered.

It was the last I heard before Belle crushed the earpiece.

30

"WE HAVE TO DO SOMETHING," CHAE RIN SAID frantically for the twentieth time in thirty minutes. "She could still be in there!"

"You guys don't know. Maybe he's doing something different with Belle. Maybe he won't . . ." Lake stopped.

I could tell she was shaking. I almost wish I hadn't told them what the Surgeon was capable of. And if I remembered Brendan correctly, it wasn't just torture. Head games. Hours of emotional manipulation. Belle was mentally strong, but even she had her buttons. And buttons were easier to press when your prisoner's defenses were being battered by intense pain.

"Howard. Howard!" Chae Rin called again. "Eveline! Are you there?"

After a few minutes: "I'm sorry. It's me, Eveline." She lowered her voice. "I had to find an empty room. I . . . I heard everything. I know about Belle." The tremor in her voice as she said the name made that too clear. "I just couldn't respond."

"You guys have been gone for, like, years! Where were you?" I yelled.

"Getting ready to deploy," she said. "Howard's already down in the hangar. They need reinforcements in Oslo. Thing are getting worse."

"The APD?" Lake sounded too afraid to ask.

"They've started evacuations of the city."

I crouched down by the door. "We need to get out as soon as possible. We need to free Belle."

"You won't get another chance until they come for you. Just make sure that after you get out of the Hole, you follow her directions exactly."

"Whose directions?" I asked. "Eveline?" I tapped my ear because the sound was shorting out. "Eveline?"

She was gone. There wasn't anything more I could do but wait, each minute stretching into infinity until my door creaked open again. Quickly, I grabbed the syringe, tucked inside a clean napkin, and held it in my fist.

"Mellie."

The skin of my lips cracked and thinned as I pressed them together. One of Dot's assistants entered my room with a security agent in tow. I slid back until I was against the wall, but she didn't seem to care. Without greeting me, she pulled her hand out of the pocket of her long white lab coat and began opening the silver briefcase she carried.

"I thought the R & D department was under investigation after the stunt you pulled, and yet here you are." I smirked. "Guess you passed the loyalty test."

"Yes, I did," she answered coolly, her bob tilted to the left with her head as she began fiddling around in the case. "Unlike Dot and Pete. But then, I've always been loyal."

Dot and Pete. Those two had run from the Sect. But had they run because they were guilty? Or because they were scared?

Mellie used a pad to clean the area around my neck. And not for the first time.

"You were the one who injected me with that mind-control crap."

She laughed a little at my limited technical vocabulary, but it didn't deter me. I peered up at the bodyguard by the door, who stared down at the both of us through his thick shades.

"Tell me the truth," I said. "Did Dot tell you to do all that?"

"Dot's a brilliant mind in her field," Mellie replied. "She also needs help remembering what day it is. You really think that's the kind of player you want on board for a conspiracy?"

"But you are, right?" I flinched at her touch, the wetness of the alcohol pad picking up the chill from the room. "They had nothing to do with it, did they?" A wave of relief washed over me, but it was short-lived. Mellie pulled out the inoculation gun from the briefcase. I eyed the pen-like device as Mellie checked its contents, then turned my attention to the agent standing at the door. "So who do you take your orders from?"

He didn't answer.

"Don't worry." Mellie flicked the gun with her finger. "We'll take you to see him soon enough."

"You really think so, don't you?" I gave her a generous smile as she lifted her arm. "Poor you."

A crash. It was from Chae Rin's room. Mellie turned around sharply, her eyes wide as the commotion began. Without wasting another second, I took advantage of her distraction, punching her as hard as I could across the face, knocking her out. "I really don't feel sorry for that," I said, jumping to my feet with the syringe in hand.

I was fast, too fast for the agent to overcome his shock as he reached for his gun. I kicked the weapon out of his hand, ducking his swing. He managed to grab my neck as I straightened back up, but he'd left his exposed.

This was my chance.

I jammed the syringe into his neck. Only one shot—and this shot hit its mark. He sputtered and gasped, letting me go as I squeezed the pump. Even with the chemicals coursing into his system, he still had enough strength to continue attacking before the effects set in. And while his next punch was less focused, I couldn't afford to be hit. Taking advantage of his sluggishness, I cracked his kneecap with another hit, and when he doubled over in pain, I gave him a swift uppercut. My powers weren't back yet, so the impact battered my knuckles, but the attack did the trick. He fell back through the door, hitting the ground with a satisfying *thud*.

"I've had just about enough of the Sect's bullshit," I said, striding out the door after him as he moaned and struggled to get up. "We're *done* with you." One kick to the head and he was out cold.

Lake and Chae Rin had come out at the same time to watch me deliver the final blow.

"Damn, kid," Chae Rin said, "you're—"

"Search their pockets," I said, crouching down over the agent's unconscious body. "They use a keycard to get into the interrogation cell."

They didn't waste any time, disappearing back inside their cells to search for what we needed. This agent's pockets were empty. So were Mellie's.

"Found one!" Lake said, and she ran out into the hall with the same little white keycard Brendan had used to get inside.

Grabbing it from her, I swiped the pad. The door opened.

Tears were swelling in my eyes before I even saw the blood wetting Belle's blond hair and dripping down her stomach. Her T-shirt was discarded on the floor, so I could see all the cuts he'd made on her stomach, the holes, the burns. I thought, if anyone, Belle would be strong enough to take it. But mingled with the sweat and blood were tears staining her cheeks. For me, it was three hours of her silence. In reality, it was just that I couldn't hear her screaming.

The Surgeon didn't seem to care as we ran across the deep, white cell to get to her. He didn't put up a fight, either. Brendan was right about him. He wasn't a Sect agent in the sense of duty. He'd already gotten what he wanted. Stepping back, he put up his hands in surrender as a crying Lake helped to unstrap Belle from the operating table.

"You learn a lot when you're inside someone," he said suddenly. "This one . . . has a lot of pain. She told me many things."

I grabbed his bloody scalpel off the table.

"I don't think you're capable of that." His eyes were serene as he watched me approach him, half his expression obscured behind his mask. "But she is capable of many things under the right circumstances. Or so I've learned. Especially now. You don't know what torture can do to someone."

"Maia!"

Only after Chae Rin's cry did I realize that I'd already raised the scalpel above my head.

"We have to go," she said. Lake and Chae Rin had helped Belle put her shirt back on. One of Belle's arms was around each of their necks.

They were right. Besides, June wouldn't have wanted to see me like this. I lowered my hand, dropping the scalpel, but the Surgeon had one last thing to say.

"I think you'll be surprised soon, little one."

A hard punch in the face was all it took to shut him up. He went down hard, unconscious.

"Let's go," I told them.

We dragged the unconscious bodies into our cells and shut the door behind them before we took off. With Belle disabled, we had to march up the long, dark stairwell slowly, but with each step, I felt my power stir up inside me. Our magic was coming back. Which was good, because we were going to have to fight our way through security.

Up the stairs, through the corridors. They were shooting at us the moment the door slid open. We ducked behind a corner as the bullets whizzed over our heads. Belle was groaning from the impact, covering her head feebly with shaking hands.

"Someone do something!" I said, trying to call forth fire, but while I felt the energy swell inside of me, it wasn't powerful enough to even make my fingers spark.

"Trap and release, trap and release, trap and release," Lake muttered furiously under her breath before she let out a cry. "Ugh, I'm tired of all you people!"

A spontaneous burst of wind funneled through the room and crashed into the security. I got to my feet in time to see their bodies smashing against walls, landing at odd positions across the room, their weapons flying several feet away from them.

Lake blinked. "I guess my powers are coming back."

"Well, you were always better at it than us." Chae Rin picked Belle's arm up again. "Let's go. Come on, Ice Princess, heal fast. We can't carry you around forever."

Belle muttered something incoherent as we went through the scanners and out the entrance. We were free, for the time being. Only problem was, we had no idea where to go.

"Hello." I tapped my comm as we turned a corner into an empty hallway. "Eveline? Howard? Anyone?"

"If we can find the parking lot, maybe we can swipe a car. I know how to hot-wire," Lake said. And when we all stared at her, she shrugged her shoulders, indignant. "*What?* I can't know how to hot-wire cars?"

"That won't be necessary. We have a car waiting for you."

In the middle of the hallway, I froze at the sound of her voice in my ear. I couldn't believe it. "S-Sibyl?"

"Duck!" Lake hissed, and pulled me into the nearest corridor while some agents came around the corner.

"Sibyl," I whispered. "Where are you?"

"Later." She was all business as usual. I didn't have time to question her. The agents disappeared into another room without seeing us, but it would only be a matter of time before we were caught. "Nathan, tell me their coordinates."

Too many things had happened in the past few minutes, and I wasn't sure if my mind was just playing tricks on me. That couldn't have been my uncle who'd answered Sibyl with a calm and assured voice.

"They're in the east wing of Building A-4."

"Uncle . . ." My breath hitched in my throat. "Uncle Nathan . . ."

"*Later,*" Sibyl repeated, and I knew how much she hated having to do that.

"Maia, take the emergency stairwell three doors down until you get to the basement floor." It sounded like he was reading off of a computer screen, monitoring our movements. "Then go out exit two into the parking lot. We have people waiting for you."

I wasn't having it. Even as we made our way through the exit and down the stairwell, I didn't stop until I prodded an answer out of them.

"You know as well as I do, Maia," Sibyl said. "There's something going on inside the Sect. I set up this communication line for only those people I knew I could trust."

"Wait, *you're* the one who set this line up?" Lake stumbled under Belle's weight. Belle muttered something, but no one heard her.

"You didn't think I was back home twiddling my fingers this entire time, did you?" For the first time maybe ever, I was happy to hear the twang of bossy annoyance in Sibyl's voice. "The Sect is a very large organization, girls, and if it's compromised, then the world has a reason to be afraid. If we're going to fix what's happening, we'll have to work together on this."

"That's why she sent someone to pick me up in New York and take me to her safe house," said Uncle Nathan. "Someone from the MDCC was onto me. Sibyl intercepted a message they sent the Sect."

"So there really was a leak at the MDCC." I grasped the baluster tightly.

"More like leaks. Saul couldn't have gotten all those APDs down with only one person helping."

"Saul's in Oslo right now," Chae Rin said. "We've got to stop him. How do you plan on getting us there, Langley? Or do you have a jet waiting for us too?"

"You're not going to Oslo," she said. "You're going to Communications. You have to stop Director Prince Senior."

Rhys's dad?

Lake stumbled again, earning an angry grumble from Chae Rin, who had Belle's other arm around her neck. It was Belle herself who gently pushed them both away, waving her hand to stop them when they approached her again.

"I'm okay," she said, though she was still wincing in pain. "I'm starting . . . to heal."

Her eyes didn't show it. They were off focus, their blue pupils dulled. Shutting them, she shook her head and took in a deep breath. "It's okay."

Our feet finally touched the pavement of the basement floor. Running out the second exit, we searched for our accomplices. Section B-2, Uncle Nathan told us. And there they were, two agents standing by our getaway car, waving us forward.

Shots rang out. The elevator several feet away had just spat out two security guards, who started firing the moment they saw us. The agents flung open the car door and hid behind it for cover.

"Get in!" they yelled.

We made a run for it. Chae Rin had just enough power to cause a sinkhole underneath the security guards, but even when we hopped into the van and the agents drove out into the night, more security streamed out of another exit in the parking lot.

"Sirens," I said as they began to ring out over the entire facility. They knew we'd escaped. "Sibyl, we need to get out of here. Why the hell are you guys taking us to *Communications*?"

"Because according to my sources there, Brendan Prince can't stop his father with words, and he's too cowardly to do it through action," Sibyl answered. "But Arthur Prince is between a rock and a hard place. Oslo is a war zone. Saul promised death and he's delivering. With the phantoms around the perimeter of the city, nobody can go in or out. It'll become another Seattle Siege."

Chae Rin pounded her fist against the back of a seat. "Then we should be there," she said. "If we can get to Oslo before—"

"Soon there won't *be* an Oslo."

The van fell silent as it cut across the grounds.

"What . . . ?" My breath struggled in my throat. "What . . . do you mean?"

"It's something I found on the flash drive not too long ago," Uncle Nathan said. I could hear the fear creeping up in his voice. "Not about those soldiers. But about the weapon the Sect has been building for years without anyone knowing. Not even Sibyl. It's about Minerva."

Minerva. The third phase of Project X19.

Chae Rin narrowed her eyes. "Minerva? What about it?"

"It's the name of a secret Sect satellite that can fire a particle beam at any target in the world," Sibyl said. "And if we don't stop him, Arthur will use it to kill Saul. Even if it destroys the city—and everyone inside it."

31

"SO THE SECT JUST HAS A DEATH WEAPON lying around?" I yelled so loudly the agent driving squirmed a little in his seat. I didn't care. My fingernails were practically ripping the leather of his headrest, but I didn't even notice.

"Apparently," Uncle Nathan said. "According to the file I read, the Sect built it a decade ago, a last resort in case of a cataclysmic phantom attack. But it was never used. Only certain members of the Council know about its existence. If Director Prince is using it, then either he knew about it all along or one of those Council members told him the big company secret and gave him the controls. Either way, looks like we're about to see Phase III."

"Phase III is to nuke a city?" I pounded the headrest with a fist. It was too much to believe. *"Why?"*

"I don't know," Sibyl said. "I don't know whether Director Prince is aware of Project X19. But if he does this, it's only going to make things worse. Even if he succeeds in taking Saul out, he will sacrifice lives. And he will start something I'm not sure any of us will be able to finish. You have to stop him, Maia. Even if that means killing him."

Chae Rin's and Lake's expressions said it all. We were battered, starved, and exhausted. I didn't know how much any of us had left. And I didn't know if I could stomach taking another parent away from Rhys. . . .

Rhys.

"Rhys is in Oslo!" I sat back against the seat, my hands shaking. "He was deployed there . . . by his father."

Chae Rin looked horrified. "God, that's messed up. Either he sent him there knowing from the beginning, or he's willing to sacrifice his own son."

"He couldn't. He wouldn't!" I turned to Belle, waiting for some kind of affirmation. But she was lying against the side of the door, staring at nothing through lidded eyes. "Belle!" I shook her. "Are you okay?"

She jerked her arm away at my touch and dragged herself up. "I'm fine," she said, a little sluggishly. "I'm okay. Just leave me alone."

"But, Belle—"

"Stop," she snapped, and laid her head in her hands. "My body's . . . healing."

But was her mind? This was the wrong time for Belle to be incapacitated, though I couldn't even imagine what she'd just been through. I could still see the scars along her neck, the burn marks scorching her left temple, searing off a bit of the hair there. She caught me staring and let her hair out of its binds to cover it.

"He told me something strange." Belle's eyes lost focus again.

I leaned over as she wiped her face. "What?"

"He said something strange. About me. That I would always be alone."

She looked at me. Whatever the Surgeon had done to her . . . had said to her . . . it wasn't just physical. It had emptied her out. Hollowed her. She looked at me as if she didn't know me. As if she never had.

"But that isn't true, is it? Maia . . . you're on my side, aren't you? You're on Natalya's side."

I pulled back from her.

From the backseat, Chae Rin gave her a rough shove. "Snap out of it. We've got more important things to deal with." But behind her gruffness, even she looked worried.

"More important," Belle repeated as if trying to feel the words in her mouth. She lowered her head, her hands shaking. "Like Vasily said . . . no one cares anymore . . . about Natalya. . . ."

"Great." Chae Rin shook her head. "Just fucking great."

We were nearing the south building, which housed the Communications department, but we weren't alone. Three rows of agents were waiting for us right in front of the entrance, the bottom two rows kneeling and crouching so we could see the barrels of each one of their guns pointed at us as they fired. The driver swerved, trying to avoid the bullets, but one punctured the windshield, narrowly grazing Lake's head.

"Press the gas!" Chae Rin yelled.

The driver didn't need telling twice. I could hear the screams of the agents diving out of our way as we crashed into the building. We hopped out of the car and started running. Belle shrugged off my hand when I tried to help her. Her feet carried her through the halls just fine. We didn't have much of a plan when we kicked open the doors to the main communications center.

I expected the guns pointed at us, though not all the agents at their terminals and computer screens had their weapons in hand and aimed. What I didn't expect was to see Saul on the main video screen at the front of the room. He stood in front of a magnificent white building surrounded by his gang of criminals with Sect-grade weapons. NOBELS FREDSSENTER, it read on a strip above the high, arched windows. And next to those words, the English translation: NOBEL PEACE CENTER.

Saul certainly had a sense of irony. Probably Alice's. Yet I couldn't discount that Nick could be so twisted, for as he told me in Morocco, the differences between them didn't matter much these days. They were both dangerous.

I could see phantoms flying off in the distance, slithering in the air, weaving through funnels of smoke and patches of fire tearing through the city. Several dead men and women in Sect uniforms were strewn about the cobbled pavement. Only three were left alive. All had been forced onto their knees, their backs to us, their heads lifted as they stared down the barrel of rifles.

Saul told someone to adjust the camera, and the image shook.

"He's livestreaming this," Lake whispered. That much was clear from the progress bar at the bottom of the screen. Maybe he was just streaming this to us.

Or maybe to the whole world.

"What is this?" In front of the computer terminals, Director Prince's eyes bulged as he ripped his stern gaze from the screen and saw us standing there. "What are you doing here?"

"Yeah, we're not gonna let your dumb ass nuke a city, asshole," Chae Rin eloquently explained. "Look at that screen! You've still got people alive in there!"

But Director Prince wasn't listening. "What are you all doing? Capture them and take them back to the Hole!"

"No!" Brendan strode out from behind him, his hands raised. "Hold your fire!"

Prince was furious. "Brendan—"

"No, Dad! This has to stop! They're right. People are going to die!"

"They're evacuating the city. It'll be minimal loss of life. We have to stop Saul *now*."

"Even if it means killing your own son?"

Slowly, I looked back at the screen, at the three agents kneeling on the ground. Two were women. The other was a young man, his dark hair noticeable even under the veil of night. And when Vasily stepped into the frame, his frightening grin wide as he grabbed the young man's hair and yanked his head up, I didn't have to see his face to know who he was. Vasily's malicious glee told me everything.

"You can't . . ." I took several shaky steps forward, barely flinching even when many of the agents by the terminal cocked their guns. "You can't do this. He's your son. Please . . . *please* don't kill him. . . ."

It wasn't that Prince had no feelings toward his son. It was obvious he was fighting with himself from the way he screwed up his face and leaned over slightly, as if trying and failing to hide the physical pain the decision caused him.

Finally: "Open negotiations," he told someone sitting in the front row of terminals.

After a few swift *click*s of a keyboard from the Communication techs, Prince stood up straight, visually assuming the mantle of the head of the Sect even if he couldn't be seen by his enemy.

"Saul," he said. "We're sending reinforcements to the city. Surrender now before this goes any further."

"Oh, Arthur, Arthur, Arthur." Saul wagged a finger from his metal hand at the screen, like a child playing a wicked game. So Alice was in charge this time. That much I knew. "How many times do I have to say that we're on the same side? I'm doing this for you—for the Sect."

"Stop trying to confuse the people! The Sect has nothing to do with you," Prince spat. His anger was convincing. Too convincing. In fact, he very well may have believed it. "Let your prisoners go!"

"My prisoners?" Saul grabbed a rifle from one of his thugs and shot a female agent in the head without missing a beat. She was on the ground dead in seconds. "Two to go."

Terror swept through me as he swung his gun toward Rhys. I could hear Jessie laughing behind the camera, not surprisingly finding a kindred spirit in Alice, another young girl as twisted as she. Saul took his time cocking the gun, lifting it, pointing it at Rhys's head. . . .

"Stop!" Brendan cried.

"Stop," Prince said at the same time—it was defeat that carried the sound from his lips. "Don't . . . kill my son."

"Oh, right, this is your son. I almost forgot."

He nodded to Vasily, who kicked Rhys in the face so hard, his body twisted around and hit the ground on his side. But Vasily only let Rhys writhe in pain for so long before grabbing his hair again and twisting his head forward so we could all see his bruised, bloody features. *Rhys* . . .

"But then," Saul continued, "I wonder. Maybe he does deserve to die. Maybe you shouldn't save him. After all, he isn't innocent." Saul walked across the cobbled pavement and knelt next to Rhys. "He's a murderer. Killed when he was a child. Killed as an agent. Who was the last person, Vasily?"

My lips parted in a silent cry, my hand rising as if there were something I could do from inside this room to stop the next words out of Vasily's mouth.

"Natalya," Vasily said simply with a shrug. "Natalya Filipova."

My hand fell back to my side.

The room went still as a grave. No one moved. No one breathed.

"Did you hear that?" Saul shook his head, his smug smile facing the screen. "I hope the whole world heard that correctly, but I'll repeat it for those not listening. Aidan Rhys, second son of the Sect's North American Division's director, murdered the legendary, heroic Natalya

Filipova. And she didn't even see it coming." He looked at Rhys. "Do you deny it?"

When Rhys struggled to speak, Vasily responded by letting go of his hair and slapping him in the face. His forehead hit the pavement so hard I could hear the *thud*, but he was still conscious. Vasily grabbed his sleeve and dragged him up to his knees.

"Do you deny it?" Saul repeated patiently.

"N-no." The word was almost indiscernible, but I'd heard it.

Saul leaned in, cocking his head toward him. "What was that?"

"No," Rhys said more strongly despite the blood dripping from his mouth. "I don't. I don't deny it. I killed Natalya."

The few agents who still had their guns pointed at us lowered them as they shifted back to the screen and stared in awe. In this room filled with dozens of people, you could hear nothing but gasps. Brendan stumbled back until he bumped into a terminal, his eyes glistening with tears. Director Prince continued to stand stoically, though his hands curled into fists that twitched against his thighs.

And behind me, someone finally stirred.

Belle.

I twisted around to meet her . . . her eyes. They were on me. Still hollow. Still empty. But with a flash of something else I couldn't name. A chasm had opened in them, her face like crumbling stone, as she stared at me, *through* me, without blinking. Her pupils darted to the right and left, trying and failing to grab hold of anything. She was undone.

"A suicide turns to murder in a matter of seconds. Games played by the Sect." Saul turned his back. "And he's not the only guilty party."

The crowd of armed criminals made room for the young woman making her way to the front. She kept her head low, her thick, curly chestnut hair flowing down over her sandy skin. Immediately, I felt a pain in my chest, sudden, unexplainable. Something wasn't right. Something deep inside me was screaming it.

"Don't think that the Effigies are your friends," Saul said.

The girl lifted her head to show her face.

My face.

I fell to my knees. Everyone was looking at me, but I was looking at me too. At the girl who looked exactly like me from the shape of her forehead to the stub of her nose to the point of her chin. The girl who wasn't me stared blankly at the cameras as Saul passed her a gun. And she didn't seem to feel anything when she raised it and shot the second agent in the head, killing the woman instantly.

"See?" Saul used the one hand he had left to grip her shoulder, giving it an almost loving squeeze. "You never know what someone is capable of. Right, Maia?"

But that wasn't "Maia."

In that moment, I heard Saul's words echoing in the back of my mind. The words he'd spoken to me that day in Morocco, an evil promise whispering unknown horrors to come.

This is a world of shadows, Maia. And the secrets hide themselves there in the dark. You'll understand that soon enough. I'll give you a sign.

You won't miss it.

"It can't be." I leaned over, propping myself up against the floor with my hands as I whispered her name. "June?"

32

THE WORLD FELL AWAY. PEOPLE WERE YELL-
ing things. None of it mattered, not until Chae Rin lifted me back to
my feet.

"Pull it together!" Chae Rin shoved me. "I'm tired of saying it to
you people, ugh!"

But I could barely hear her. "June . . . June . . . J—" I nearly collapsed
again, but it was Chae Rin who held me upright.

Chae Rin and Lake appeared as spooked as the rest of the room,
everyone looking from the Maia on-screen to me standing limply in
the back. But it wasn't Maia. That wasn't Maia.

June.

No, it couldn't have been.

June. My sister. The girl who shared my face. That was *my* face. My
face staring back at me. But my face was hers. Every crevice was the
same. My eyes welled up with tears. She'd had acne before she'd died,
but it wasn't there anymore. Maybe it wasn't her after all. Maybe it *was*
me. But it couldn't be. I was here. And it couldn't be my dead sister
either.

Unless . . . June was alive?

Back in Madrid . . . Naomi's shooting. I'd been so careful about hiding my face, but people had seen me anyway. Could it have been—

No. It was impossible.

But what if it wasn't? What if June was alive?

June . . . alive. June was here. She'd come back from the dead. Was it to punish me? Was this Saul's divine justice? But June would never hurt anyone. She certainly wouldn't *kill* someone. I swayed on my feet, propping myself up by the knees as I gulped up air in short, frantic breaths.

Lake bent down and grabbed my shoulders, shaking me. "Maia, *please* get ahold of yourself! Breathe in and out, okay? Like this."

As I tried to follow her lead, elsewhere in the room, Prince expressed his frustration in a low, baritone grumble.

"Cut the communications." Prince motioned to the techs. "Make sure he can't hear us. This has gone on long enough. Resume the weapons launch."

"Dad!" Brendan cried, grabbing his arm.

"Enough!" He yanked his arm out of his son's grip. "We need to take out Saul. Now!"

Take out Saul. I straightened my back and looked at him, horrified. He was going to use Minerva. But Rhys was there.

And June.

"Get ready to launch—"

"Not happening!" Chae Rin raised her hands and the ground began to rumble beneath us, but before she could get started, a gunshot cut her off, the bullet burying itself in her arm.

"Chae Rin!" Lake caught her before she could fall to the ground.

"What are you doing?" Brendan stared at his father, whose gun was still pointed and smoking.

"Saul is making us look . . . look like fools." Prince's arm trembled. "The world is watching. We need to take action."

"The world will watch us destroy a city!"

"The world will watch us *save* a lot of other cities. We need this. We need this for the Sect. I will not allow this terrorist to crush what I've built."

This was the desperate man who'd shaken hands with political devils at Blackwell's party, sullying his name if it meant rebuilding the Sect in the eyes of the world. Only here, his desperation was obvious. It curled off of him like the pungent smell of alcohol.

He was willing to kill them. His own son and the girl who shared my face.

Brendan couldn't conceal his fury. "You won't let them destroy the Sect you built, but you'll destroy your son with your own hands."

"He's already been branded in front of the world. *My* son. It's too late for him." Prince turned his back to his eldest. "And I . . ."

"No. You don't care." I walked forward dazedly, as if in a dream. The face of my sister weighted each of my steps. June was alive. And now both she and Rhys were about to die. All because of this man. All because of him. "You don't care if your son lives or dies. That's what you're trying to say."

Prince met my gaze defiantly, his back tall with the grim pride of a thousand cowardly fathers before him. "I raised a warrior, not a murderer."

"You dare be ashamed of him?" Brendan gripped his own gun, still in its holster against his waist. "The way you trained him. The way you brutalized him. Brainwashed him. Did you think he would see the difference?"

Prince's eyes flashed. "Start the launch."

"No!"

We all yelled it. Brendan's gun was pointed at the technicians, but he didn't know where or who to shoot. I wanted to set everything on fire. My mind was screaming. Rhys, Natalya, June. Ghosts swirled around me, goading me to finish everything. But as my mind conceived of the fire, as my fingers began to spark, I thought of my parents, my sister, being rolled away on stretchers in body bags. I thought of their charred bodies, and my hands gripped my own forehead instead.

June *couldn't* be alive.

It had to be a trick Saul was playing.

Psychotic Alice's sick game. Cruel Nick's malicious assistance.

It was . . . it was . . .

"Father." Brendan stumbled back against the terminal, his knees buckling. He fell to the ground. "What have you done?"

"What I had to," Prince replied coldly.

Nobody said anything.

I could see the digital clock running down from five minutes on the right-hand corner of the screen. Saul didn't know. Rhys didn't know. June didn't know. And no one else still in the city knew. They were going to be hit. They were all going to die.

Someone's terminal began to beep. "Sir, we're getting a video call," said one technician on the other side of the room.

"Patch him in."

If Director Prince had known that it would be Blackwell's smug face appearing on the screen, he may not have given the order. The man looked livid as Blackwell rested his elbow on his chair's armrest and rubbed his forehead, amused and exasperated all at once.

"Arthur," he said. "I didn't think you could go through with such a thing. The Council is very disappointed."

"The Council?" Prince sputtered.

"We've been watching the situation closely. I told them you

shouldn't be allowed to handle such a situation, but after all, you are a high-ranking official in the Sect." Blackwell tapped his fingers against his crossed knee. "Perhaps that was the problem from the beginning."

The skin hanging on Prince's chin trembled as he shook with fury. "It was the Council who told me to finish this. Senator Abrams himself told me to take this course of action. I have dealt with Saul. I've finally ended this nightmare."

"And so you have." Blackwell grinned. "And now I'm dealing with you."

A troop of police burst through the door behind us. Lake, Chae Rin, Belle, and I scrambled out of the way as they came in fully armed in riot gear, their shields up, their guns pointing at everyone in the room.

"The building is surrounded," one yelled. "Director Prince Senior and Junior, and all present Sect personnel—you are under arrest for treason and acts of terrorism."

Both Princes blanched, neither knowing where to move or where to look. Some members of the Communications department already had their hands up in defeat, while some looked as utterly baffled as their leaders standing in front of them.

"Acts . . ." Director Prince stared up at Blackwell. "Acts of *terrorism?*"

"You made the wrong move this time, Arthur." Blackwell shook his head with an almost theatrical sweep of his head. "It's a wonder why Abrams would tell you such a thing. Or how he would get such an awful idea in the first place."

"Blackwell." Prince gathered the situation with flaring eyes, his neck reddening by the second. "Did you—"

"Yes, I called the police," he answered. "And don't worry, we'll also be taking Abrams into custody, as well as anyone else in the Council who shared his views. My meetings with various foreign dignitaries have been fruitful indeed. We've already decided that the Sect can no longer be allowed to run amok in dealing with affairs that should be in their hands. This latest infraction is just proof that you're not fit to rule. And your kingdom isn't fit to stand."

"We said, put your hands up," the police officer repeated. "Sir, we will not ask you a third time."

As more officers spilled into the room and began taking the willing into custody, Blackwell cleared his throat, gathering Prince's attention again.

"It's better if you cooperate. As criminals under the law."

"I am not . . ." Prince's teeth clenched tight. "I am—"

"What you are, Arthur," Blackwell began, "is a father willing to kill your own son in order to hold on to the power and reputation your family has given you. A spoiled, sad little boy with blood on his hands." And he grinned wide. "Like father, like son, I suppose."

"Effigies! Come with us!"

Several police officers surrounded us, cornering us against the wall. They looked terrified as they pointed their guns at us, one holding out handcuffs with shaking hands. The metal jingled in his grip.

"Yeah," Chae Rin said. "No."

Lake sent a gale crashing into them, and before the rest could raise their hands to shoot, Chae Rin broke open a hole in the wall for us to escape through. We leapt out and began running once again down the hall. Belle's wall of ice sealed the hole after us and blocked off the path so that the other officers in the corridor couldn't follow. I could hear their gunshots *clink* against the ice.

"Belle," I started. "You—"

My next words vanished as I remembered Rhys's confession. Her devastation. Belle didn't look back at me as she ran. She didn't say a word as we made our way through the building.

"Blackwell," Sibyl said quietly once the communication link was back up. "If he manipulated Director Prince into using Minerva . . . then he was part of this too. A part of Project X19. But all they did was turn the world against the Sect, against the Effigies. Maybe that was the plan all along. Maybe *that* was Phase III, not the weapon itself."

"Where can we go?" Lake said once we stopped to catch our breath. "Those police said the building was surrounded!"

"There's an underground pathway beneath the building that will take you outside the facility," Sibyl said. "Not many people know about it. You need to leave the city until we can get you transportation to our safe house. Dot, Pete, and Cheryl are all already on their way. Keep going down the hall, and at the first bend, turn left."

We followed Sibyl's instructions. My thoughts were racing, blurring pain and confusion together as my legs carried me down stairs, through corridors. We couldn't stop Saul. We hadn't stopped Prince. And now Rhys and who knew how many others were dead. And June? It didn't make any sense. But even if I could piece it together, it was too late to save any of them.

Five minutes had already passed.

"The beam hit." Uncle Nathan had whispered it. "It . . . the city . . ."

He didn't need to say anything more. We were failures. And now we were fugitives.

Rhys . . . I'm sorry. Tears stung my eyes. I was broken.

I'd lost someone again.

So many words left unsaid because of my own cowardice. My body felt as if it would collapse into pieces on the floor. I was already haunted by it: his smile, that beautiful smile I would never see again. The boy who'd confessed that he'd fallen in love with me. I wanted to scream, to cry, to curse, to die. But I had to keep going. I *had* to. He would have wanted me to. I blinked my tears away as Sibyl guided us to a small underground hangar, empty but for two cars. Once again, there were agents waiting.

"From here, we should split up," Belle suggested suddenly.

"I would advise against that," Sibyl said. "I don't understand exactly what *I* just saw, but people around the world saw Maia Finley, an Effigy, help Saul essentially cause the destruction of a city."

My stomach lurched. "Uncle Nathan . . ."

"I know. I saw her too."

He sounded so small. I'm sure he could hear the sob in my voice as I breathed in, trying to keep myself together.

"This is a catastrophe on the level of the Seattle Siege," Sibyl said. "And in the eyes of the world, the Effigies—the entire Sect is implicated. You have to stay together."

"We're fugitives now," Belle pressed. "They'll be looking for all four of us. If we split up, it'll be harder for them to capture us all."

Sibyl went quiet. But after a moment, she acquiesced with a sigh. "Two per car."

"Maia." Belle was already staring at me, the dark circles under her eyes deep and unforgiving. "Come with me."

I didn't argue as the agent opened the backseat doors for us.

"Is this really happening?" Lake said. "We're splitting up?"

The four of us stood in a circle, close together and yet still separated by the chasm of the unknown. Belle was the only one who avoided our gazes. Her bloodshot eyes remained steadfastly low as the rest of us joined hands.

"It's going to be okay," I told them, mustering up what little bravery I could through the pits of despair and fear. "It'll just be for a little while."

"I don't have the best feeling about this," Chae Rin said. "I'm kind of with Sibyl. But maybe splitting up really is the best way to go. In that case . . . well, just don't get caught. Or killed. Or I'll be super pissed, okay?"

Lake laughed a little, and the strain in her voice made it obvious that the gesture hadn't been easy. I felt her squeeze my hand. But when I looked over at Belle, she was still in her own head, staring at the floor. I grabbed her hand, trying to smile. She didn't look up.

"Okay," I said, letting go of both girls. "Let's go. I'll see you guys again at the safe house."

"Right, then. See you in a bit!" Lake's cheerfulness may have been artifice, but it gave me courage like I suspected she'd meant it to.

We entered our own cars and drove out of the hangar, down the underground path, until we surfaced outside the facility. We came to a fork in the road, and there, under the night sky, we separated. I twisted around, watching the other car until it disappeared into the darkness.

"Where are we heading?" I asked carefully.

"The Straits of Dover," the agent answered, looking at me in the rearview mirror. "We'll rendezvous with some people who'll help us cross into France."

"France," Belle repeated lifelessly. "My home. The place I was . . . born."

She fell silent.

I half expected her to be limp against the door again, but this time she was surprisingly stiff. Her back was straight as if held up by a metal rod. Her hands were placed on her lap, her fingers curled at an odd angle against her knees. She said nothing. She didn't even look at me throughout the almost two-hour drive. The entire time, I kept to my side of the bench, my hand awkwardly gripping my seat belt as I tried to keep my eyes on the antiphantom threads weaving across the highway, keeping us safe from the horrors outside. I made sure my gaze stayed on them. I'd been awake for so many hours I'd lost count. I was running on nothing, but I couldn't let my eyelids flutter closed like they wanted to. Because if I did, I'd see his face. I'd see Rhys obliterated by a weapon that to him would have looked simply like a beautiful light from above. Before absolution.

I held my sobs in for the ride until we came to the White Cliffs. It was somewhat still under the glow of nearby antiphantom protection, so we didn't have to worry about phantoms here. But the strait wasn't protected. The agent had told us to expect a fishing ship coming down the strait. I was sure it would come with its own APD, lest we let the monsters lurking beneath the waves drag us down into the deep with them. We waited patiently for the rendezvous, but after we stood close to the edge of the cliffs for several minutes, nothing showed up.

"They're late." The agent checked his watch impatiently.

"Redman." Belle approached the young man. "I need to speak with Maia."

Surprised, I turned from looking over the cliffs.

"What?" Redman cocked his head. "Look, miss, I'm sorry, but we're in a bit of a—"

Belle knocked him out.

"What are you *doing*?" I yelled as he fell limp over her arm.

Reaching into her ear, she took out his earpiece and crushed it. Before I could move out of the way, she'd grabbed my arm, yanking me close so she could dig out mine as well. She threw both into the strait.

Real fear started to colonize my body. I was backing away from her, away from the cliff, before I'd even realized it. "What are you doing?" I asked again as I watched her throw Redman's unconscious body to the ground.

"I told you. That man told me many things." The dark circles cast poisonous shadows under her eyes. "Strange things."

"The Surgeon?" My feet slid and scuffled across the gravel.

"He said I would always be alone." Belle's head was low, but tilted slightly. She'd lost focus again. "I think he was right."

She began closing the distance between us.

"Belle," I started, wrapping my arms around myself to keep from shaking. "I don't know what he did to you. . . ."

But I did. I knew that he'd tortured her physically, mentally, and emotionally. He had twisted her for an entire hour while I was locked in my cell, unable to do anything. Yet what he'd done to her maybe wasn't as important as what I had done.

"I wanted to believe that he was wrong. That I had finally found friends I could believe in."

Her blue eyes snapped back into focus and she looked up at me desperately.

"Y-you have," I said, shaking. "We're . . . We *are* friends, Belle."

"Then, as a friend, let me ask you this."

I already knew what she would ask. My lips began trembling.

"And as a *friend*, answer me truthfully." Belle placed a hand on her stomach, touching a hole through the tears her torturer had made in her shirt. "Did you know?"

Tears stung my eyes once again. "Belle . . ."

"Did you know this entire time?"

What could I say? We'd all heard the confession. The whole world had heard Aidan Rhys admit that he had murdered Natalya.

"*Please*, Maia." She was begging me now. "Please, just tell me."

But I couldn't. I pressed my lips together to seal up my whimpers. I'd stopped moving, my stomach turning so terribly that I doubled over from the pain. But she was still approaching me.

"Maia, just tell me. Remember . . ."

The wind chilled, snowflakes slipping out from the air around her, gathering by her hand, forming the shape of her sword.

"I'm asking as a friend."

I saw the edge of the beautiful sword I'd once admired and suddenly, in that moment, I realized that it was Belle who'd suggested we travel in separate cars.

I could lie. I could tell her I hadn't known. That I'd been as surprised as anyone. But I didn't want to. The man whose secrets I was protecting was dead. I would never see him again. And I was tired. I was tired of everything.

"Did you know, Maia? That Aidan killed Natalya?"

"I've known for a long time."

She was too fast. The sword came down on my head before I knew what was happening, but by pure instinct alone, I avoided her. She was emotional, too emotional to be precise. That was my advantage. I dodged her clumsy swings, her enraged, sorrowful cries splitting the air. I called my own weapon, my scythe emerging out of a whirl of flame to counteract her strikes, but she pressed me back, back, and back still. It wasn't until I felt the rocks crumble and fall down from my heel that I realized she'd pinned me against the cliff.

One more swing and she broke my scythe. It dissipated into nothingness.

This was insane. This couldn't be happening. "Belle, I'm sorry!"

"You *knew*!" Belle dragged the tip of her sword against the cliffs. "You saw me going through hell. I opened myself to you—to all of you. And you betrayed me!"

"I know!" I put out my hands to stave her fury, to save my own life. The tears were falling freely now, dripping into my lips, down my chin. "I know, and I'm sorry. I was scared. I was scared you would do something crazy!"

"Like kill your lover?" Belle's hair was a shambles across her face.

When she swept it back, I saw her eyes glinting with malevolence, with disdain, with *pain*. She smiled the mocking grin of a girl who knew her world was over and she had nothing left to lose. "But he's already dead. It was all for nothing."

A strangled cry escaped my lips as I thought of him, the pain of his death made real by her malicious words. "It wasn't just for him. It was for you! Belle, this isn't you. You're not a killer. Natalya's gone, but it's killing you! It's twisting you! Natalya wouldn't—"

She pointed her sword at my heart. "*Don't* tell me what Natalya would want," she said, breathing wildly. "You weren't there. You didn't see me. You didn't see Madame Bisette beat me. You didn't see Natalya save me. All you saw were heroes. You were never there! You didn't save me!" She gripped her own head, crying openly. "You *betrayed* me. You were my friend and you betrayed me! Why? *Why?*" she shrieked. "*Why, Maia?* Wh—"

The stream of angry cries died as she looked down and realized what I already knew, what I could already feel.

The elegant tip of her blade pierced through my chest.

She stared at it, her tear-soaked face catching the moonlight. She stared as if she did not understand what it was. As if she didn't recognize the blood dripping down my stomach, down the edges of my mouth.

It was beyond pain. It was mercy. Numb. Forgiving. The tears continued to slip quietly down my cheeks as my lips quivered, my hands shaking as they reached up to the blade, whose steel surface I'd memorized all those nights I watched clips of her fighting alone in my room, dreaming that her strength was mine. I touched it, the sword that had pierced through my flesh, blood, and bone. As I felt the steel beneath my fingers, my lips parted one last time.

"I . . . just . . ." I sucked in a shaky breath. And then I did the only thing I could. I smiled at her. "I just . . . didn't want to lose anyone . . . ever again."

The sword ripped out of me just as a gasp tore out of my throat and into the chilly air. I stumbled back, the stars, the moon, the night spinning and tilting above me until my eyes rolled to the back of my head and darkness washed over me.

The smile never quite left my face as I fell off the cliff and into the waters below.

ACKNOWLEDGMENTS

First, I want to thank my endlessly supportive mother and my older brothers, who never stop reminding me how amazing it is to have a published book. I also want to thank my cousins, aunts, uncles, and extended family, who told their friends. I need to mention Chandrima, Don, and Daniel, my thesis committee, who oversaw the completion of my dissertation while I was writing the Effigies series—and no, that was not easy. Thank you to the Simon Pulse team, including my wonderful editor, Sarah McCabe, who continues to help steer the series in the right direction. Thanks also to Simon & Schuster Canada for helping to organize events and promotions. And finally, to all the fans and supporters of the Effigies, who continue to inspire me to keep writing—I'm where I am today only because of all of you. Thank you.

ABOUT THE AUTHOR

Sarah Raughley grew up in Southern Ontario writing stories about freakish little girls with powers because she secretly wanted to be one. She is a huge fangirl of anything from manga to sci-fi/fantasy TV to Japanese role-playing games, but she will swear up and down at book signings that she was inspired by Jane Austen. On top of being a young adult writer, Sarah has a PhD in English, which makes her a doctor, so it turns out she didn't have to go to medical school after all.